jGN WARTMAN Peter
Through the moon /
Wartman, Peter,

DEC 3 1 2020

wonderstorm

All rights reserved. Published by Scholastic Inc., *Publishers since 1920.* SCHOLASTIC and
associated logos are trademarks and/or registered trademarks of Scholastic Inc.

The publisher does not have any control over and does not assume any responsibility
for author or third-party websites or their content.

This book is a work of fiction. Names, characters, places, and incidents are either the
product of the author's imagination or are used fictitiously, and any resemblance to
actual persons, living or dead, business establishments, events, or locales is entirely
coincidental.

ISBN 978-1-338-60881-6 (paperback)

10 9 8 7 6 5 4 3 2 1   20 21 22 23 24

Printed in the U.S.A.   113

Edited by Chloe Fraboni, Rachel Stark, and Katie Woehr

Book design by Betsy Peterschmidt

Letters by Olga Andreyeva

Additional assistance with colors by Cynthia Cheng, Farrah Su, Boya Sun,
Adeetje Bouma, Eva Cone, Katie Mitroff

AN ORIGINAL GRAPHIC NOVEL

THE DRAGON PRINCE

Through the Moon

Story by **AARON EHASZ**
and **JUSTIN RICHMOND**

Written by **PETER WARTMAN**

Illustrated by **XANTHE BOUMA**

An Imprint of **SCHOLASTIC**

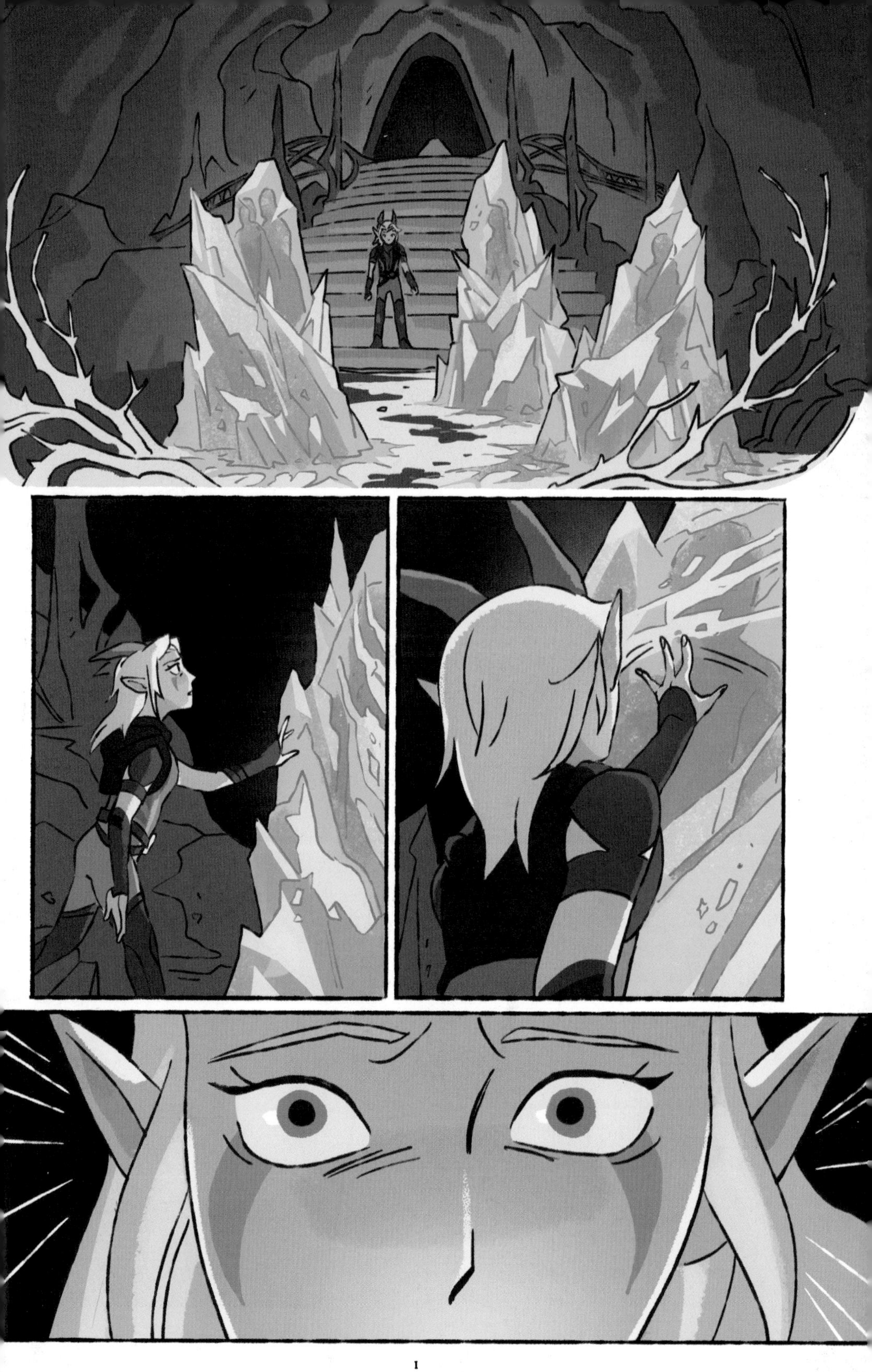

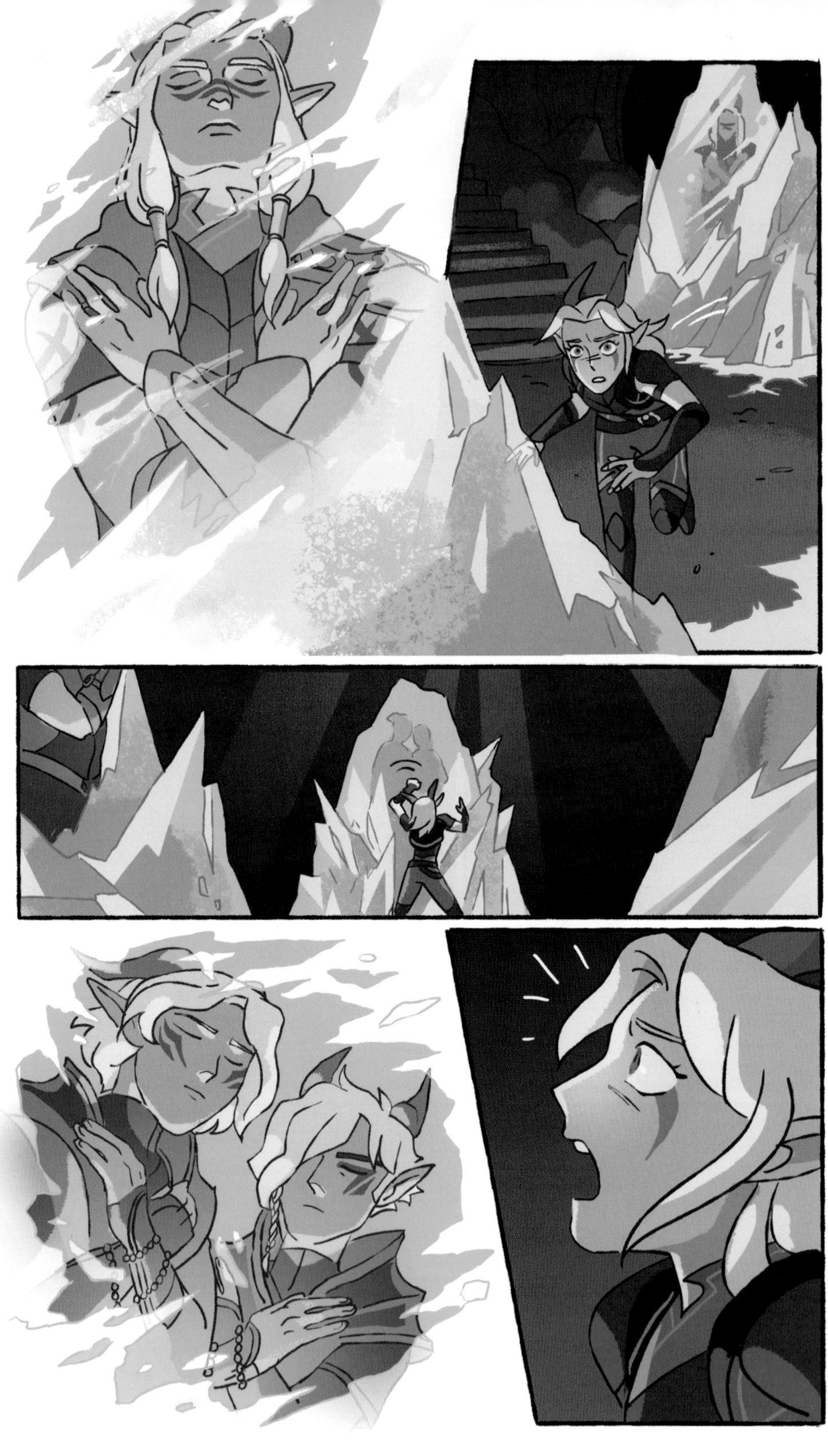

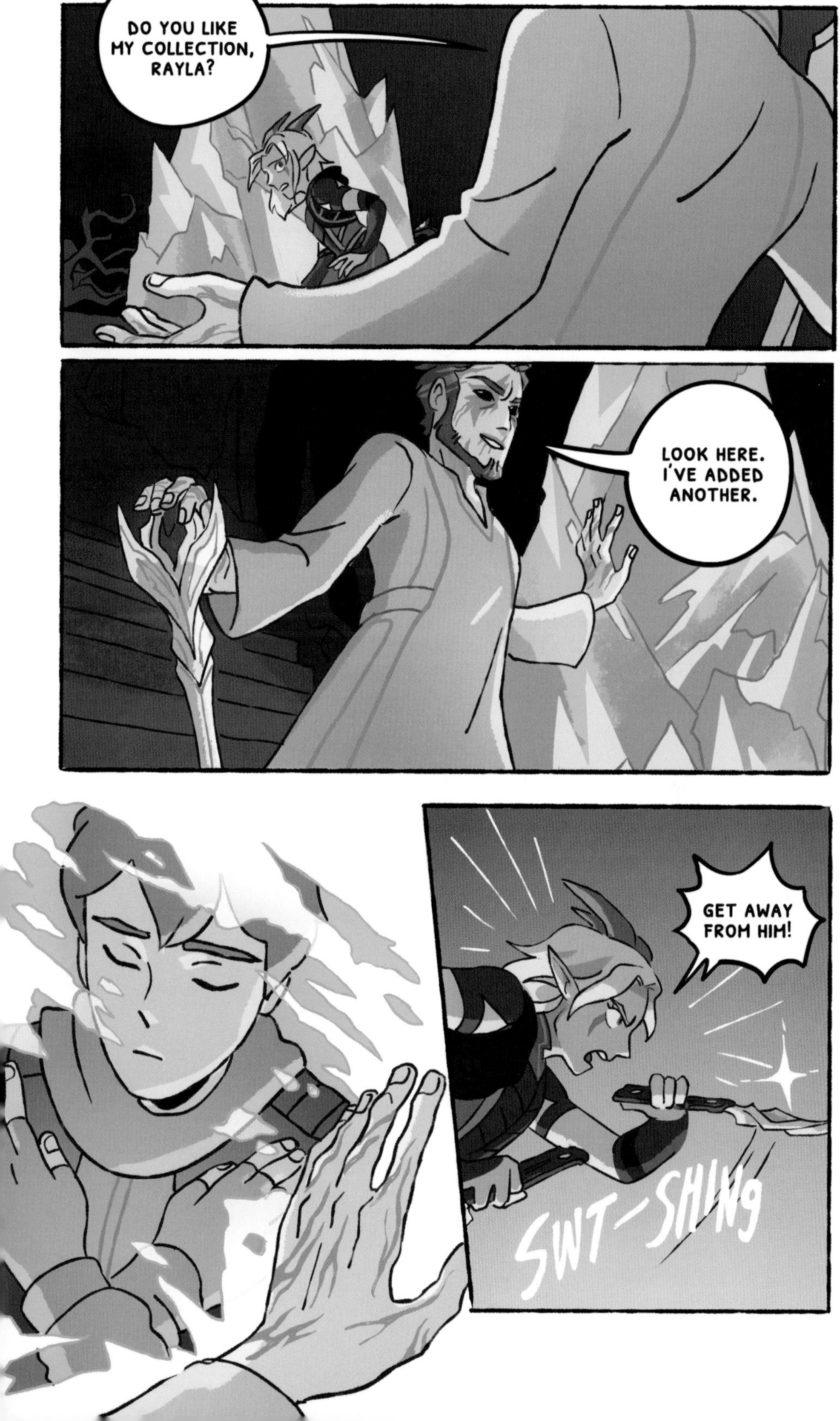
DO YOU LIKE MY COLLECTION, RAYLA?
LOOK HERE. I'VE ADDED ANOTHER.
GET AWAY FROM HIM!
SWT-SHING

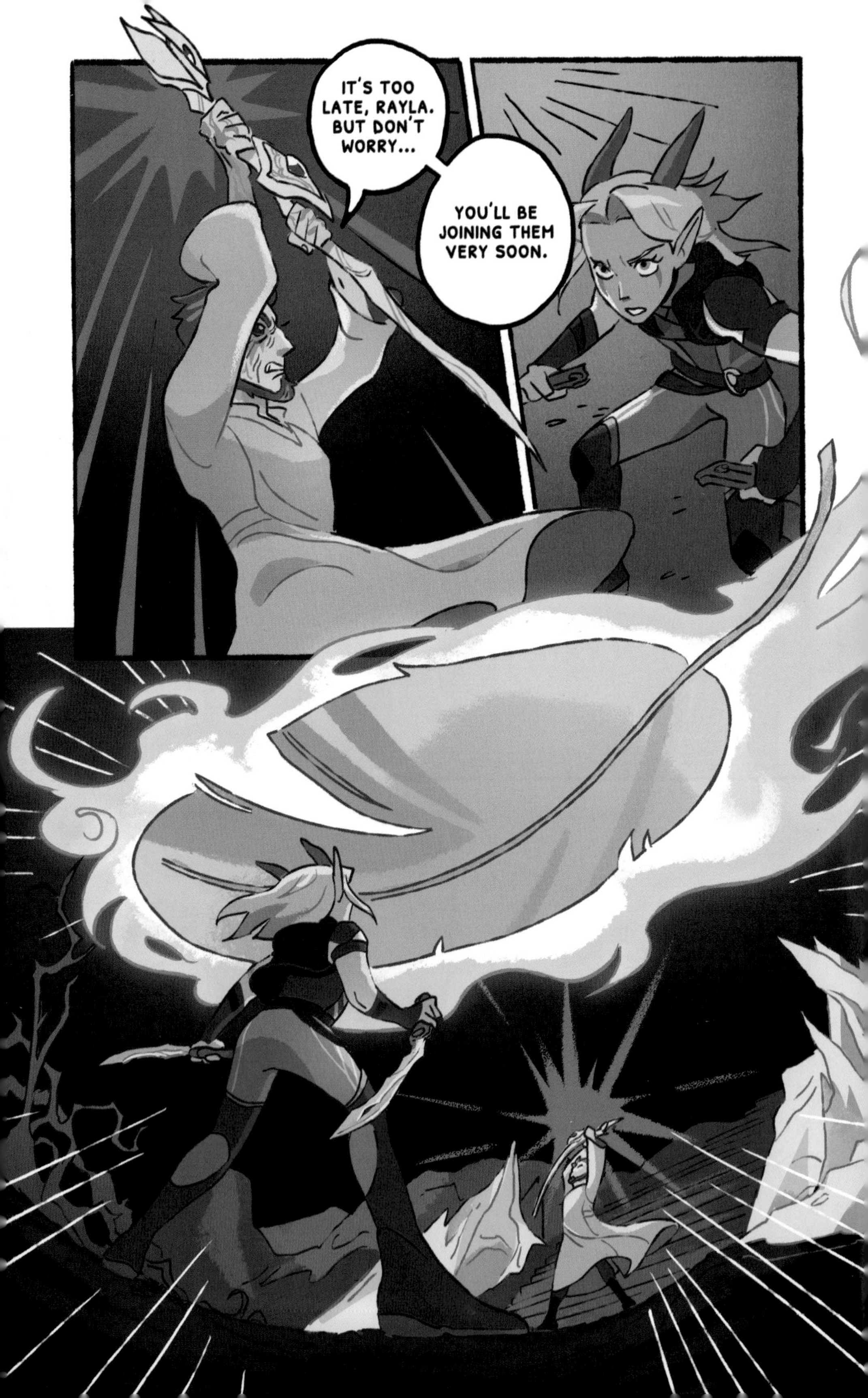
IT'S TOO LATE, RAYLA. BUT DON'T WORRY...
YOU'LL BE JOINING THEM VERY SOON.

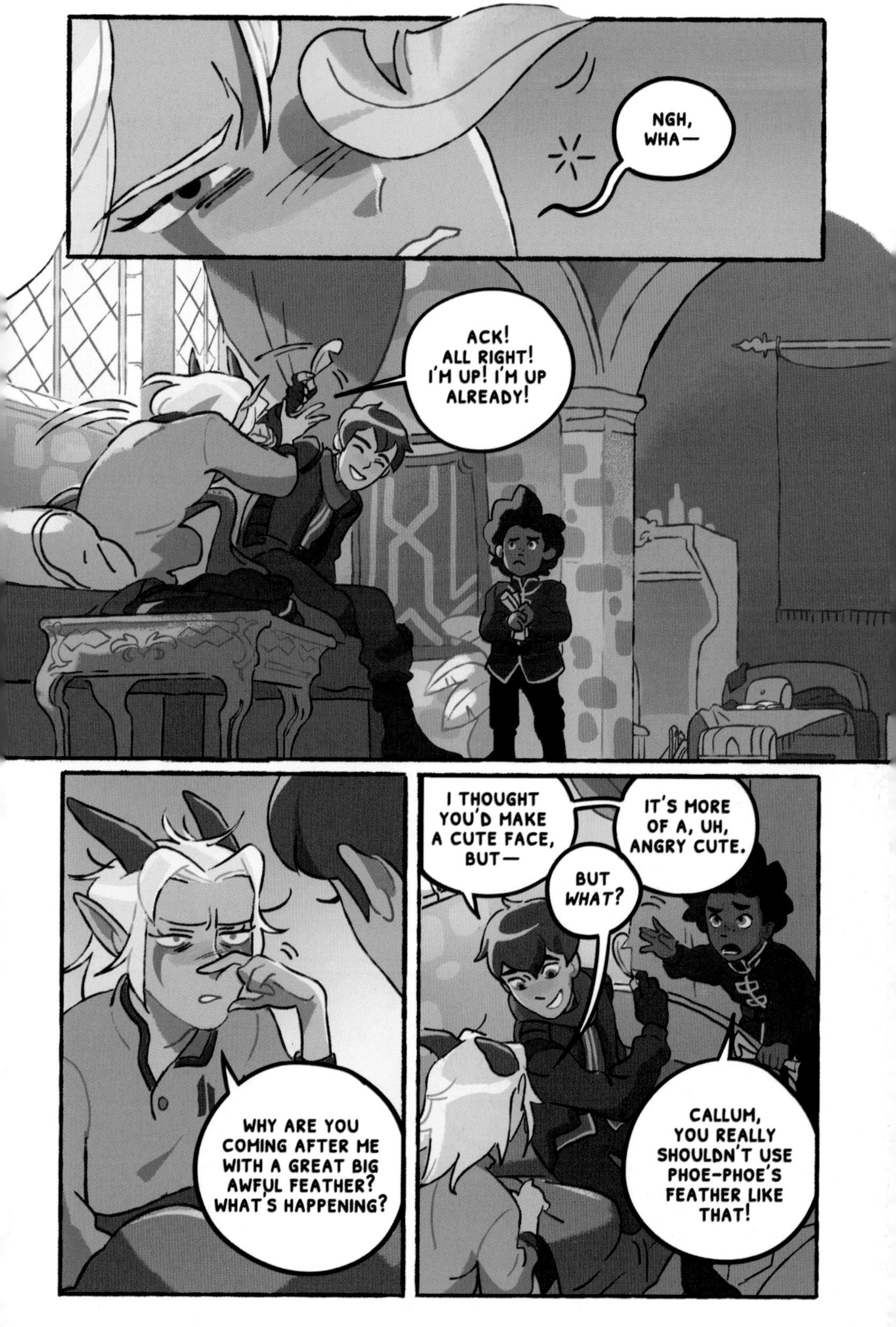
NGH, WHA—
ACK! ALL RIGHT! I'M UP! I'M UP ALREADY!
WHY ARE YOU COMING AFTER ME WITH A GREAT BIG AWFUL FEATHER? WHAT'S HAPPENING?
I THOUGHT YOU'D MAKE A CUTE FACE, BUT—
BUT WHAT?
IT'S MORE OF A, UH, ANGRY CUTE.
CALLUM, YOU REALLY SHOULDN'T USE PHOE-PHOE'S FEATHER LIKE THAT!

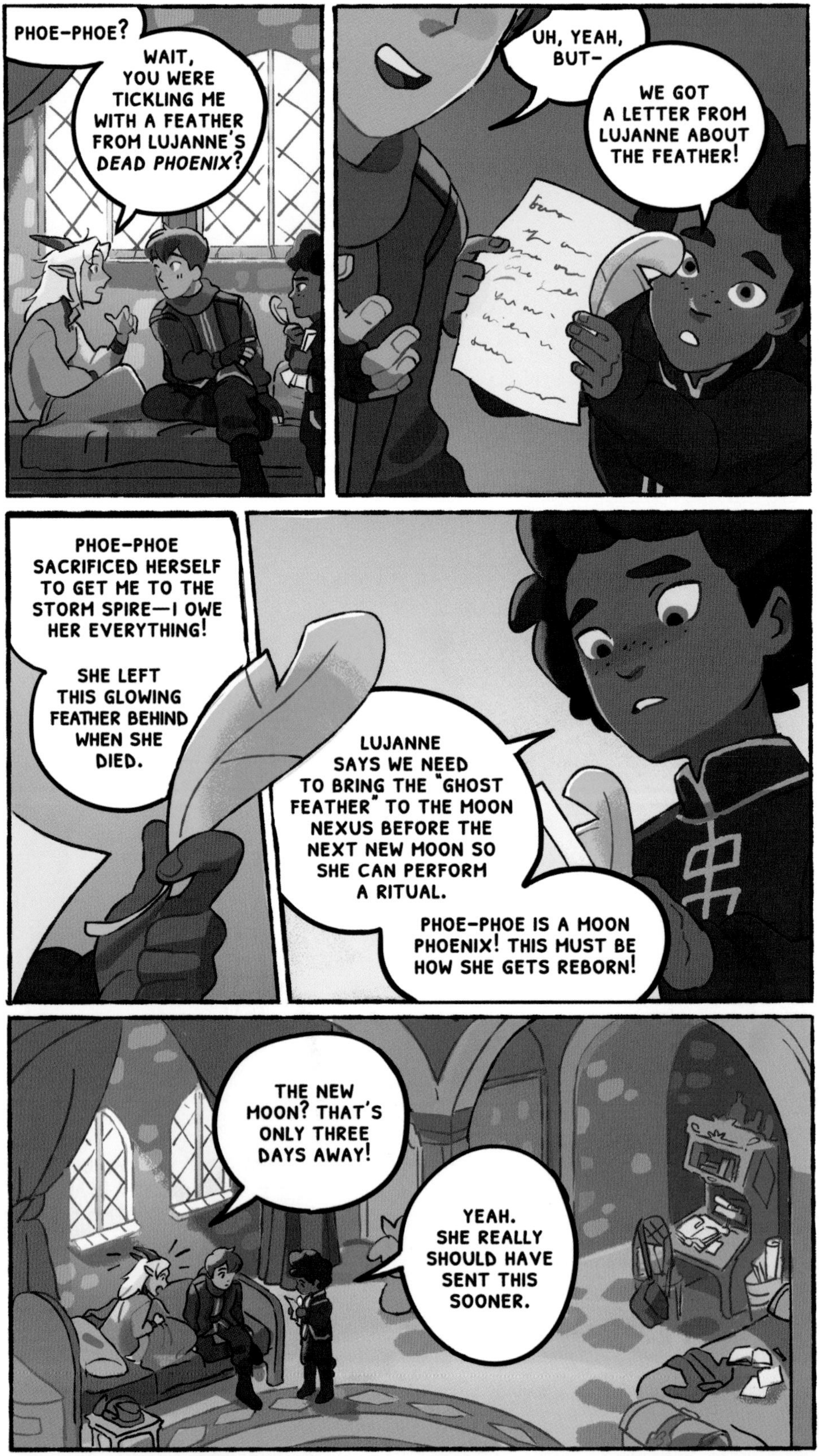
PHOE-PHOE?
WAIT, YOU WERE TICKLING ME WITH A FEATHER FROM LUJANNE'S *DEAD PHOENIX*?
UH, YEAH, BUT—
WE GOT A LETTER FROM LUJANNE ABOUT THE FEATHER!
PHOE-PHOE SACRIFICED HERSELF TO GET ME TO THE STORM SPIRE—I OWE HER EVERYTHING!
SHE LEFT THIS GLOWING FEATHER BEHIND WHEN SHE DIED.
LUJANNE SAYS WE NEED TO BRING THE "GHOST FEATHER" TO THE MOON NEXUS BEFORE THE NEXT NEW MOON SO SHE CAN PERFORM A RITUAL.
PHOE-PHOE IS A MOON PHOENIX! THIS MUST BE HOW SHE GETS REBORN!
THE NEW MOON? THAT'S ONLY THREE DAYS AWAY!
YEAH. SHE REALLY SHOULD HAVE SENT THIS SOONER.

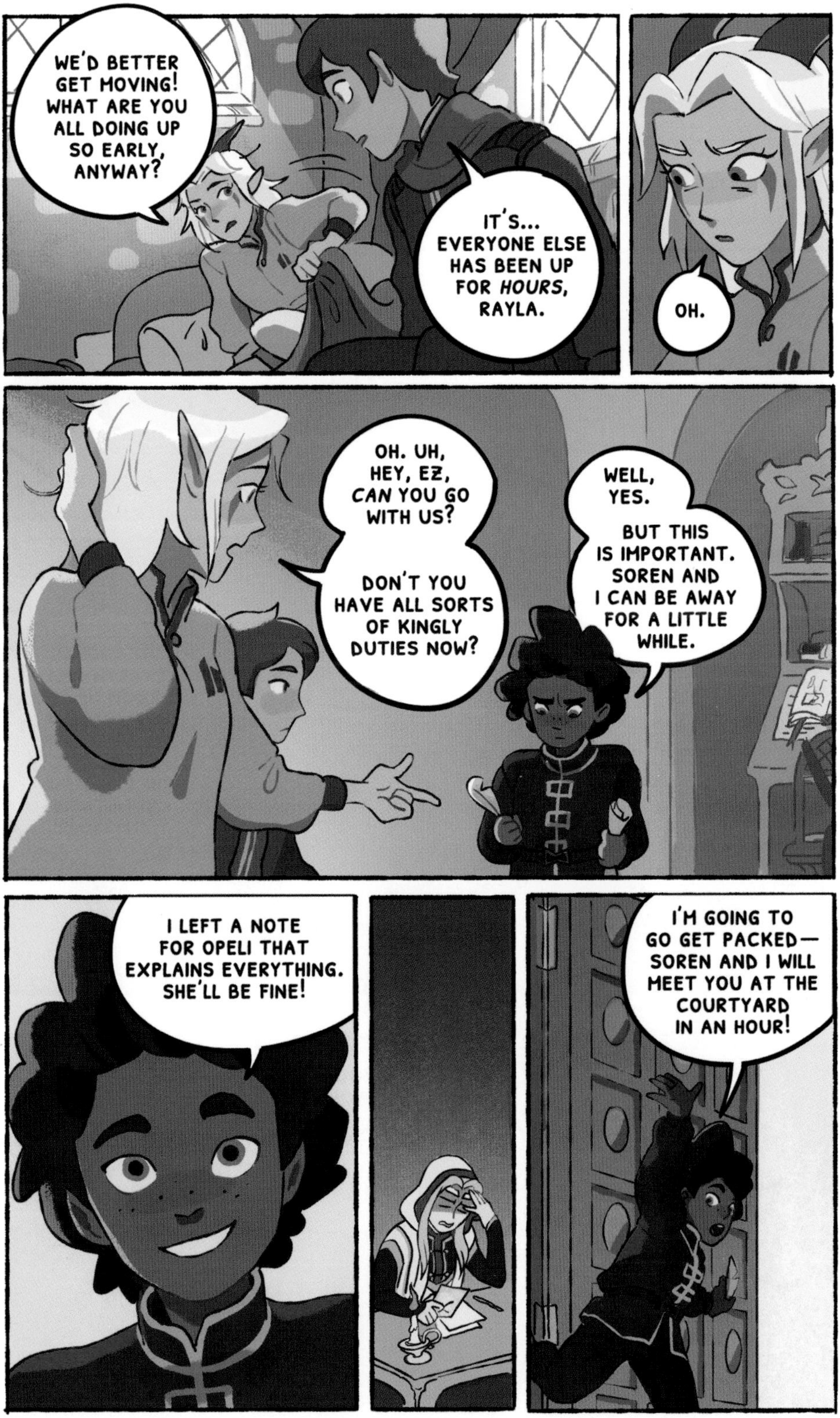
WE'D BETTER GET MOVING! WHAT ARE YOU ALL DOING UP SO EARLY, ANYWAY?
IT'S... EVERYONE ELSE HAS BEEN UP FOR *HOURS*, RAYLA.
OH.
OH. UH, HEY, EZ, *CAN* YOU GO WITH US?
DON'T YOU HAVE ALL SORTS OF KINGLY DUTIES NOW?
WELL, YES.
BUT THIS IS IMPORTANT. SOREN AND I CAN BE AWAY FOR A LITTLE WHILE.
I LEFT A NOTE FOR OPELI THAT EXPLAINS EVERYTHING. SHE'LL BE FINE!
I'M GOING TO GO GET PACKED—SOREN AND I WILL MEET YOU AT THE COURTYARD IN AN HOUR!

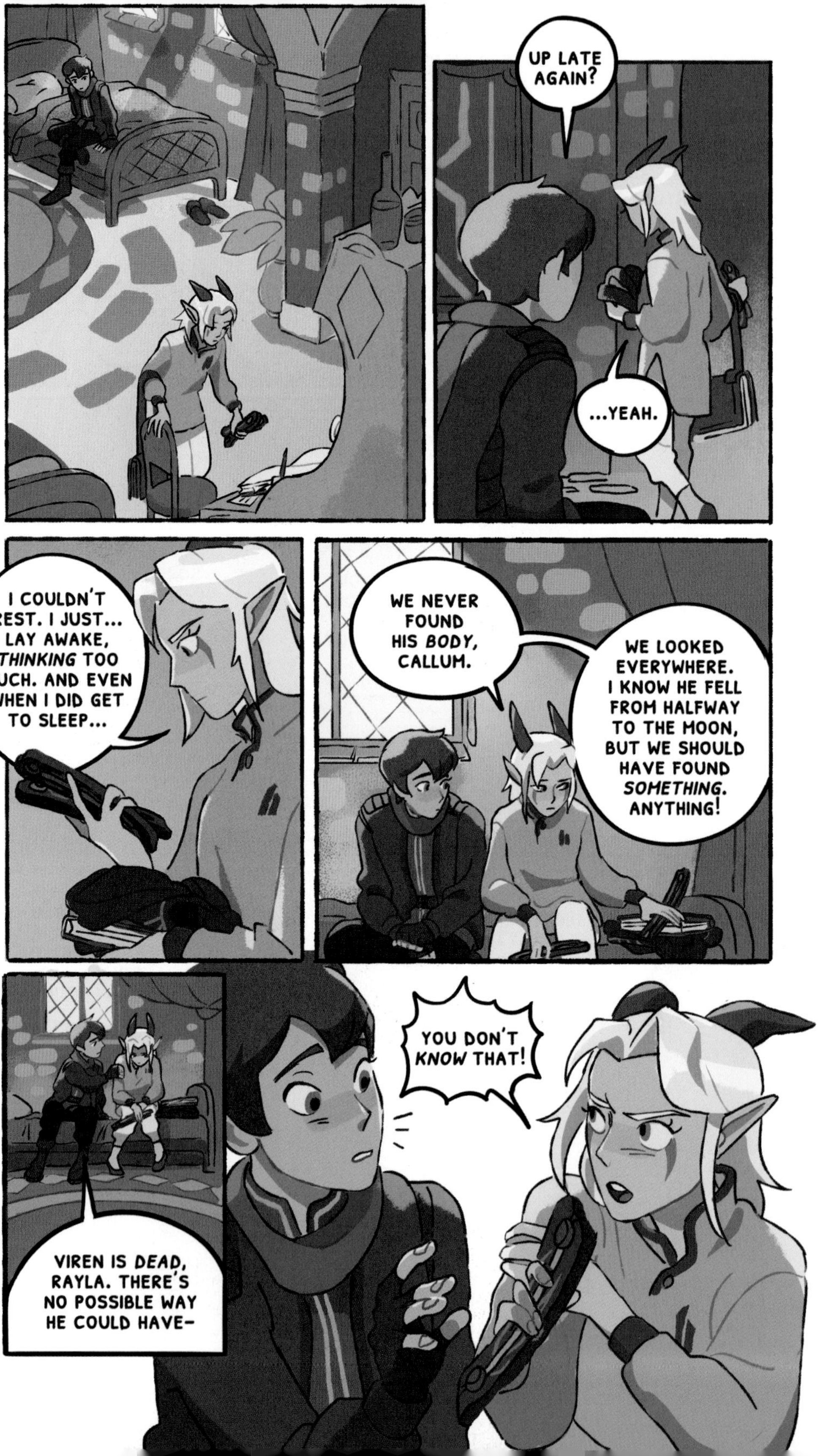
UP LATE AGAIN?
...YEAH.
I COULDN'T REST. I JUST... LAY AWAKE, *THINKING* TOO MUCH. AND EVEN WHEN I DID GET TO SLEEP...
WE NEVER FOUND HIS *BODY*, CALLUM.
WE LOOKED EVERYWHERE. I KNOW HE FELL FROM HALFWAY TO THE MOON, BUT WE SHOULD HAVE FOUND *SOMETHING*. ANYTHING!
VIREN IS *DEAD*, RAYLA. THERE'S NO POSSIBLE WAY HE COULD HAVE-
YOU DON'T *KNOW* THAT!

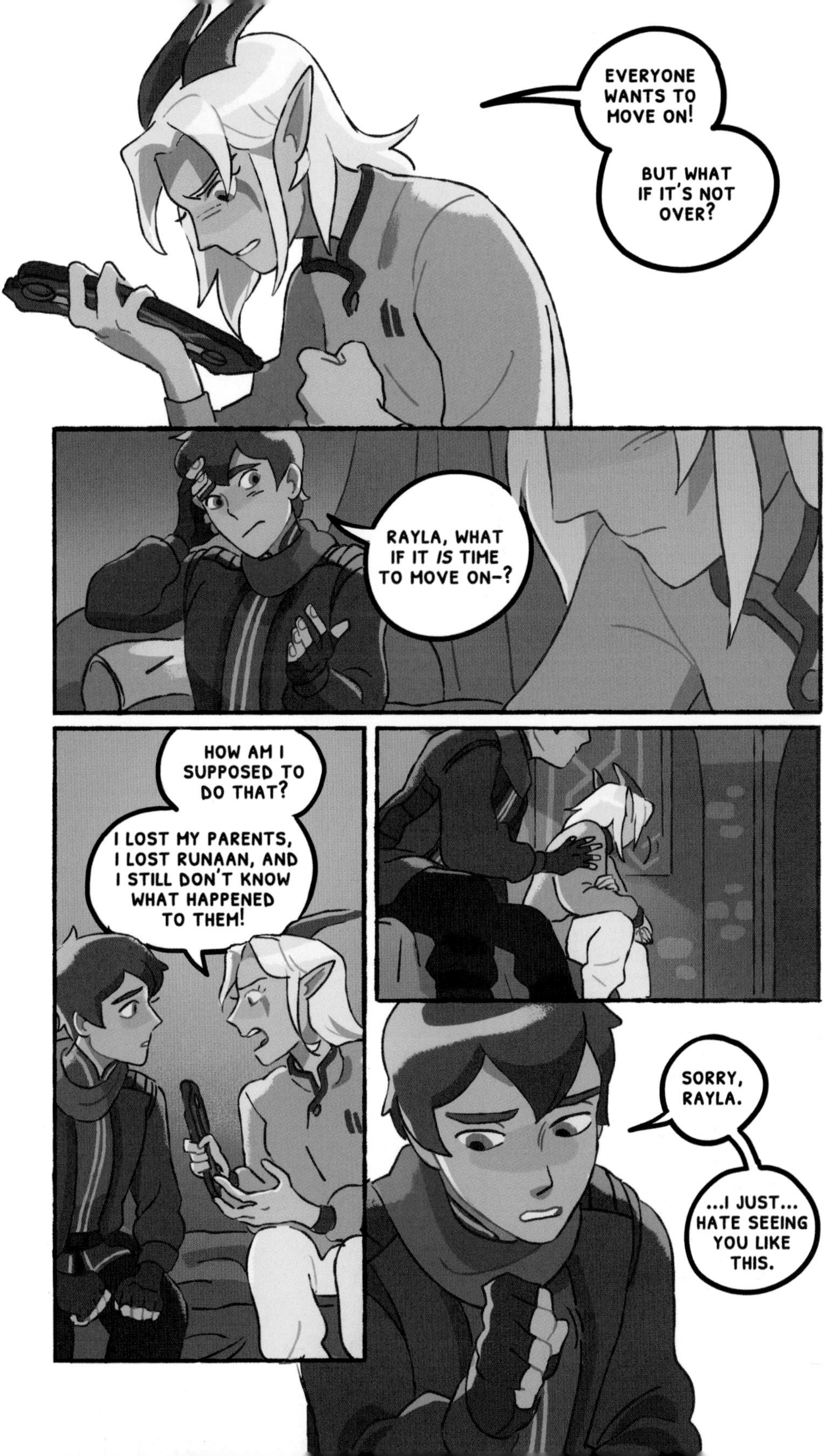
EVERYONE WANTS TO MOVE ON!
BUT WHAT IF IT'S NOT OVER?
RAYLA, WHAT IF IT *IS* TIME TO MOVE ON-?
HOW AM I SUPPOSED TO DO THAT?
I LOST MY PARENTS, I LOST RUNAAN, AND I STILL DON'T KNOW WHAT HAPPENED TO THEM!
SORRY, RAYLA.
...I JUST... HATE SEEING YOU LIKE THIS.

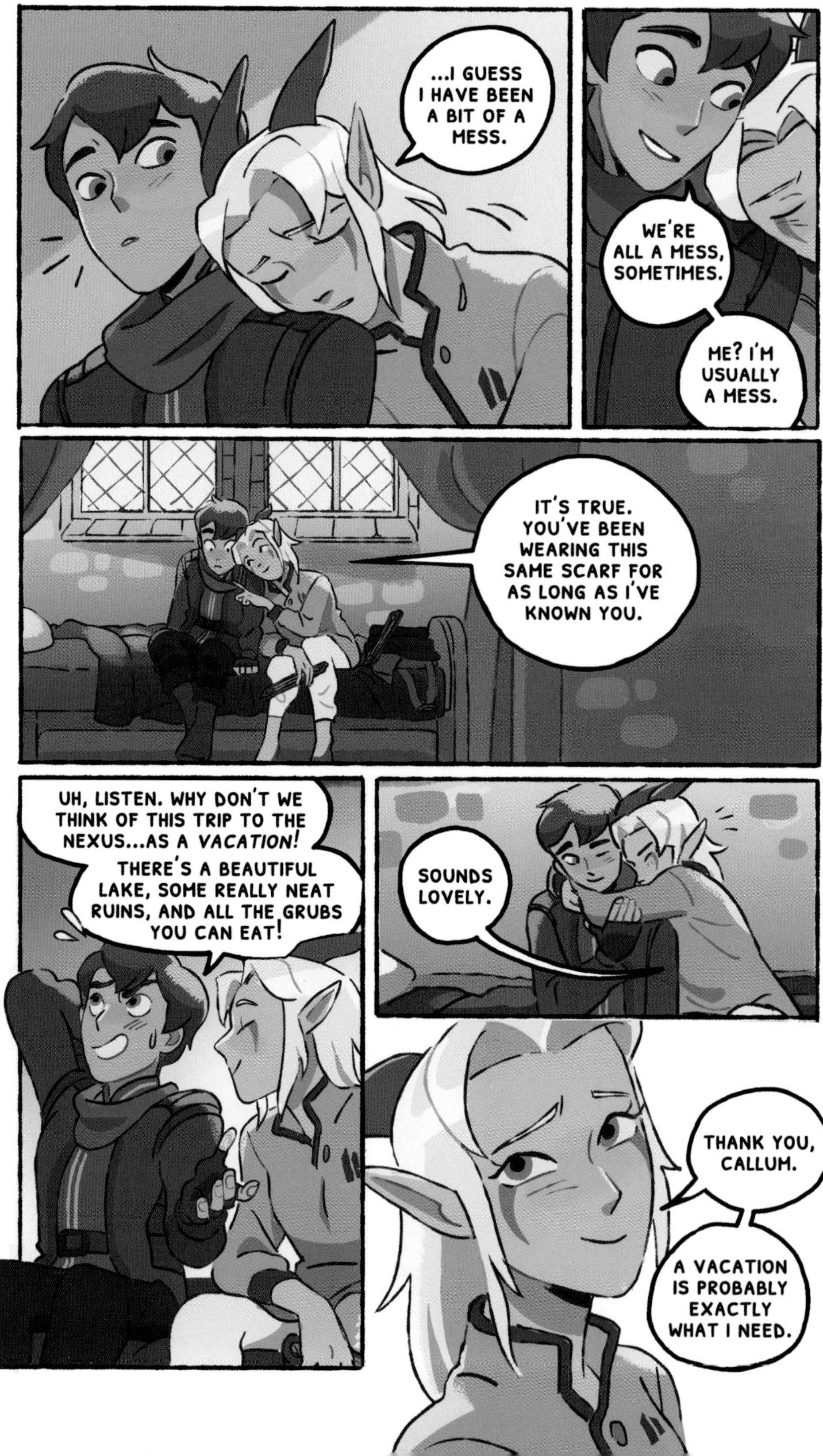
...I GUESS I HAVE BEEN A BIT OF A MESS.
WE'RE ALL A MESS, SOMETIMES.
ME? I'M USUALLY A MESS.
IT'S TRUE. YOU'VE BEEN WEARING THIS SAME SCARF FOR AS LONG AS I'VE KNOWN YOU.
UH, LISTEN. WHY DON'T WE THINK OF THIS TRIP TO THE NEXUS...AS A *VACATION*!
THERE'S A BEAUTIFUL LAKE, SOME REALLY NEAT RUINS, AND ALL THE GRUBS YOU CAN EAT!
SOUNDS LOVELY.
THANK YOU, CALLUM.
A VACATION IS PROBABLY EXACTLY WHAT I NEED.

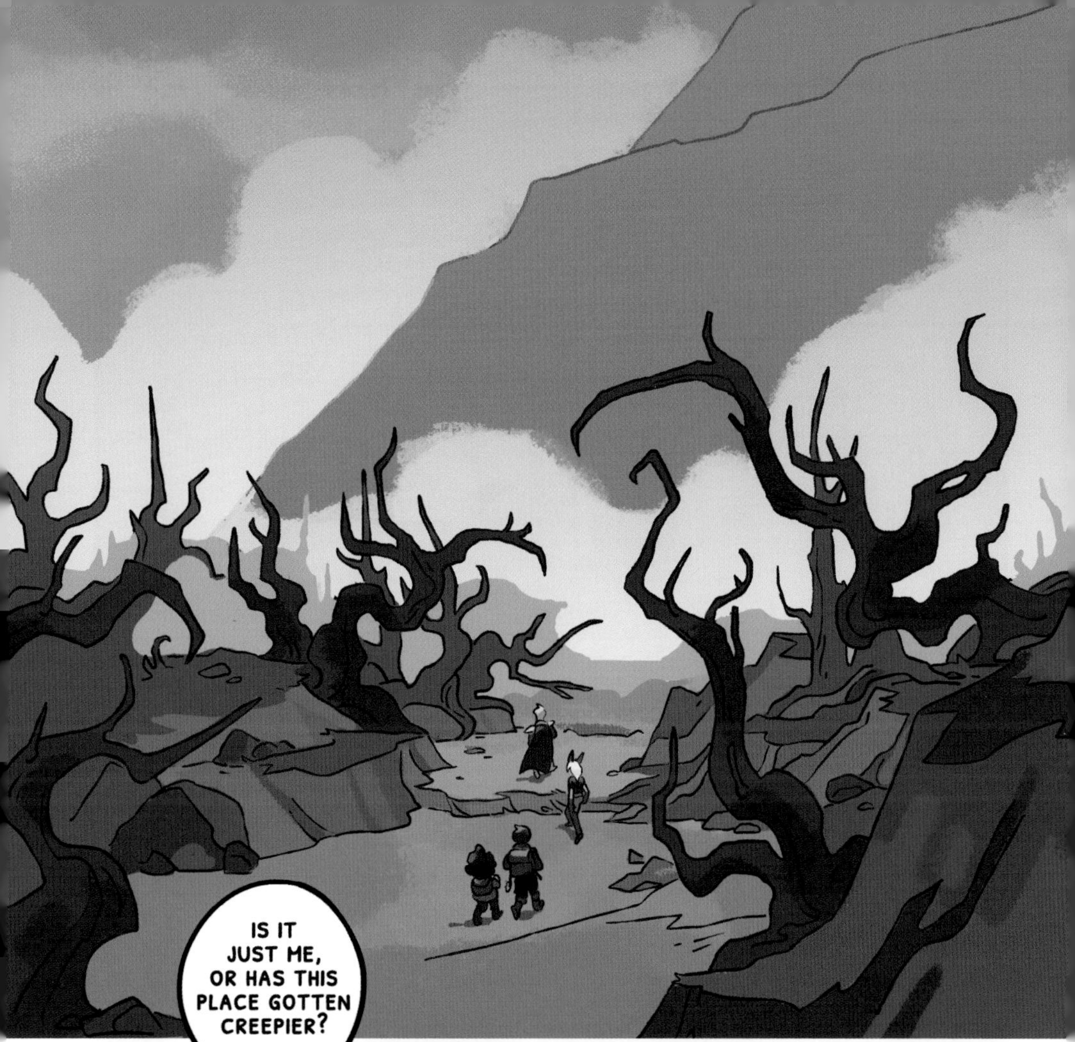
IS IT JUST ME, OR HAS THIS PLACE GOTTEN CREEPIER?

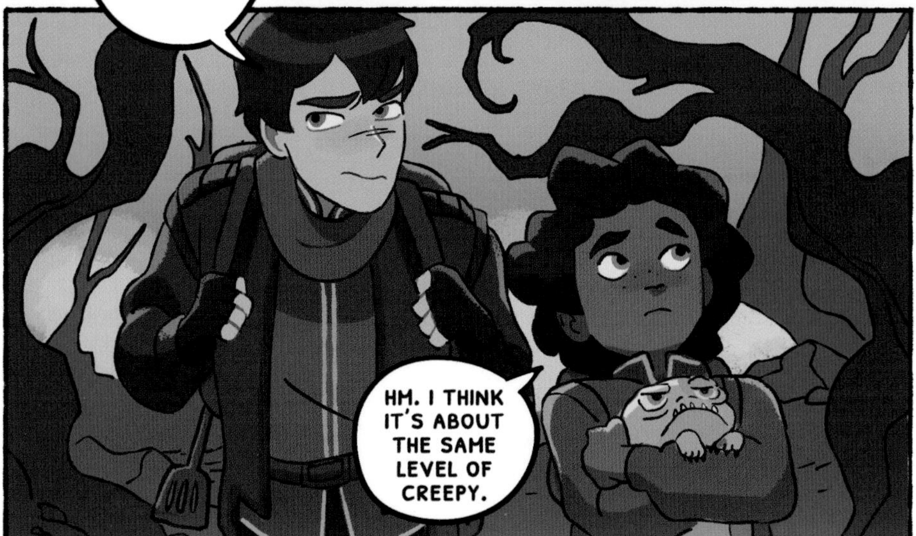
HM. I THINK IT'S ABOUT THE SAME LEVEL OF CREEPY.

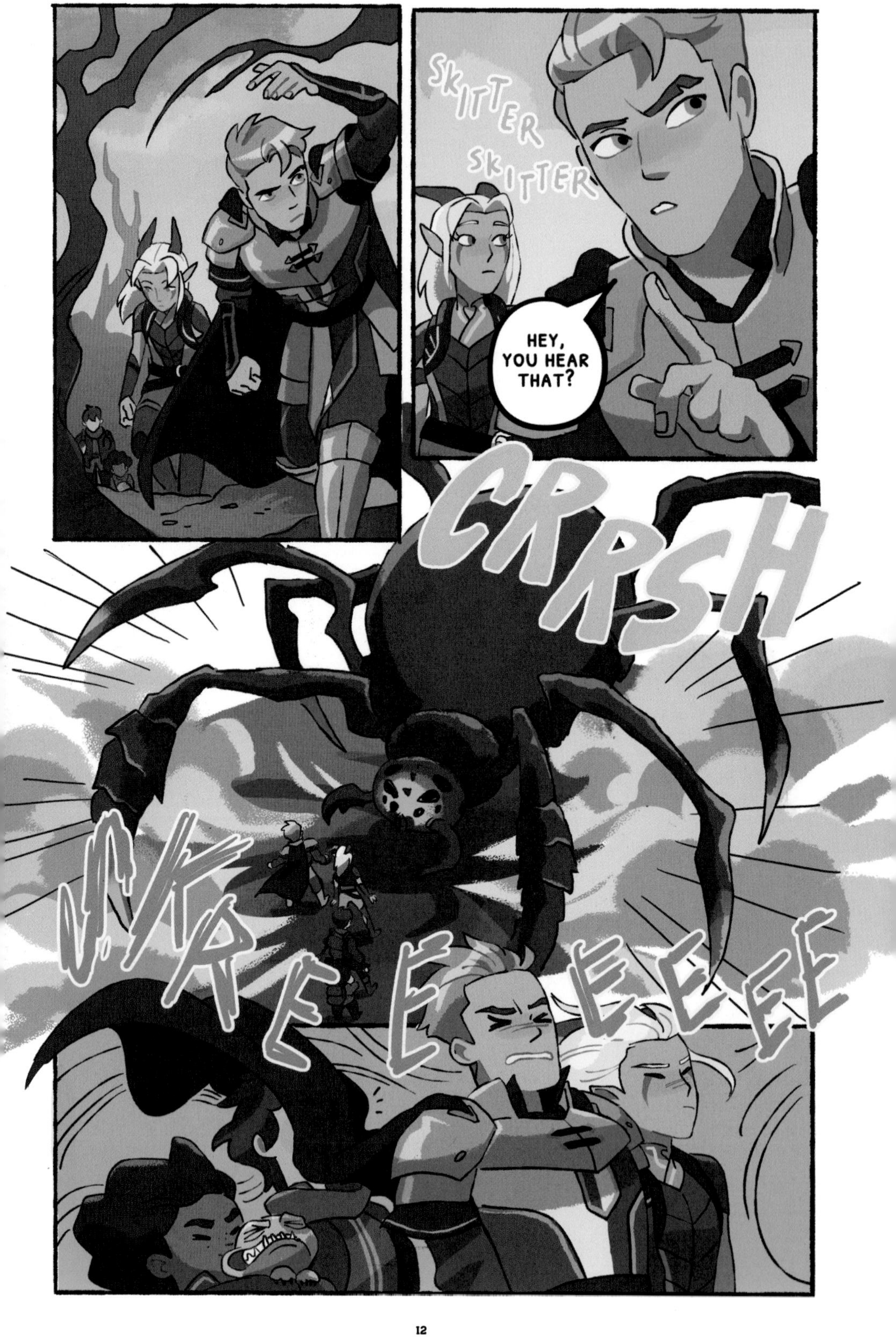
SKITTER
SKITTER
HEY, YOU HEAR THAT?
CRRSH

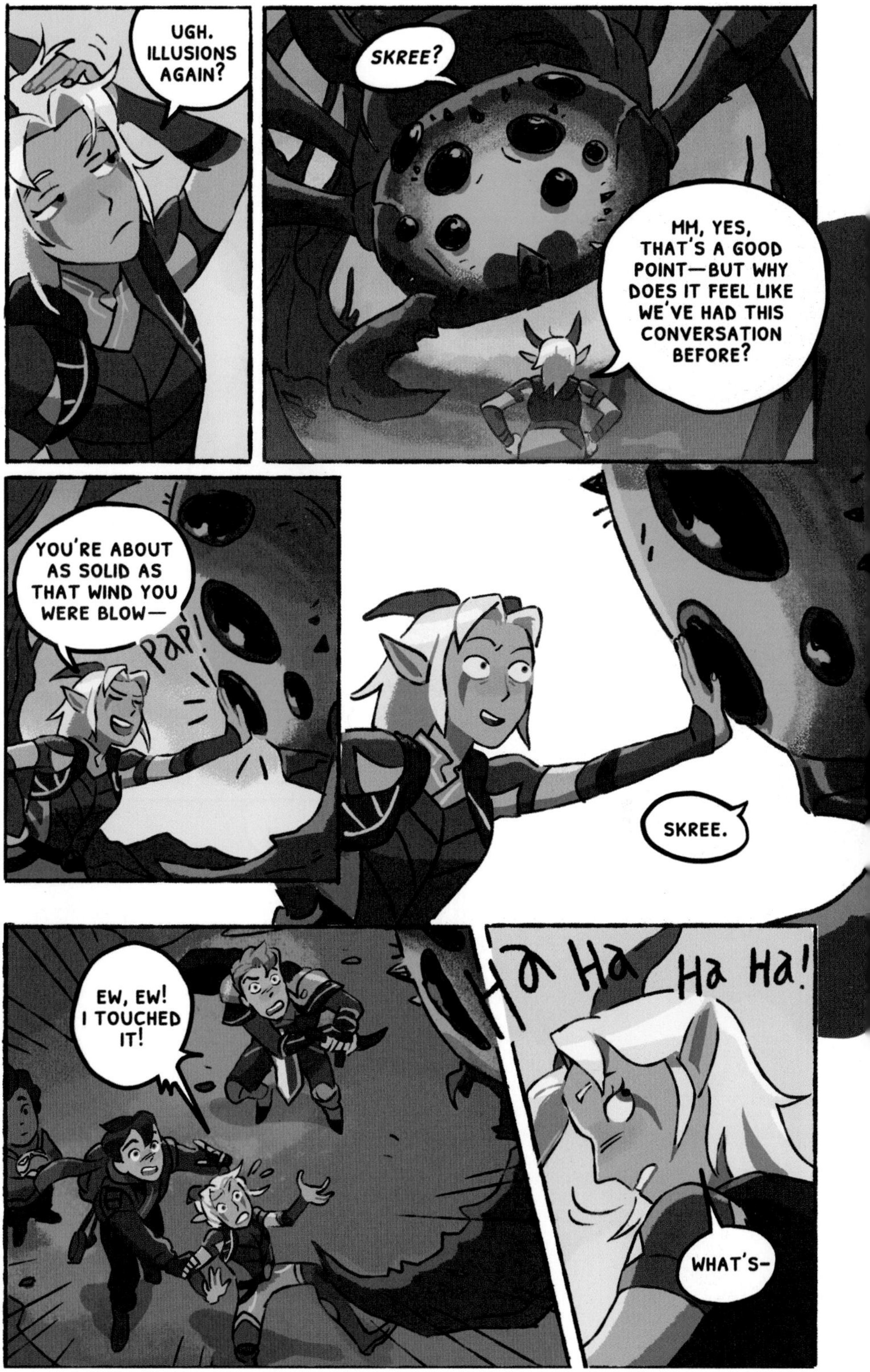
UGH. ILLUSIONS AGAIN?
SKREE?
MM, YES, THAT'S A GOOD POINT—BUT WHY DOES IT FEEL LIKE WE'VE HAD THIS CONVERSATION BEFORE?
YOU'RE ABOUT AS SOLID AS THAT WIND YOU WERE BLOW—
PAP!
SKREE.
EW, EW! I TOUCHED IT!
HA HA HA HA!
WHAT'S-

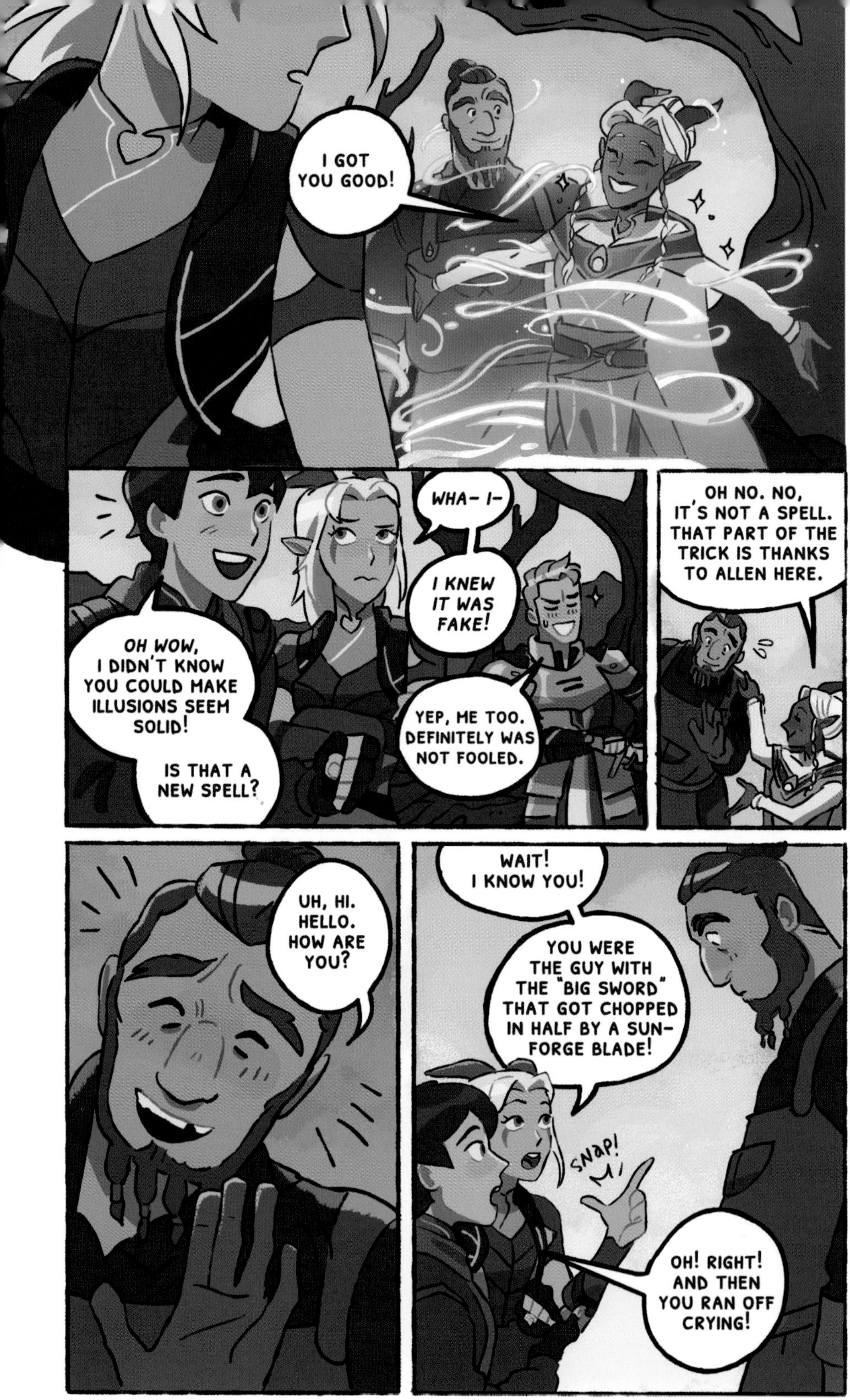
I GOT YOU GOOD!
WHA- I-
I KNEW IT WAS FAKE!
OH WOW, I DIDN'T KNOW YOU COULD MAKE ILLUSIONS SEEM SOLID!
IS THAT A NEW SPELL?
YEP, ME TOO. DEFINITELY WAS NOT FOOLED.
OH NO. NO, IT'S NOT A SPELL. THAT PART OF THE TRICK IS THANKS TO ALLEN HERE.
UH, HI. HELLO. HOW ARE YOU?
WAIT! I KNOW YOU!
YOU WERE THE GUY WITH THE "BIG SWORD" THAT GOT CHOPPED IN HALF BY A SUN-FORGE BLADE!
SNAP!
OH! RIGHT! AND THEN YOU RAN OFF CRYING!

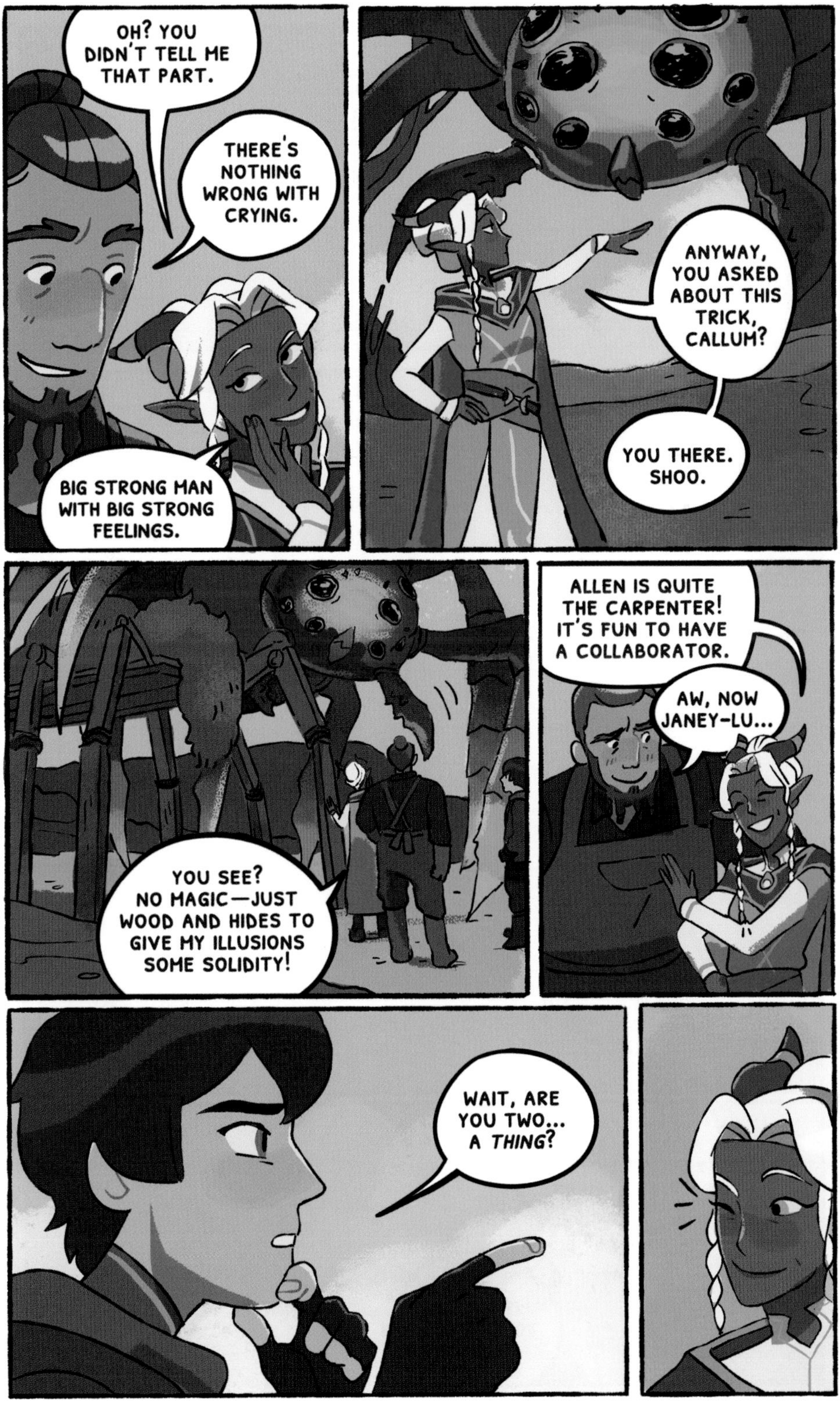
OH? YOU DIDN'T TELL ME THAT PART.
THERE'S NOTHING WRONG WITH CRYING.
BIG STRONG MAN WITH BIG STRONG FEELINGS.
ANYWAY, YOU ASKED ABOUT THIS TRICK, CALLUM?
YOU THERE. SHOO.
YOU SEE? NO MAGIC—JUST WOOD AND HIDES TO GIVE MY ILLUSIONS SOME SOLIDITY!
ALLEN IS QUITE THE CARPENTER! IT'S FUN TO HAVE A COLLABORATOR.
AW, NOW JANEY-LU...
WAIT, ARE YOU TWO... A *THING*?

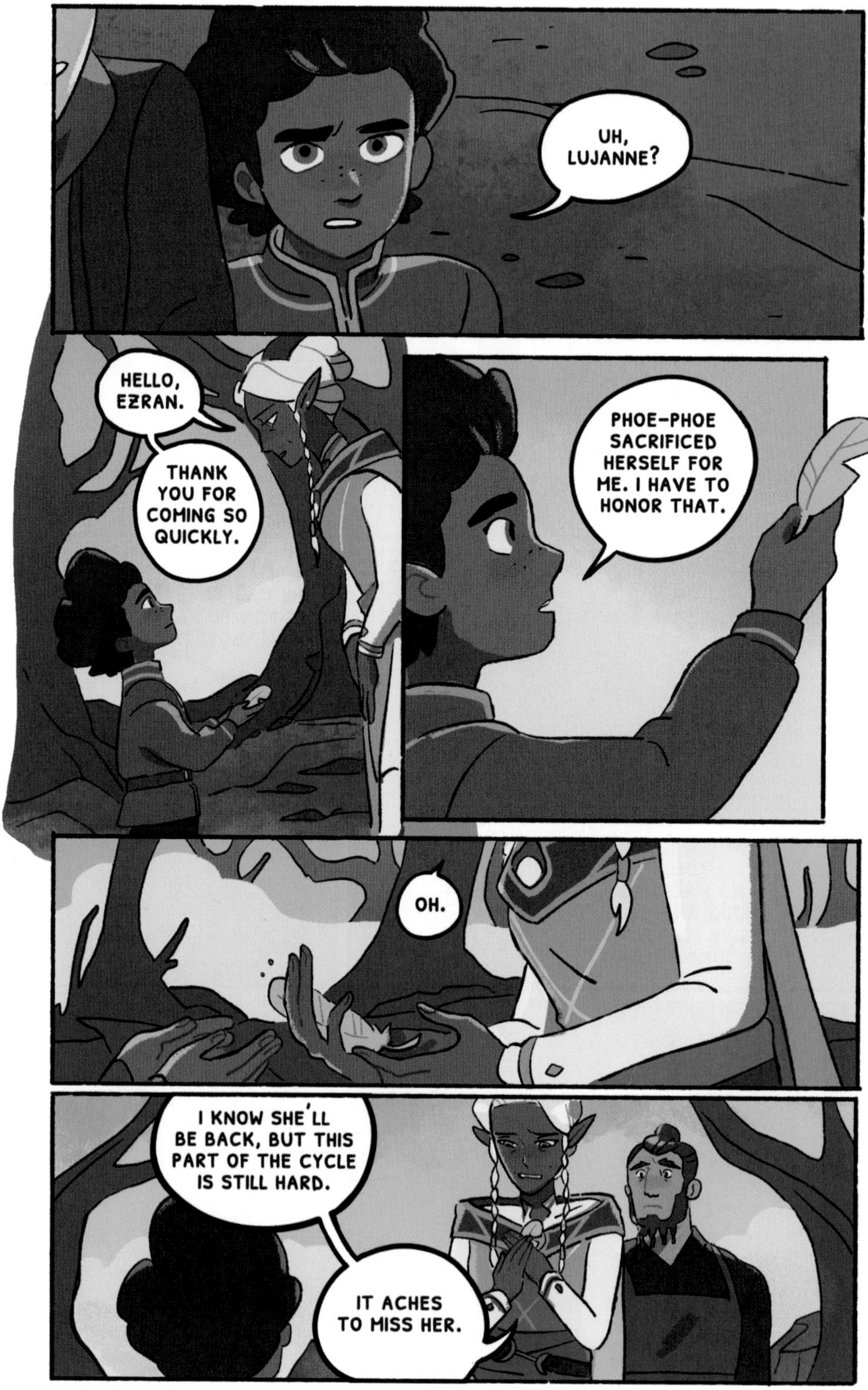
UH, LUJANNE?
HELLO, EZRAN.
THANK YOU FOR COMING SO QUICKLY.
PHOE-PHOE SACRIFICED HERSELF FOR ME. I HAVE TO HONOR THAT.
OH.
I KNOW SHE'LL BE BACK, BUT THIS PART OF THE CYCLE IS STILL HARD.
IT ACHES TO MISS HER.

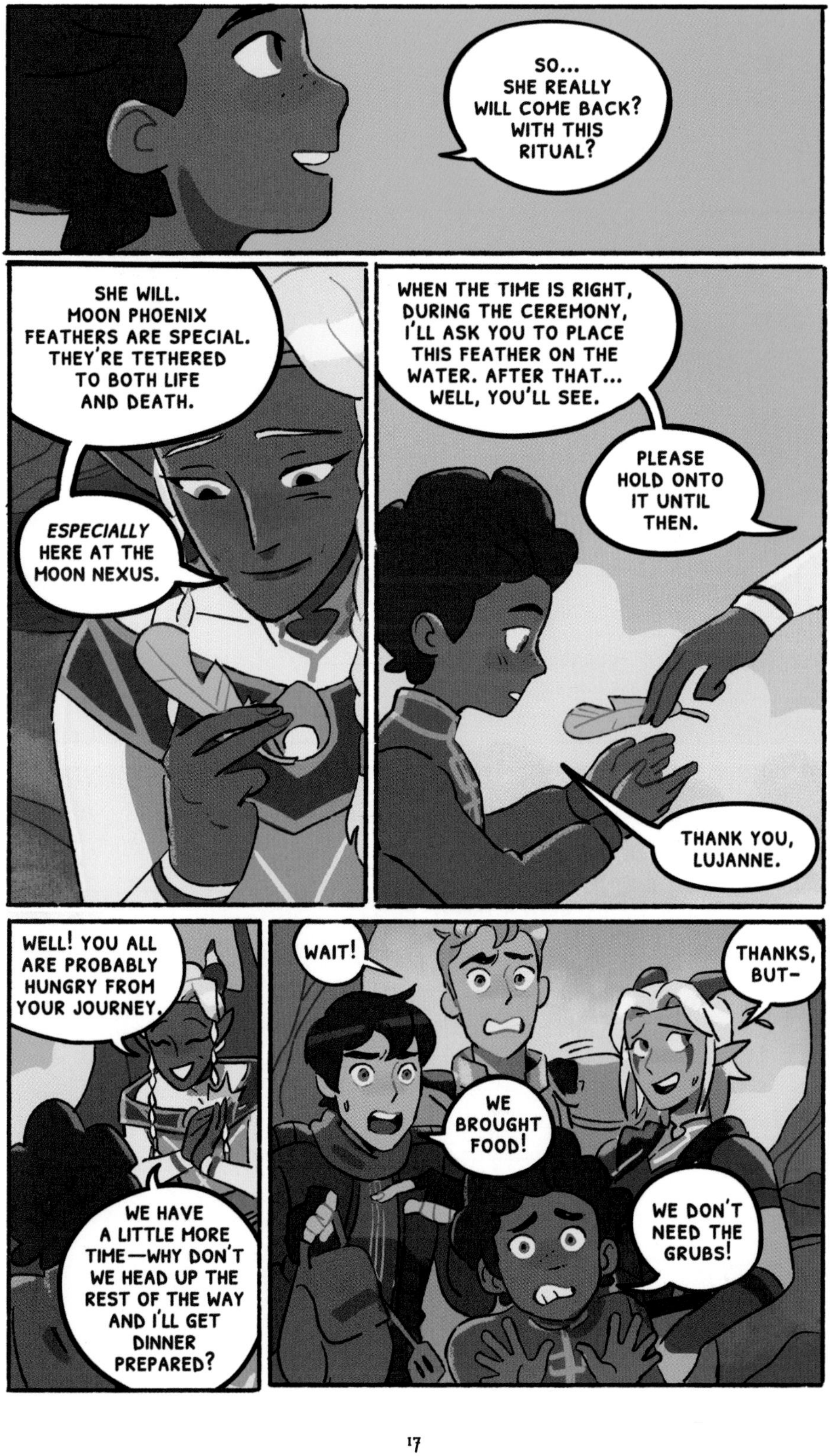
SO... SHE REALLY WILL COME BACK? WITH THIS RITUAL?
SHE WILL. MOON PHOENIX FEATHERS ARE SPECIAL. THEY'RE TETHERED TO BOTH LIFE AND DEATH.
ESPECIALLY HERE AT THE MOON NEXUS.
WHEN THE TIME IS RIGHT, DURING THE CEREMONY, I'LL ASK YOU TO PLACE THIS FEATHER ON THE WATER. AFTER THAT... WELL, YOU'LL SEE.
PLEASE HOLD ONTO IT UNTIL THEN.
THANK YOU, LUJANNE.
WELL! YOU ALL ARE PROBABLY HUNGRY FROM YOUR JOURNEY.
WE HAVE A LITTLE MORE TIME—WHY DON'T WE HEAD UP THE REST OF THE WAY AND I'LL GET DINNER PREPARED?
WAIT!
THANKS, BUT-
WE BROUGHT FOOD!
WE DON'T NEED THE GRUBS!

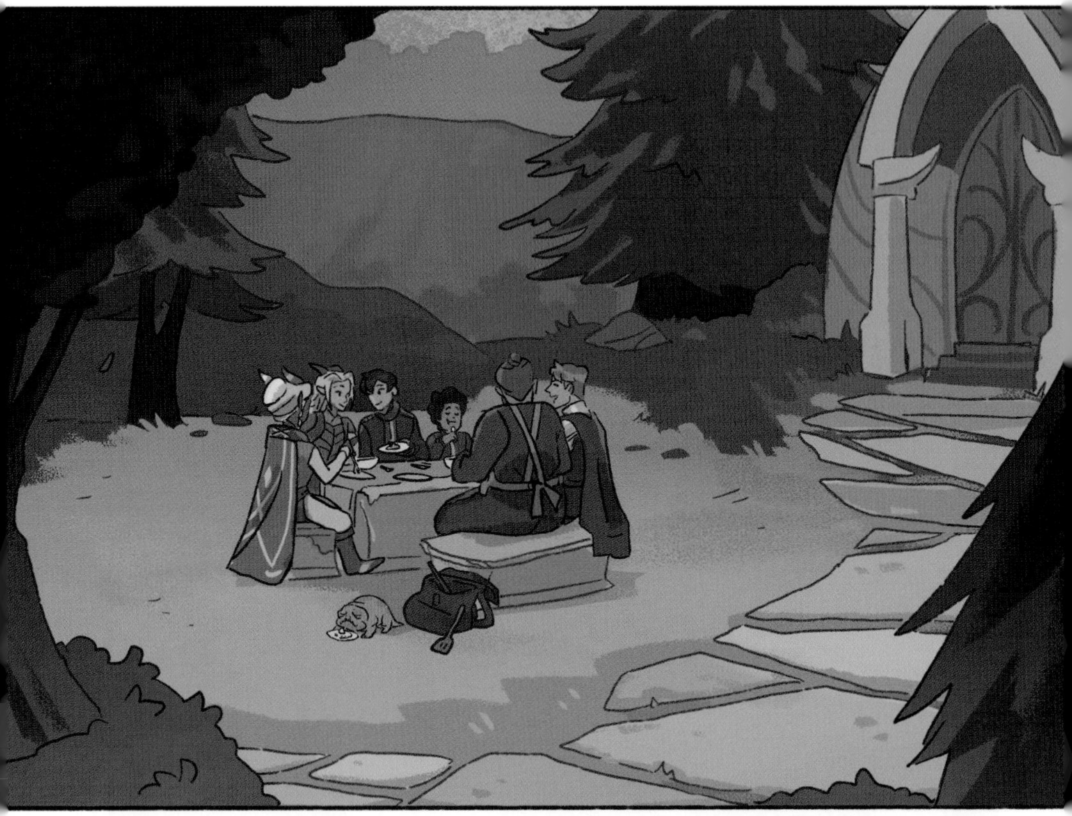

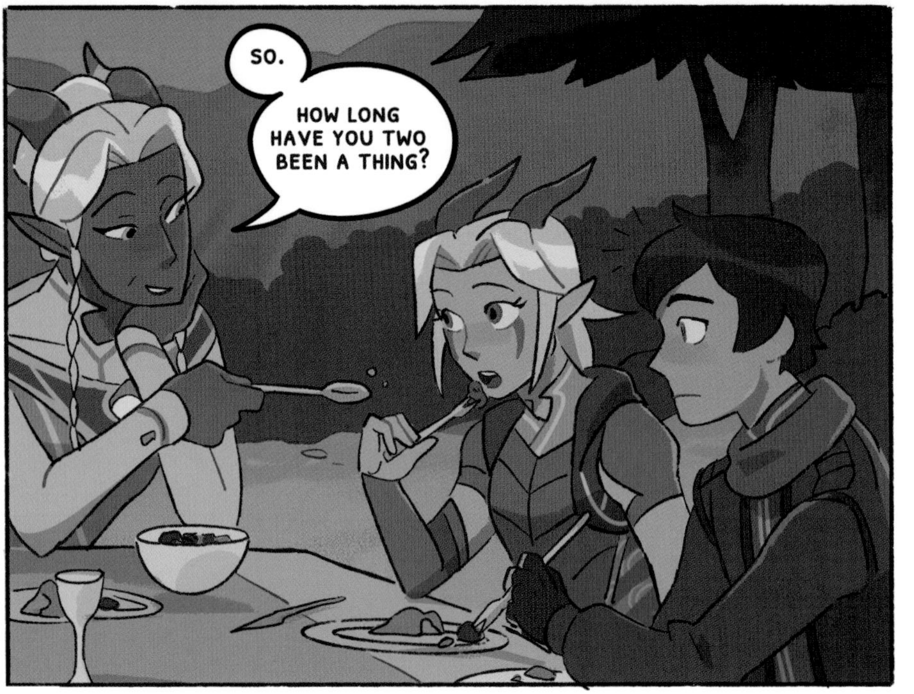
SO.
HOW LONG HAVE YOU TWO BEEN A THING?

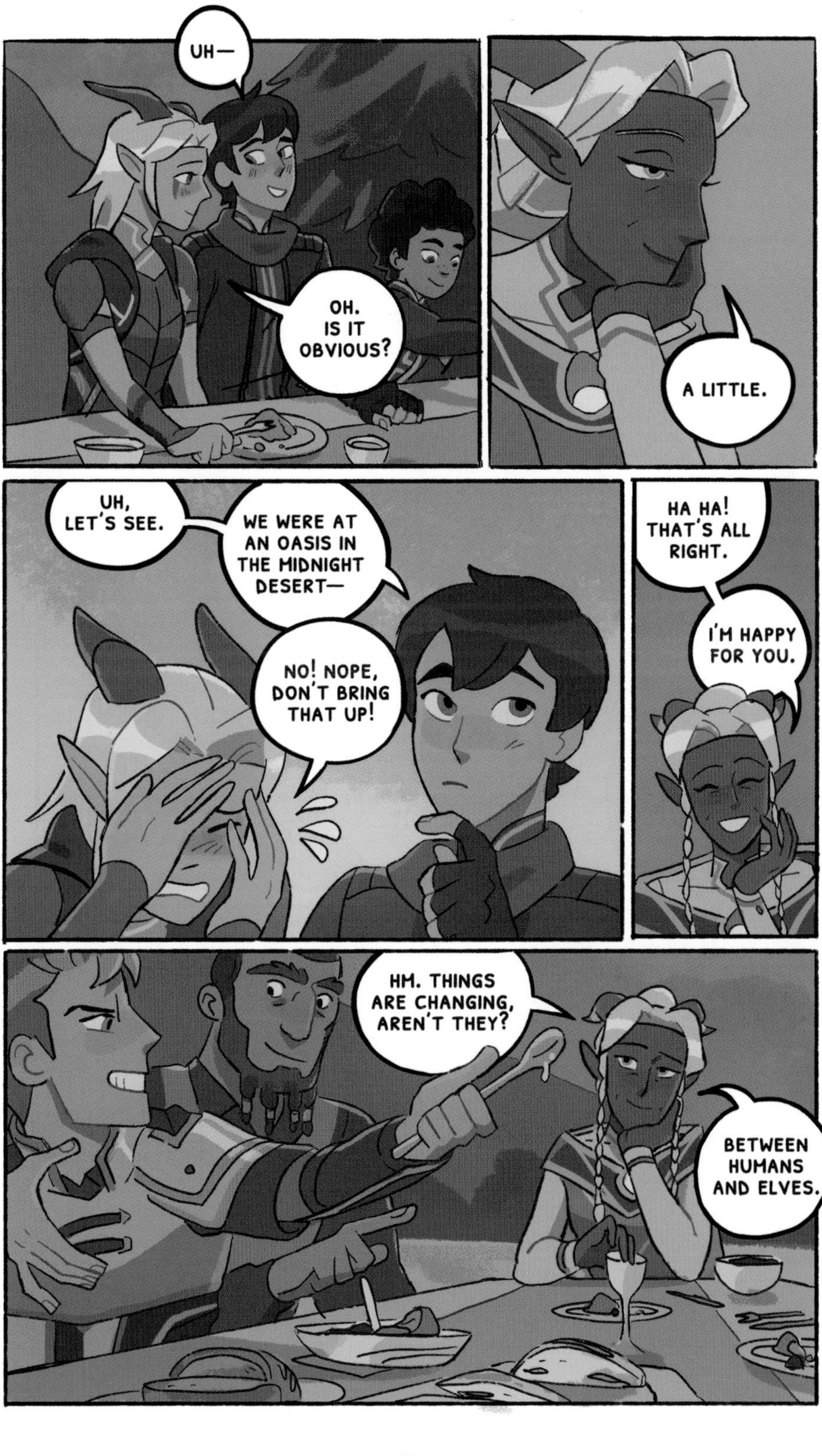
UH—
OH. IS IT OBVIOUS?
A LITTLE.
UH, LET'S SEE.
WE WERE AT AN OASIS IN THE MIDNIGHT DESERT—
NO! NOPE, DON'T BRING THAT UP!
HA HA! THAT'S ALL RIGHT.
I'M HAPPY FOR YOU.
HM. THINGS ARE CHANGING, AREN'T THEY?
BETWEEN HUMANS AND ELVES.

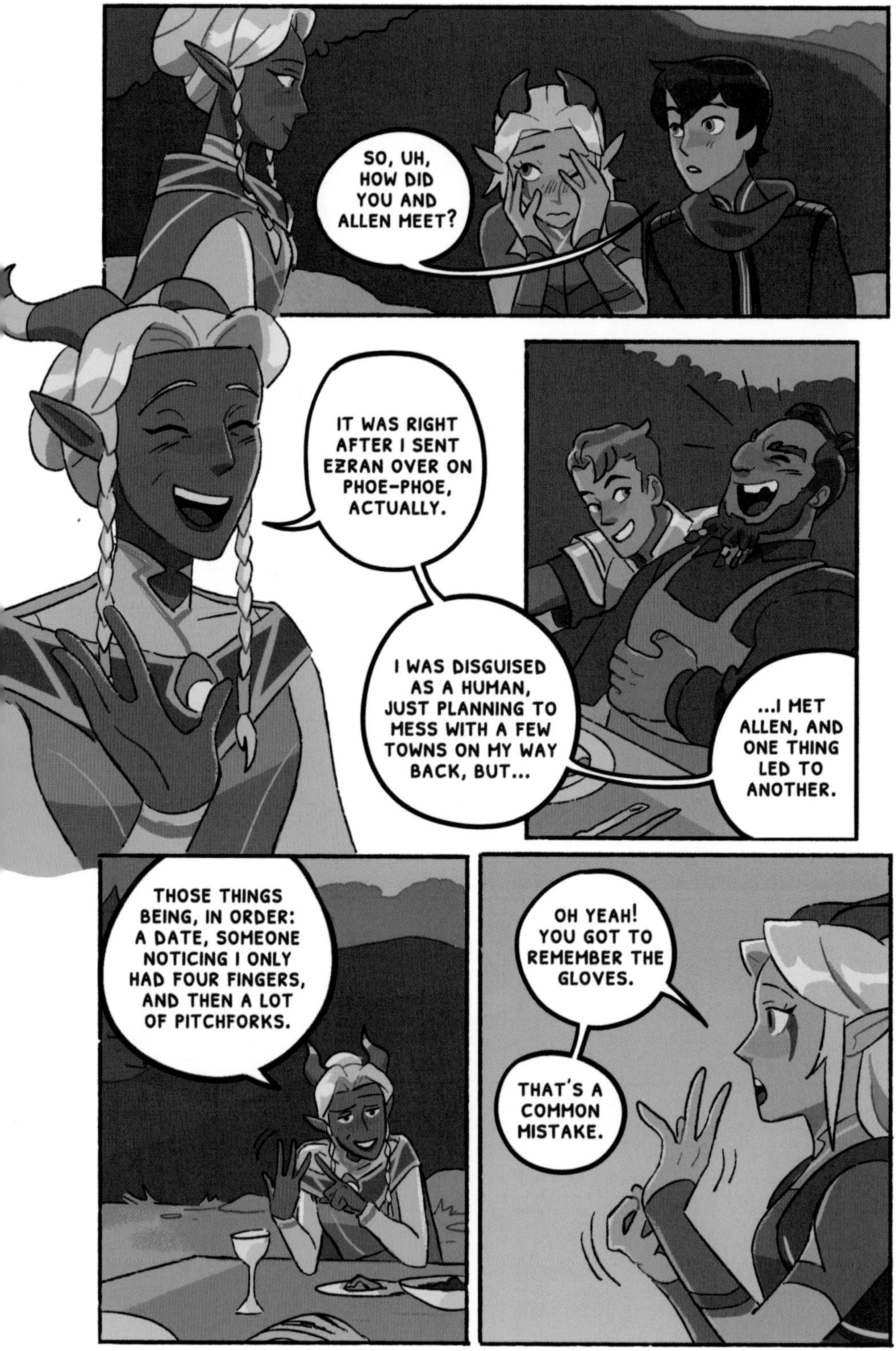
SO, UH, HOW DID YOU AND ALLEN MEET?
IT WAS RIGHT AFTER I SENT EZRAN OVER ON PHOE-PHOE, ACTUALLY.
I WAS DISGUISED AS A HUMAN, JUST PLANNING TO MESS WITH A FEW TOWNS ON MY WAY BACK, BUT...
...I MET ALLEN, AND ONE THING LED TO ANOTHER.
THOSE THINGS BEING, IN ORDER: A DATE, SOMEONE NOTICING I ONLY HAD FOUR FINGERS, AND THEN A LOT OF PITCHFORKS.
OH YEAH! YOU GOT TO REMEMBER THE GLOVES.
THAT'S A COMMON MISTAKE.

I'M GLAD PHOE-PHOE WAS ABLE TO HELP EZRAN.

GLAD THAT HER SACRIFICE MADE A DIFFERENCE.

AND IT SEEMS LIKE EVERYTHING WORKED OUT IN THE END!

DID IT?

VIREN, THE MOST DANGEROUS MAN IN THE WORLD, UP AND DISAPPEARED. JUST, *POOF*, GONE!

AND EVERYONE WANTS TO BELIEVE THAT HE'S DEAD, BUT—

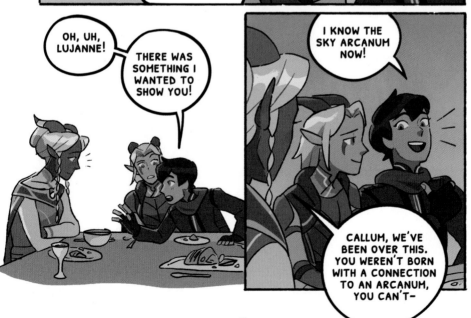

OH, UH, LUJANNE!

THERE WAS SOMETHING I WANTED TO SHOW YOU!

I KNOW THE SKY ARCANUM NOW!

CALLUM, WE'VE BEEN OVER THIS. YOU WEREN'T BORN WITH A CONNECTION TO AN ARCANUM, YOU CAN'T—

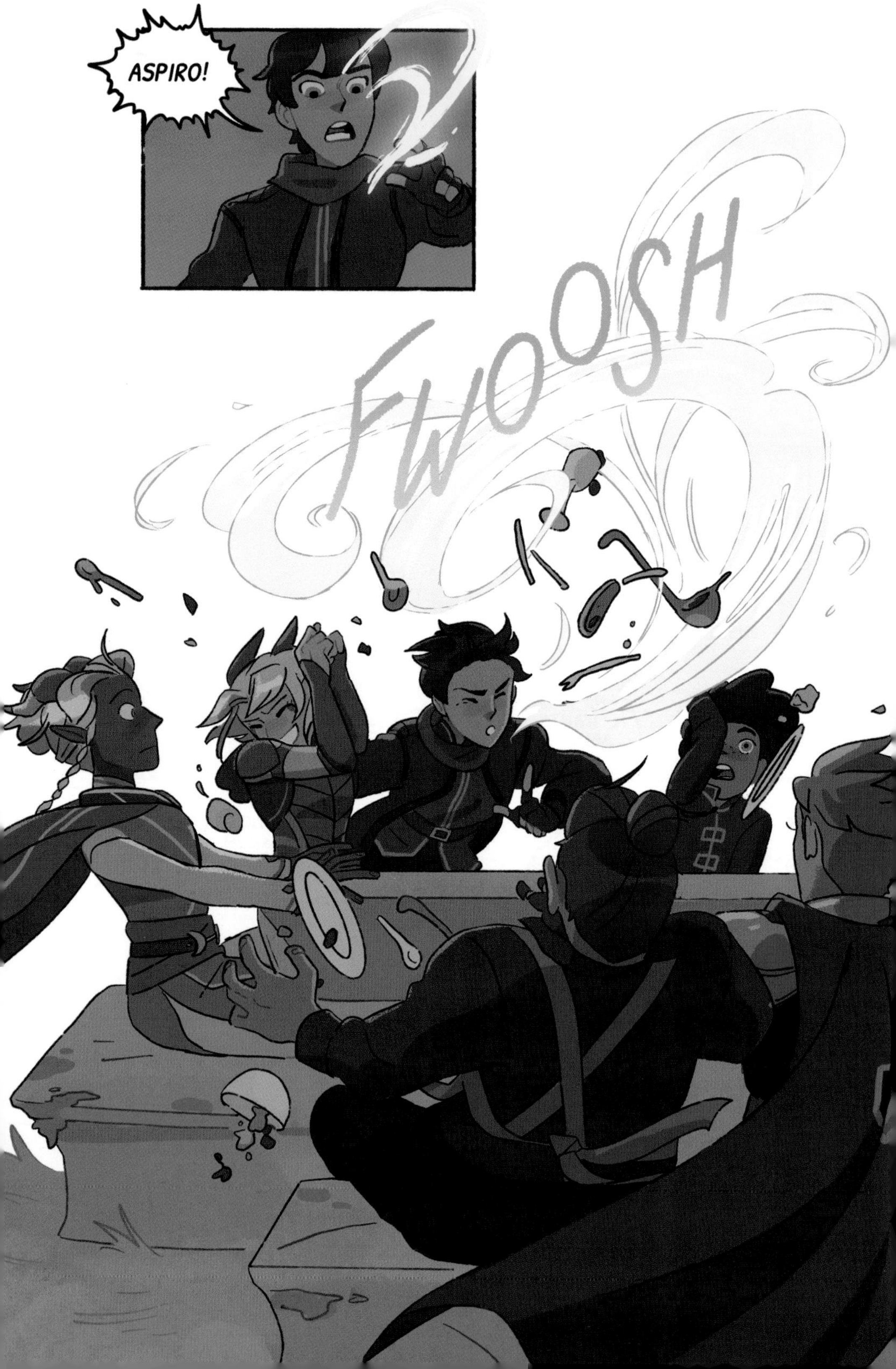
ASPIRO!
FWOOSH

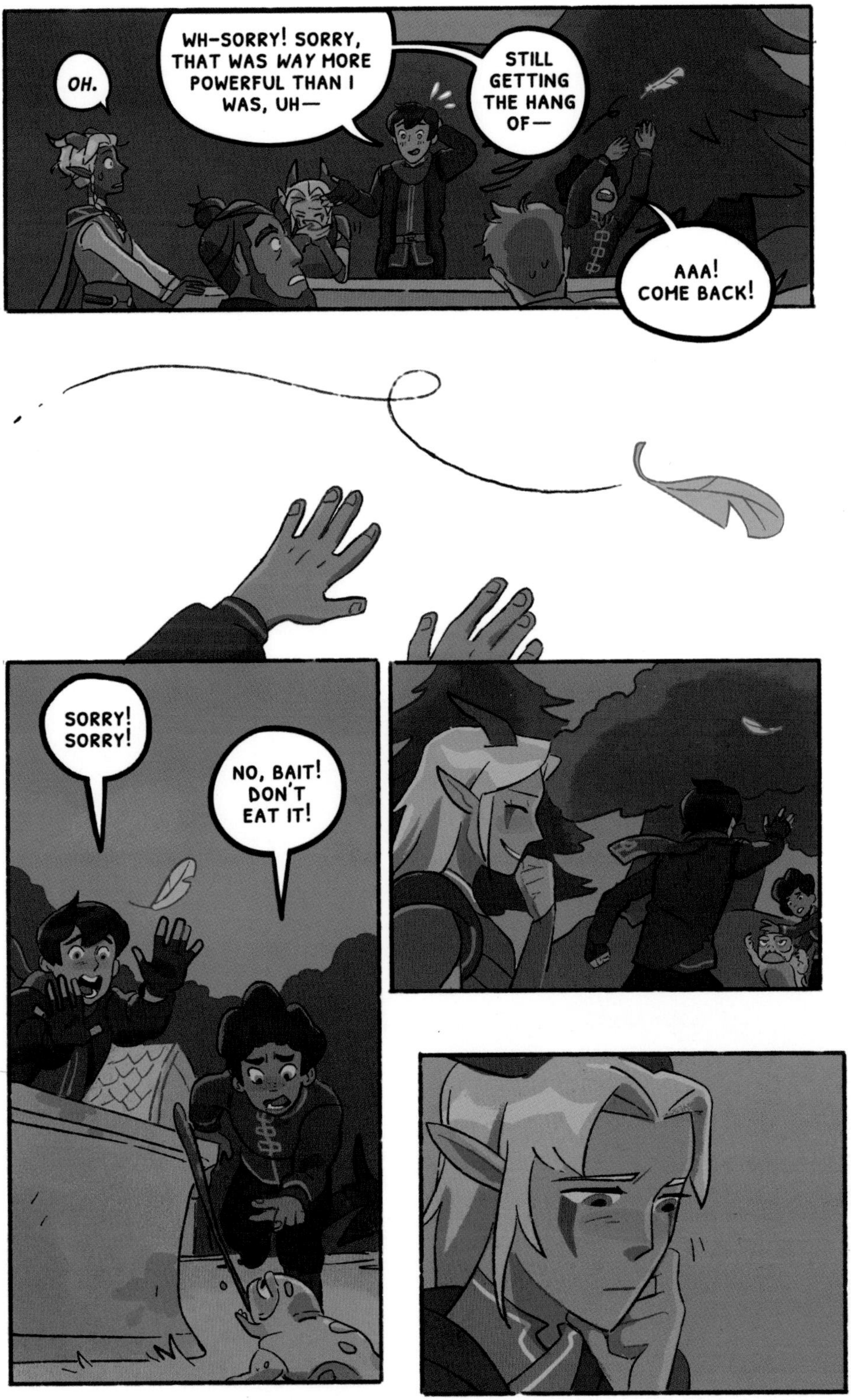
OH.
WH-SORRY! SORRY, THAT WAS WAY MORE POWERFUL THAN I WAS, UH—
STILL GETTING THE HANG OF—
AAA! COME BACK!
SORRY! SORRY!
NO, BAIT! DON'T EAT IT!

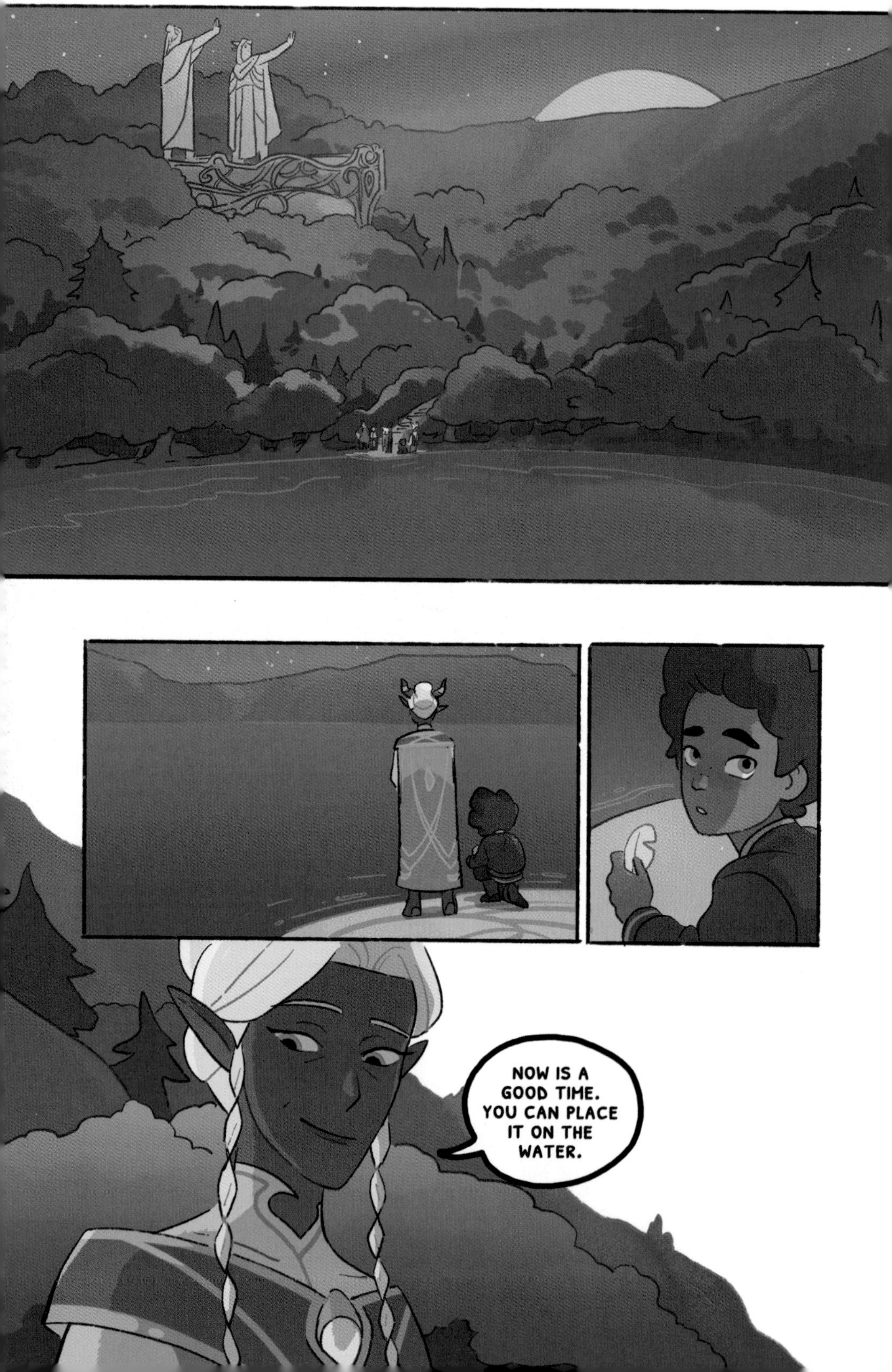
NOW IS A GOOD TIME. YOU CAN PLACE IT ON THE WATER.

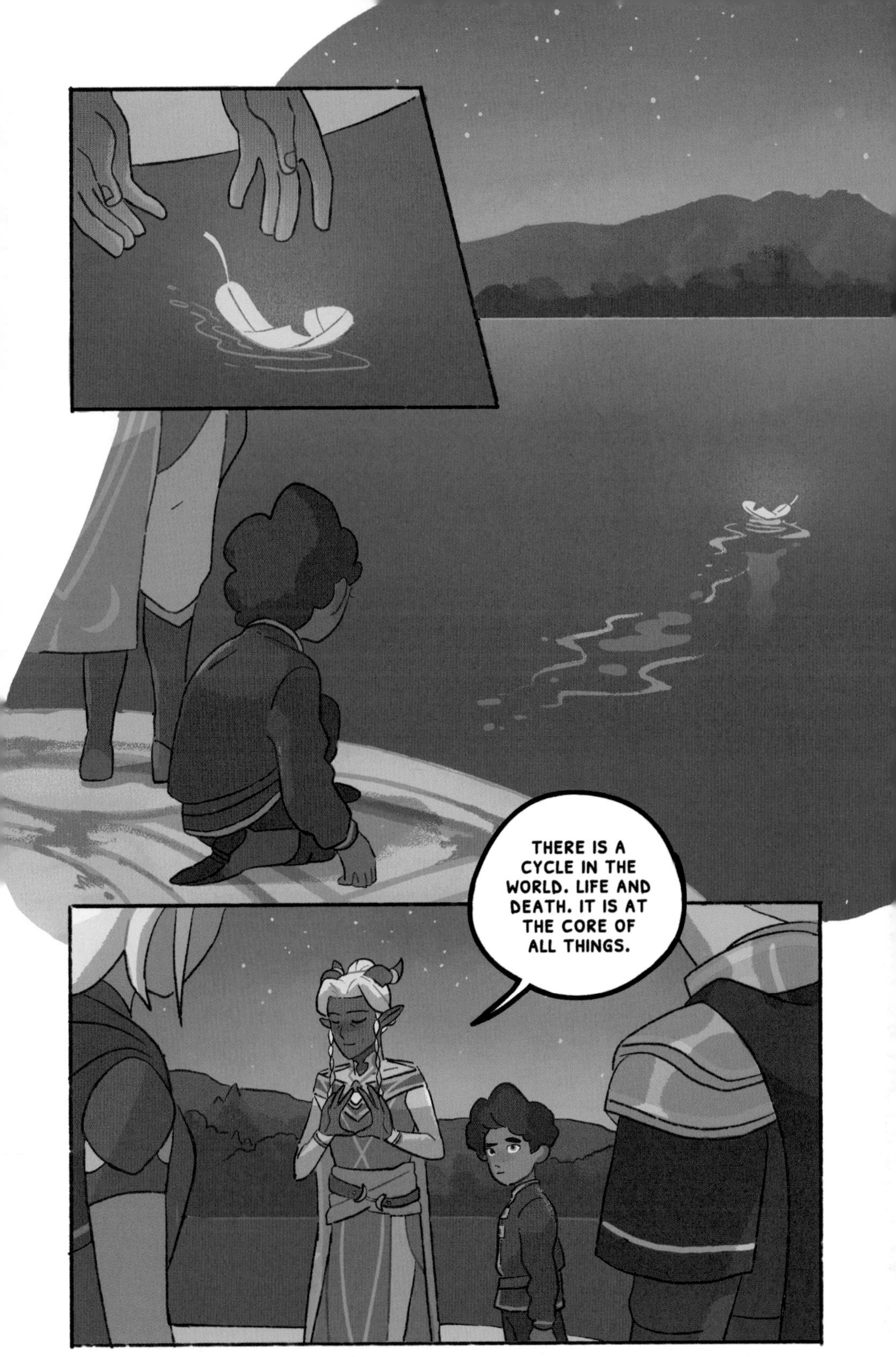
THERE IS A CYCLE IN THE WORLD. LIFE AND DEATH. IT IS AT THE CORE OF ALL THINGS.

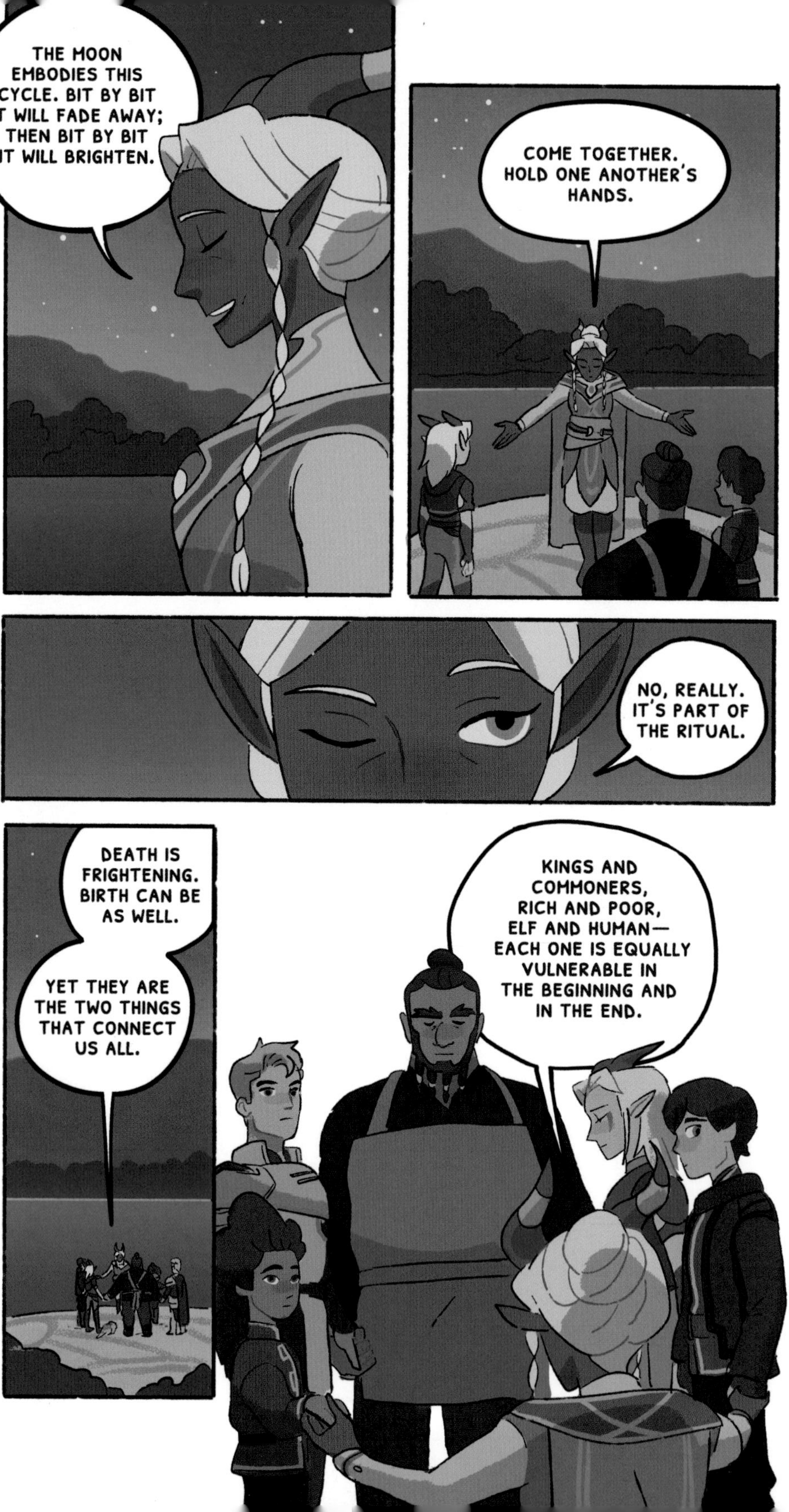
THE MOON EMBODIES THIS CYCLE. BIT BY BIT IT WILL FADE AWAY; THEN BIT BY BIT IT WILL BRIGHTEN.
COME TOGETHER. HOLD ONE ANOTHER'S HANDS.
NO, REALLY. IT'S PART OF THE RITUAL.
DEATH IS FRIGHTENING. BIRTH CAN BE AS WELL.
YET THEY ARE THE TWO THINGS THAT CONNECT US ALL.
KINGS AND COMMONERS, RICH AND POOR, ELF AND HUMAN— EACH ONE IS EQUALLY VULNERABLE IN THE BEGINNING AND IN THE END.

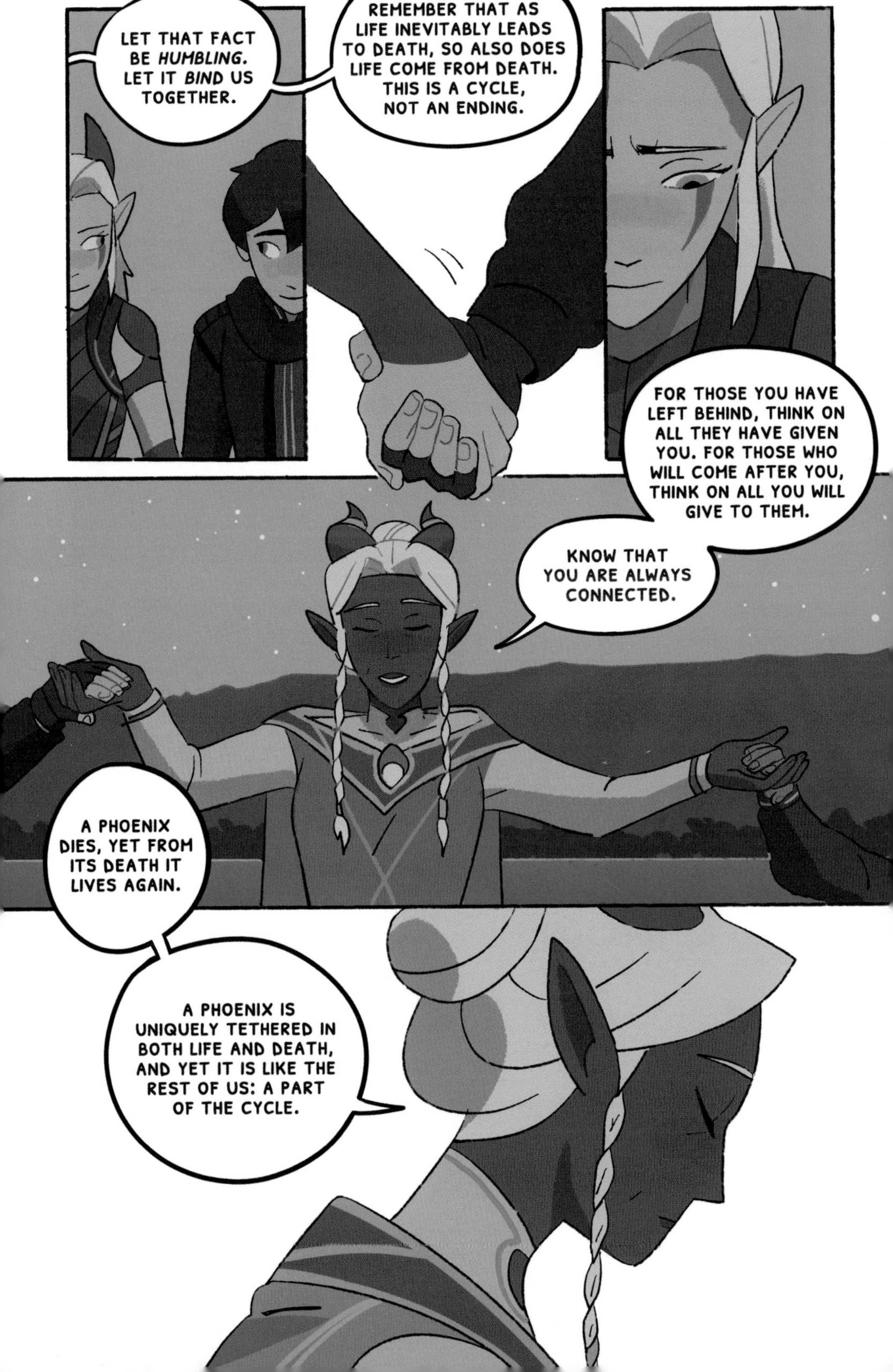
LET THAT FACT BE *HUMBLING*. LET IT *BIND* US TOGETHER.
REMEMBER THAT AS LIFE INEVITABLY LEADS TO DEATH, SO ALSO DOES LIFE COME FROM DEATH. THIS IS A CYCLE, NOT AN ENDING.
FOR THOSE YOU HAVE LEFT BEHIND, THINK ON ALL THEY HAVE GIVEN YOU. FOR THOSE WHO WILL COME AFTER YOU, THINK ON ALL YOU WILL GIVE TO THEM.
KNOW THAT YOU ARE ALWAYS CONNECTED.
A PHOENIX DIES, YET FROM ITS DEATH IT LIVES AGAIN.
A PHOENIX IS UNIQUELY TETHERED IN BOTH LIFE AND DEATH, AND YET IT IS LIKE THE REST OF US: A PART OF THE CYCLE.

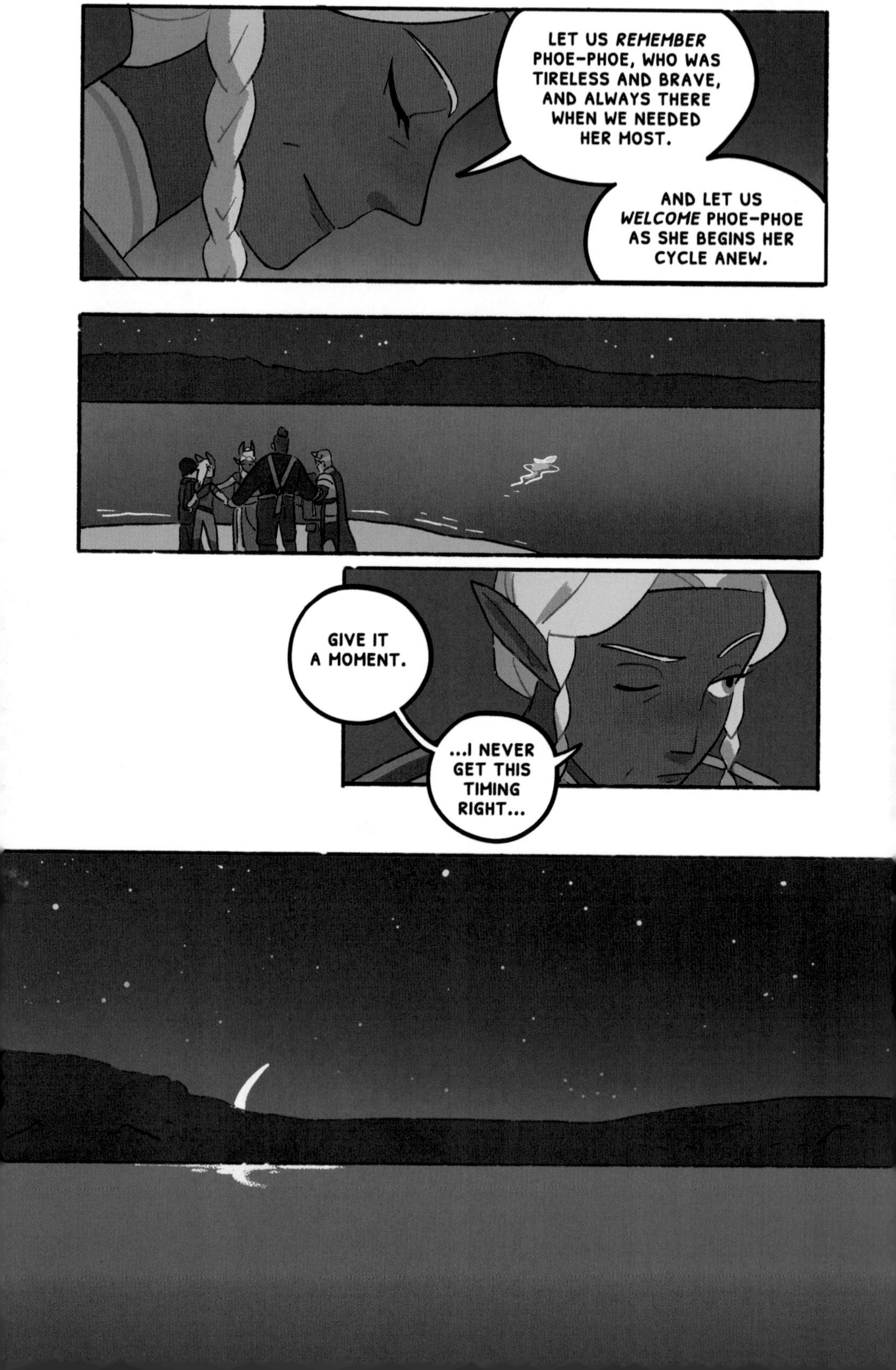
LET US *REMEMBER* PHOE-PHOE, WHO WAS TIRELESS AND BRAVE, AND ALWAYS THERE WHEN WE NEEDED HER MOST.
AND LET US *WELCOME* PHOE-PHOE AS SHE BEGINS HER CYCLE ANEW.
GIVE IT A MOMENT.
...I NEVER GET THIS TIMING RIGHT...

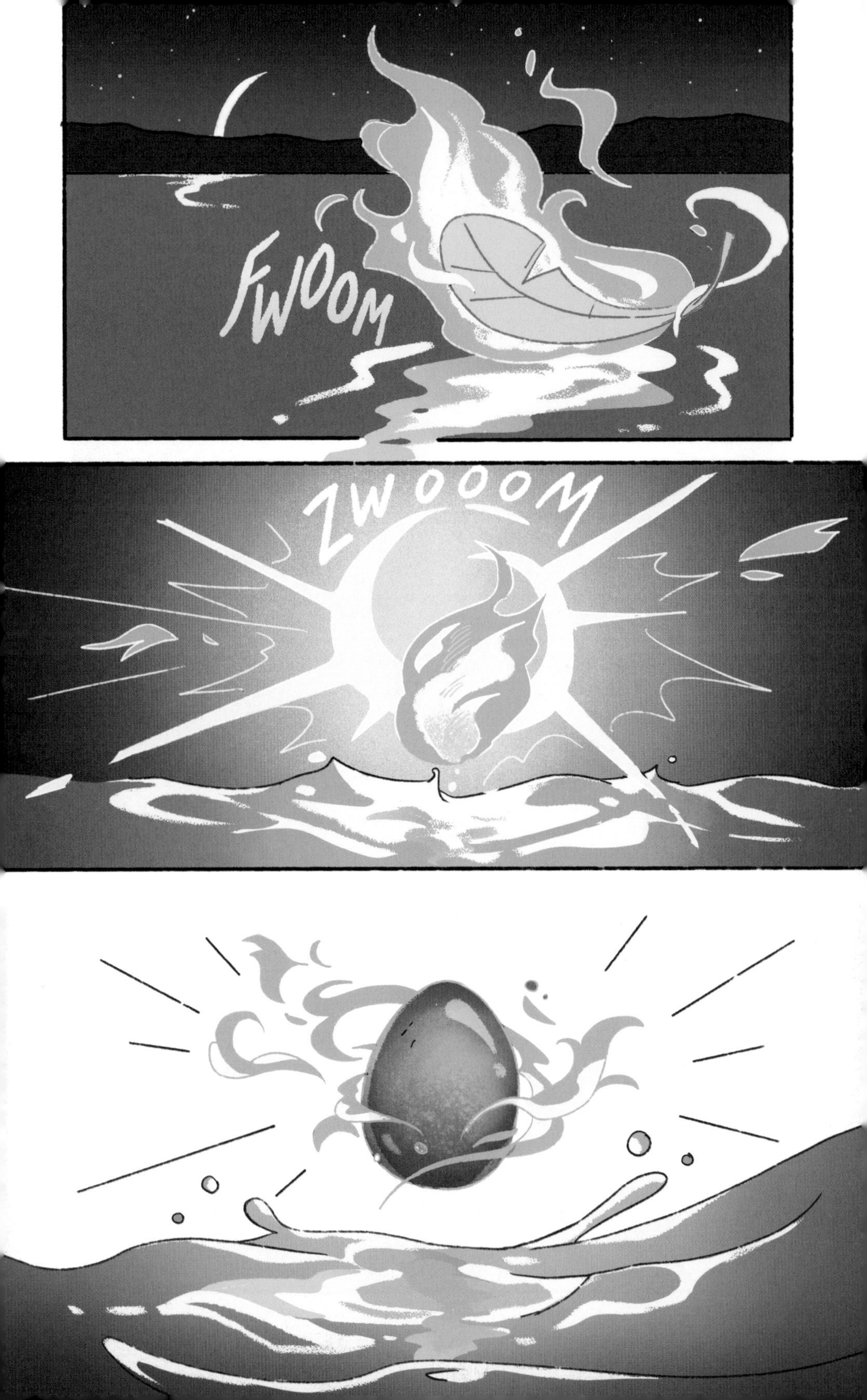
FWOOM
ZWOOOM

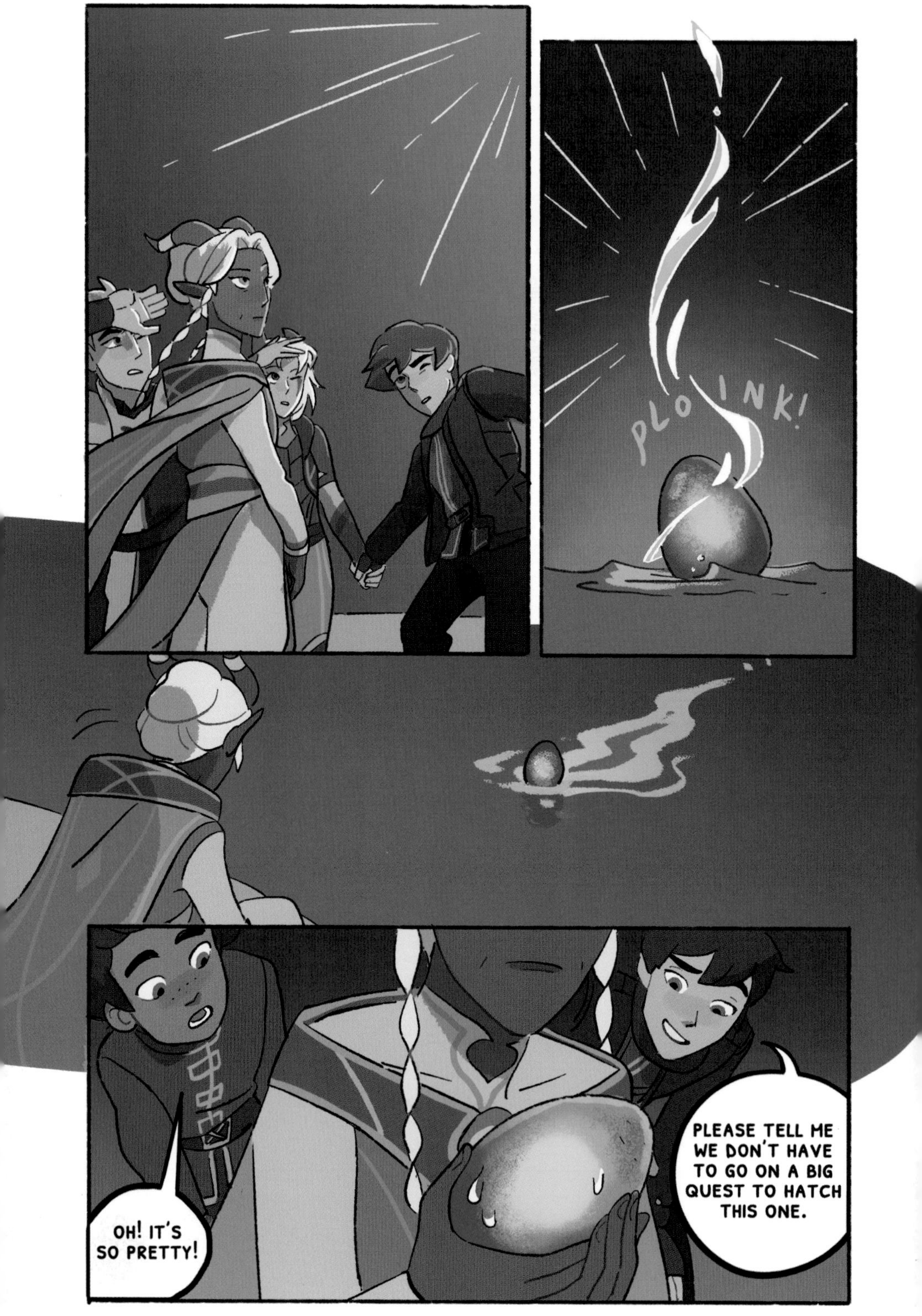
PLOINK!
OH! IT'S SO PRETTY!
PLEASE TELL ME WE DON'T HAVE TO GO ON A BIG QUEST TO HATCH THIS ONE.

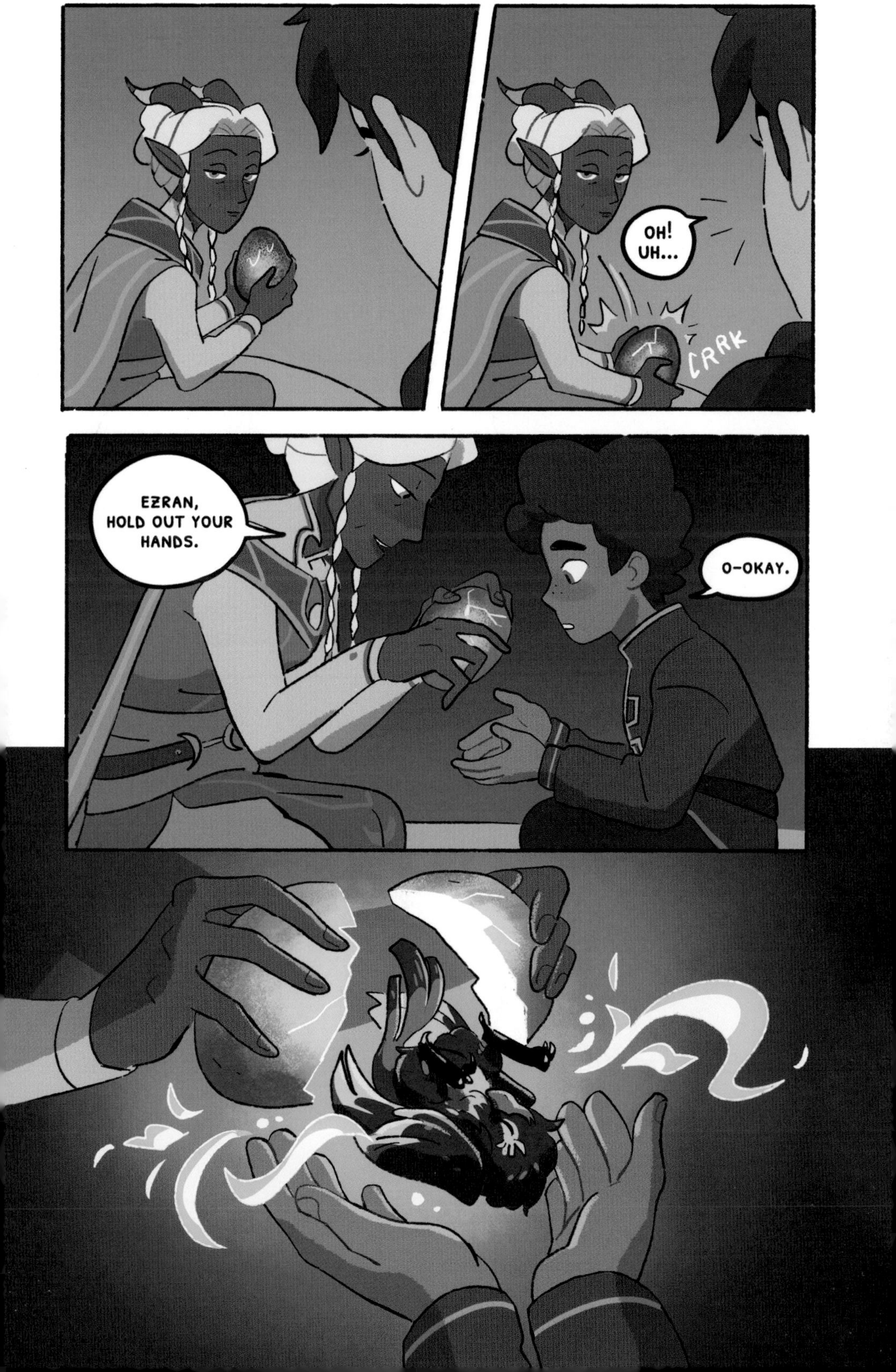
OH! UH...
CRRK
EZRAN, HOLD OUT YOUR HANDS.
O-OKAY.

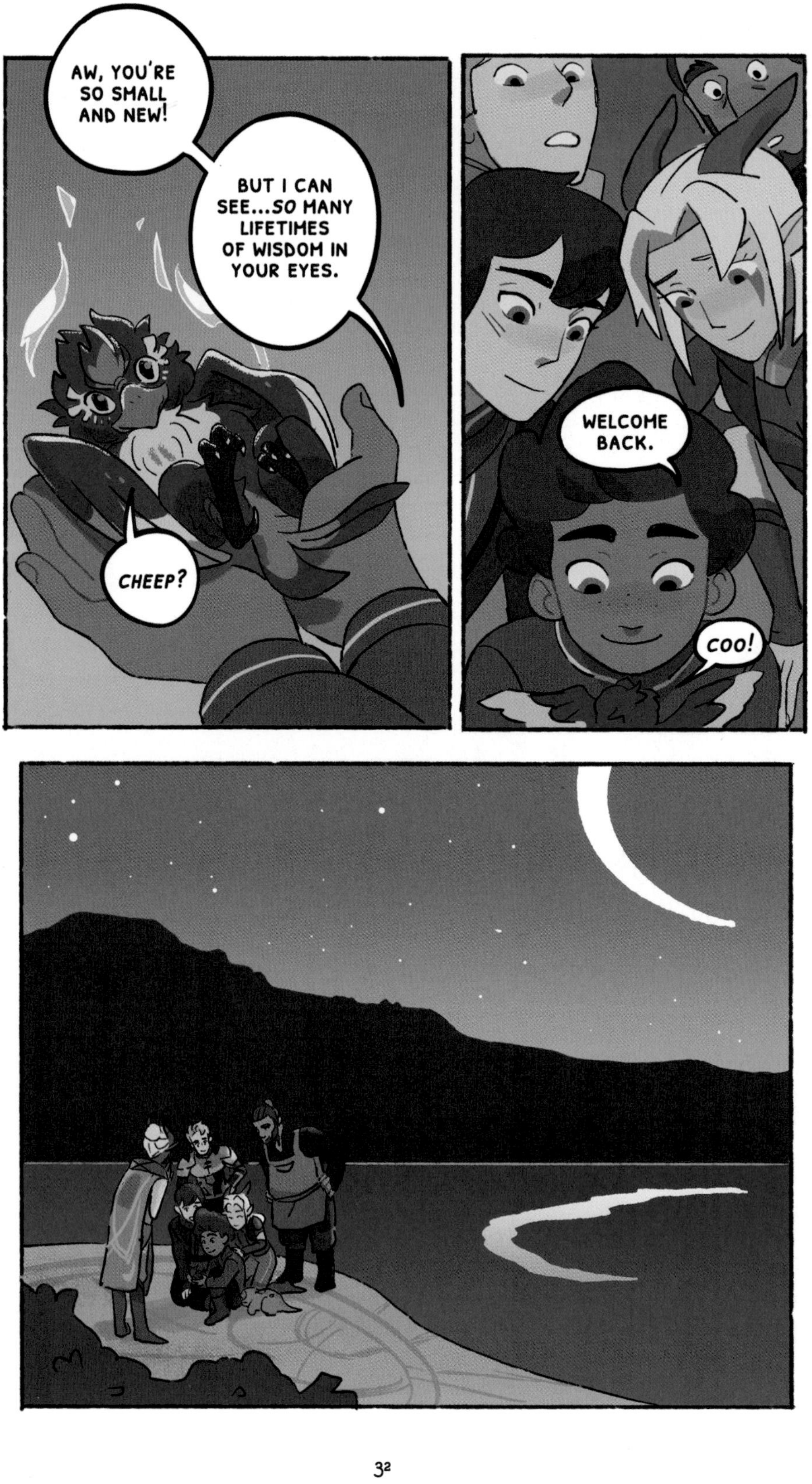
AW, YOU'RE SO SMALL AND NEW!
BUT I CAN SEE...*SO* MANY LIFETIMES OF WISDOM IN YOUR EYES.
CHEEP?
WELCOME BACK.
COO!

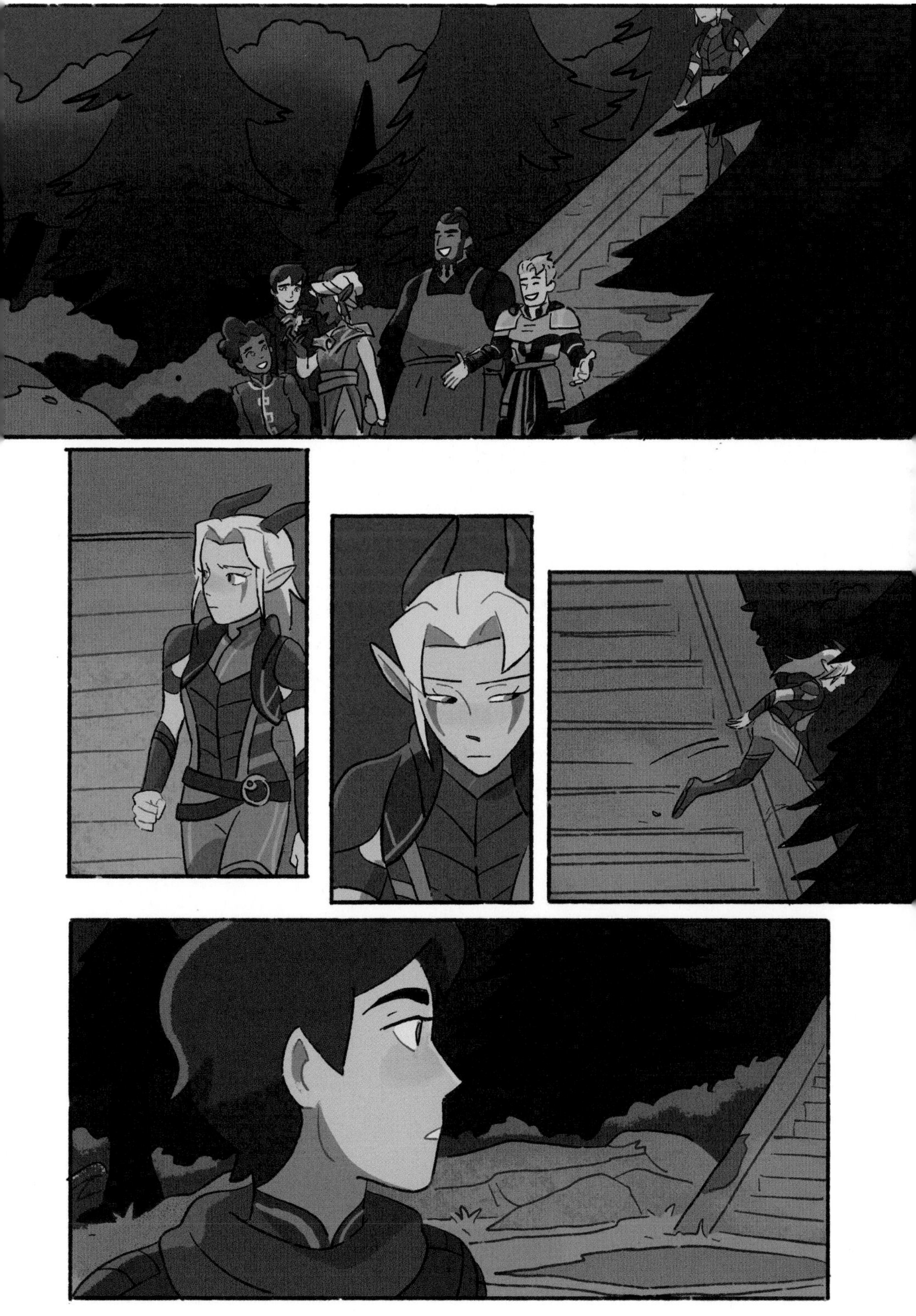

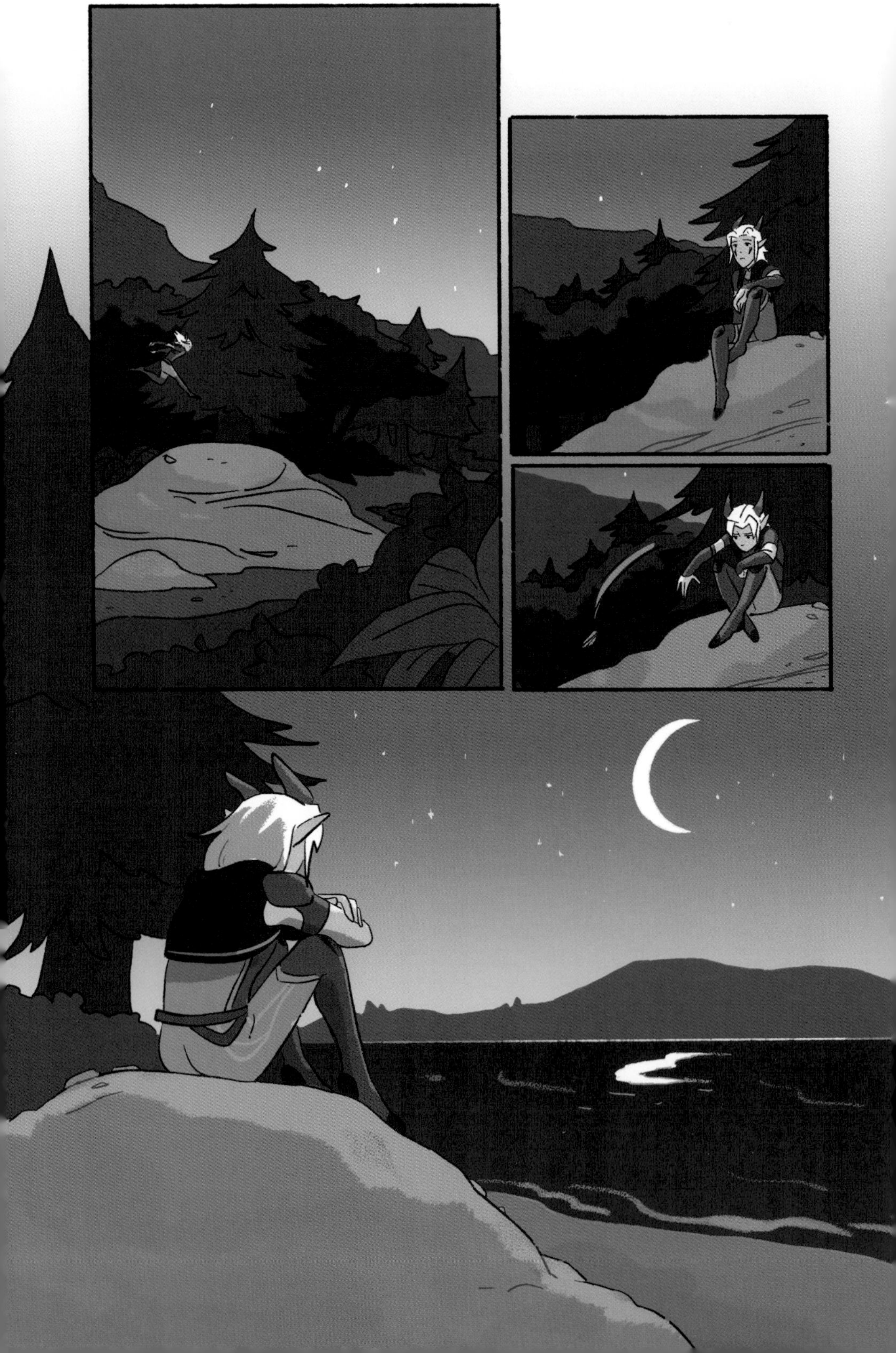

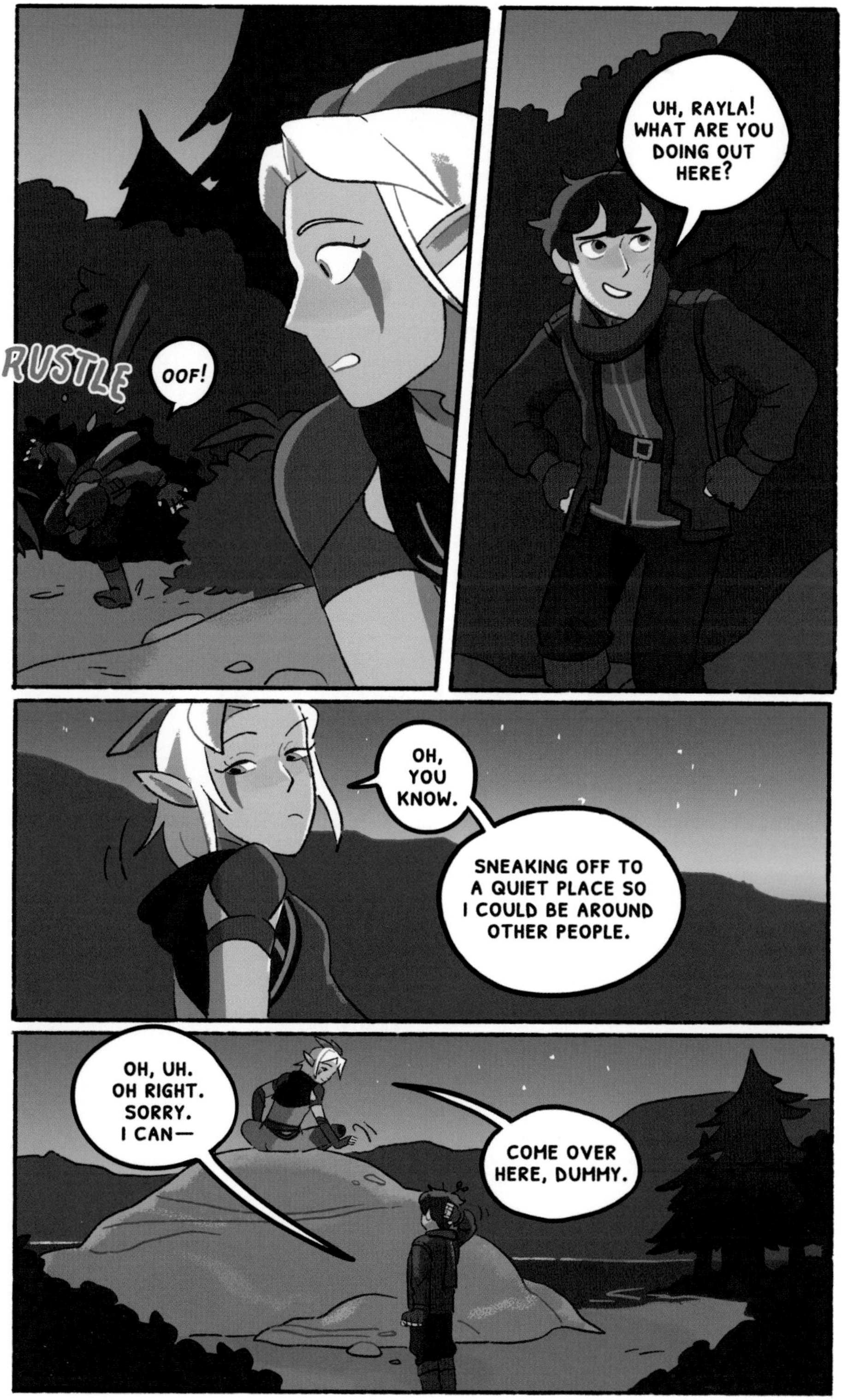
RUSTLE
OOF!
UH, RAYLA! WHAT ARE YOU DOING OUT HERE?
OH, YOU KNOW.
SNEAKING OFF TO A QUIET PLACE SO I COULD BE AROUND OTHER PEOPLE.
OH, UH. OH RIGHT. SORRY. I CAN—
COME OVER HERE, DUMMY.

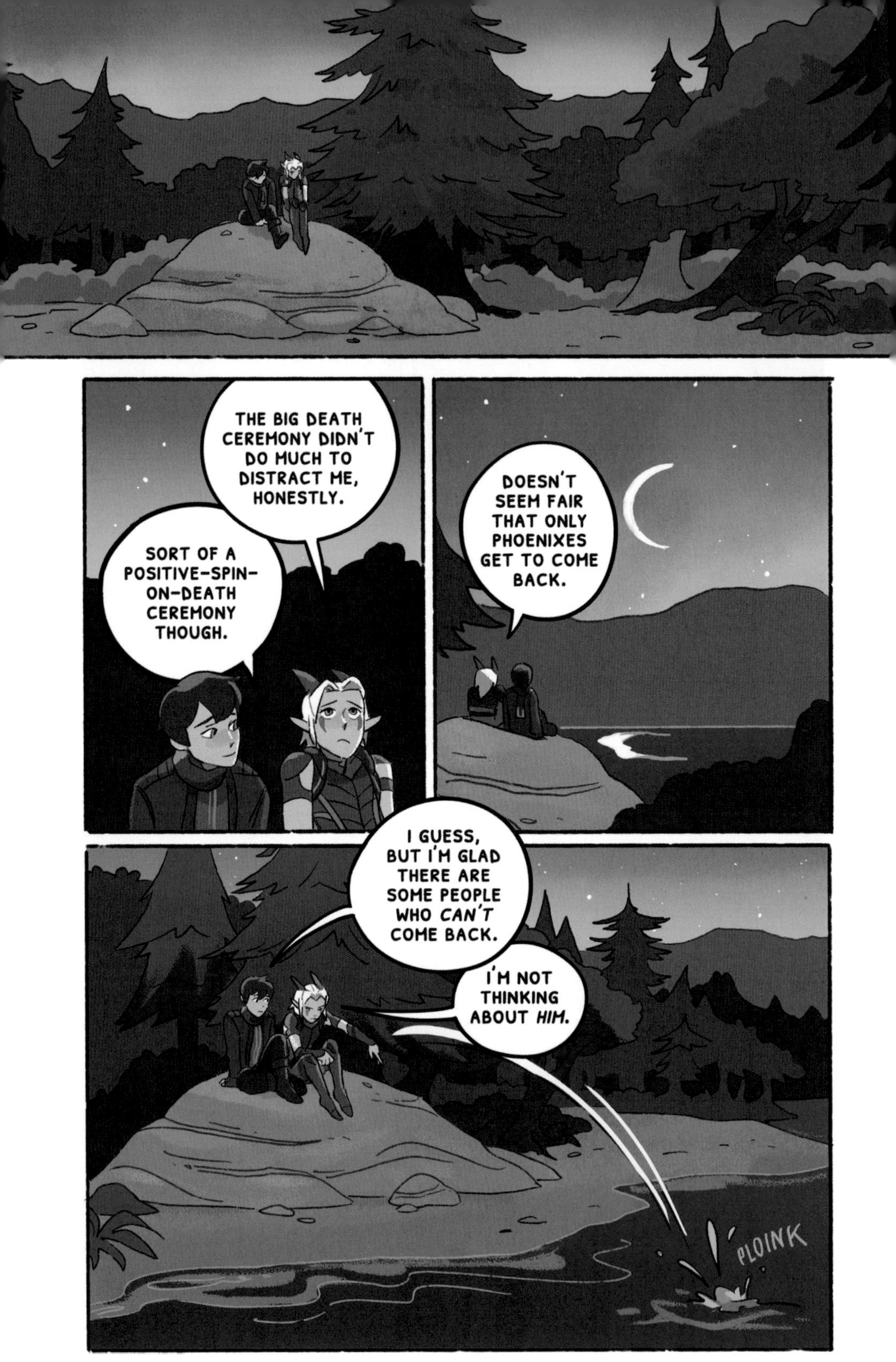
THE BIG DEATH CEREMONY DIDN'T DO MUCH TO DISTRACT ME, HONESTLY.
SORT OF A POSITIVE-SPIN-ON-DEATH CEREMONY THOUGH.
DOESN'T SEEM FAIR THAT ONLY PHOENIXES GET TO COME BACK.
I GUESS, BUT I'M GLAD THERE ARE SOME PEOPLE WHO *CAN'T* COME BACK.
I'M NOT THINKING ABOUT *HIM*.
PLOINK

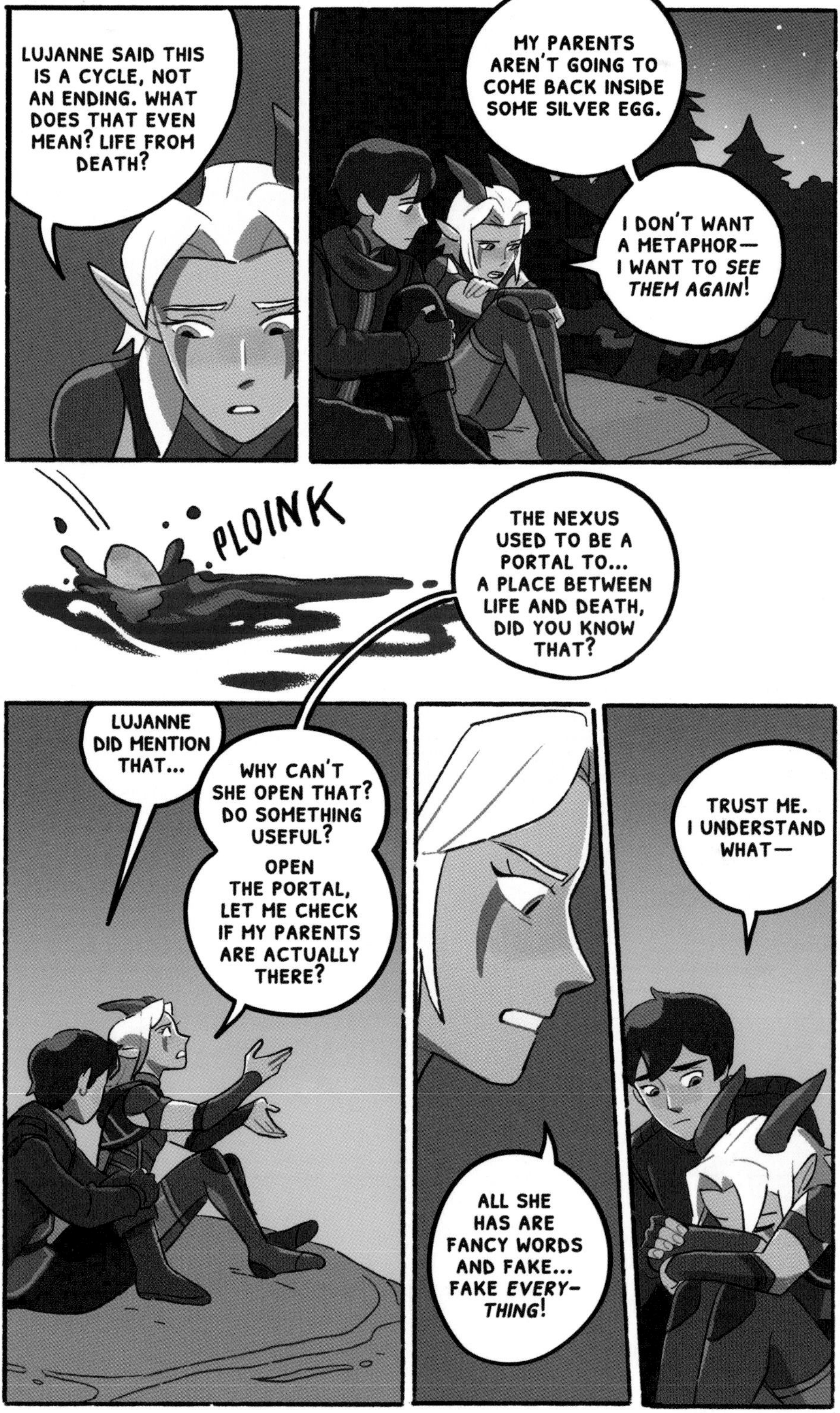
LUJANNE SAID THIS IS A CYCLE, NOT AN ENDING. WHAT DOES THAT EVEN MEAN? LIFE FROM DEATH?
MY PARENTS AREN'T GOING TO COME BACK INSIDE SOME SILVER EGG.
I DON'T WANT A METAPHOR— I WANT TO *SEE THEM AGAIN*!
PLOINK
THE NEXUS USED TO BE A PORTAL TO... A PLACE BETWEEN LIFE AND DEATH, DID YOU KNOW THAT?
LUJANNE DID MENTION THAT...
WHY CAN'T SHE OPEN THAT? DO SOMETHING USEFUL?
OPEN THE PORTAL, LET ME CHECK IF MY PARENTS ARE ACTUALLY THERE?
ALL SHE HAS ARE FANCY WORDS AND FAKE... FAKE *EVERY-THING*!
TRUST ME. I UNDERSTAND WHAT—

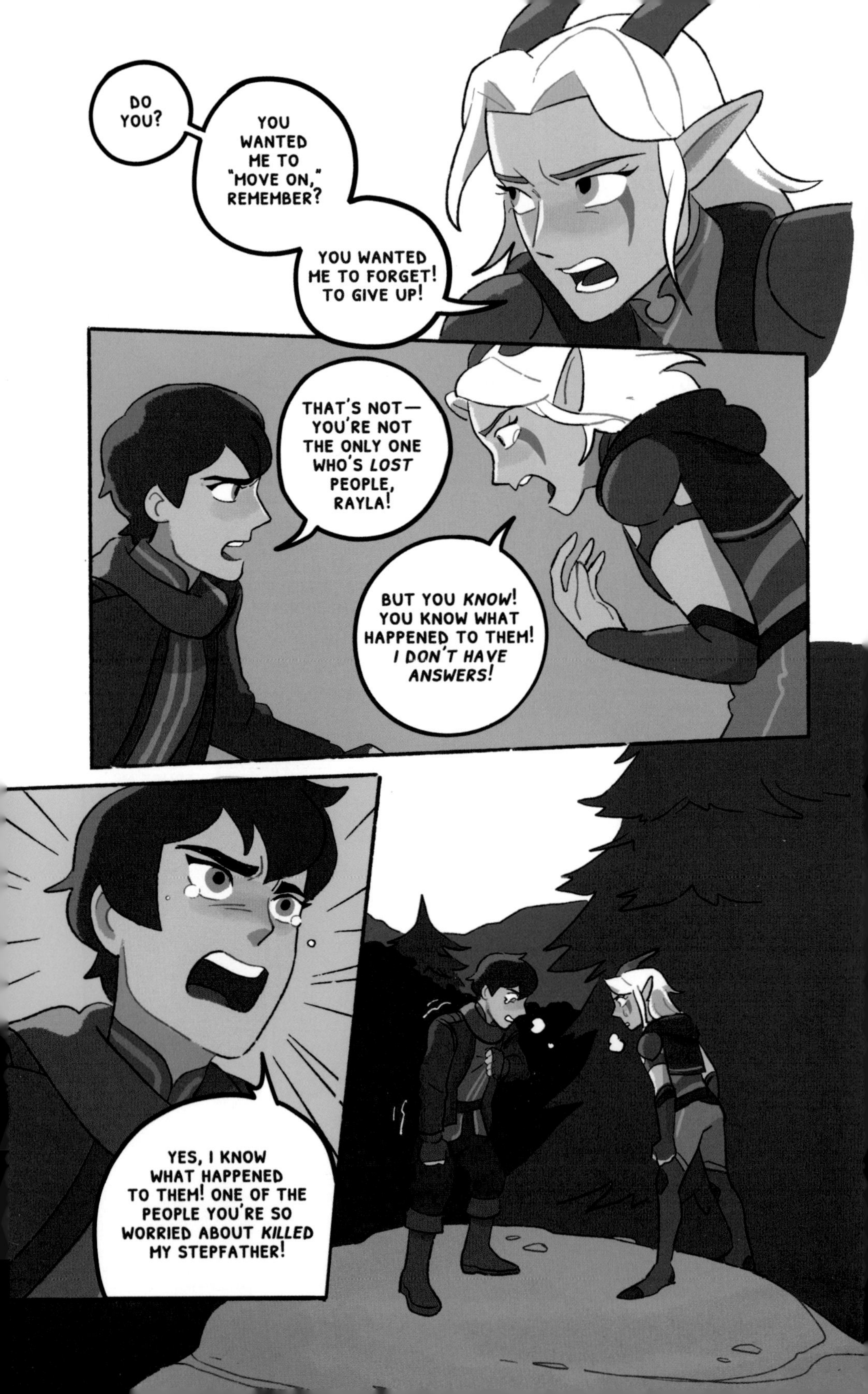
DO YOU?
YOU WANTED ME TO "MOVE ON," REMEMBER?
YOU WANTED ME TO FORGET! TO GIVE UP!
THAT'S NOT— YOU'RE NOT THE ONLY ONE WHO'S *LOST* PEOPLE, RAYLA!
BUT YOU *KNOW*! YOU KNOW WHAT HAPPENED TO THEM! *I DON'T HAVE ANSWERS*!
YES, I KNOW WHAT HAPPENED TO THEM! ONE OF THE PEOPLE YOU'RE SO WORRIED ABOUT *KILLED* MY STEPFATHER!

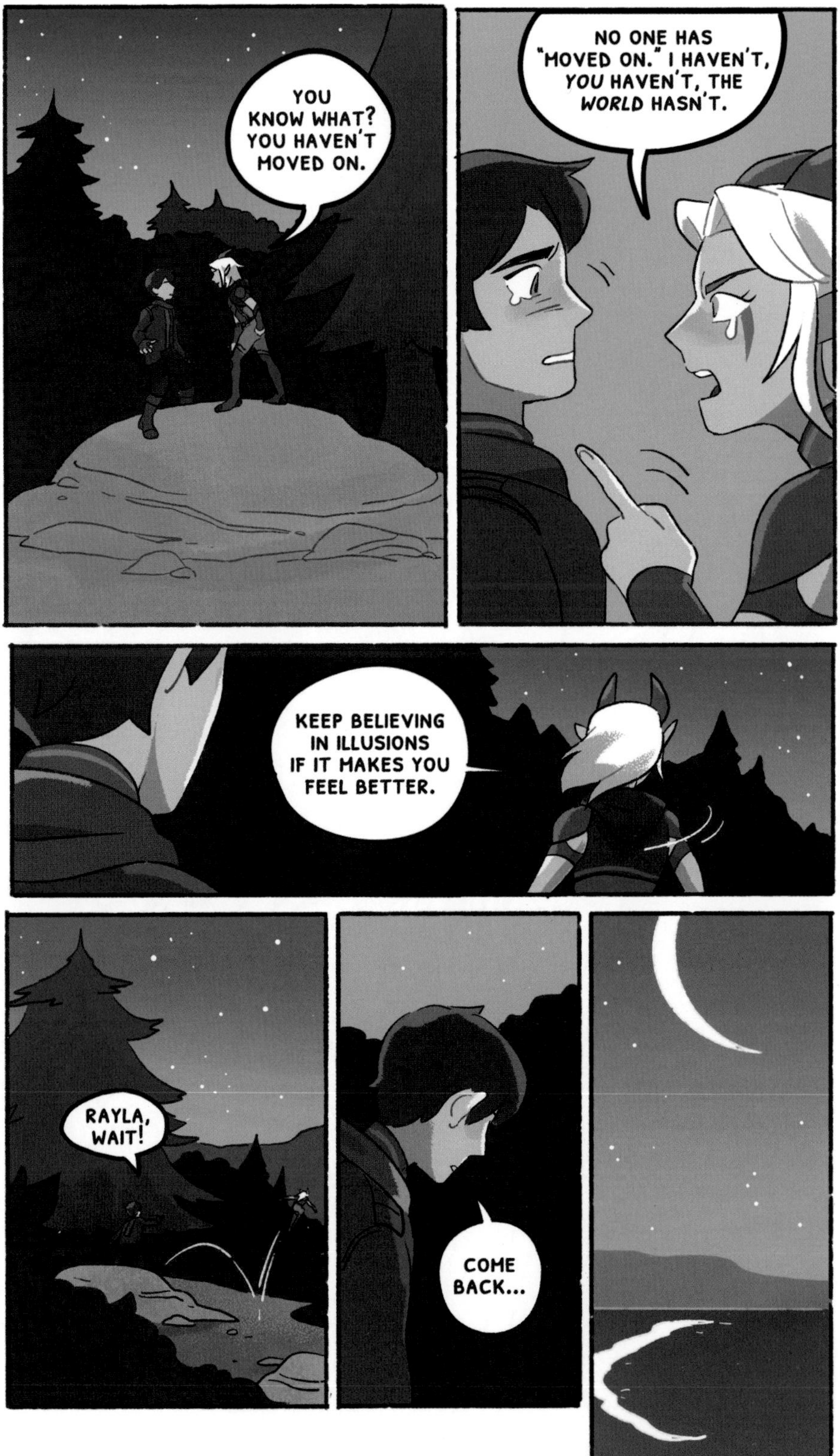
YOU KNOW WHAT? YOU HAVEN'T MOVED ON.
NO ONE HAS "MOVED ON." I HAVEN'T, *YOU* HAVEN'T, THE *WORLD* HASN'T.
KEEP BELIEVING IN ILLUSIONS IF IT MAKES YOU FEEL BETTER.
RAYLA, WAIT!
COME BACK...

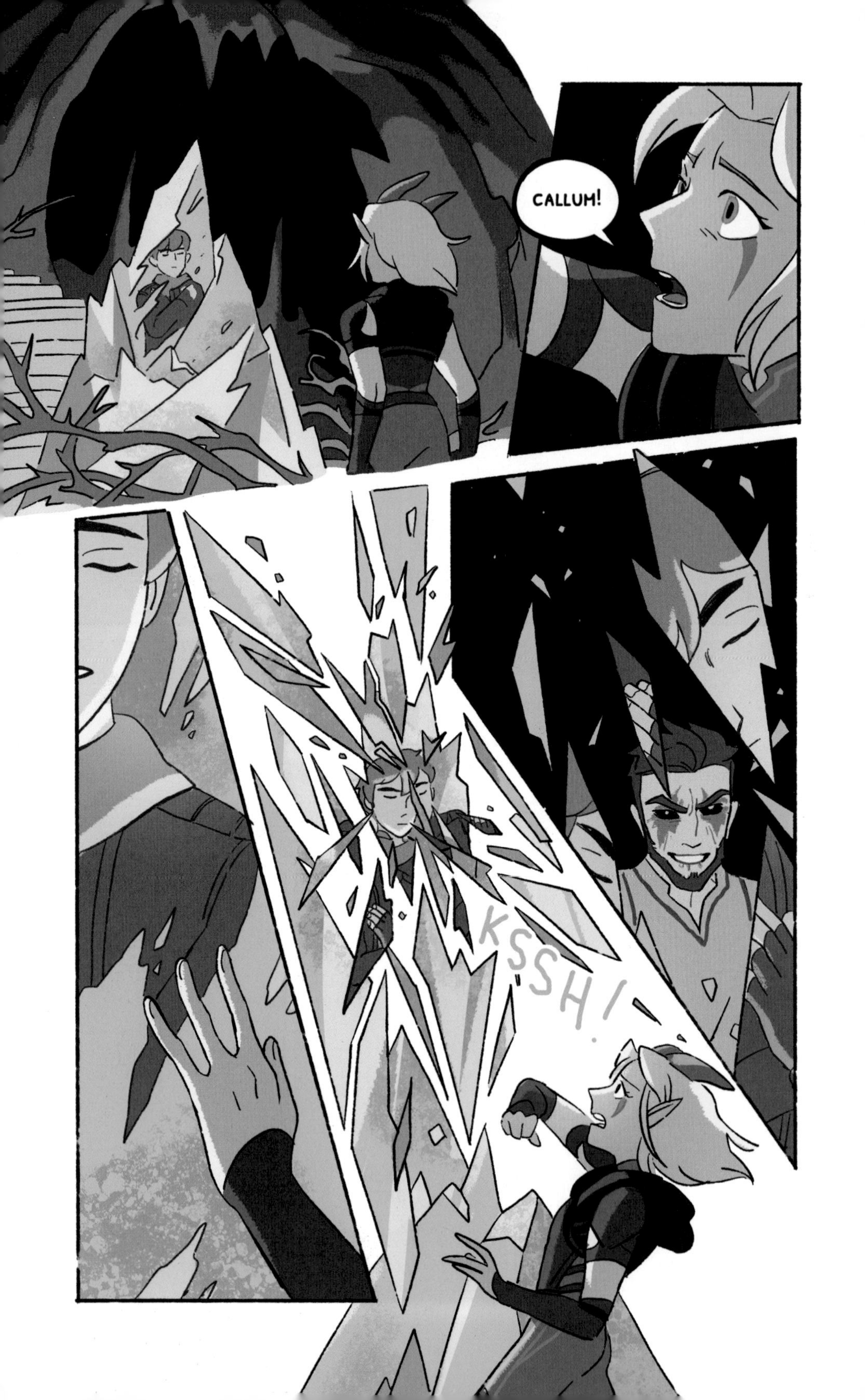
CALLUM!
KSSH!

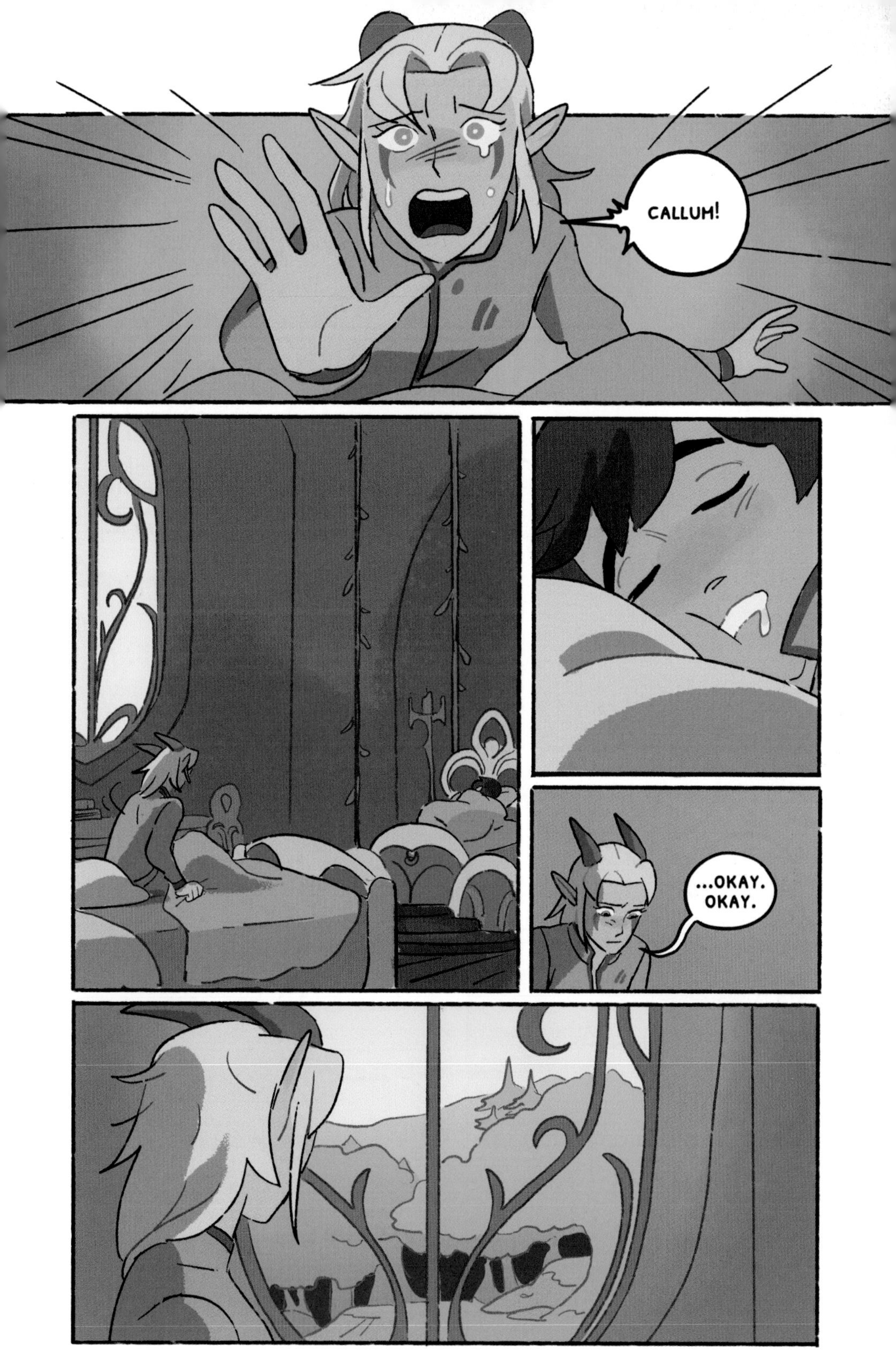
CALLUM!
...OKAY. OKAY.

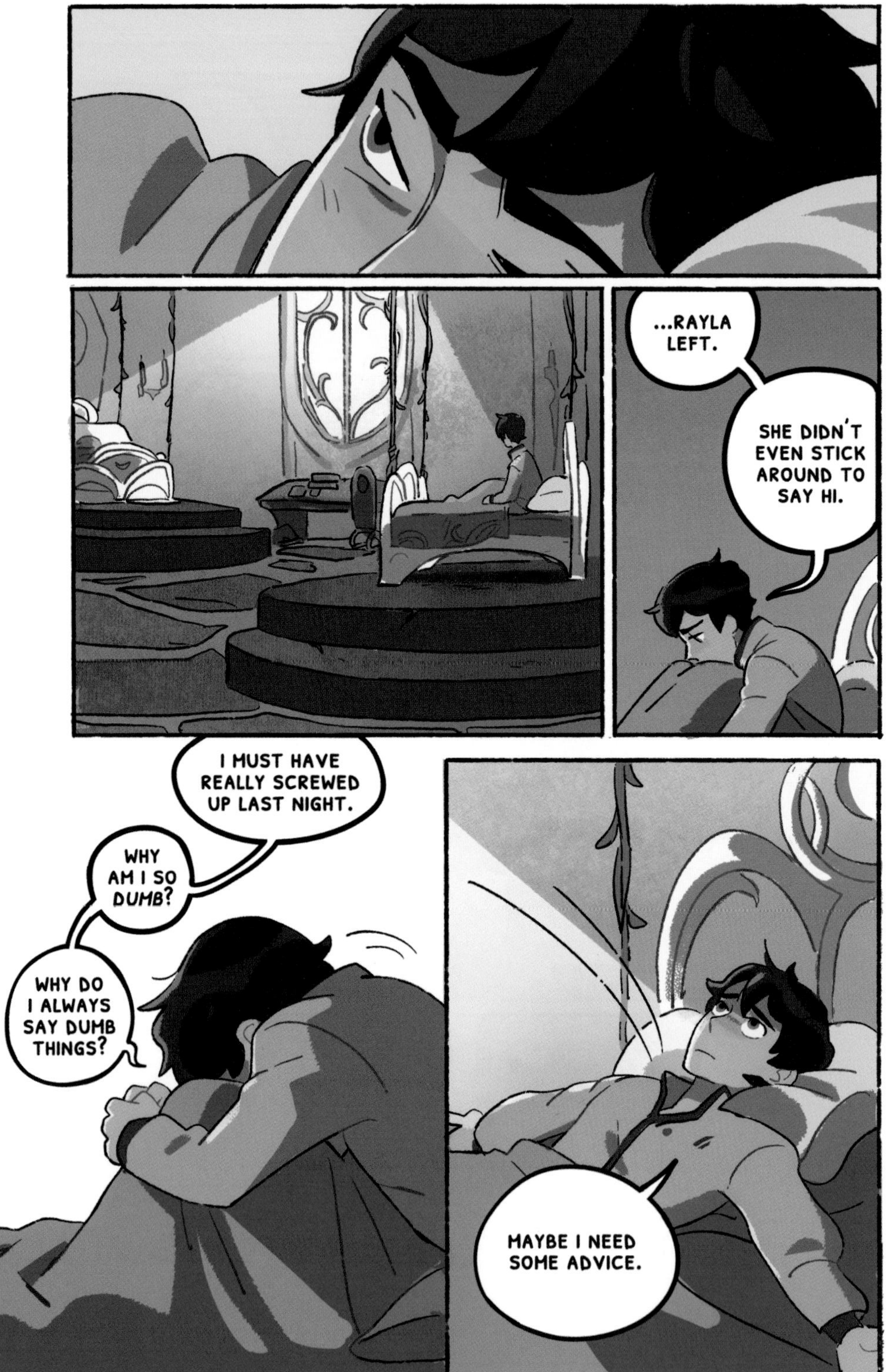
...RAYLA LEFT.
SHE DIDN'T EVEN STICK AROUND TO SAY HI.
I MUST HAVE REALLY SCREWED UP LAST NIGHT.
WHY AM I SO DUMB?
WHY DO I ALWAYS SAY DUMB THINGS?
MAYBE I NEED SOME ADVICE.

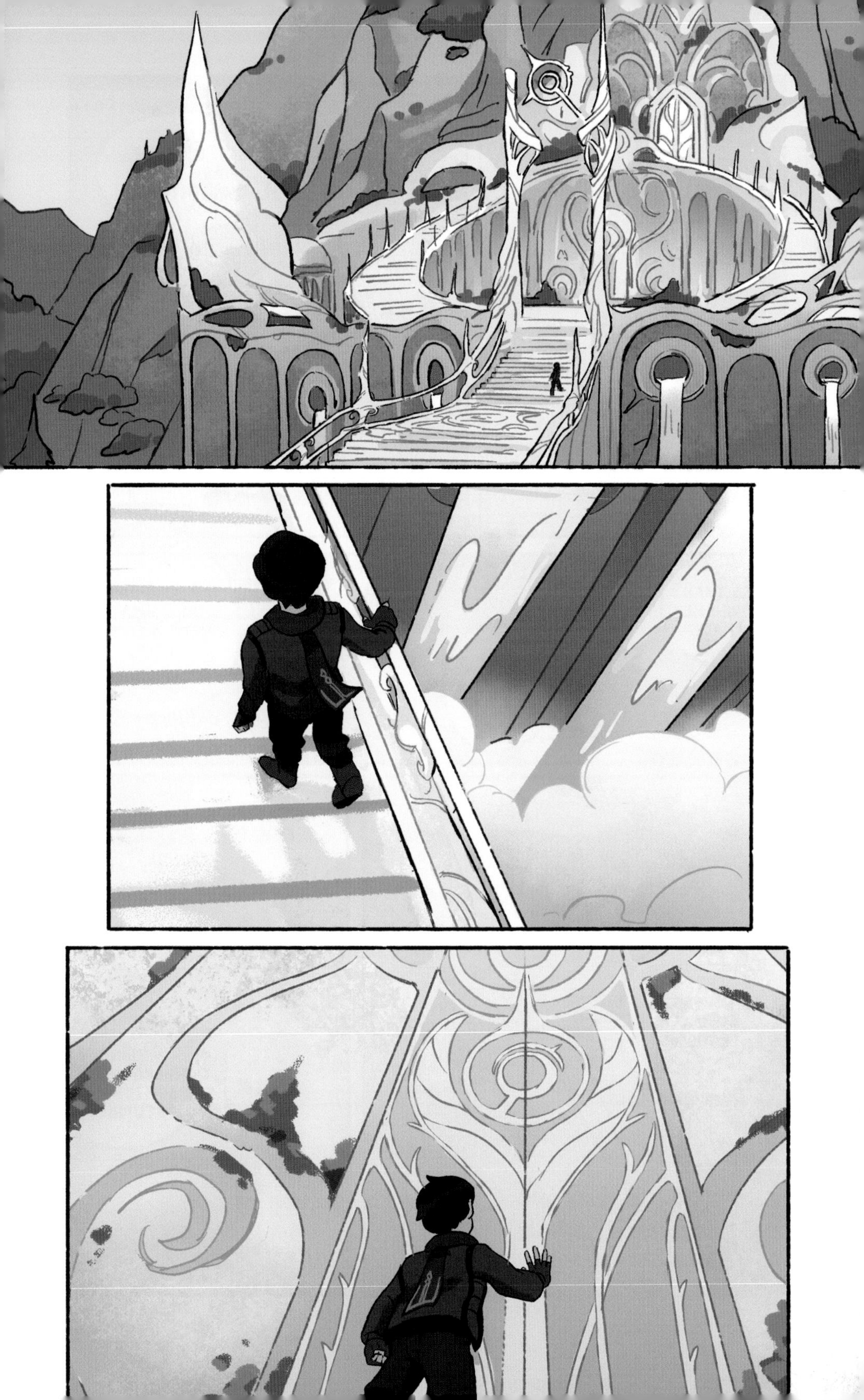

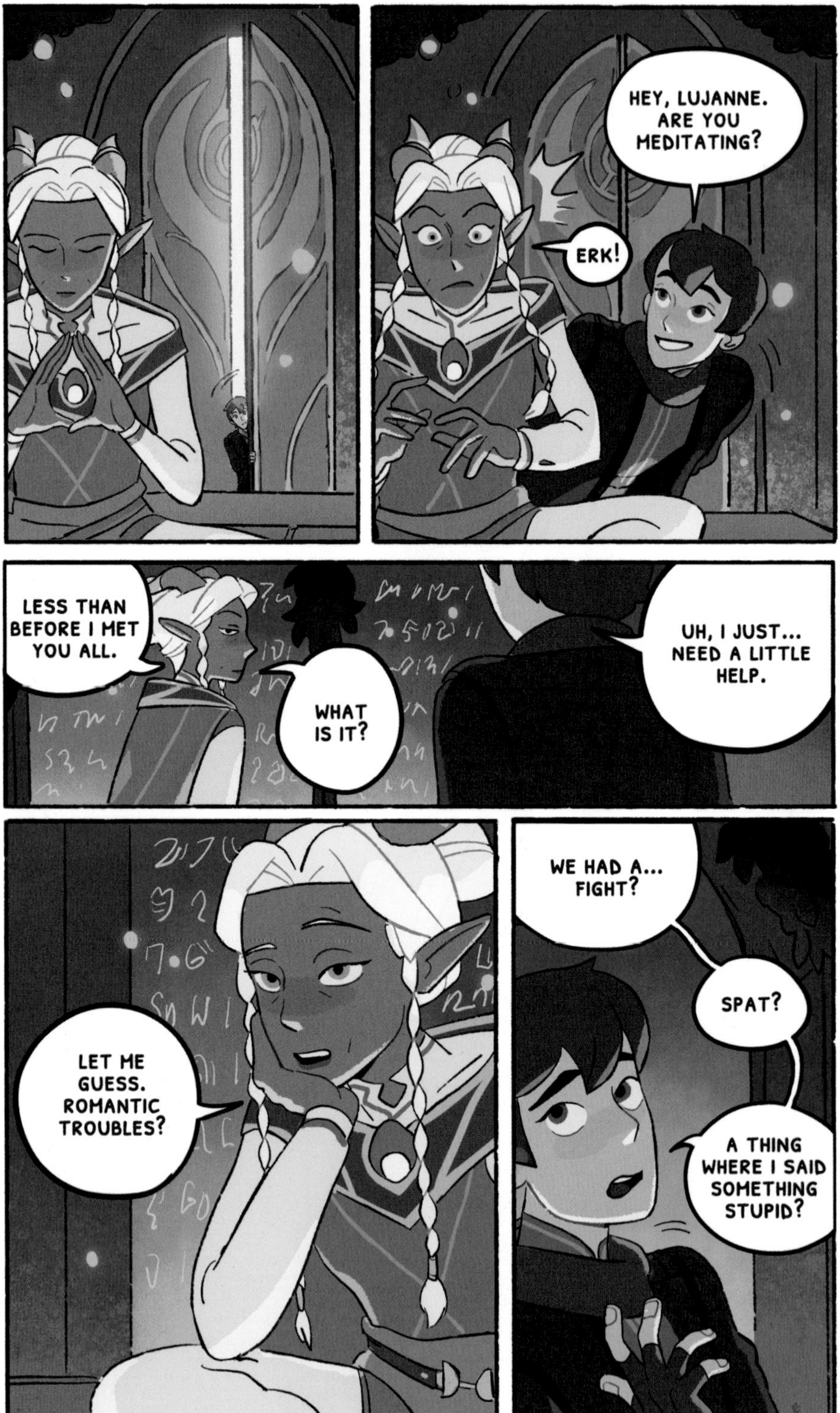
HEY, LUJANNE. ARE YOU MEDITATING?
ERK!
LESS THAN BEFORE I MET YOU ALL.
WHAT IS IT?
UH, I JUST... NEED A LITTLE HELP.
LET ME GUESS. ROMANTIC TROUBLES?
WE HAD A... FIGHT?
SPAT?
A THING WHERE I SAID SOMETHING STUPID?

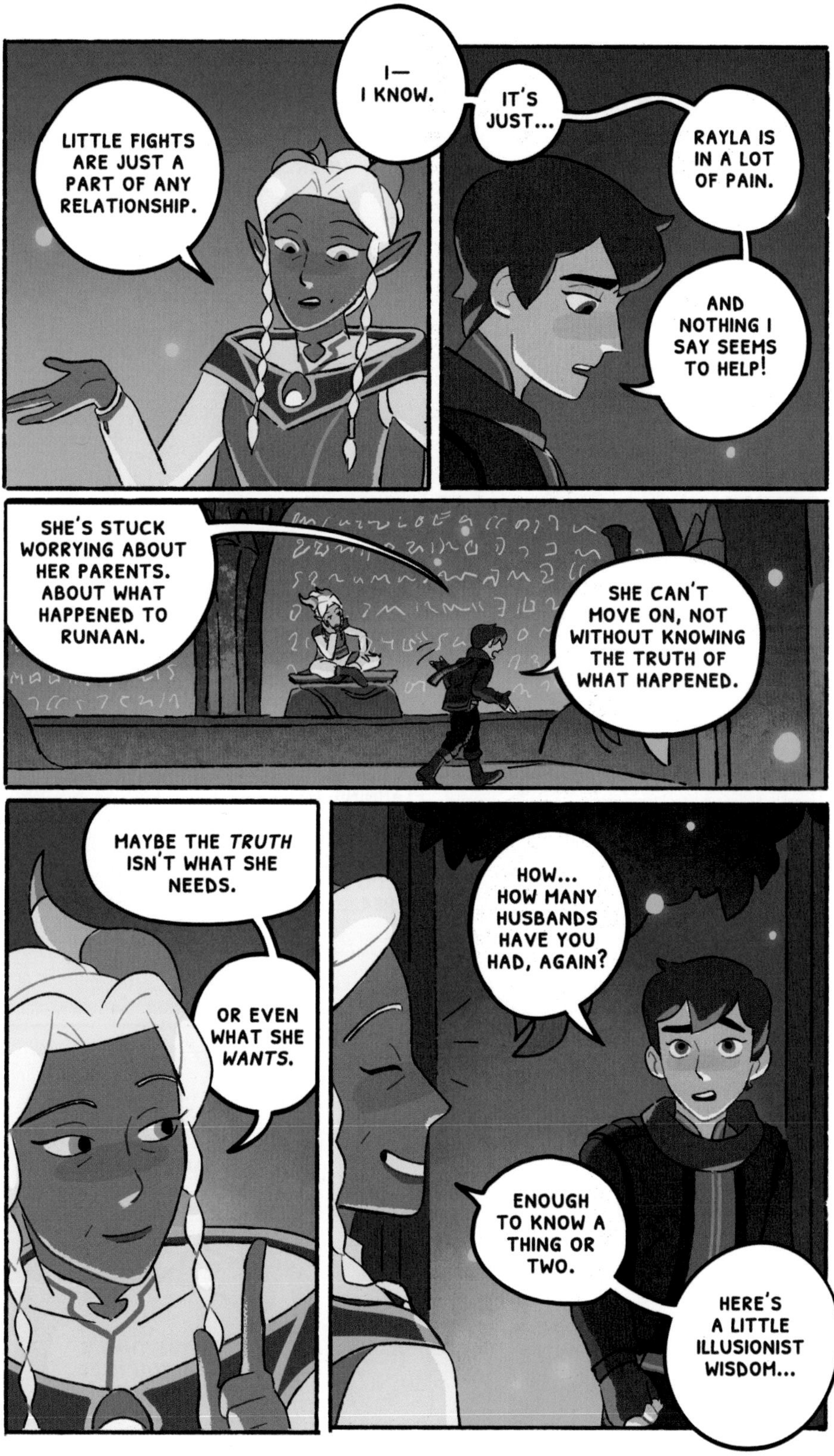
LITTLE FIGHTS ARE JUST A PART OF ANY RELATIONSHIP.
I— I KNOW.
IT'S JUST...
RAYLA IS IN A LOT OF PAIN.
AND NOTHING I SAY SEEMS TO HELP!
SHE'S STUCK WORRYING ABOUT HER PARENTS. ABOUT WHAT HAPPENED TO RUNAAN.
SHE CAN'T MOVE ON, NOT WITHOUT KNOWING THE TRUTH OF WHAT HAPPENED.
MAYBE THE *TRUTH* ISN'T WHAT SHE NEEDS.
OR EVEN WHAT SHE *WANTS*.
HOW... HOW MANY HUSBANDS HAVE YOU HAD, AGAIN?
ENOUGH TO KNOW A THING OR TWO.
HERE'S A LITTLE ILLUSIONIST WISDOM...

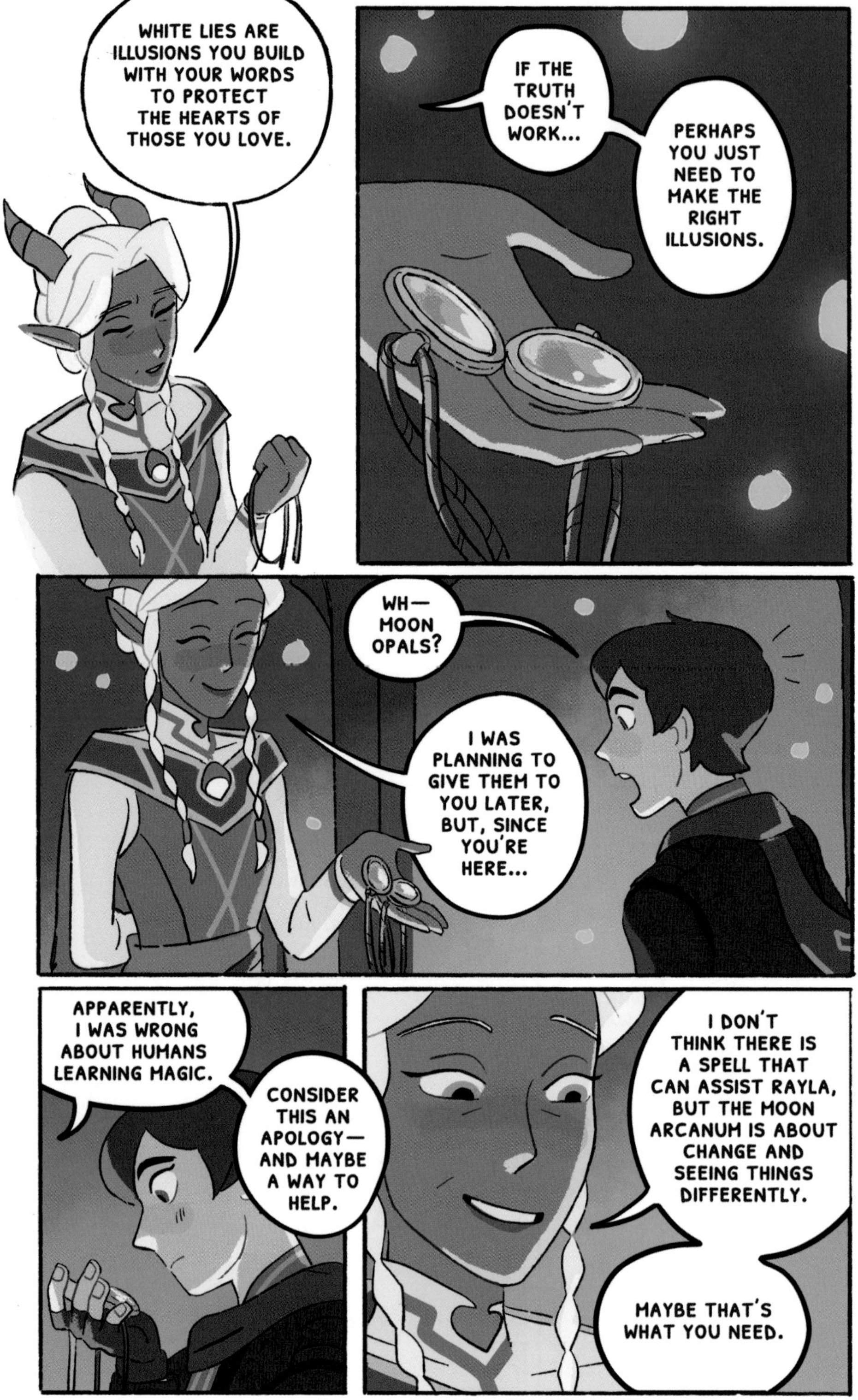
WHITE LIES ARE ILLUSIONS YOU BUILD WITH YOUR WORDS TO PROTECT THE HEARTS OF THOSE YOU LOVE.
IF THE TRUTH DOESN'T WORK...
PERHAPS YOU JUST NEED TO MAKE THE RIGHT ILLUSIONS.
WH— MOON OPALS?
I WAS PLANNING TO GIVE THEM TO YOU LATER, BUT, SINCE YOU'RE HERE...
APPARENTLY, I WAS WRONG ABOUT HUMANS LEARNING MAGIC.
CONSIDER THIS AN APOLOGY— AND MAYBE A WAY TO HELP.
I DON'T THINK THERE IS A SPELL THAT CAN ASSIST RAYLA, BUT THE MOON ARCANUM IS ABOUT CHANGE AND SEEING THINGS DIFFERENTLY.
MAYBE THAT'S WHAT YOU NEED.

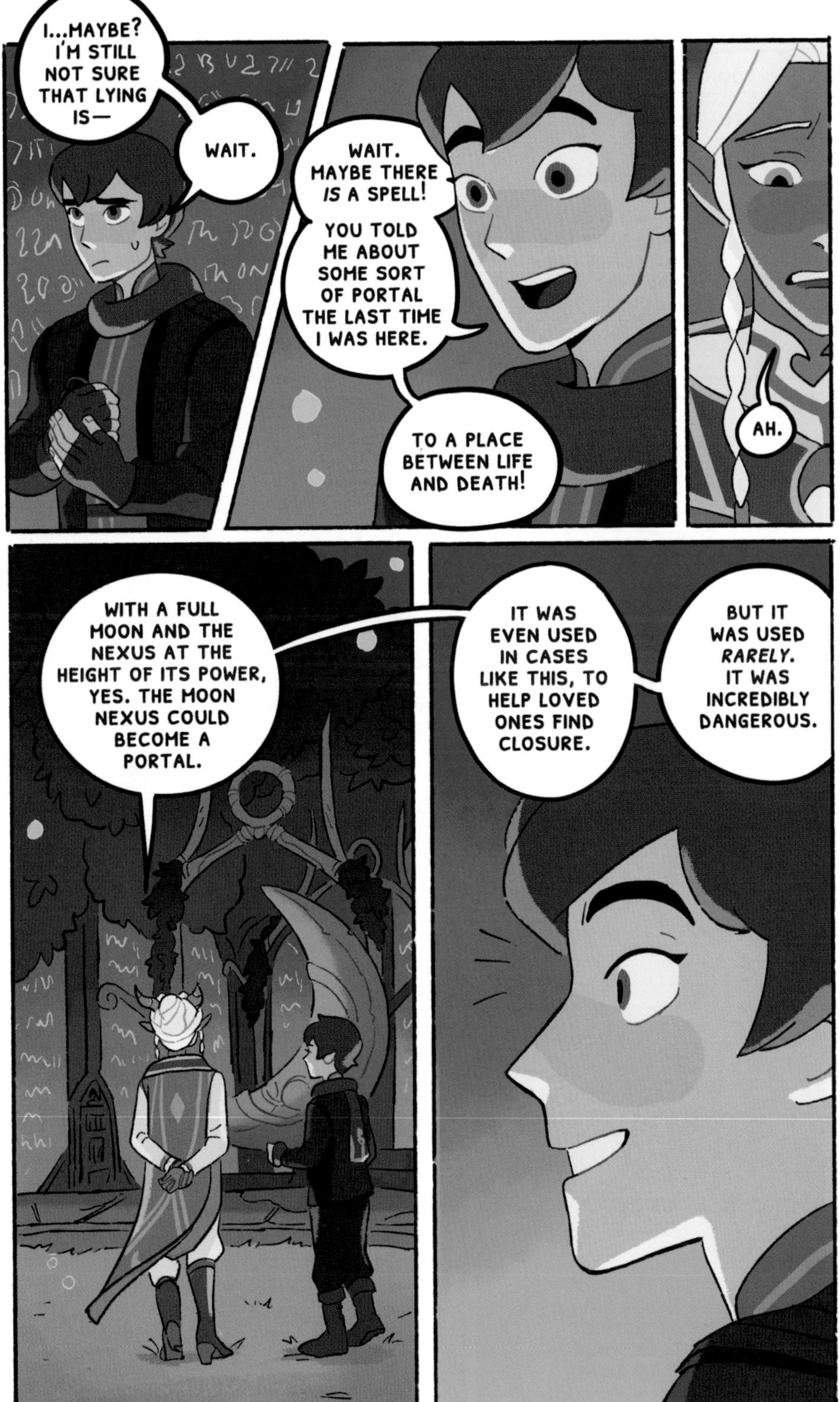
I...MAYBE? I'M STILL NOT SURE THAT LYING IS—
WAIT.
WAIT. MAYBE THERE *IS* A SPELL!
YOU TOLD ME ABOUT SOME SORT OF PORTAL THE LAST TIME I WAS HERE.
TO A PLACE BETWEEN LIFE AND DEATH!
AH.
WITH A FULL MOON AND THE NEXUS AT THE HEIGHT OF ITS POWER, YES. THE MOON NEXUS COULD BECOME A PORTAL.
IT WAS EVEN USED IN CASES LIKE THIS, TO HELP LOVED ONES FIND CLOSURE.
BUT IT WAS USED *RARELY*. IT WAS INCREDIBLY DANGEROUS.

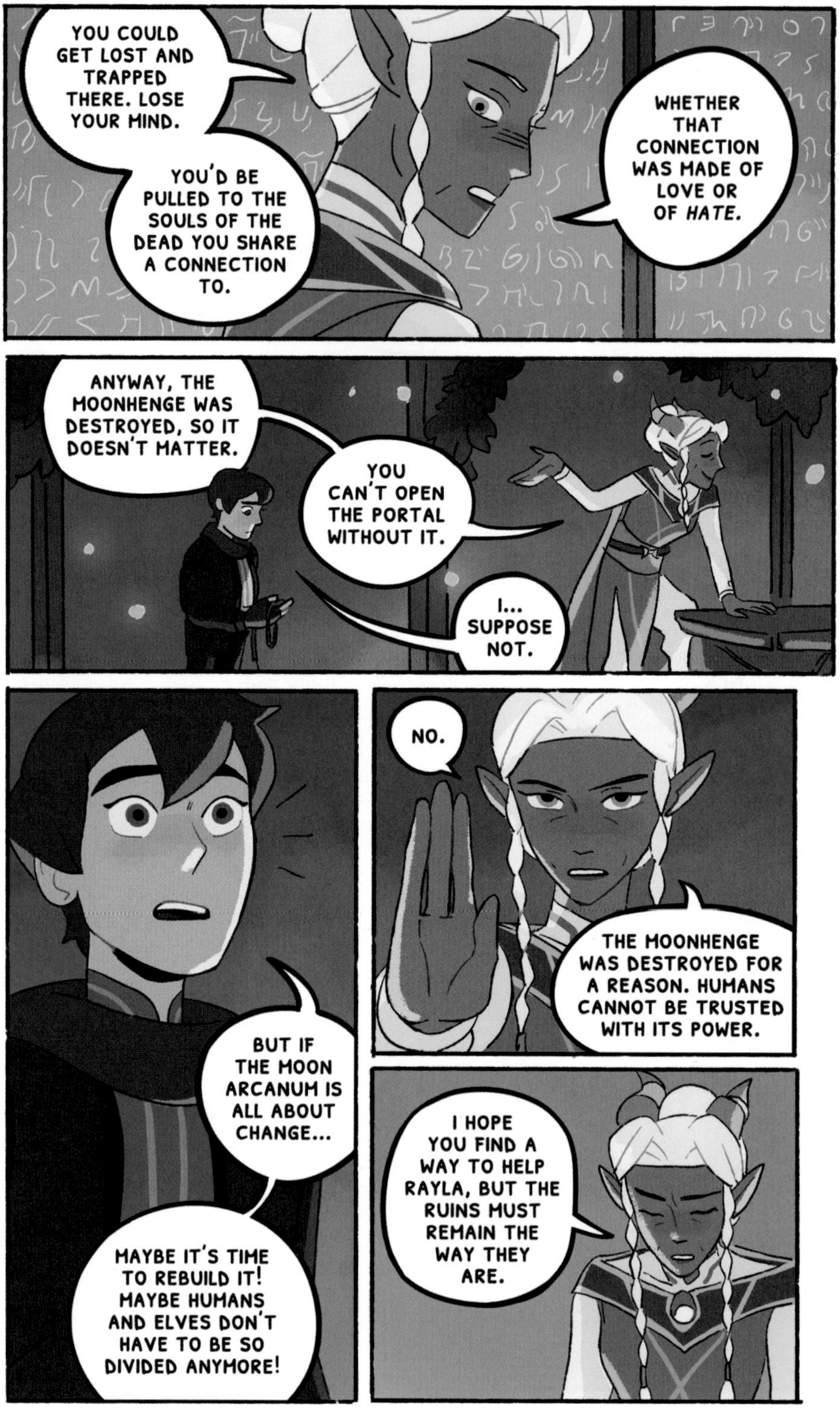
YOU COULD GET LOST AND TRAPPED THERE. LOSE YOUR MIND.
YOU'D BE PULLED TO THE SOULS OF THE DEAD YOU SHARE A CONNECTION TO.
WHETHER THAT CONNECTION WAS MADE OF LOVE OR OF *HATE*.
ANYWAY, THE MOONHENGE WAS DESTROYED, SO IT DOESN'T MATTER.
YOU CAN'T OPEN THE PORTAL WITHOUT IT.
I... SUPPOSE NOT.
BUT IF THE MOON ARCANUM IS ALL ABOUT CHANGE...
MAYBE IT'S TIME TO REBUILD IT! MAYBE HUMANS AND ELVES DON'T HAVE TO BE SO DIVIDED ANYMORE!
NO.
THE MOONHENGE WAS DESTROYED FOR A REASON. HUMANS CANNOT BE TRUSTED WITH ITS POWER.
I HOPE YOU FIND A WAY TO HELP RAYLA, BUT THE RUINS MUST REMAIN THE WAY THEY ARE.

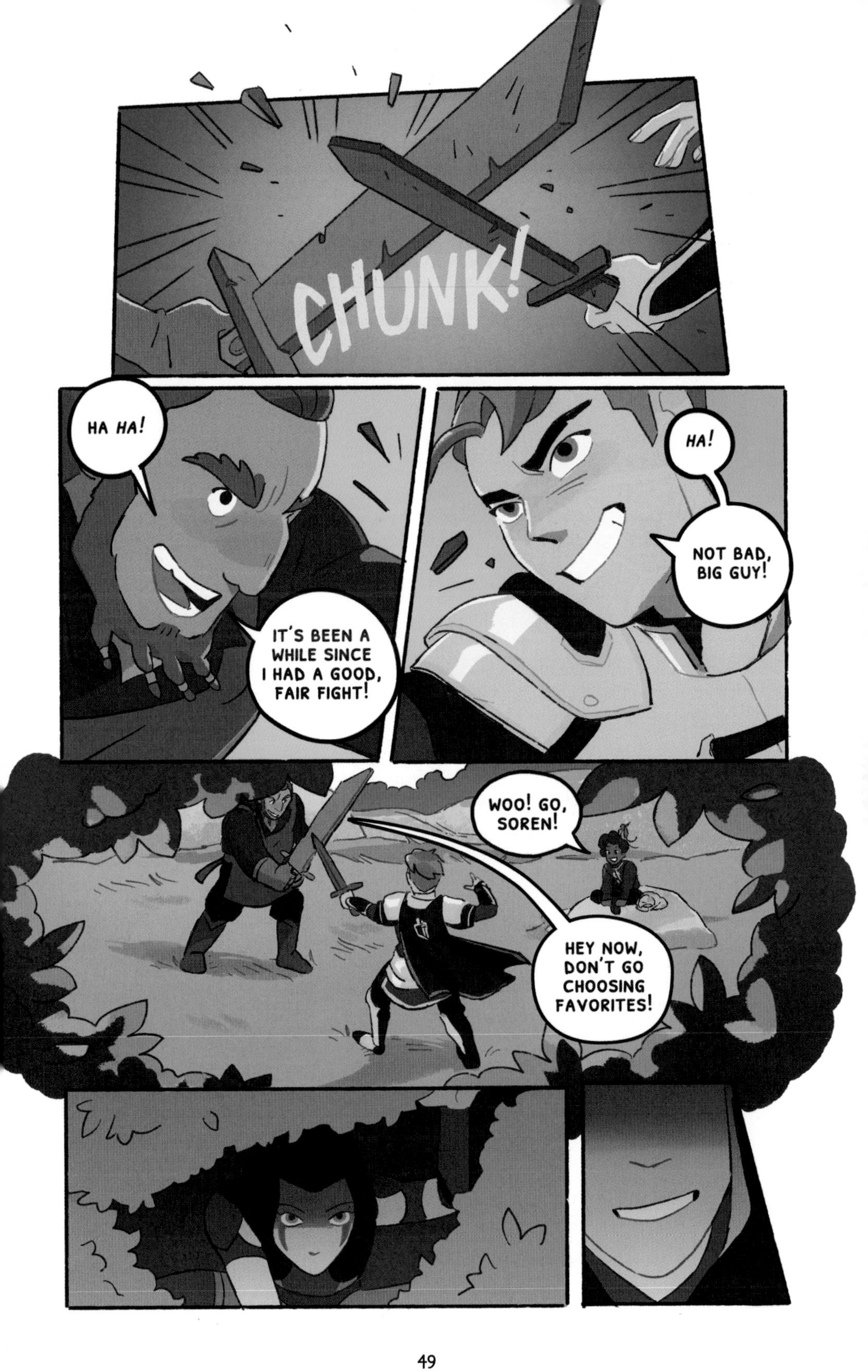
CHUNK!
HA HA!
IT'S BEEN A WHILE SINCE I HAD A GOOD, FAIR FIGHT!
HA!
NOT BAD, BIG GUY!
WOO! GO, SOREN!
HEY NOW, DON'T GO CHOOSING FAVORITES!

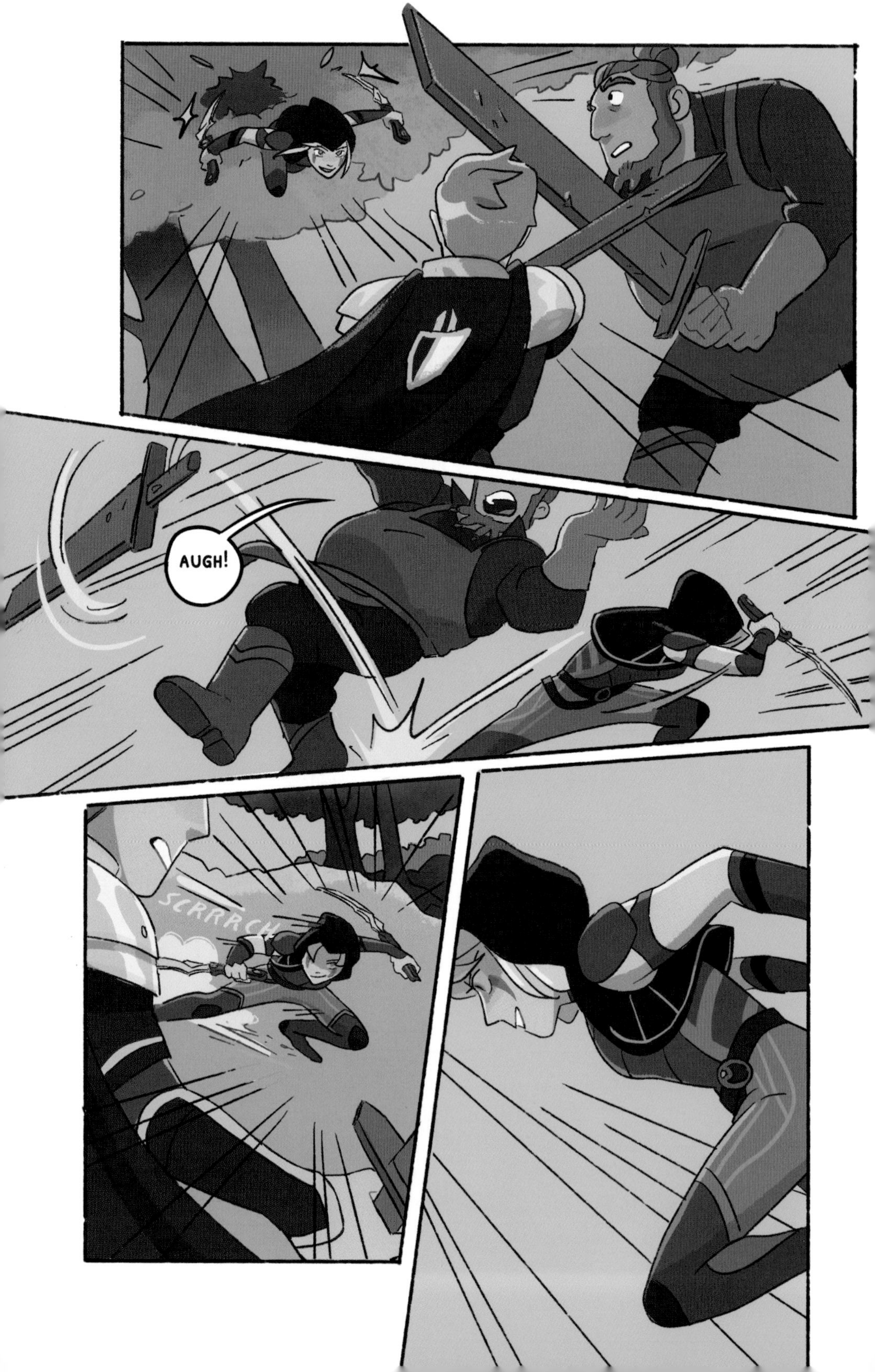
AUGH!
SCRRRCH

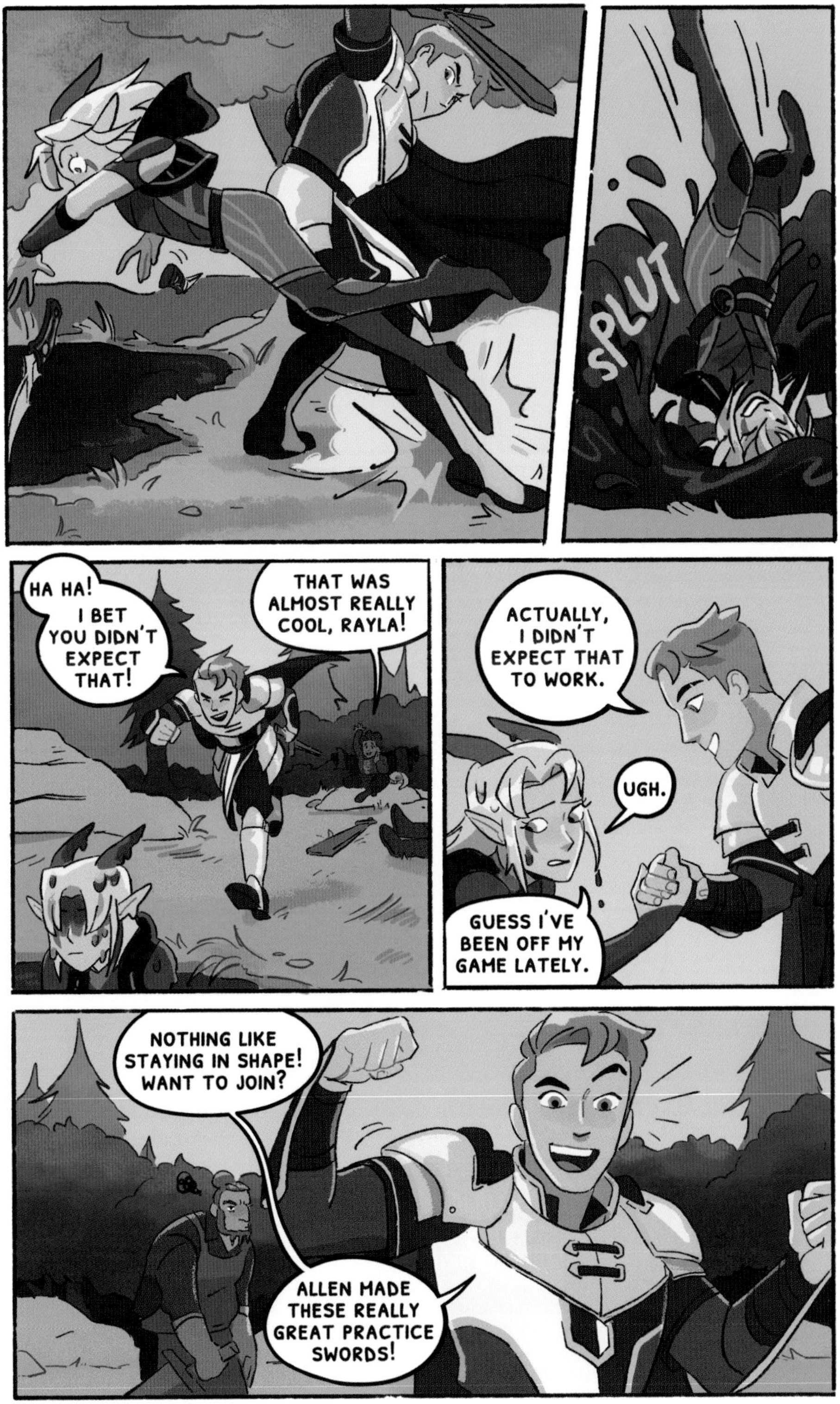
SPLUT
HA HA! I BET YOU DIDN'T EXPECT THAT!
THAT WAS ALMOST REALLY COOL, RAYLA!
ACTUALLY, I DIDN'T EXPECT THAT TO WORK.
UGH.
GUESS I'VE BEEN OFF MY GAME LATELY.
NOTHING LIKE STAYING IN SHAPE! WANT TO JOIN?
ALLEN MADE THESE REALLY GREAT PRACTICE SWORDS!

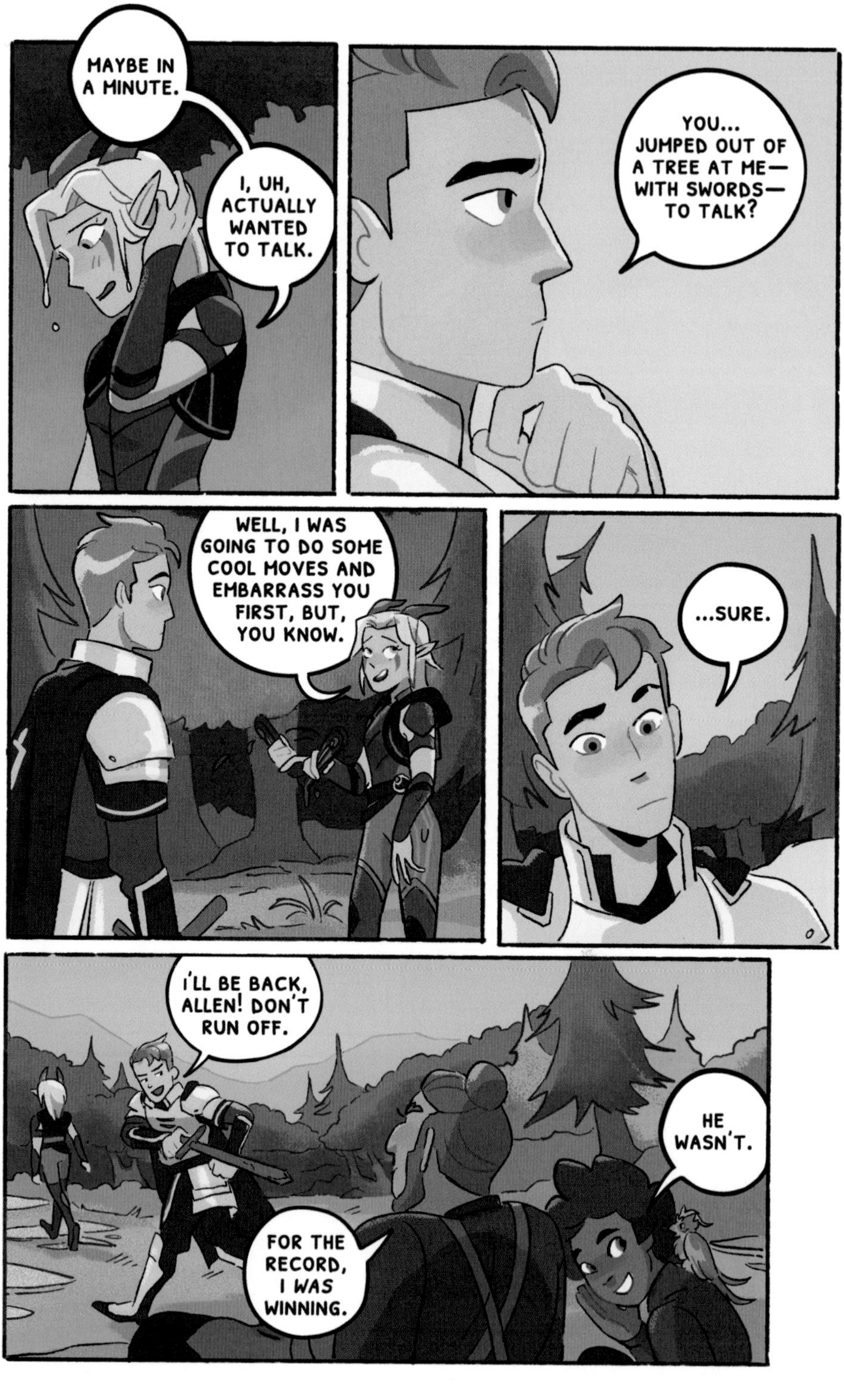
MAYBE IN A MINUTE.
I, UH, ACTUALLY WANTED TO TALK.
YOU... JUMPED OUT OF A TREE AT ME—WITH SWORDS—TO TALK?
WELL, I WAS GOING TO DO SOME COOL MOVES AND EMBARRASS YOU FIRST, BUT, YOU KNOW.
...SURE.
I'LL BE BACK, ALLEN! DON'T RUN OFF.
FOR THE RECORD, I WAS WINNING.
HE WASN'T.

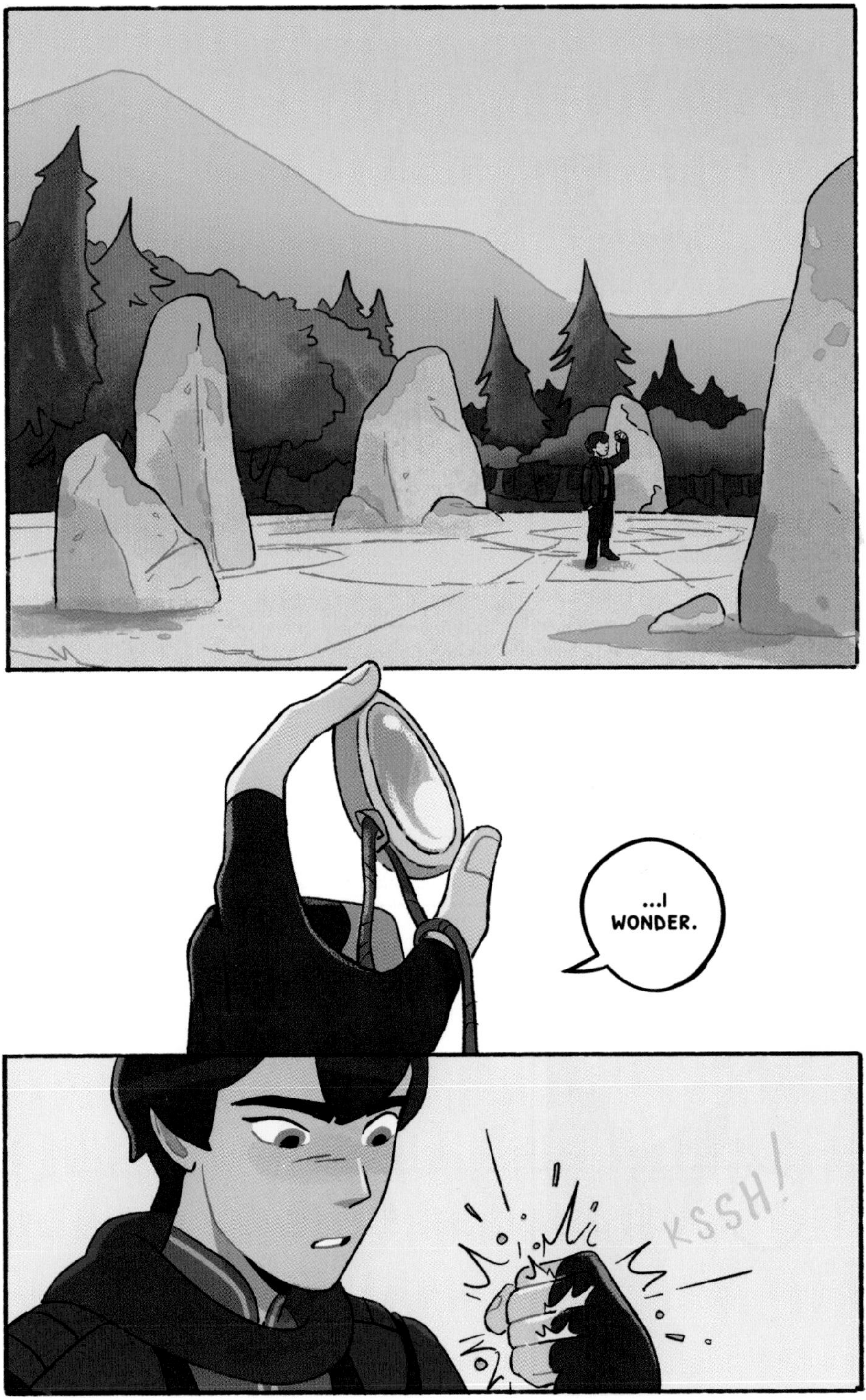
...I WONDER.
KSSH!

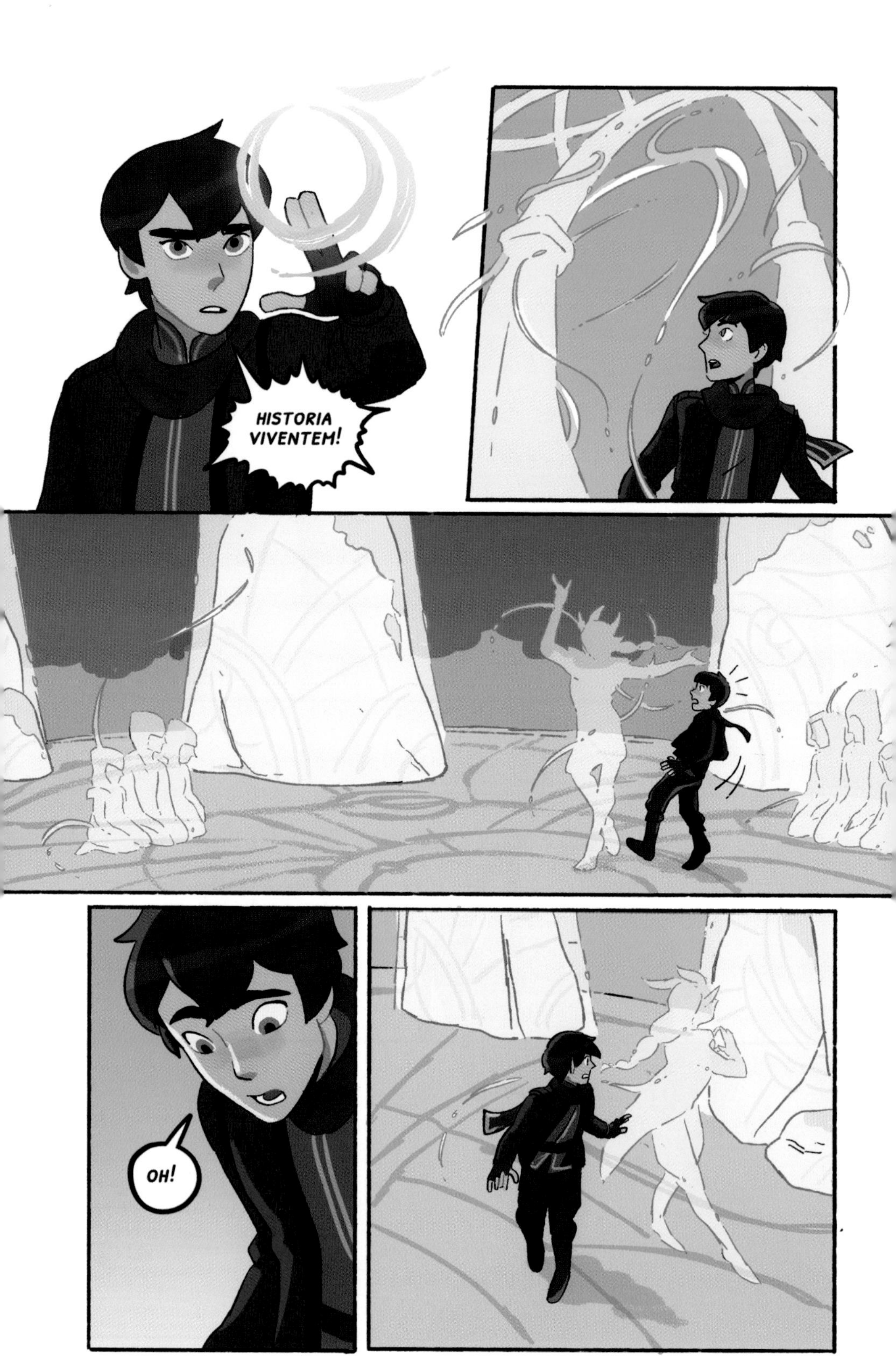
HISTORIA VIVENTEM!
OH!

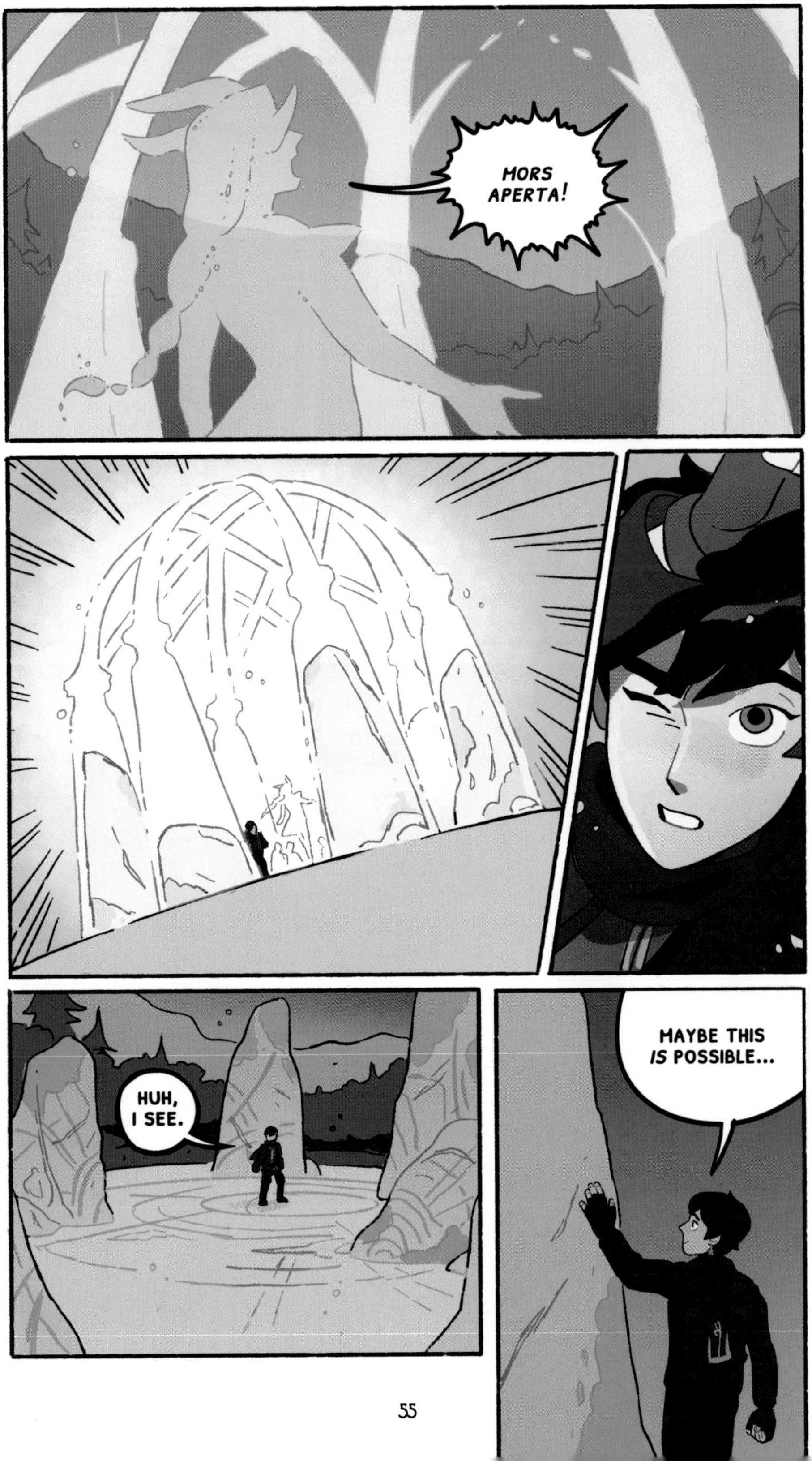
MORS APERTA!
HUH, I SEE.
MAYBE THIS *IS* POSSIBLE...

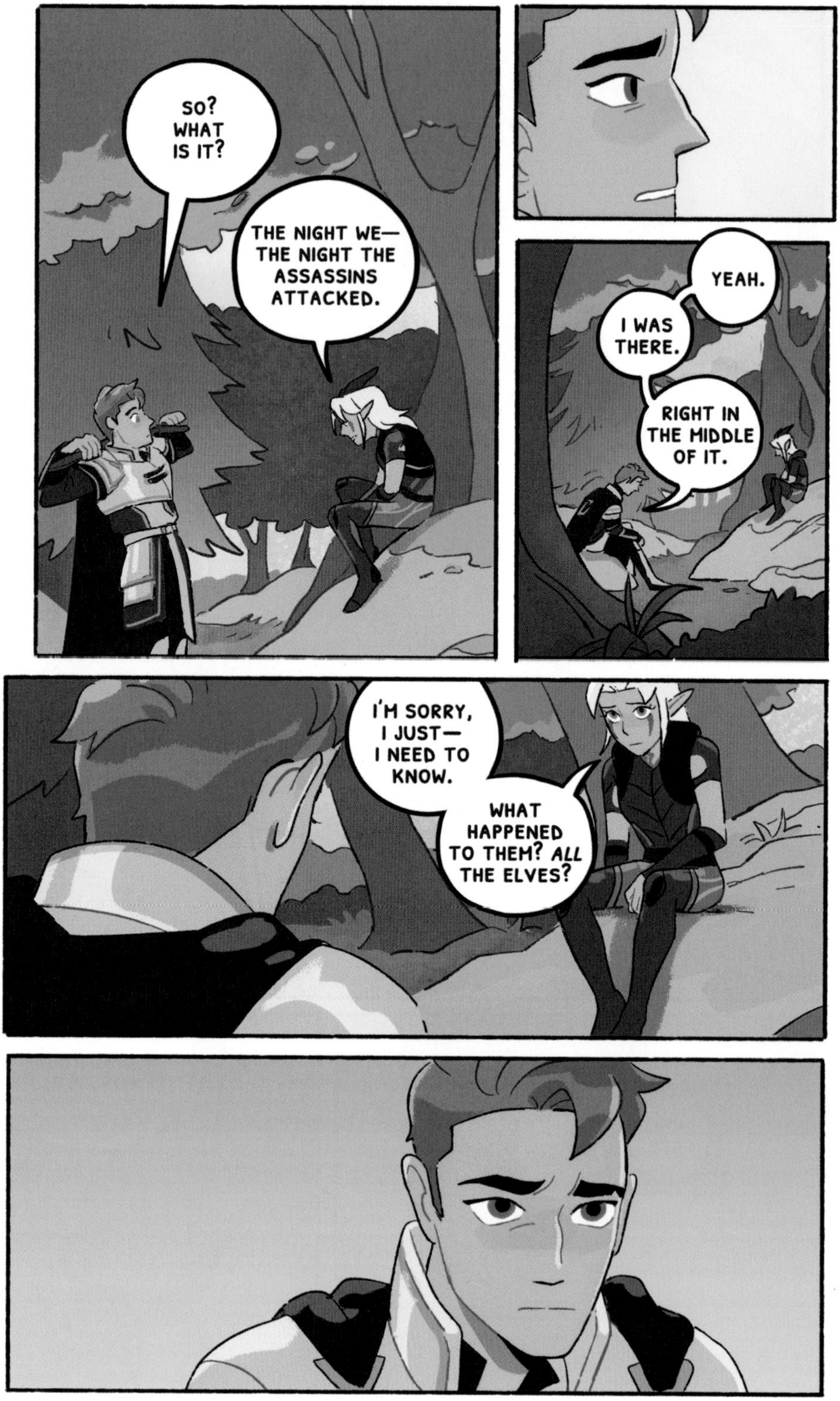
SO? WHAT IS IT?
THE NIGHT WE— THE NIGHT THE ASSASSINS ATTACKED.
I WAS THERE.
YEAH.
RIGHT IN THE MIDDLE OF IT.
I'M SORRY, I JUST— I NEED TO KNOW.
WHAT HAPPENED TO THEM? *ALL* THE ELVES?

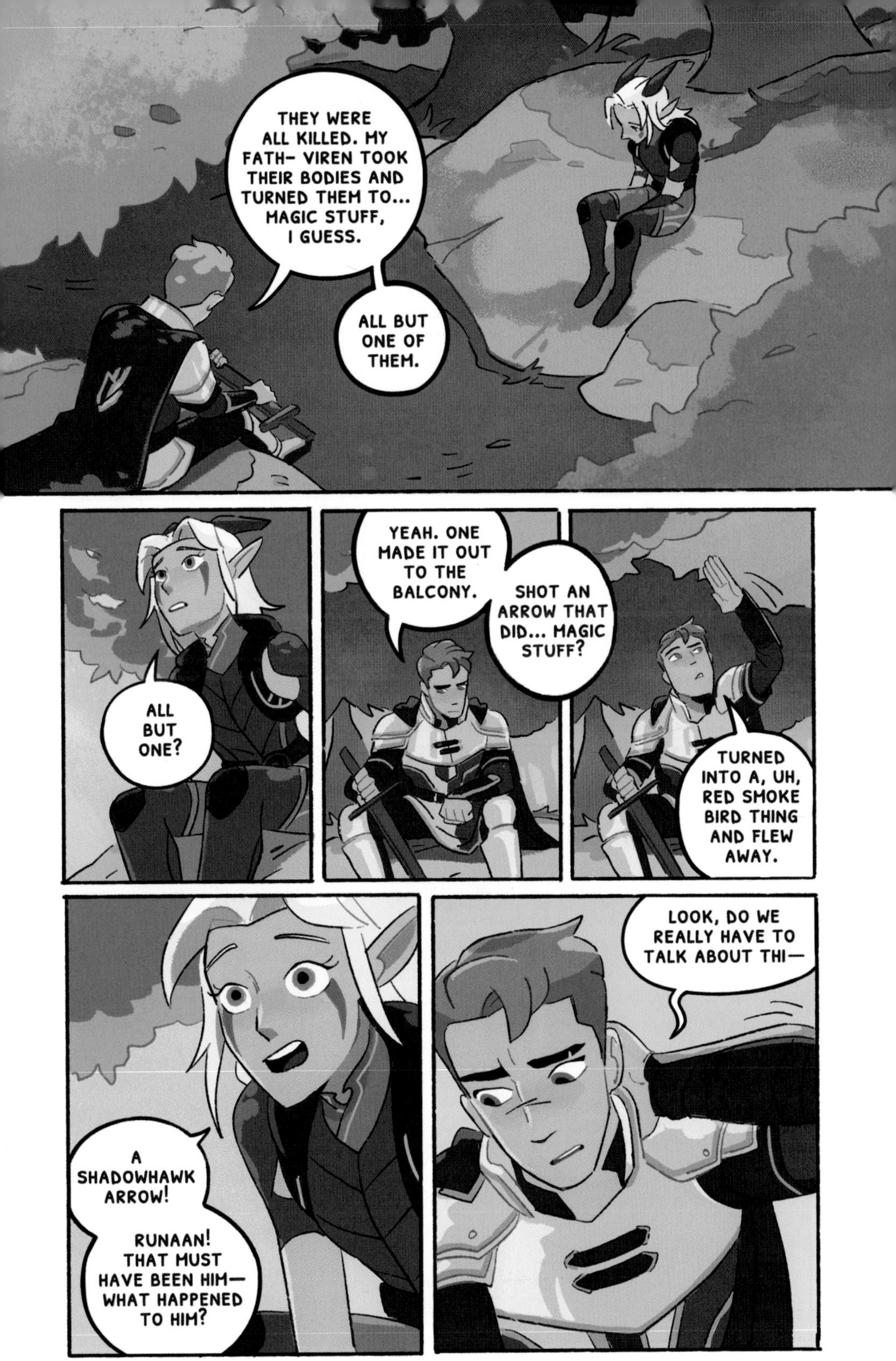
THEY WERE ALL KILLED. MY FATH— VIREN TOOK THEIR BODIES AND TURNED THEM TO... MAGIC STUFF, I GUESS.
ALL BUT ONE OF THEM.
ALL BUT ONE?
YEAH. ONE MADE IT OUT TO THE BALCONY.
SHOT AN ARROW THAT DID... MAGIC STUFF?
TURNED INTO A, UH, RED SMOKE BIRD THING AND FLEW AWAY.
A SHADOWHAWK ARROW!
RUNAAN! THAT MUST HAVE BEEN HIM— WHAT HAPPENED TO HIM?
LOOK, DO WE REALLY HAVE TO TALK ABOUT THI—

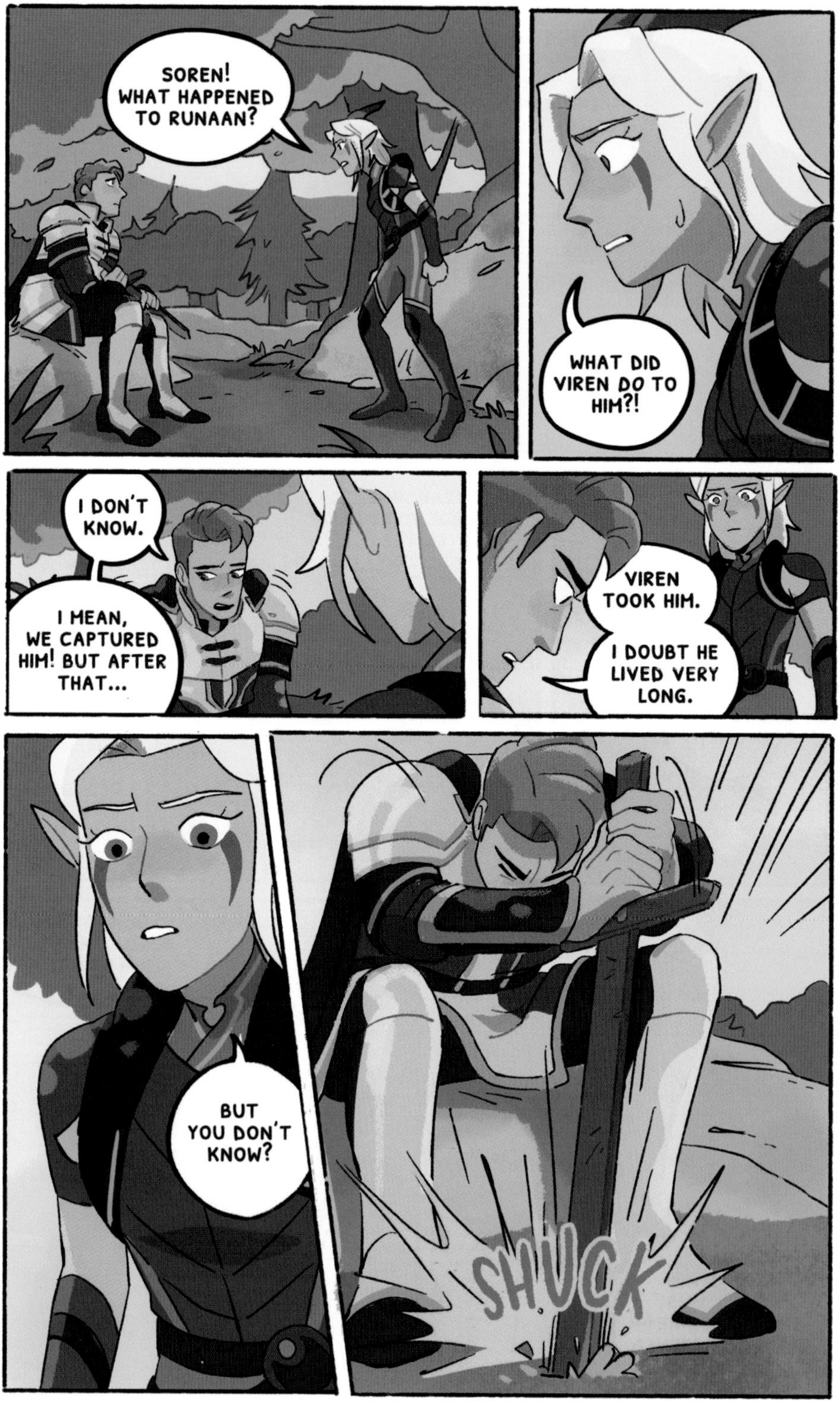
SOREN! WHAT HAPPENED TO RUNAAN?
WHAT DID VIREN DO TO HIM?!
I DON'T KNOW.
I MEAN, WE CAPTURED HIM! BUT AFTER THAT...
VIREN TOOK HIM.
I DOUBT HE LIVED VERY LONG.
BUT YOU DON'T KNOW?
SHUCK

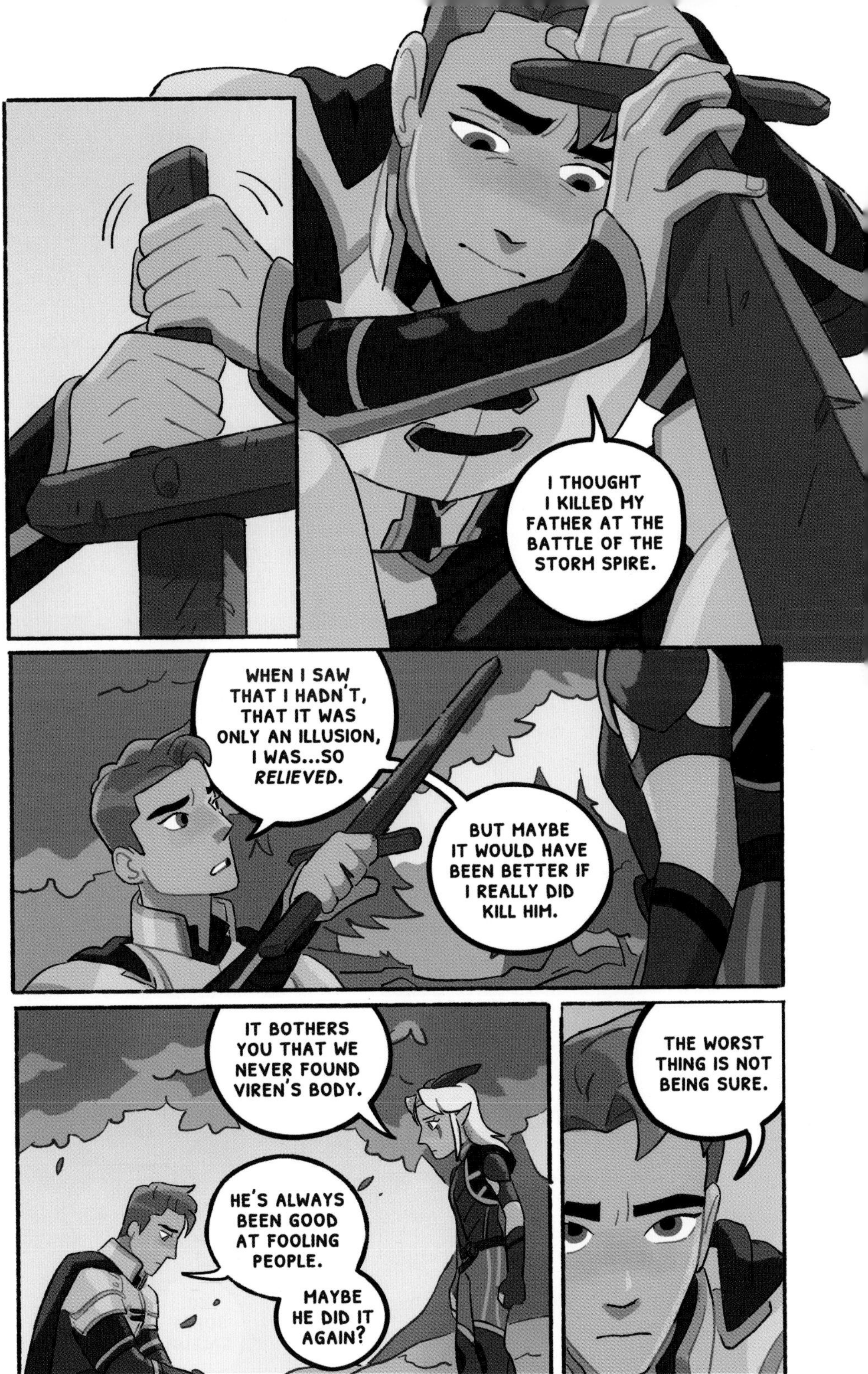
I THOUGHT I KILLED MY FATHER AT THE BATTLE OF THE STORM SPIRE.
WHEN I SAW THAT I HADN'T, THAT IT WAS ONLY AN ILLUSION, I WAS...SO *RELIEVED*.
BUT MAYBE IT WOULD HAVE BEEN BETTER IF I REALLY DID KILL HIM.
IT BOTHERS YOU THAT WE NEVER FOUND VIREN'S BODY.
HE'S ALWAYS BEEN GOOD AT FOOLING PEOPLE.
MAYBE HE DID IT AGAIN?
THE WORST THING IS NOT BEING SURE.

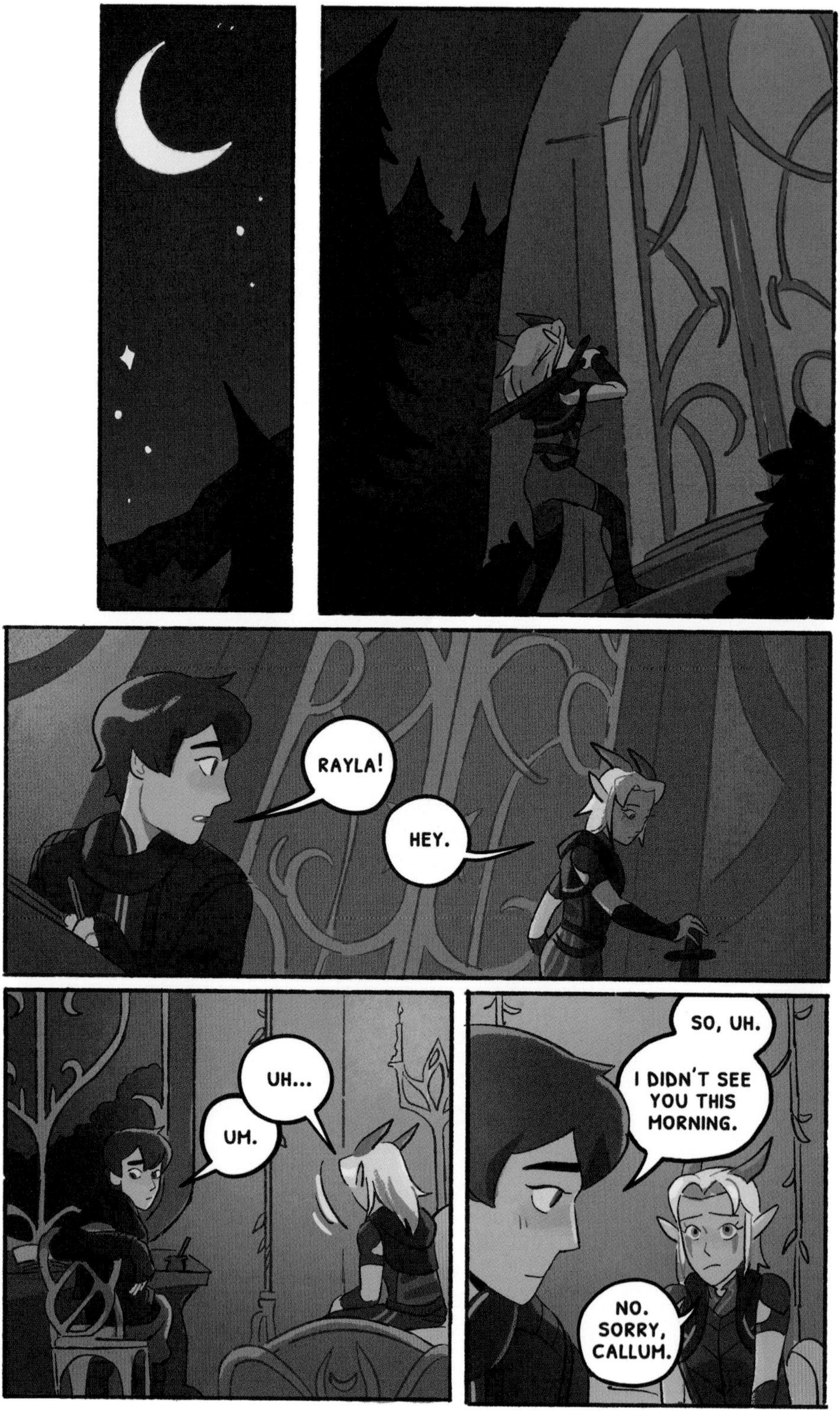
RAYLA!
HEY.
UH...
UM.
SO, UH.
I DIDN'T SEE YOU THIS MORNING.
NO. SORRY, CALLUM.

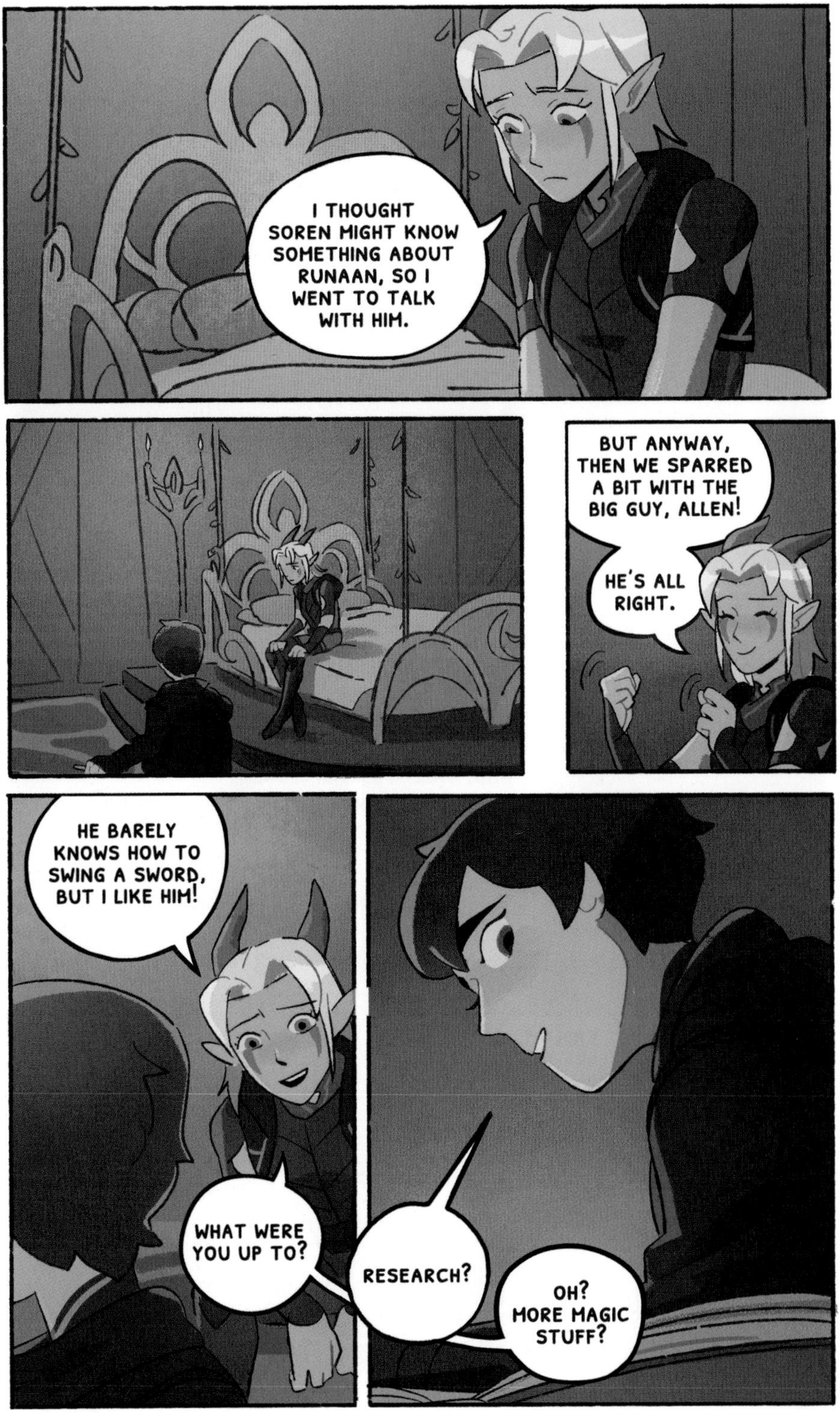
I THOUGHT SOREN MIGHT KNOW SOMETHING ABOUT RUNAAN, SO I WENT TO TALK WITH HIM.
BUT ANYWAY, THEN WE SPARRED A BIT WITH THE BIG GUY, ALLEN!
HE'S ALL RIGHT.
HE BARELY KNOWS HOW TO SWING A SWORD, BUT I LIKE HIM!
WHAT WERE YOU UP TO?
RESEARCH?
OH? MORE MAGIC STUFF?

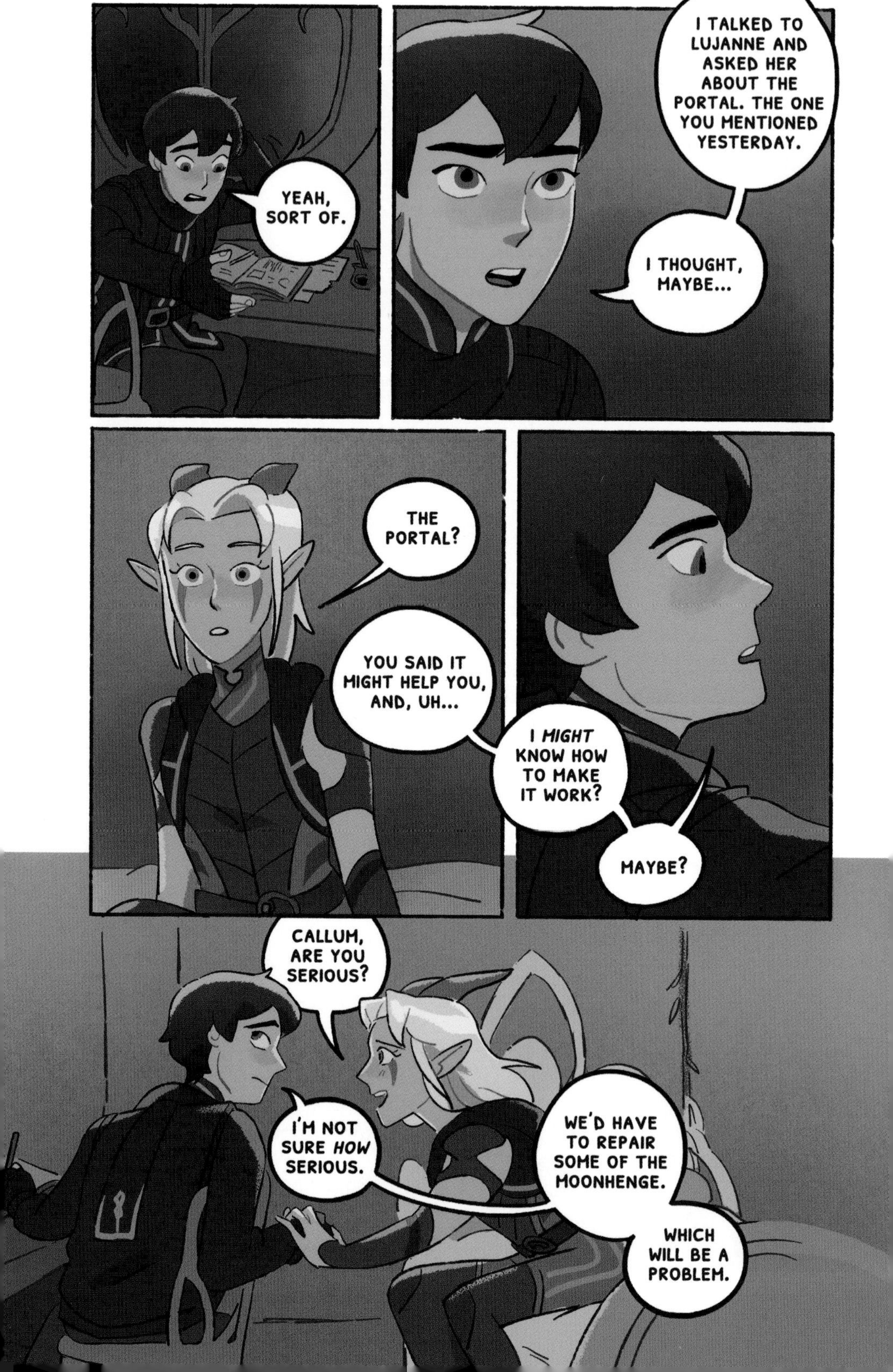
YEAH, SORT OF.
I TALKED TO LUJANNE AND ASKED HER ABOUT THE PORTAL. THE ONE YOU MENTIONED YESTERDAY.
I THOUGHT, MAYBE...
THE PORTAL?
YOU SAID IT MIGHT HELP YOU, AND, UH...
I *MIGHT* KNOW HOW TO MAKE IT WORK?
MAYBE?
CALLUM, ARE YOU SERIOUS?
I'M NOT SURE *HOW* SERIOUS.
WE'D HAVE TO REPAIR SOME OF THE MOONHENGE.
WHICH WILL BE A PROBLEM.

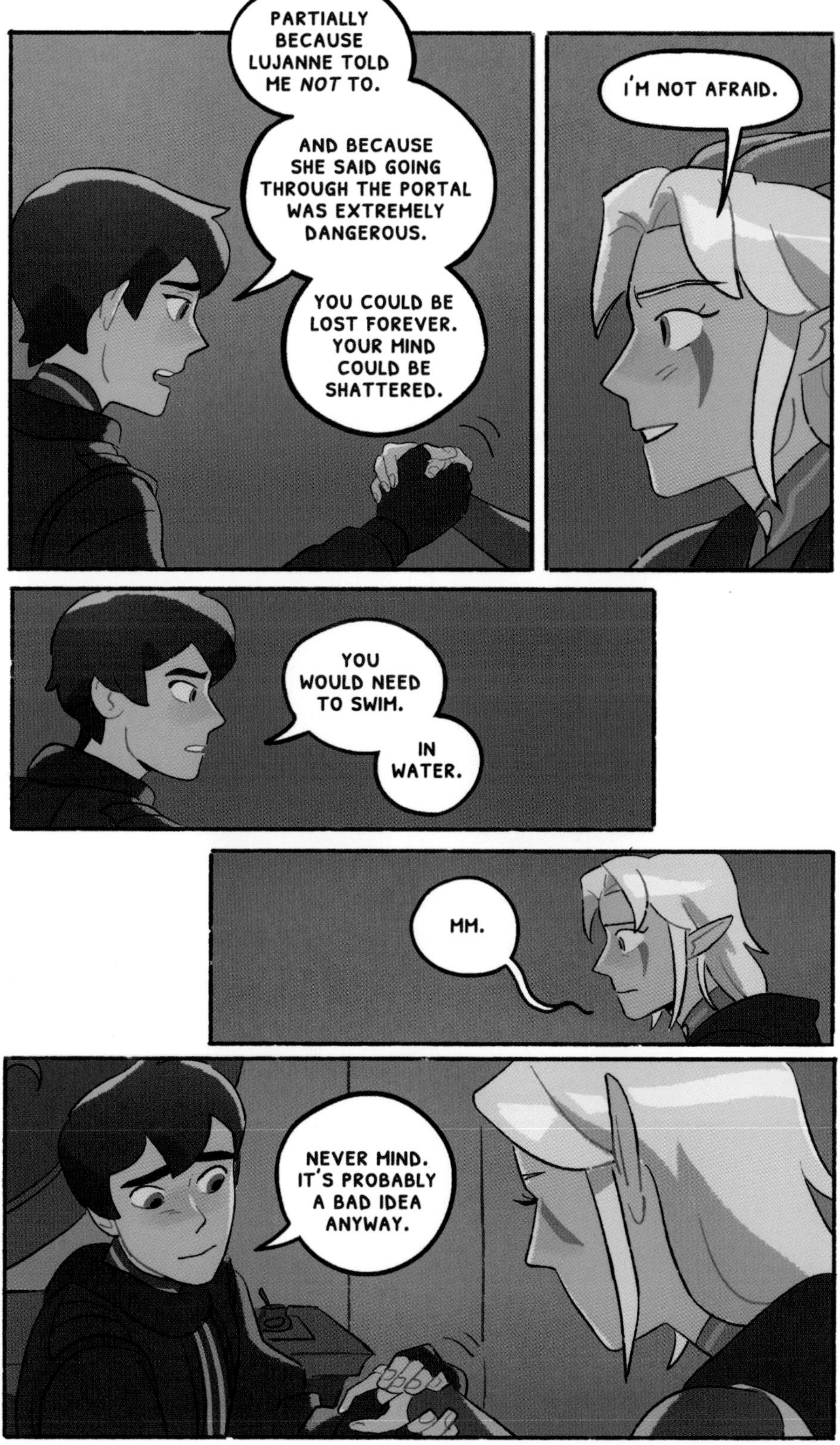
PARTIALLY BECAUSE LUJANNE TOLD ME *NOT* TO.
AND BECAUSE SHE SAID GOING THROUGH THE PORTAL WAS EXTREMELY DANGEROUS.
YOU COULD BE LOST FOREVER. YOUR MIND COULD BE SHATTERED.
I'M NOT AFRAID.
YOU WOULD NEED TO SWIM.
IN WATER.
MM.
NEVER MIND. IT'S PROBABLY A BAD IDEA ANYWAY.

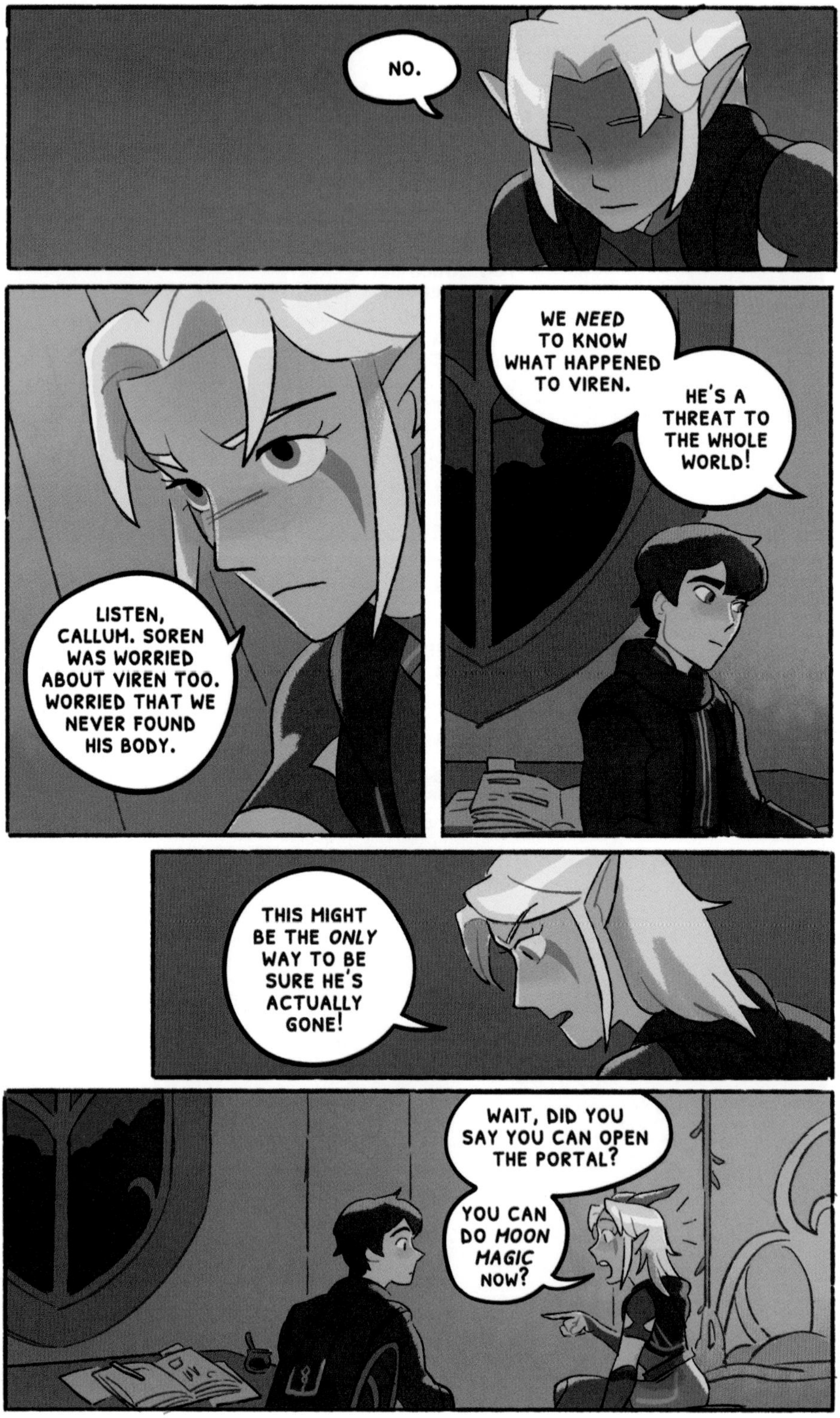
NO.
LISTEN, CALLUM. SOREN WAS WORRIED ABOUT VIREN TOO. WORRIED THAT WE NEVER FOUND HIS BODY.
WE *NEED* TO KNOW WHAT HAPPENED TO VIREN.
HE'S A THREAT TO THE WHOLE WORLD!
THIS MIGHT BE THE *ONLY* WAY TO BE SURE HE'S ACTUALLY GONE!
WAIT, DID YOU SAY YOU CAN OPEN THE PORTAL?
YOU CAN DO *MOON MAGIC* NOW?

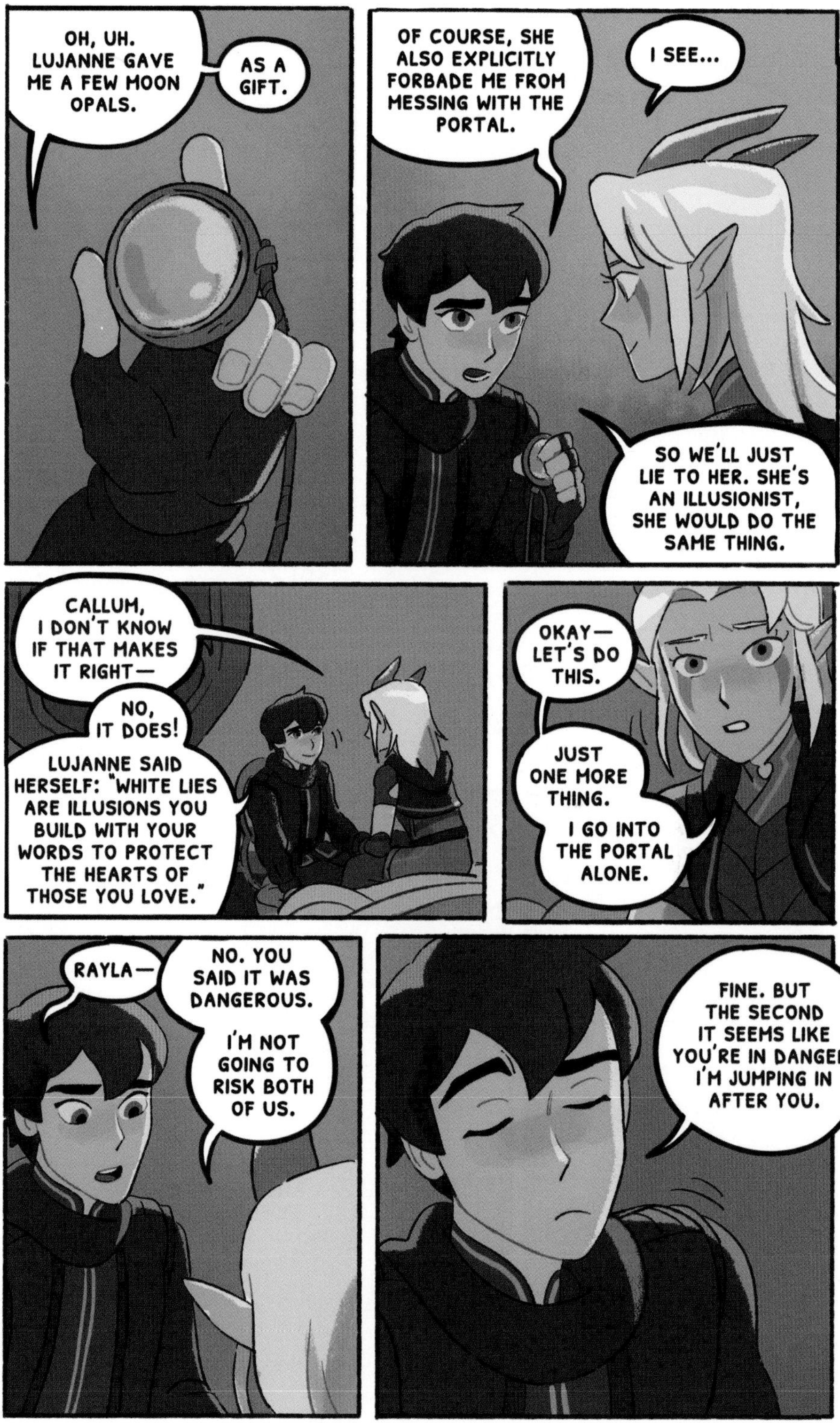
OH, UH. LUJANNE GAVE ME A FEW MOON OPALS.
AS A GIFT.
OF COURSE, SHE ALSO EXPLICITLY FORBADE ME FROM MESSING WITH THE PORTAL.
I SEE...
SO WE'LL JUST LIE TO HER. SHE'S AN ILLUSIONIST, SHE WOULD DO THE SAME THING.
CALLUM, I DON'T KNOW IF THAT MAKES IT RIGHT—
NO, IT DOES!
LUJANNE SAID HERSELF: "WHITE LIES ARE ILLUSIONS YOU BUILD WITH YOUR WORDS TO PROTECT THE HEARTS OF THOSE YOU LOVE."
OKAY— LET'S DO THIS.
JUST ONE MORE THING.
I GO INTO THE PORTAL ALONE.
RAYLA—
NO. YOU SAID IT WAS DANGEROUS.
I'M NOT GOING TO RISK BOTH OF US.
FINE. BUT THE SECOND IT SEEMS LIKE YOU'RE IN DANGER, I'M JUMPING IN AFTER YOU.

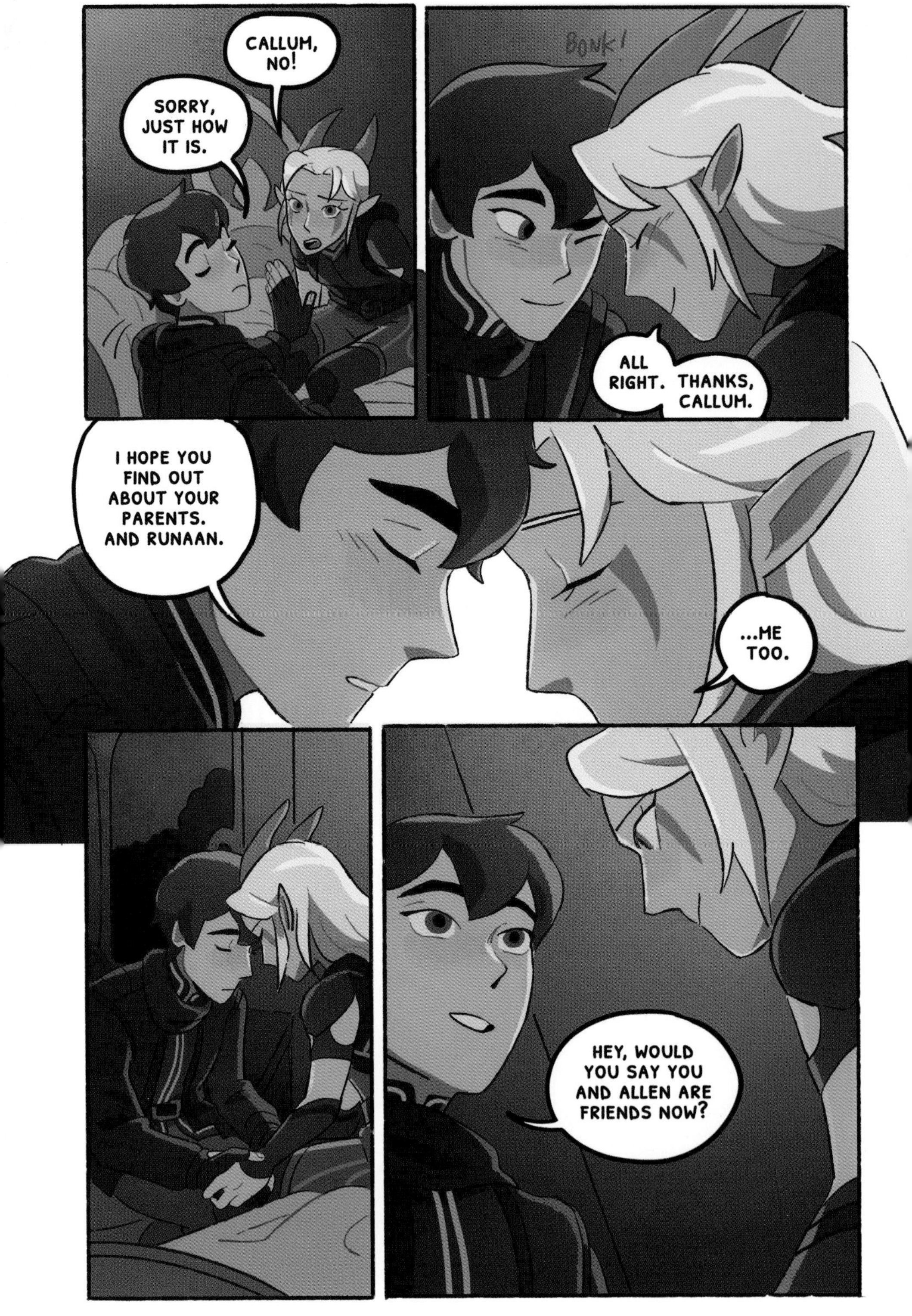
CALLUM, NO!
SORRY, JUST HOW IT IS.
BONK!
ALL RIGHT.
THANKS, CALLUM.
I HOPE YOU FIND OUT ABOUT YOUR PARENTS. AND RUNAAN.
...ME TOO.
HEY, WOULD YOU SAY YOU AND ALLEN ARE FRIENDS NOW?

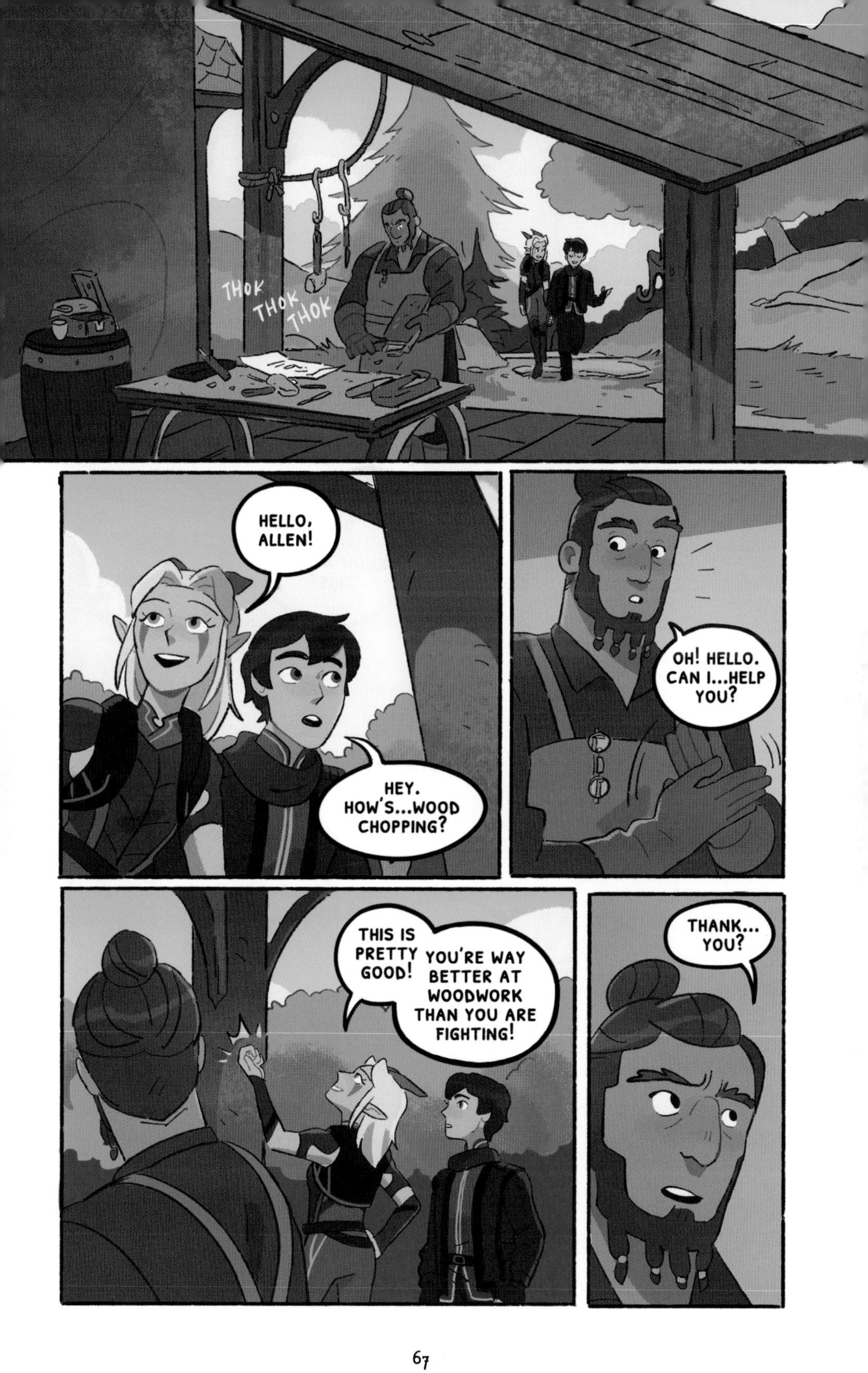
THOK
THOK
THOK
HELLO, ALLEN!
HEY. HOW'S...WOOD CHOPPING?
OH! HELLO. CAN I...HELP YOU?
THIS IS PRETTY GOOD!
YOU'RE WAY BETTER AT WOODWORK THAN YOU ARE FIGHTING!
THANK... YOU?

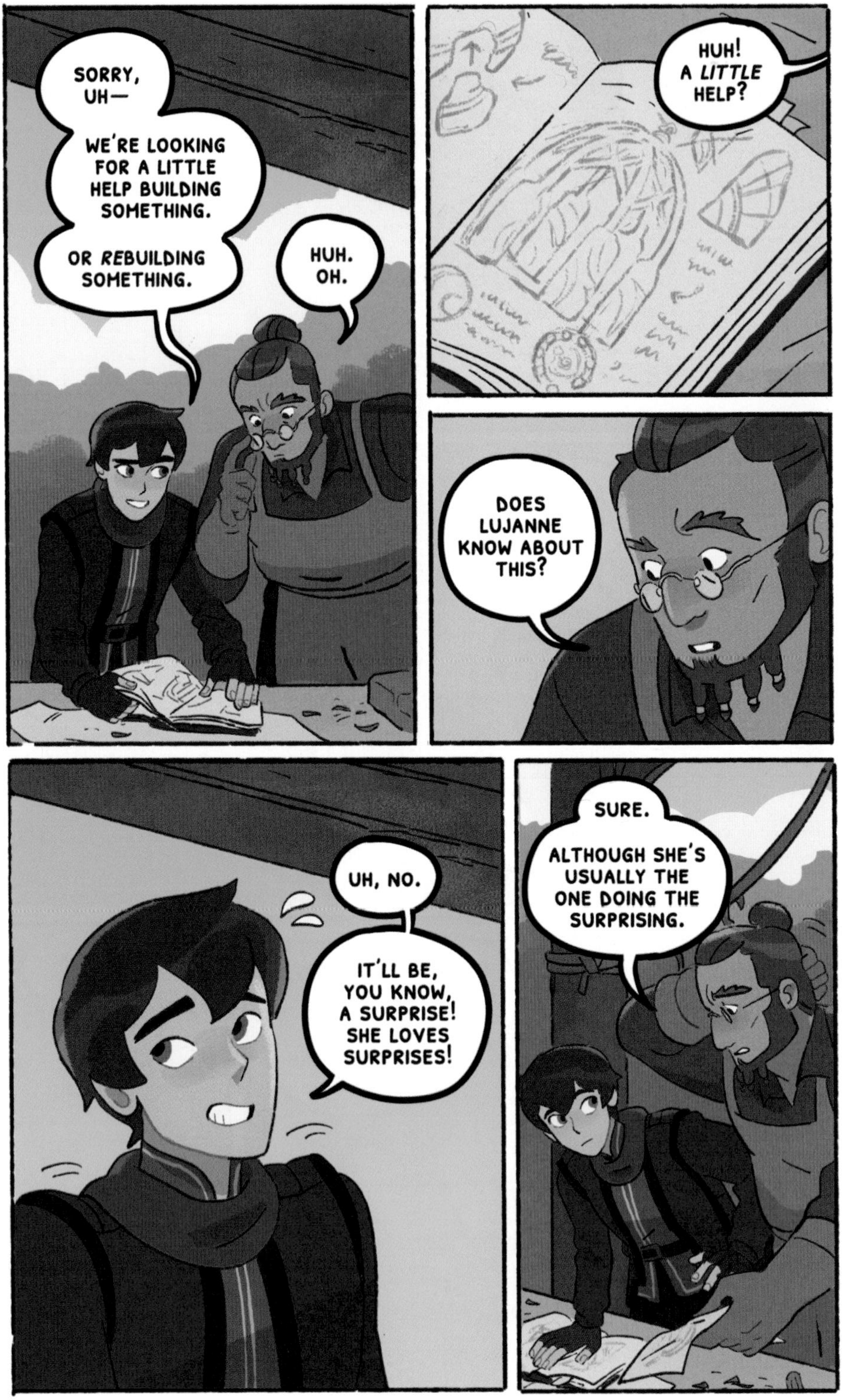
SORRY, UH—
WE'RE LOOKING FOR A LITTLE HELP BUILDING SOMETHING.
OR REBUILDING SOMETHING.
HUH. OH.
HUH! A LITTLE HELP?
DOES LUJANNE KNOW ABOUT THIS?
UH, NO.
IT'LL BE, YOU KNOW, A SURPRISE! SHE LOVES SURPRISES!
SURE.
ALTHOUGH SHE'S USUALLY THE ONE DOING THE SURPRISING.

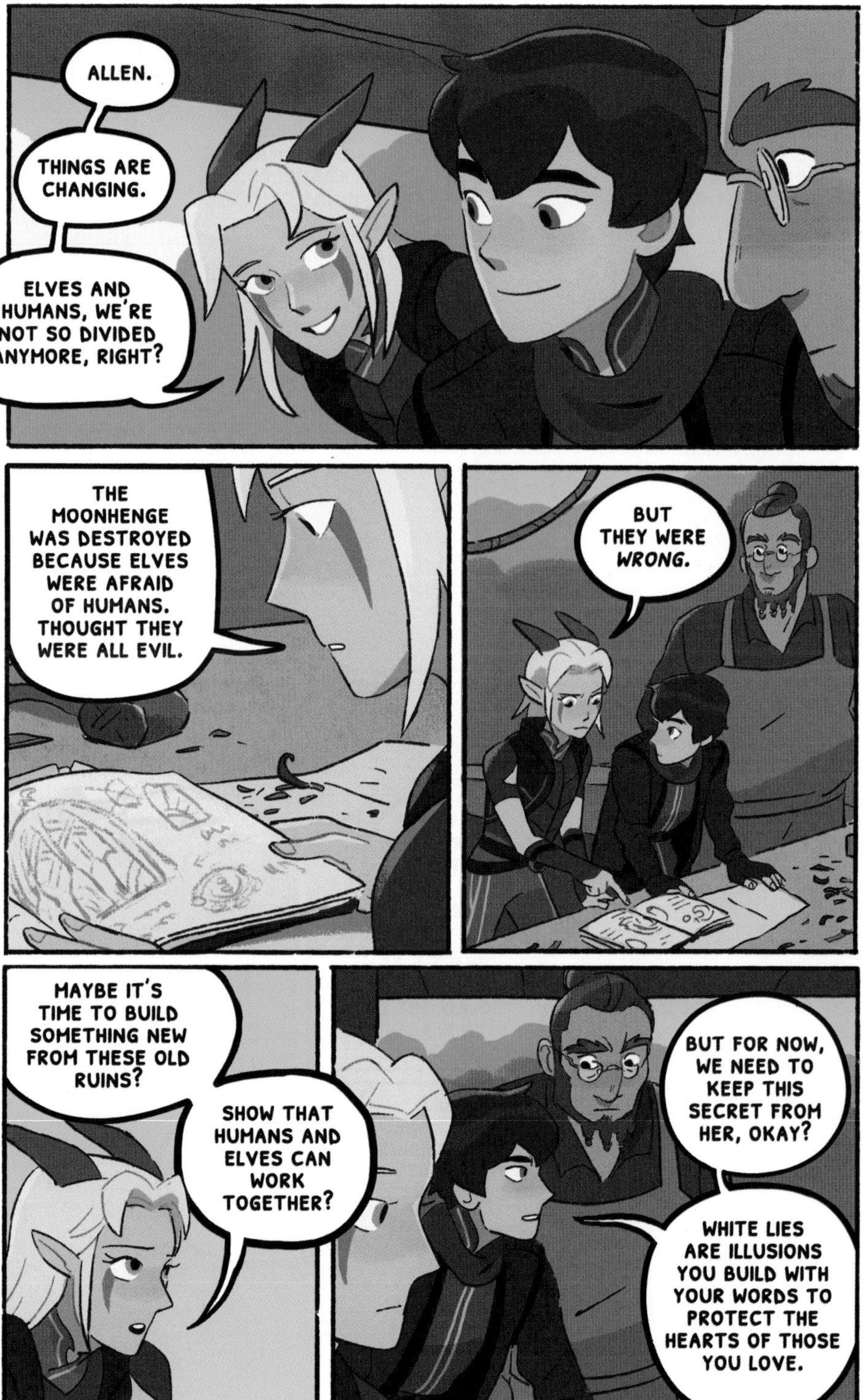
ALLEN.
THINGS ARE CHANGING.
ELVES AND HUMANS, WE'RE NOT SO DIVIDED ANYMORE, RIGHT?
THE MOONHENGE WAS DESTROYED BECAUSE ELVES WERE AFRAID OF HUMANS. THOUGHT THEY WERE ALL EVIL.
BUT THEY WERE *WRONG*.
MAYBE IT'S TIME TO BUILD SOMETHING NEW FROM THESE OLD RUINS?
SHOW THAT HUMANS AND ELVES CAN WORK TOGETHER?
BUT FOR NOW, WE NEED TO KEEP THIS SECRET FROM HER, OKAY?
WHITE LIES ARE ILLUSIONS YOU BUILD WITH YOUR WORDS TO PROTECT THE HEARTS OF THOSE YOU LOVE.

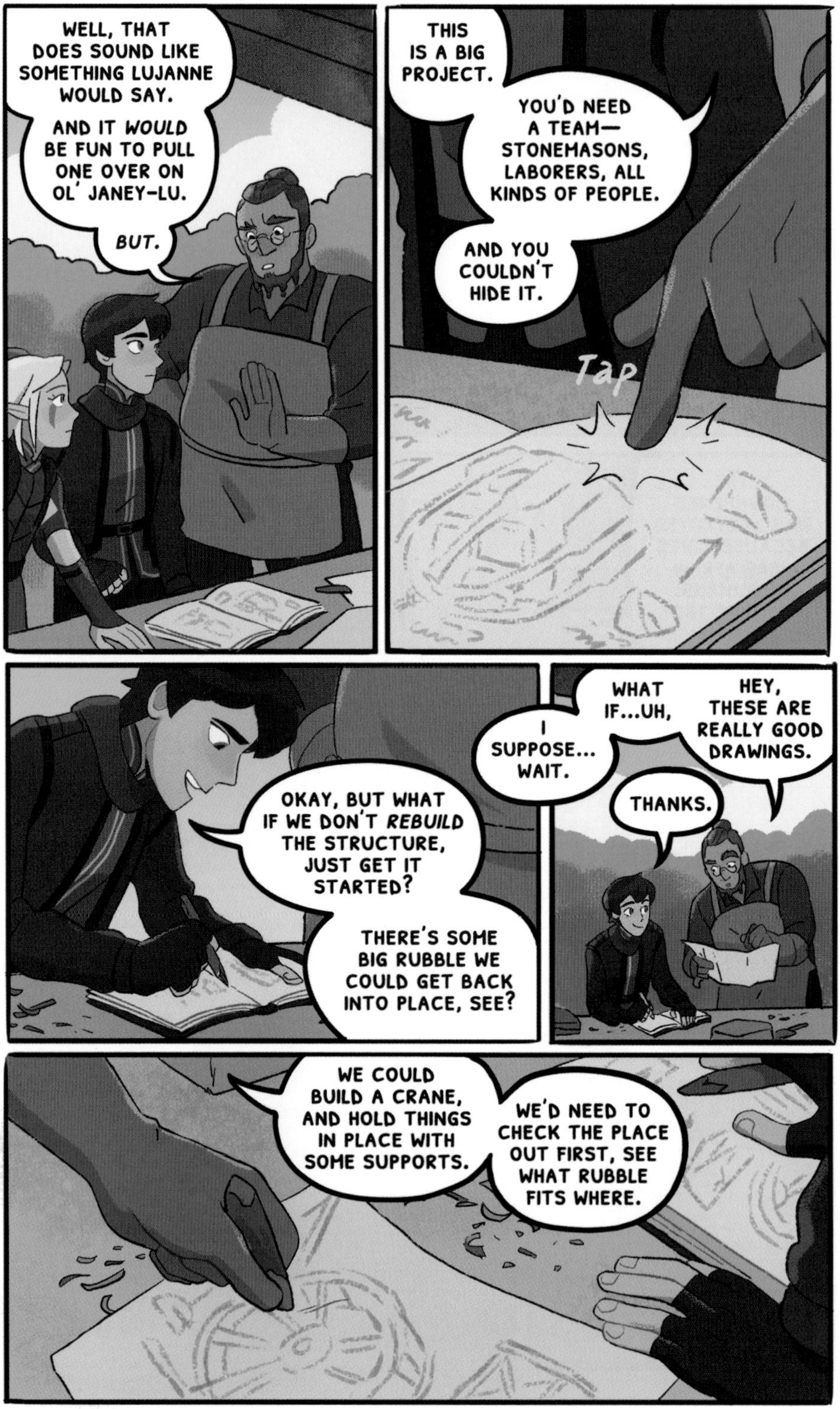
WELL, THAT DOES SOUND LIKE SOMETHING LUJANNE WOULD SAY.
AND IT *WOULD* BE FUN TO PULL ONE OVER ON OL' JANEY-LU.
BUT.
THIS IS A BIG PROJECT.
YOU'D NEED A TEAM—STONEMASONS, LABORERS, ALL KINDS OF PEOPLE.
AND YOU COULDN'T HIDE IT.
TAP
OKAY, BUT WHAT IF WE DON'T *REBUILD* THE STRUCTURE, JUST GET IT STARTED?
THERE'S SOME BIG RUBBLE WE COULD GET BACK INTO PLACE, SEE?
I SUPPOSE... WAIT.
WHAT IF...UH,
HEY, THESE ARE REALLY GOOD DRAWINGS.
THANKS.
WE COULD BUILD A CRANE, AND HOLD THINGS IN PLACE WITH SOME SUPPORTS.
WE'D NEED TO CHECK THE PLACE OUT FIRST, SEE WHAT RUBBLE FITS WHERE.

BUT WE HAVE THE SAME PROBLEM. HOW ARE WE GOING TO HIDE EVERYTHING?

TaP TaP

YOU MAKE SCAFFOLDS FOR LUJANNE ALL THE TIME, RIGHT?

WHAT IF WE DON'T HIDE IT?

...HA!

I THINK I SEE.

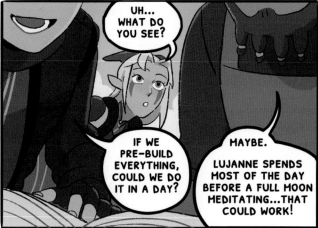

UH... WHAT DO YOU SEE?

IF WE PRE-BUILD EVERYTHING, COULD WE DO IT IN A DAY?

MAYBE. LUJANNE SPENDS MOST OF THE DAY BEFORE A FULL MOON MEDITATING...THAT COULD WORK!

HA! ALL RIGHT.

THIS WILL BE FUN.

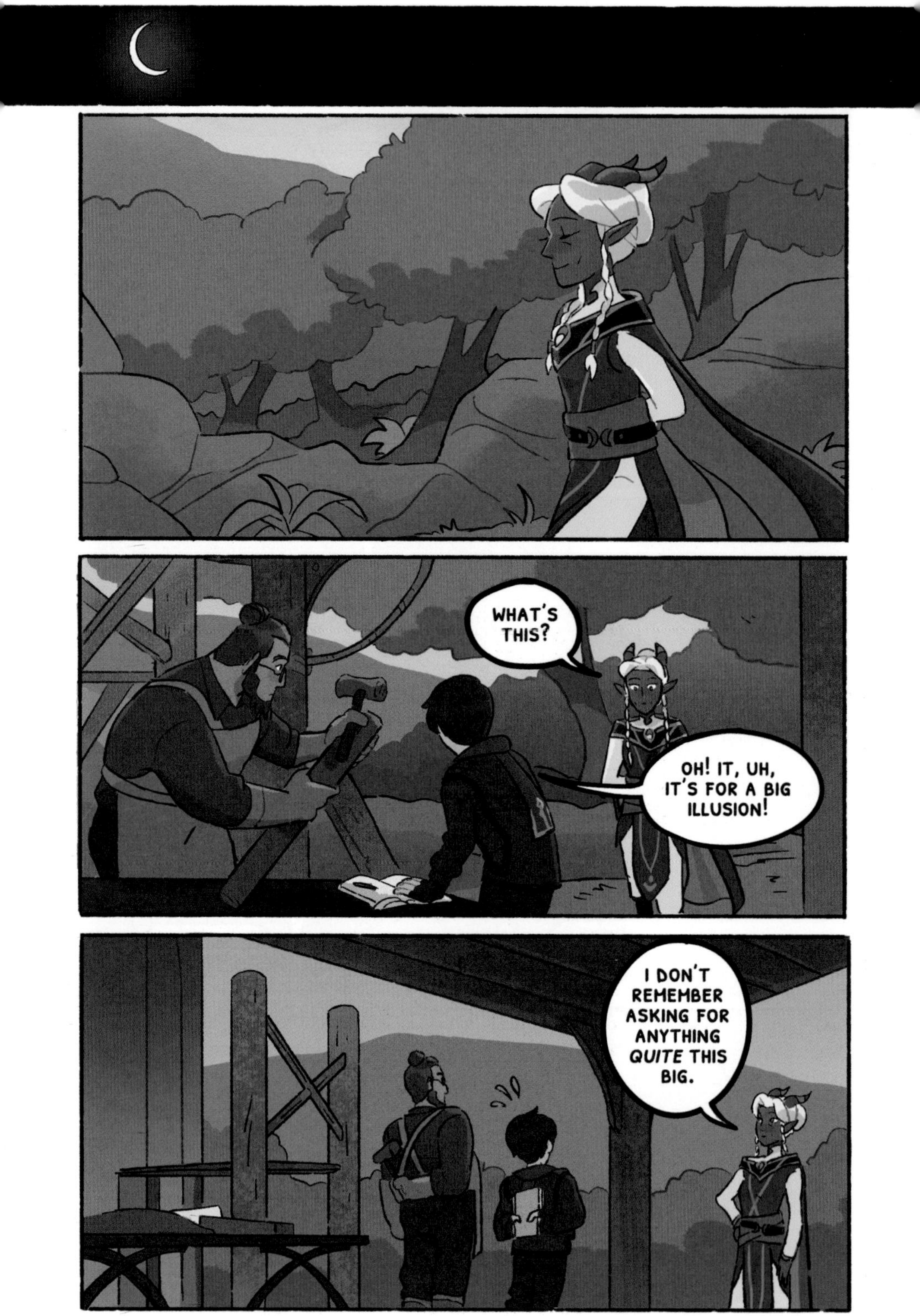
WHAT'S THIS?
OH! IT, UH, IT'S FOR A BIG ILLUSION!
I DON'T REMEMBER ASKING FOR ANYTHING *QUITE* THIS BIG.

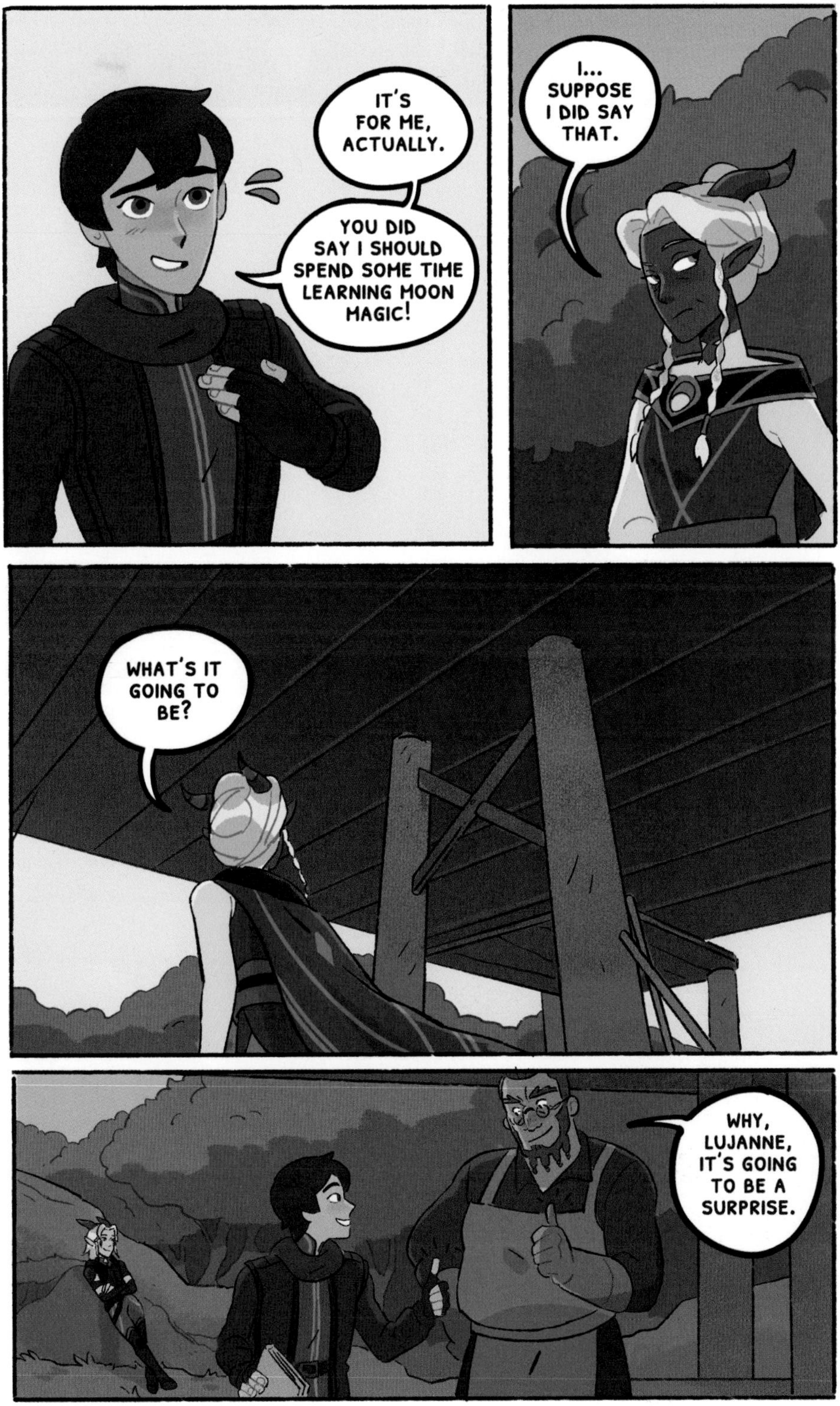
IT'S FOR ME, ACTUALLY.
YOU DID SAY I SHOULD SPEND SOME TIME LEARNING MOON MAGIC!
I... SUPPOSE I DID SAY THAT.
WHAT'S IT GOING TO BE?
WHY, LUJANNE, IT'S GOING TO BE A SURPRISE.

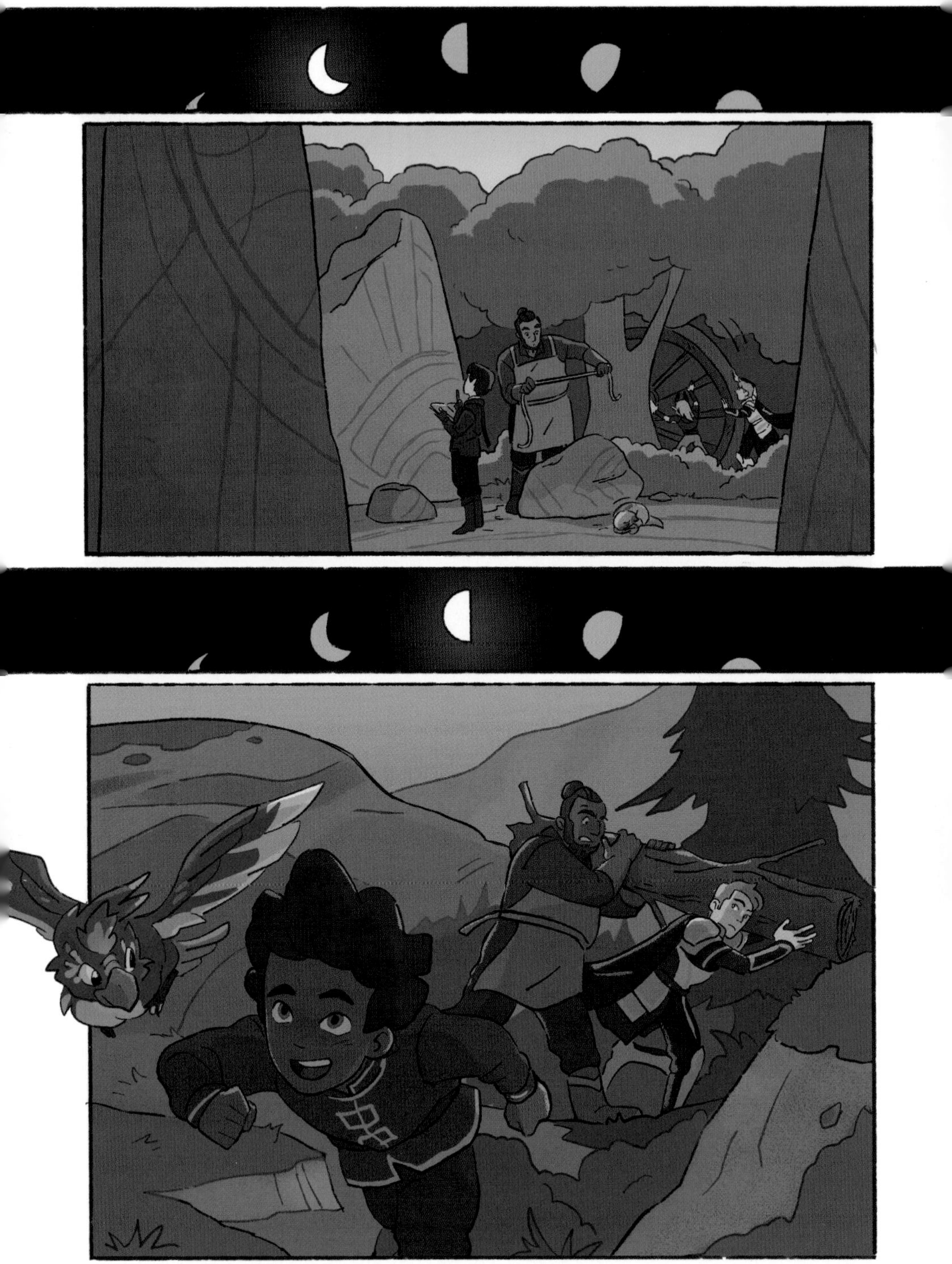

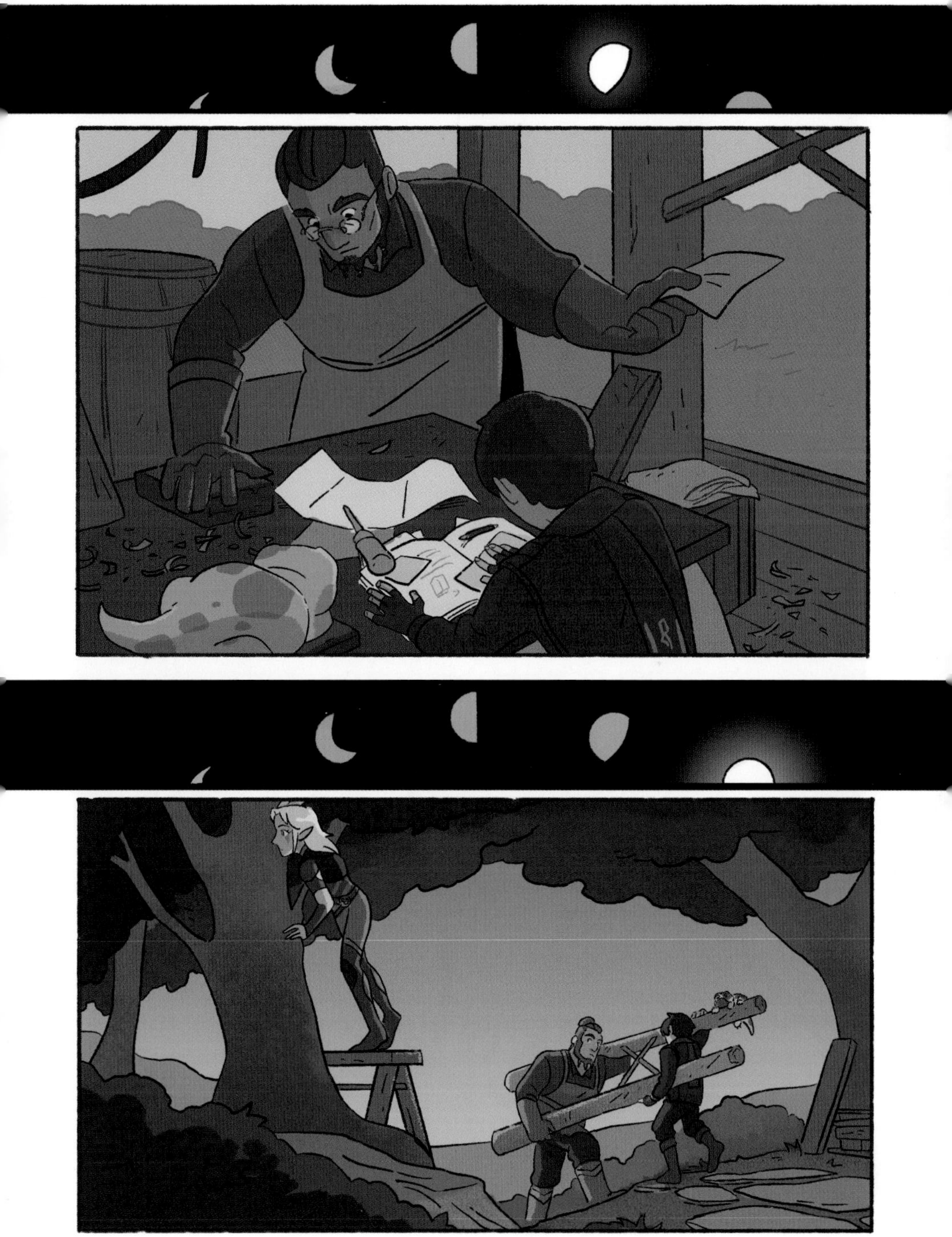

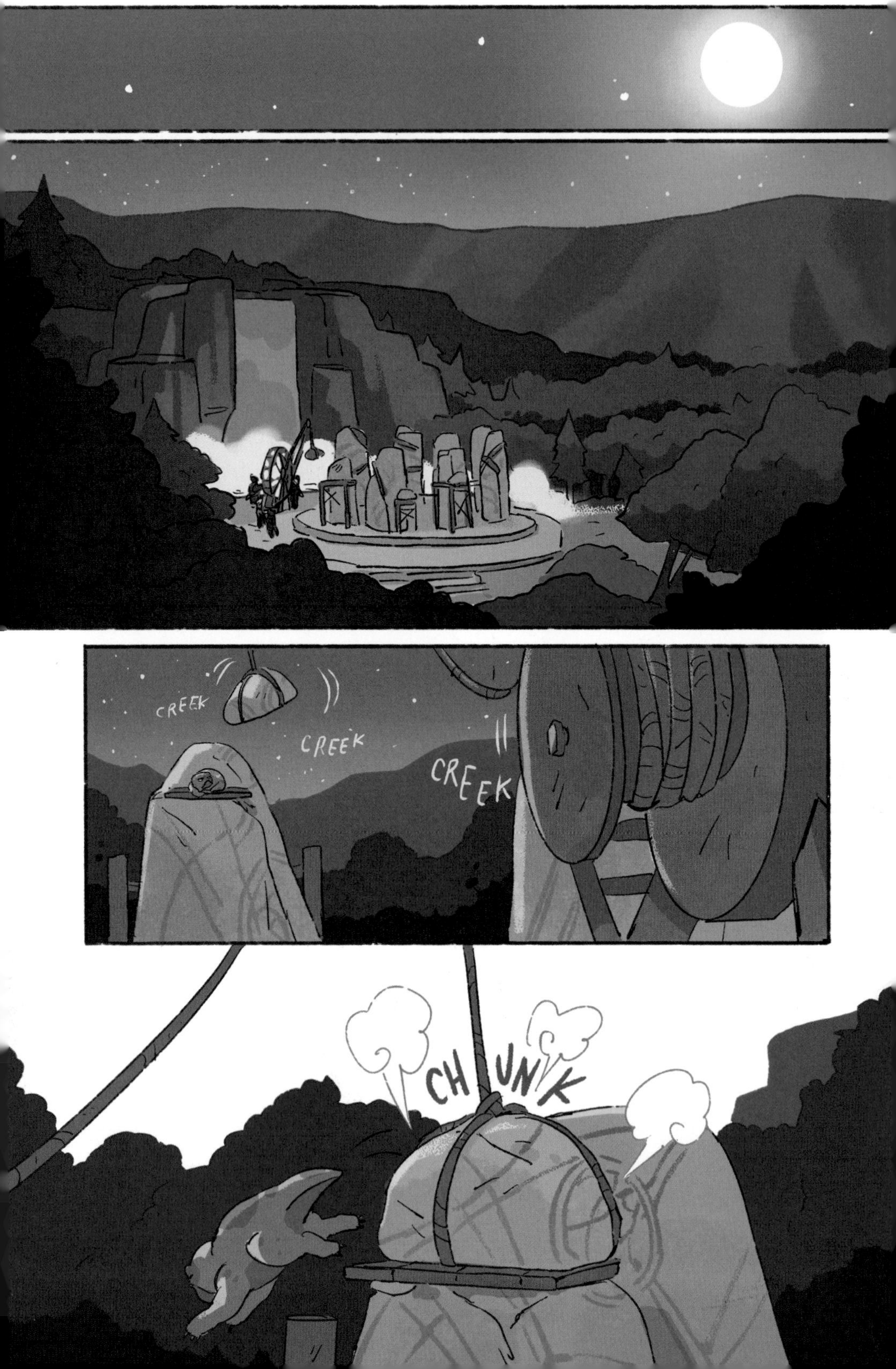
CREEK
CREEK
CREEK
CHUNK

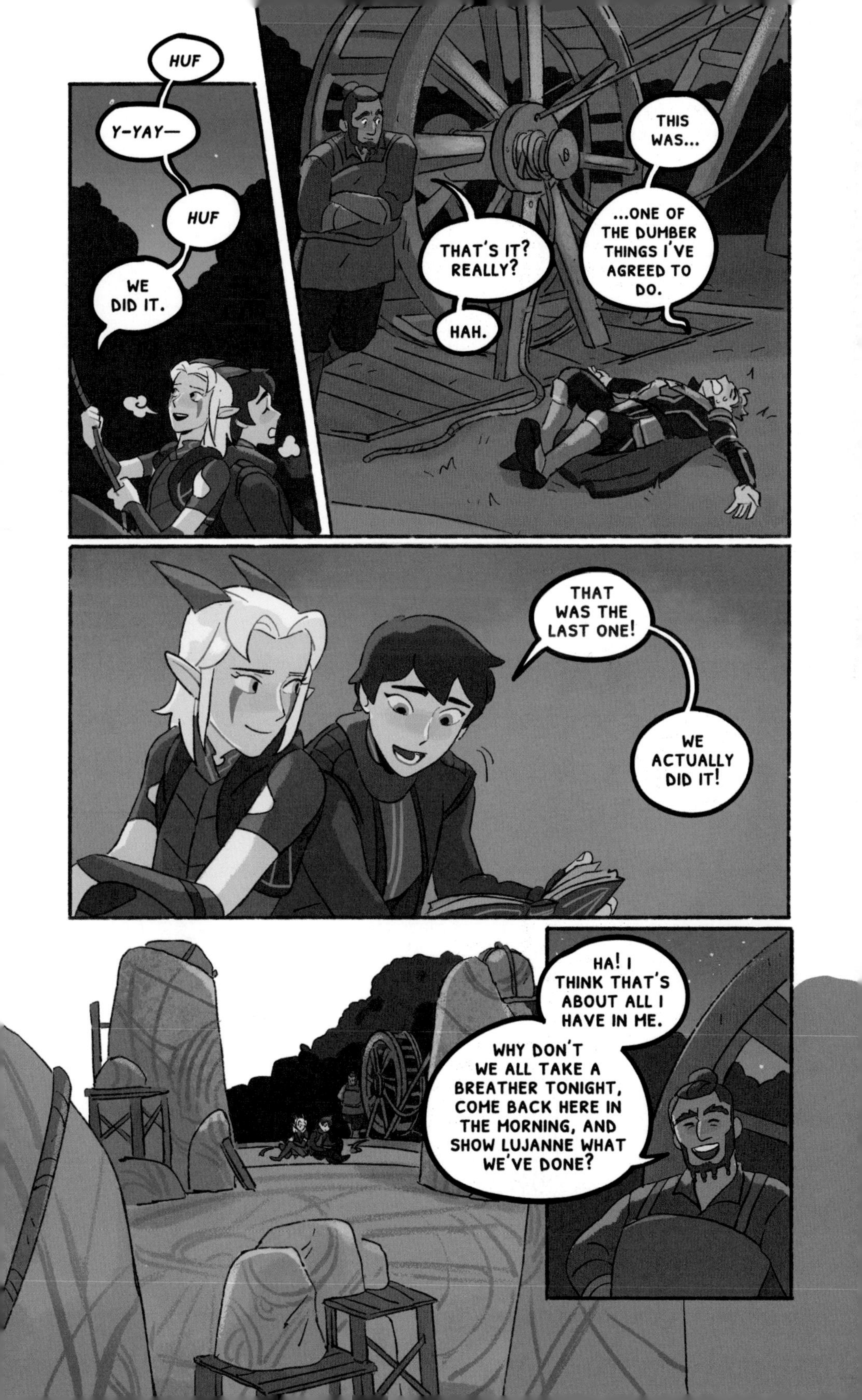
HUF
Y-YAY—
HUF
WE DID IT.
THAT'S IT? REALLY?
HAH.
THIS WAS...
...ONE OF THE DUMBER THINGS I'VE AGREED TO DO.
THAT WAS THE LAST ONE!
WE ACTUALLY DID IT!
HA! I THINK THAT'S ABOUT ALL I HAVE IN ME.
WHY DON'T WE ALL TAKE A BREATHER TONIGHT, COME BACK HERE IN THE MORNING, AND SHOW LUJANNE WHAT WE'VE DONE?

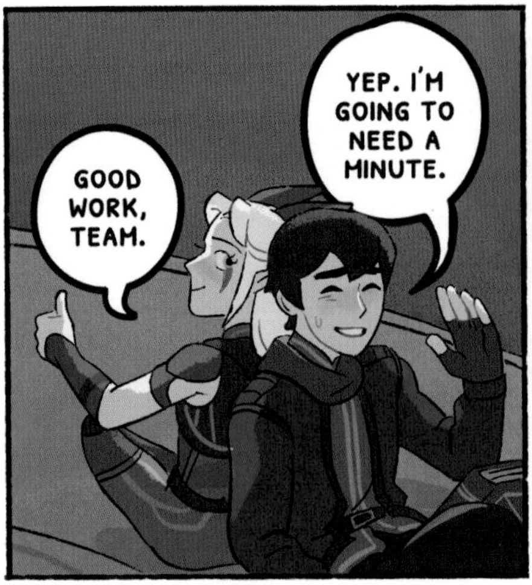
GOOD WORK, TEAM.
YEP. I'M GOING TO NEED A MINUTE.

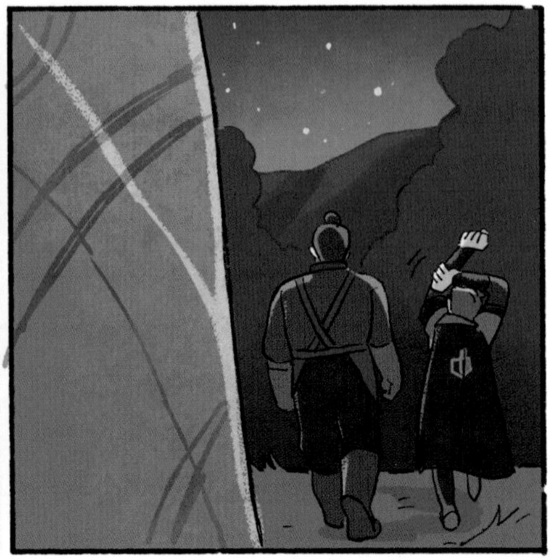

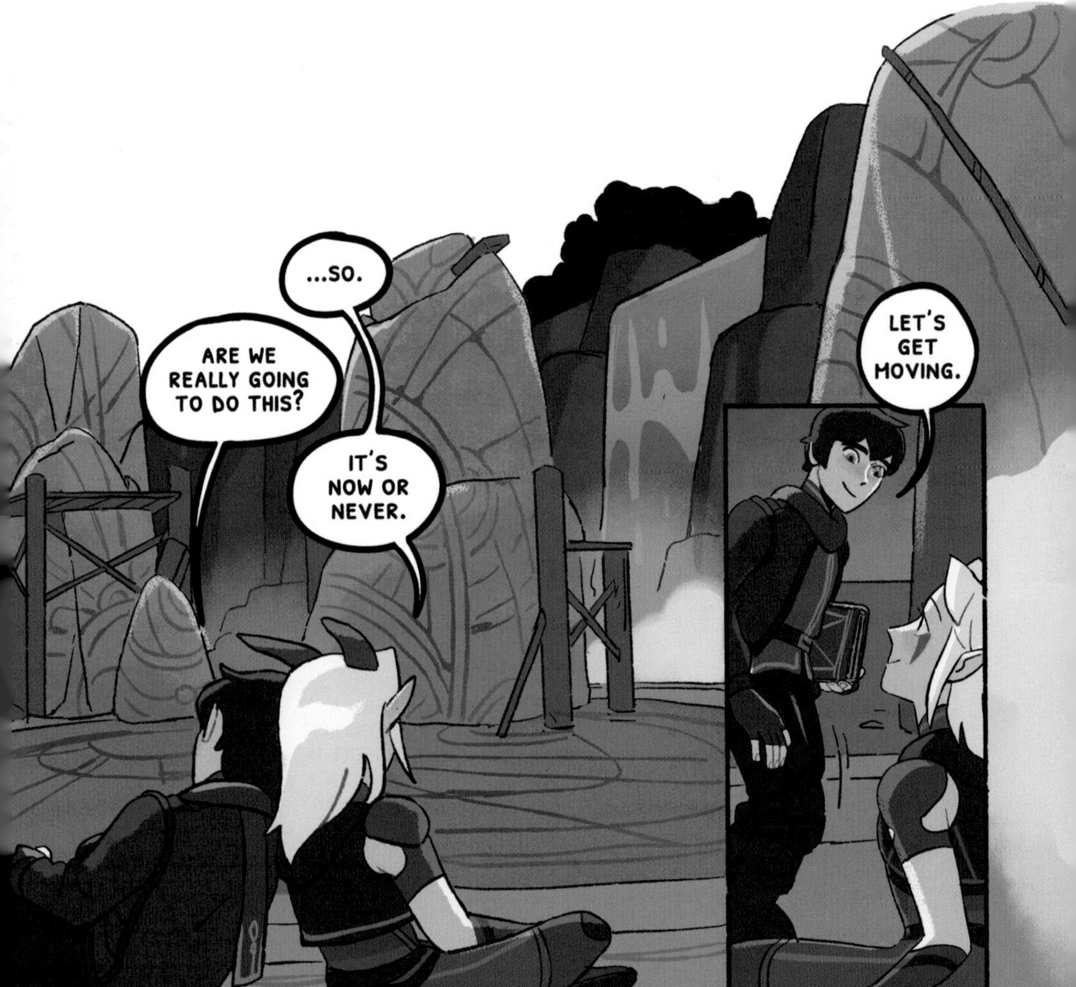
ARE WE REALLY GOING TO DO THIS?
...SO.
IT'S NOW OR NEVER.
LET'S GET MOVING.

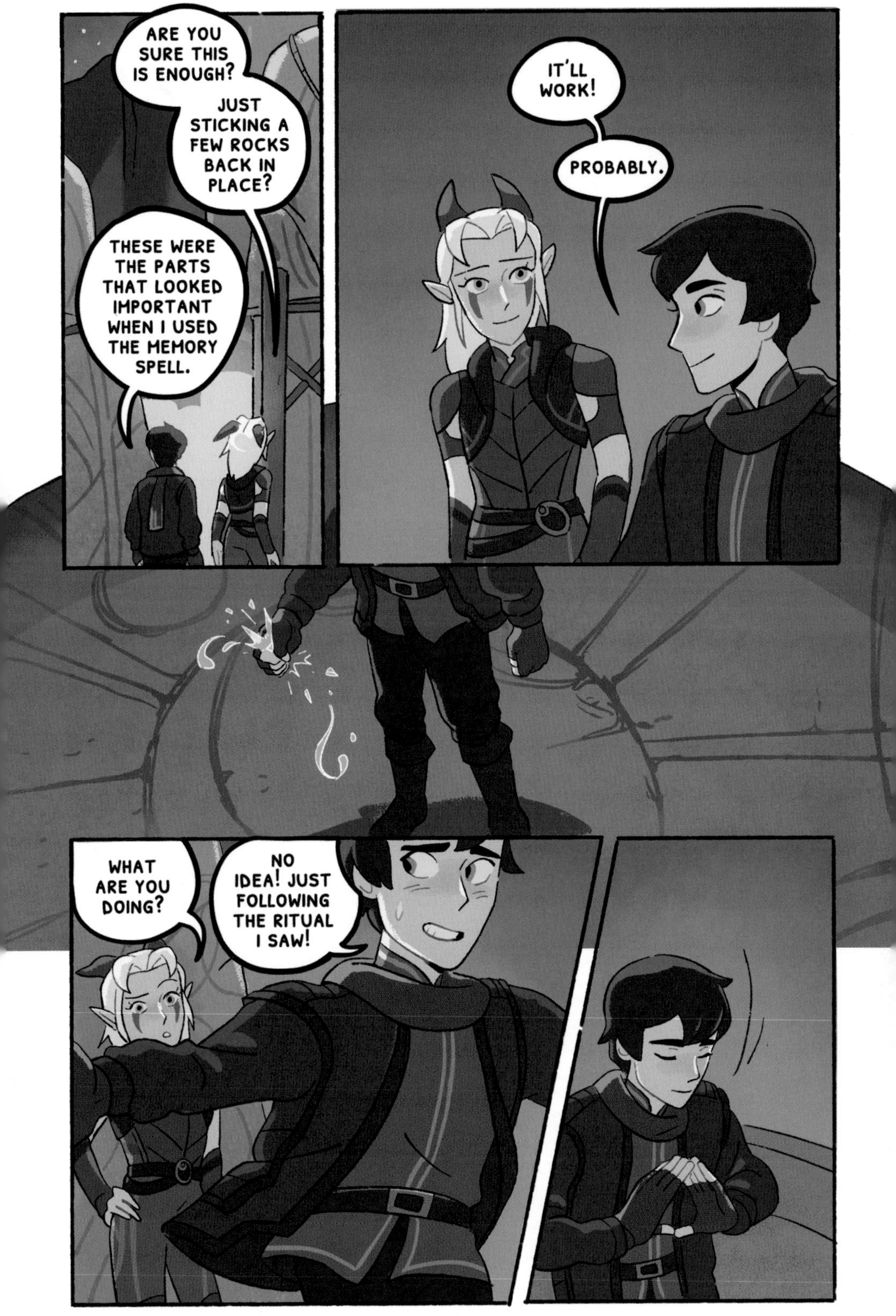
ARE YOU SURE THIS IS ENOUGH?
JUST STICKING A FEW ROCKS BACK IN PLACE?
THESE WERE THE PARTS THAT LOOKED IMPORTANT WHEN I USED THE MEMORY SPELL.
IT'LL WORK!
PROBABLY.
WHAT ARE YOU DOING?
NO IDEA! JUST FOLLOWING THE RITUAL I SAW!

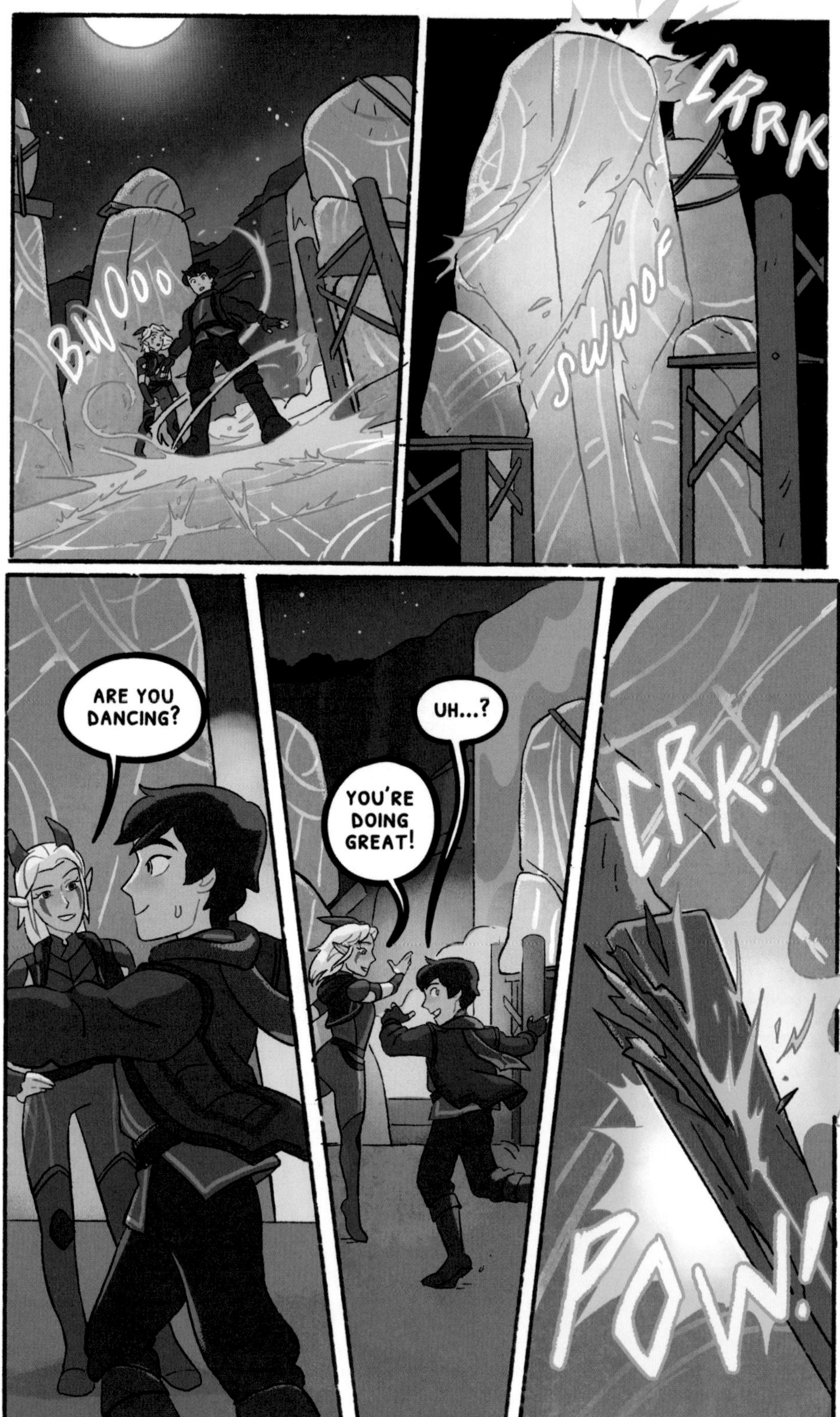
BWOOO
CRRK
SWWOF
ARE YOU DANCING?
UH...?
YOU'RE DOING GREAT!
CRK!
POW!

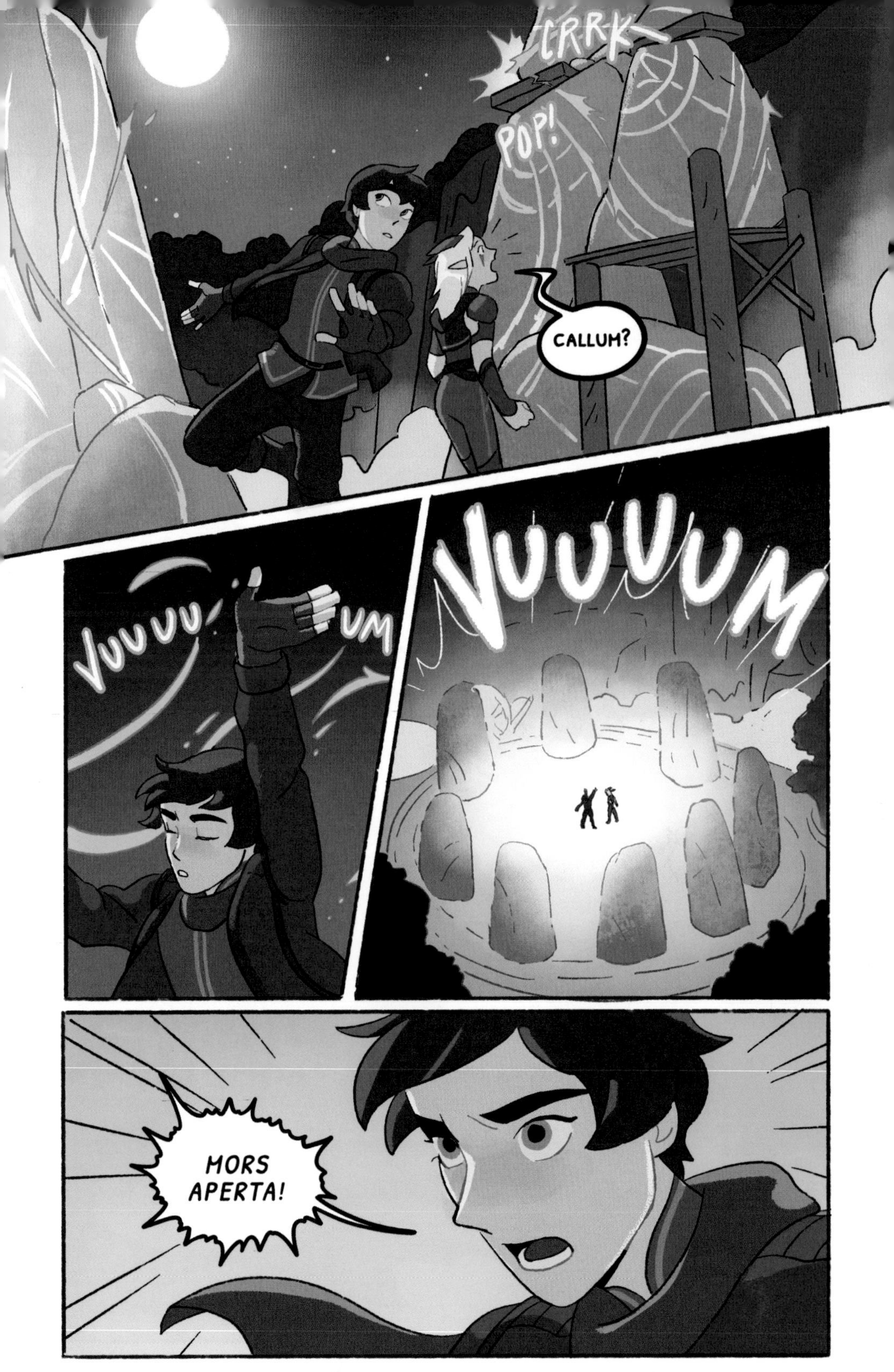
CRRK
POP!
CALLUM?
VUUUU UM
VUUUUUM
MORS
APERTA!

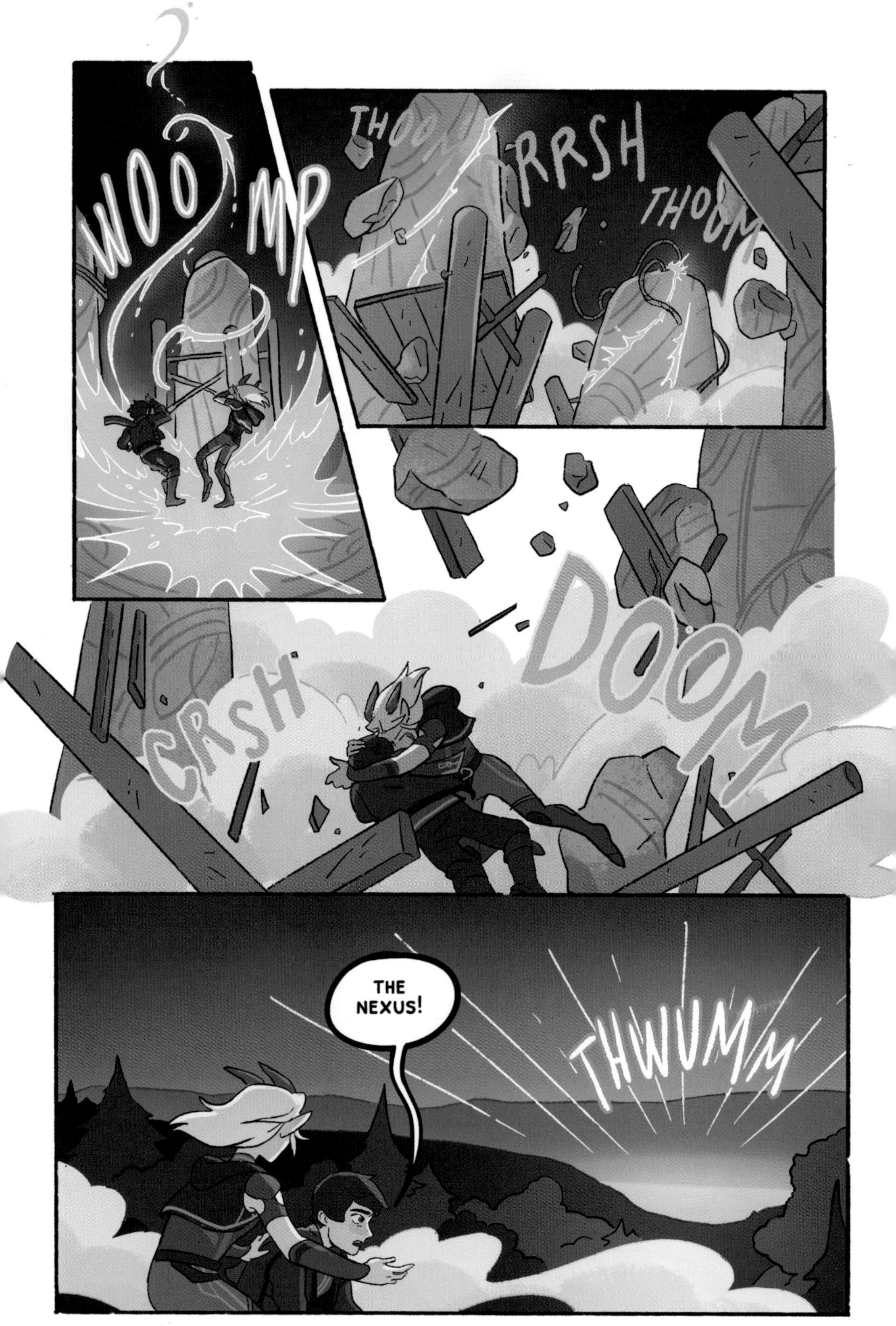
WOOMP
THOOM
CRRSH
THOOM
CRSH
DOOM
THE NEXUS!
THWUMM

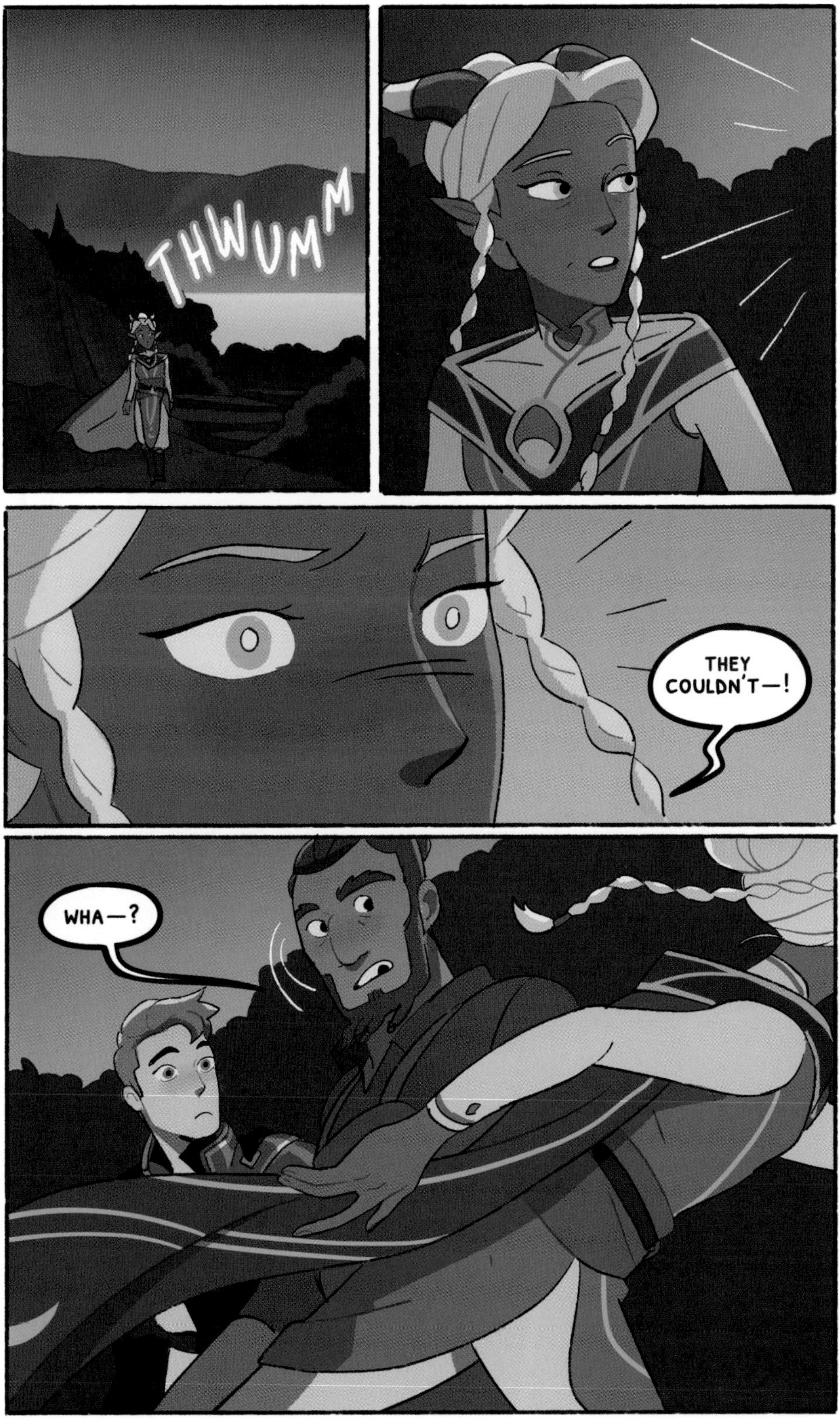
THWUMM
THEY COULDN'T—!
WHA—?

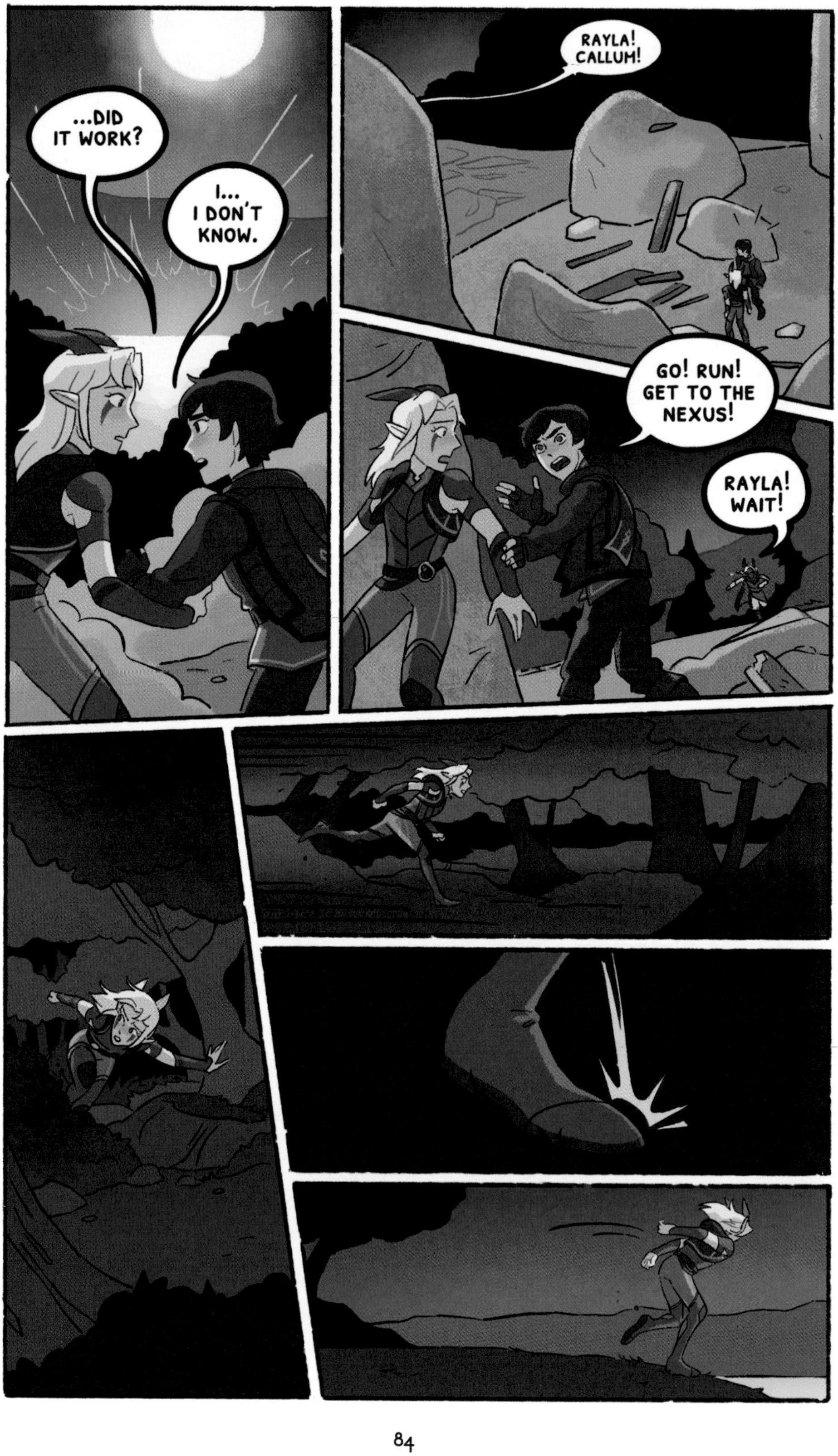
...DID IT WORK?
I... I DON'T KNOW.
RAYLA! CALLUM!
GO! RUN! GET TO THE NEXUS!
RAYLA! WAIT!

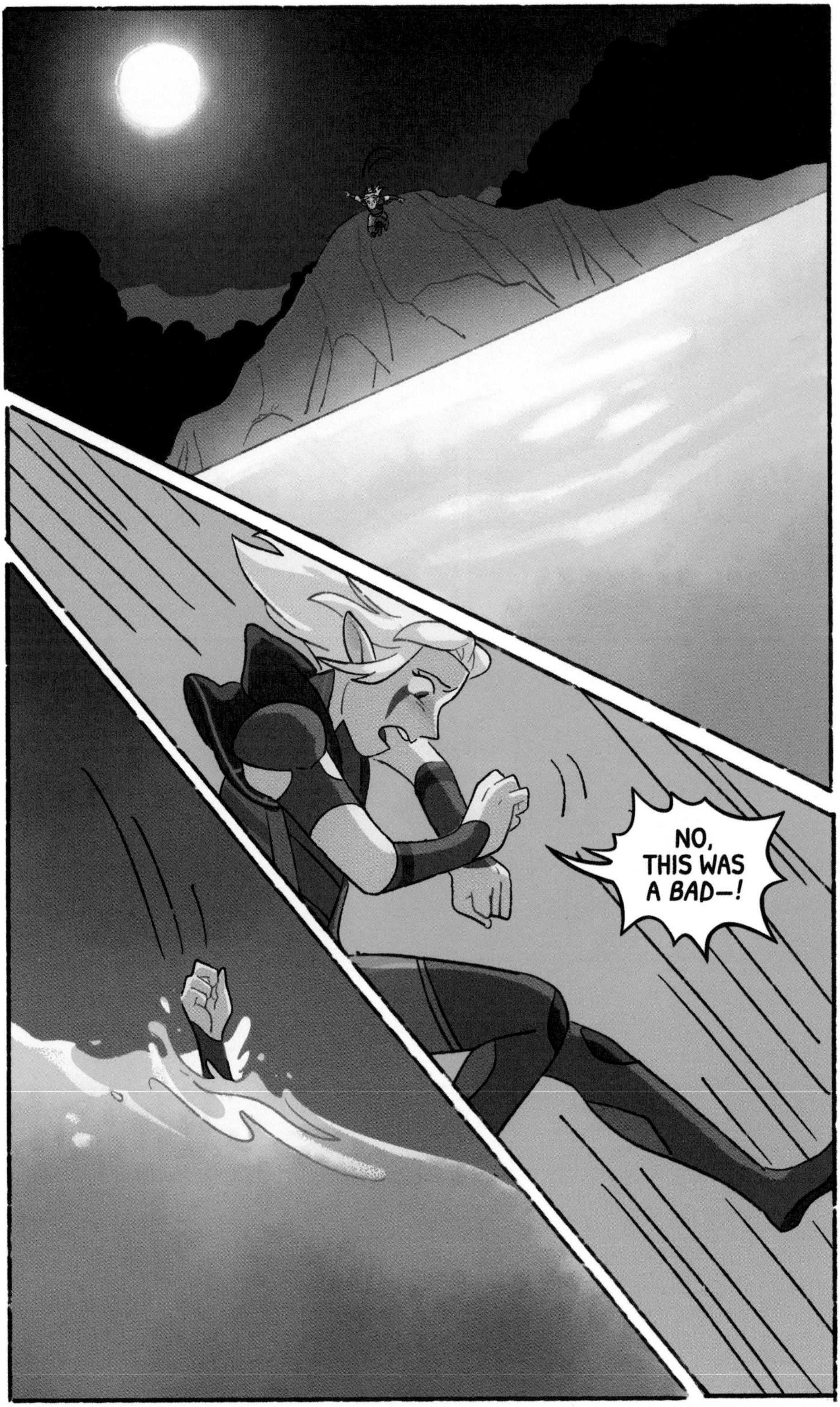
NO, THIS WAS A BAD—!

BOBB

WHAT DID YOU DO?

UH...

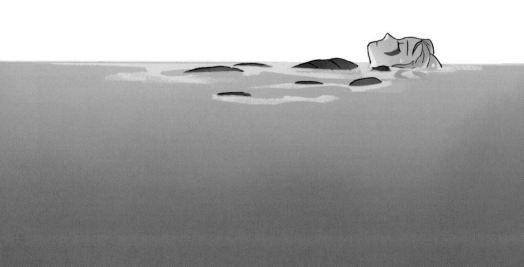

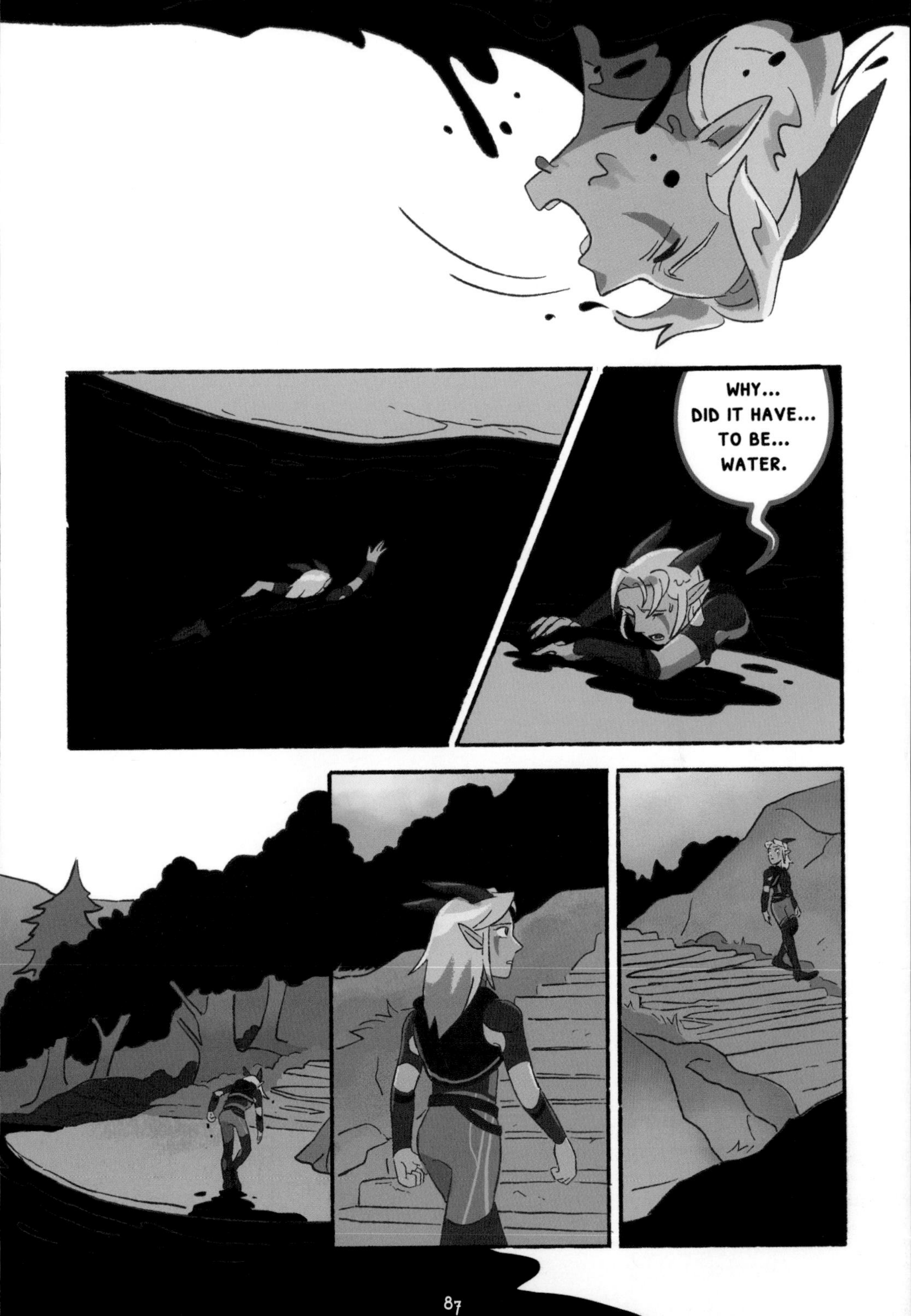
WHY... DID IT HAVE... TO BE... WATER.

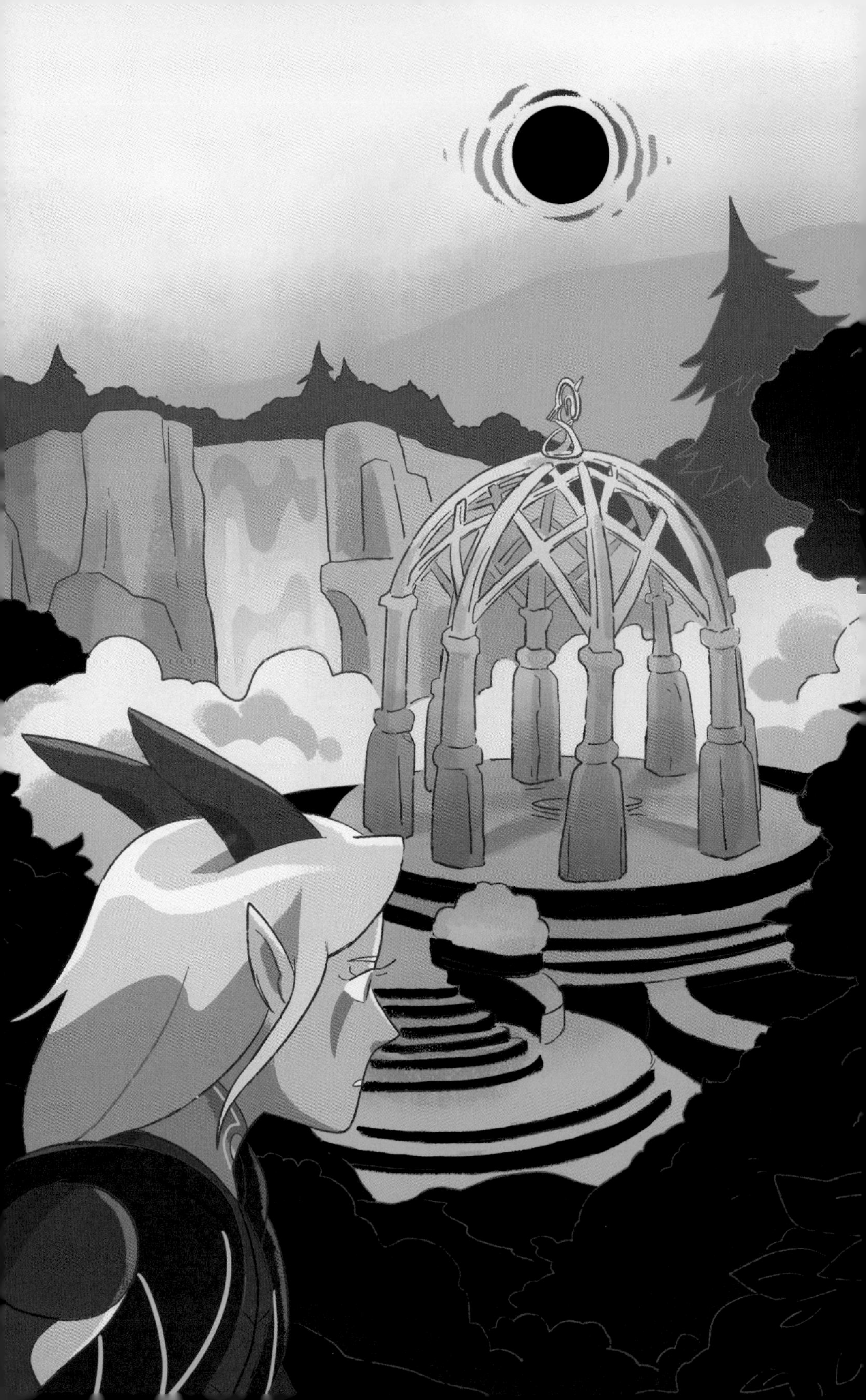

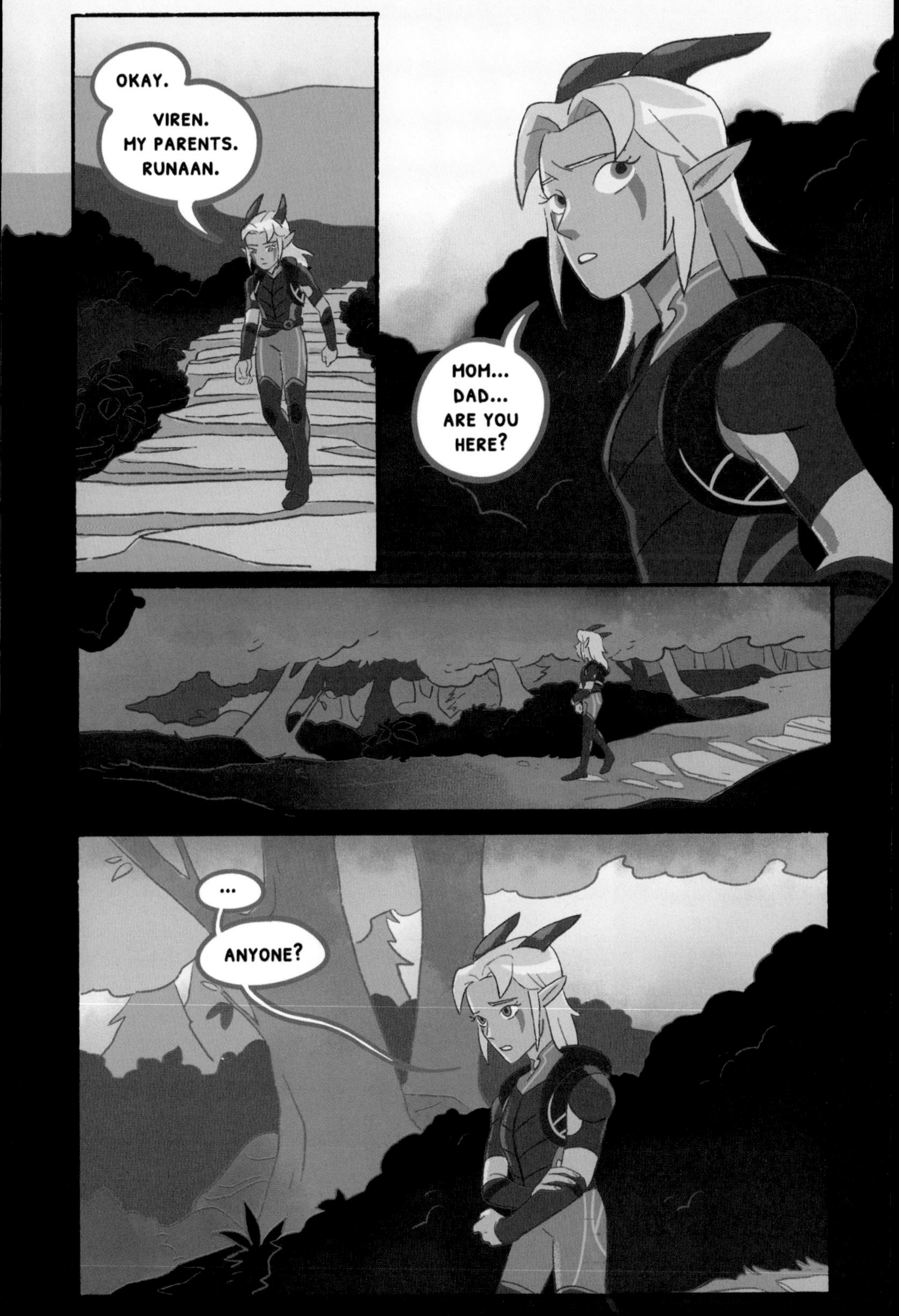
OKAY.
VIREN. MY PARENTS. RUNAAN.
MOM... DAD... ARE YOU HERE?
...
ANYONE?

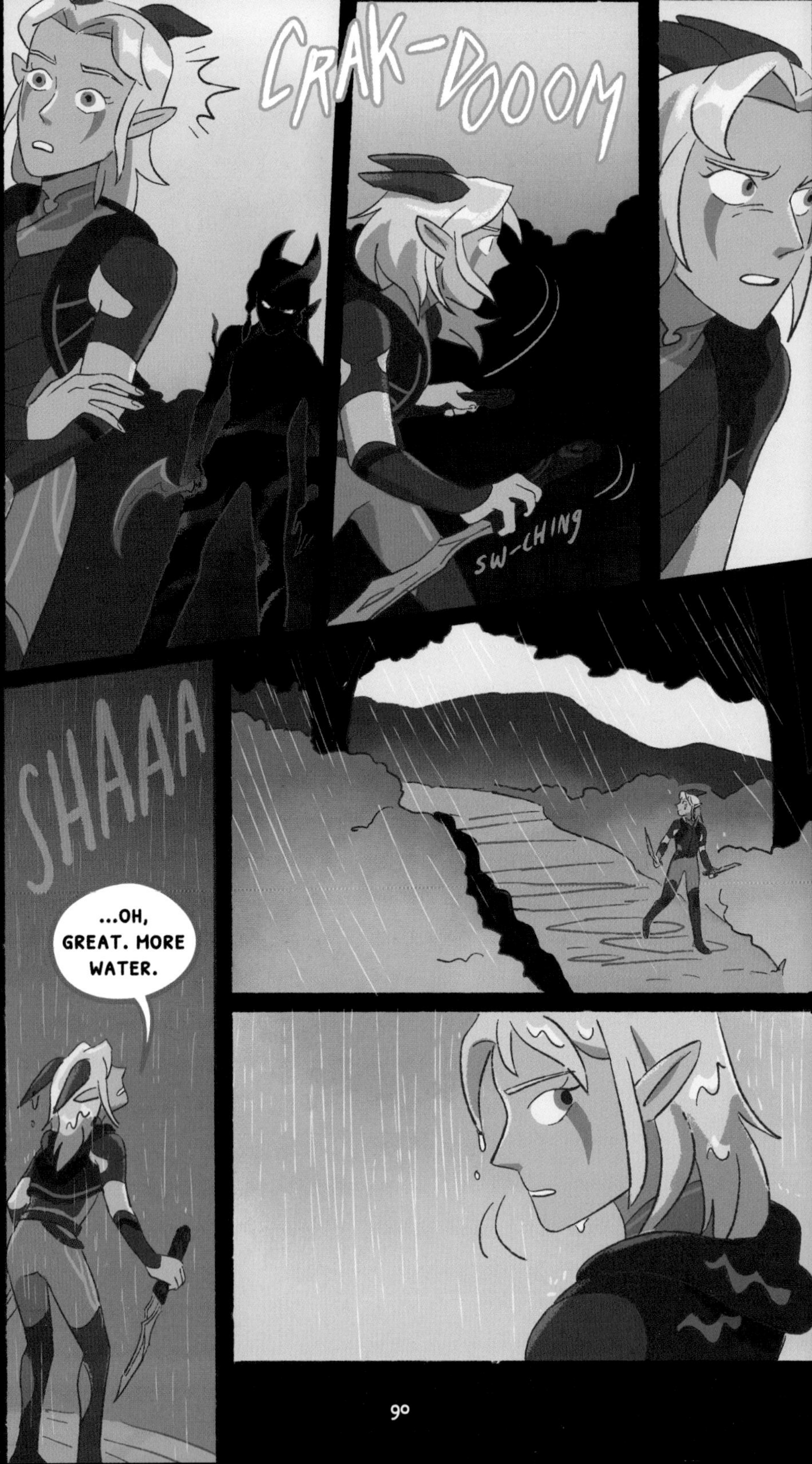
CRAK-DOOOM
SW-CHING
SHAAA
...OH, GREAT. MORE WATER.

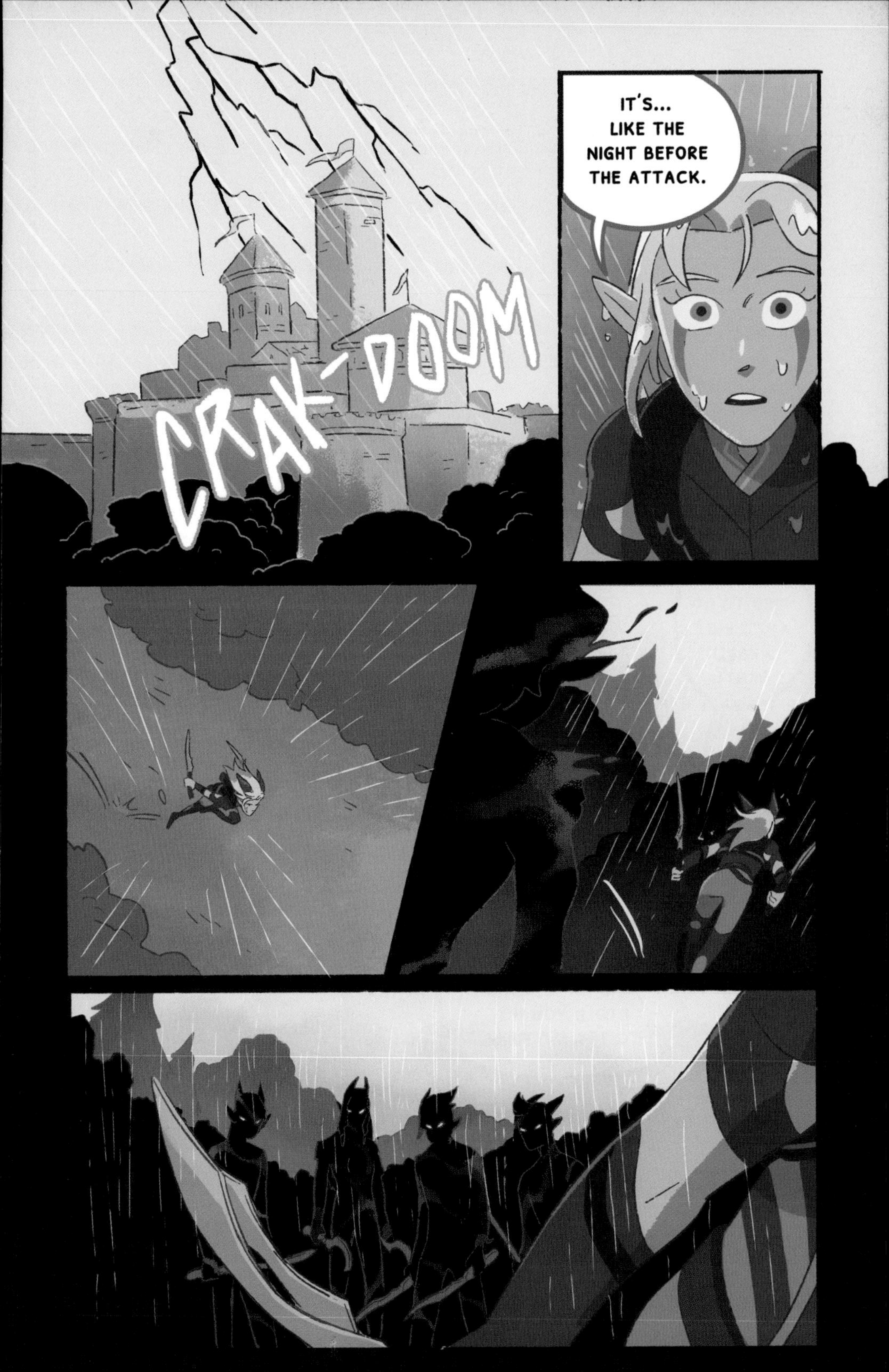
CRAK-DOOM
IT'S... LIKE THE NIGHT BEFORE THE ATTACK.

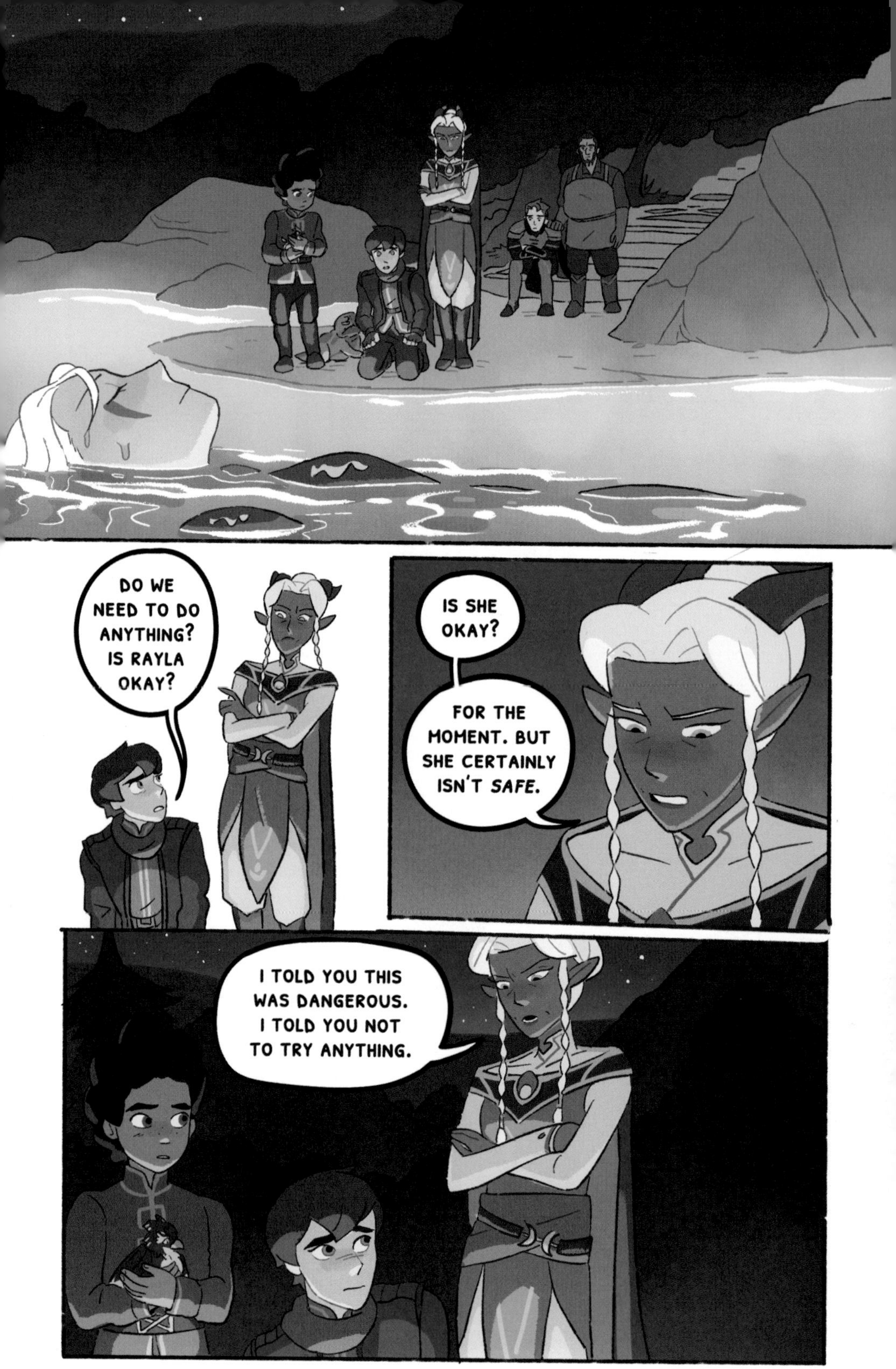
DO WE NEED TO DO ANYTHING? IS RAYLA OKAY?
IS SHE OKAY?
FOR THE MOMENT. BUT SHE CERTAINLY ISN'T *SAFE.*
I TOLD YOU THIS WAS DANGEROUS. I TOLD YOU NOT TO TRY ANYTHING.

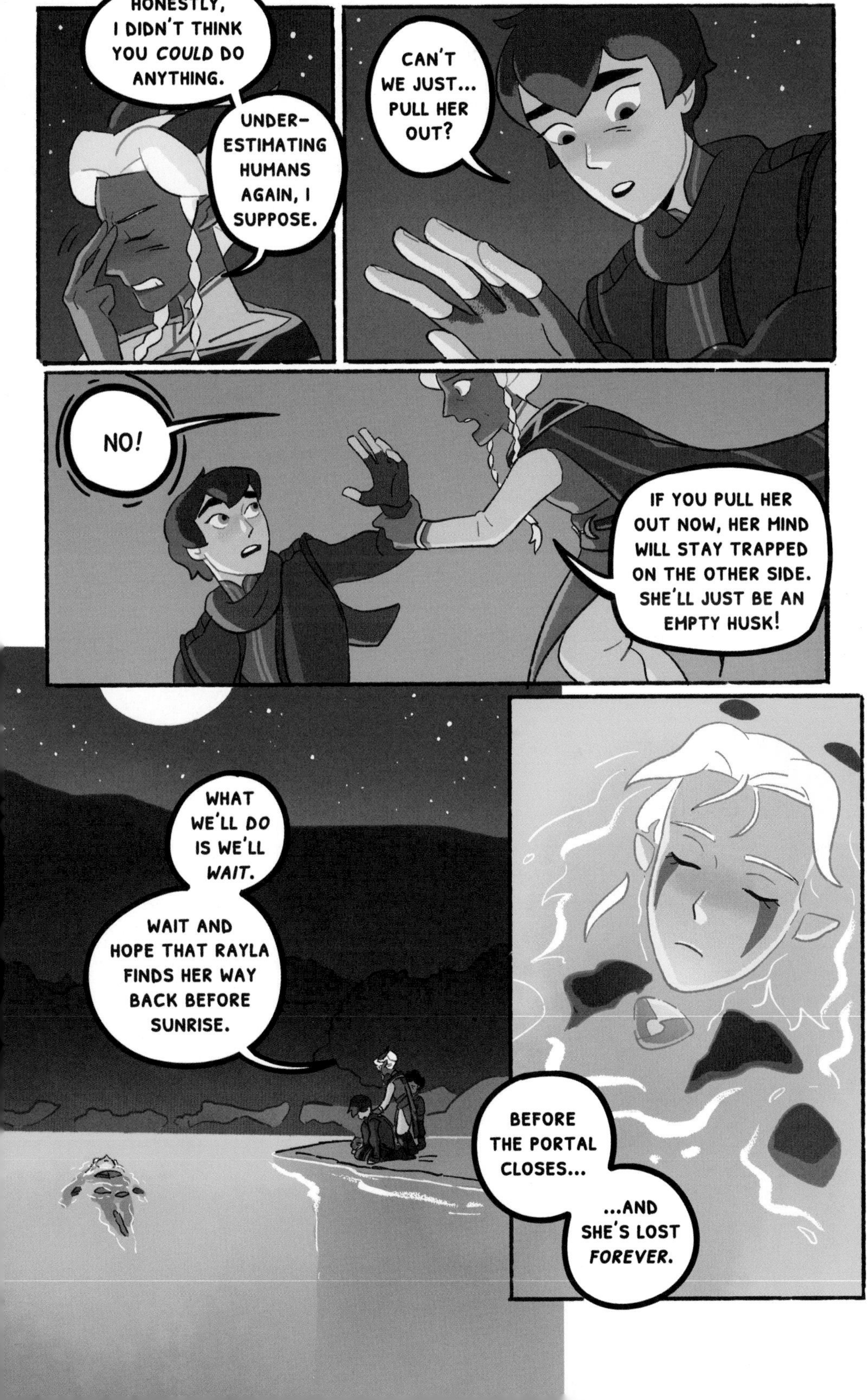
HONESTLY, I DIDN'T THINK YOU *COULD* DO ANYTHING.
UNDER-ESTIMATING HUMANS AGAIN, I SUPPOSE.
CAN'T WE JUST... PULL HER OUT?
NO!
IF YOU PULL HER OUT NOW, HER MIND WILL STAY TRAPPED ON THE OTHER SIDE. SHE'LL JUST BE AN EMPTY HUSK!
WHAT WE'LL DO IS WE'LL *WAIT*.
WAIT AND HOPE THAT RAYLA FINDS HER WAY BACK BEFORE SUNRISE.
BEFORE THE PORTAL CLOSES...
...AND SHE'S LOST *FOREVER*.

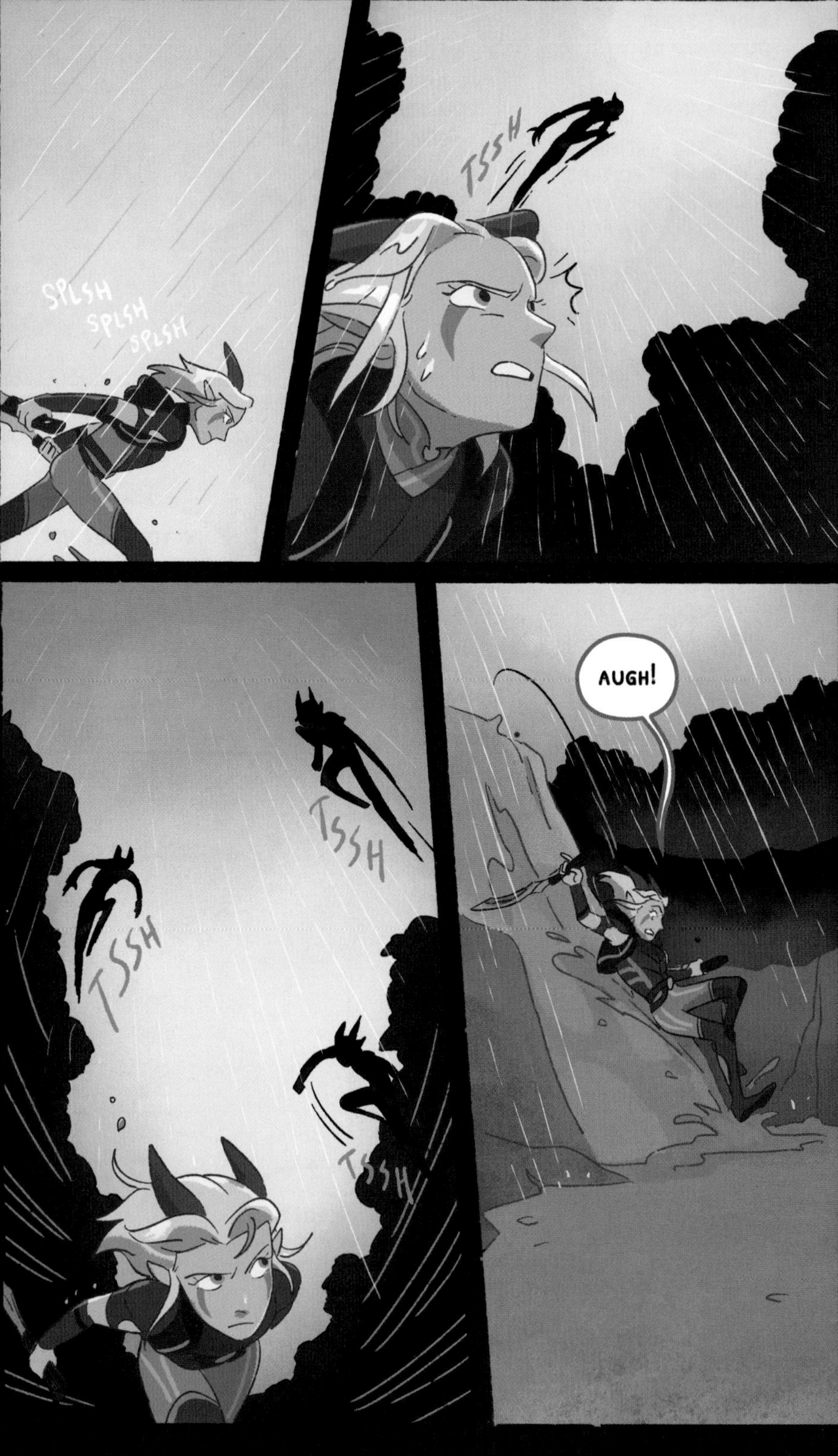
SPLSH
SPLSH
SPLSH
TSSH
TSSH
TSSH
TSSH
AUGH!

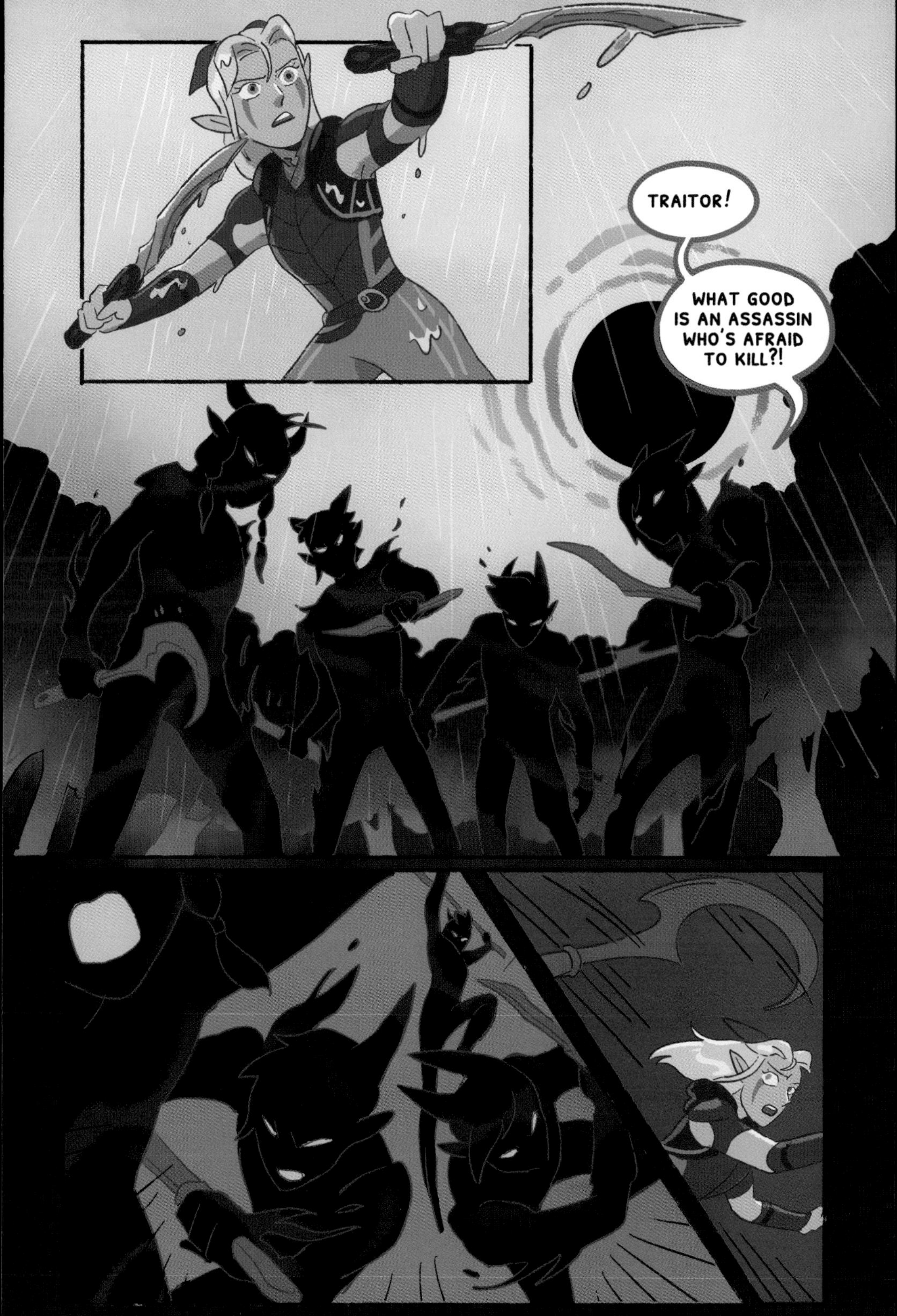
TRAITOR!
WHAT GOOD IS AN ASSASSIN WHO'S AFRAID TO KILL?!

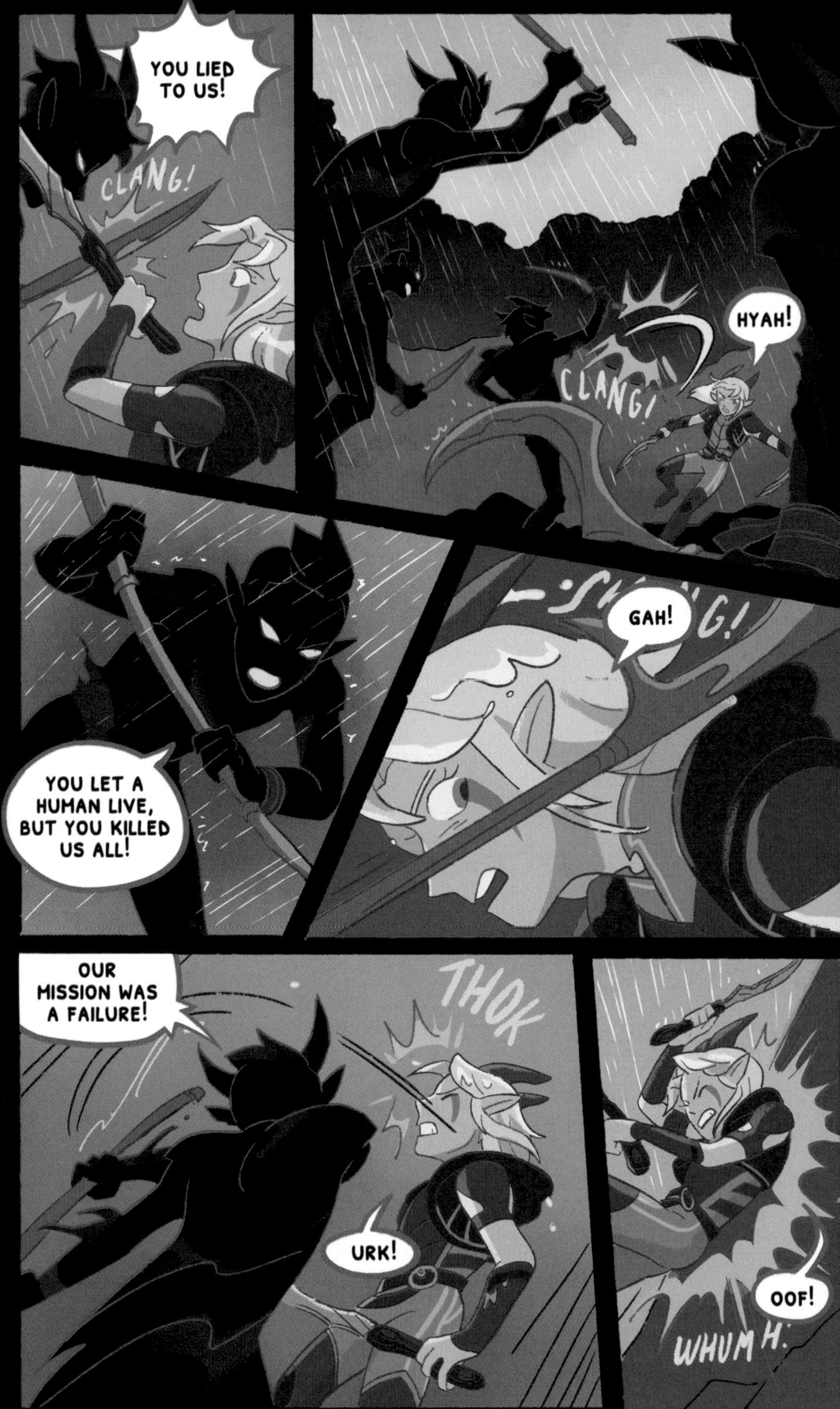
YOU LIED TO US!
CLANG!
HYAH!
CLANG!
YOU LET A HUMAN LIVE, BUT YOU KILLED US ALL!
GAH!
OUR MISSION WAS A FAILURE!
THOK
URK!
OOF!
WHUMH.

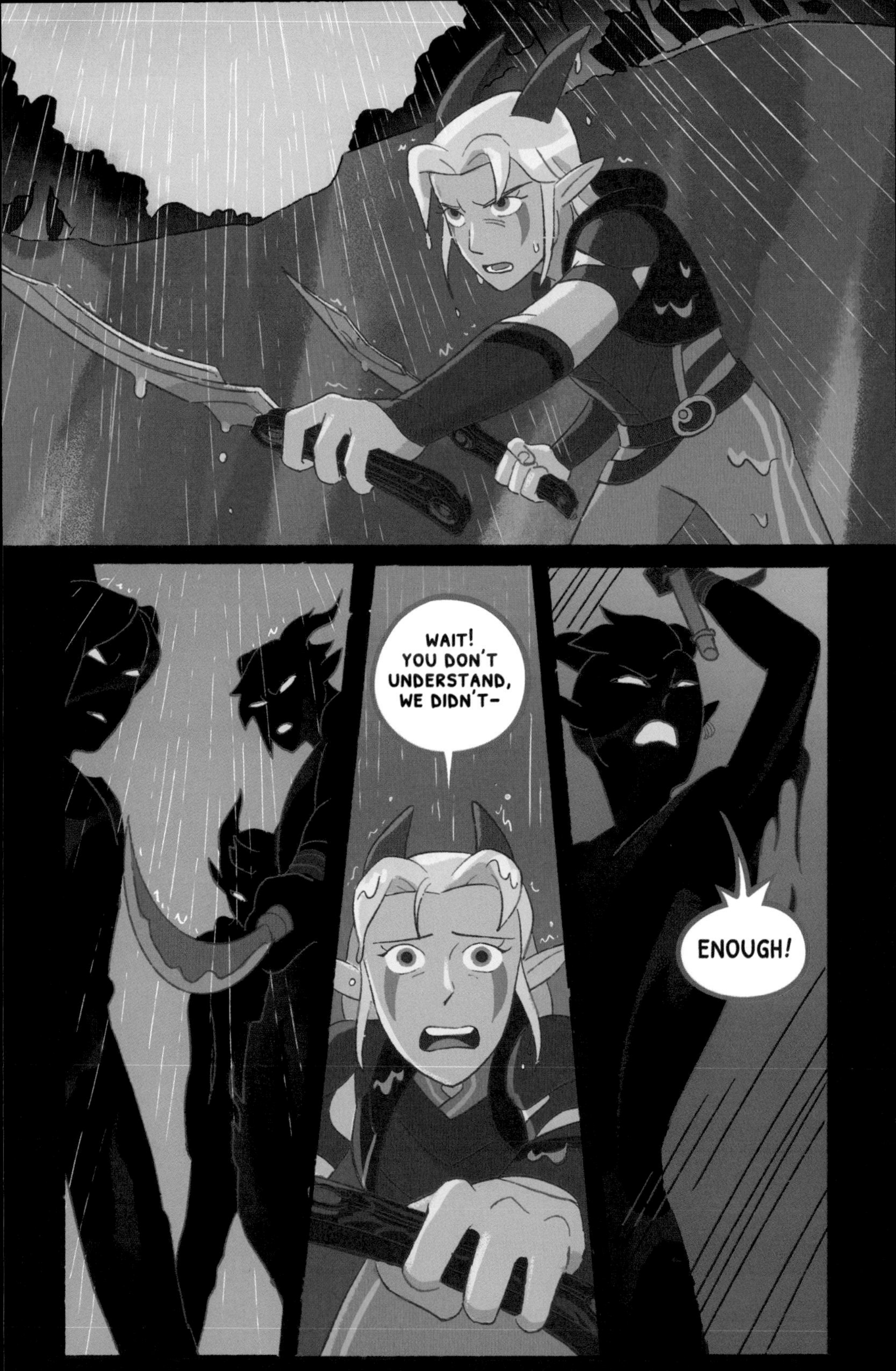
WAIT! YOU DON'T UNDERSTAND, WE DIDN'T-
ENOUGH!

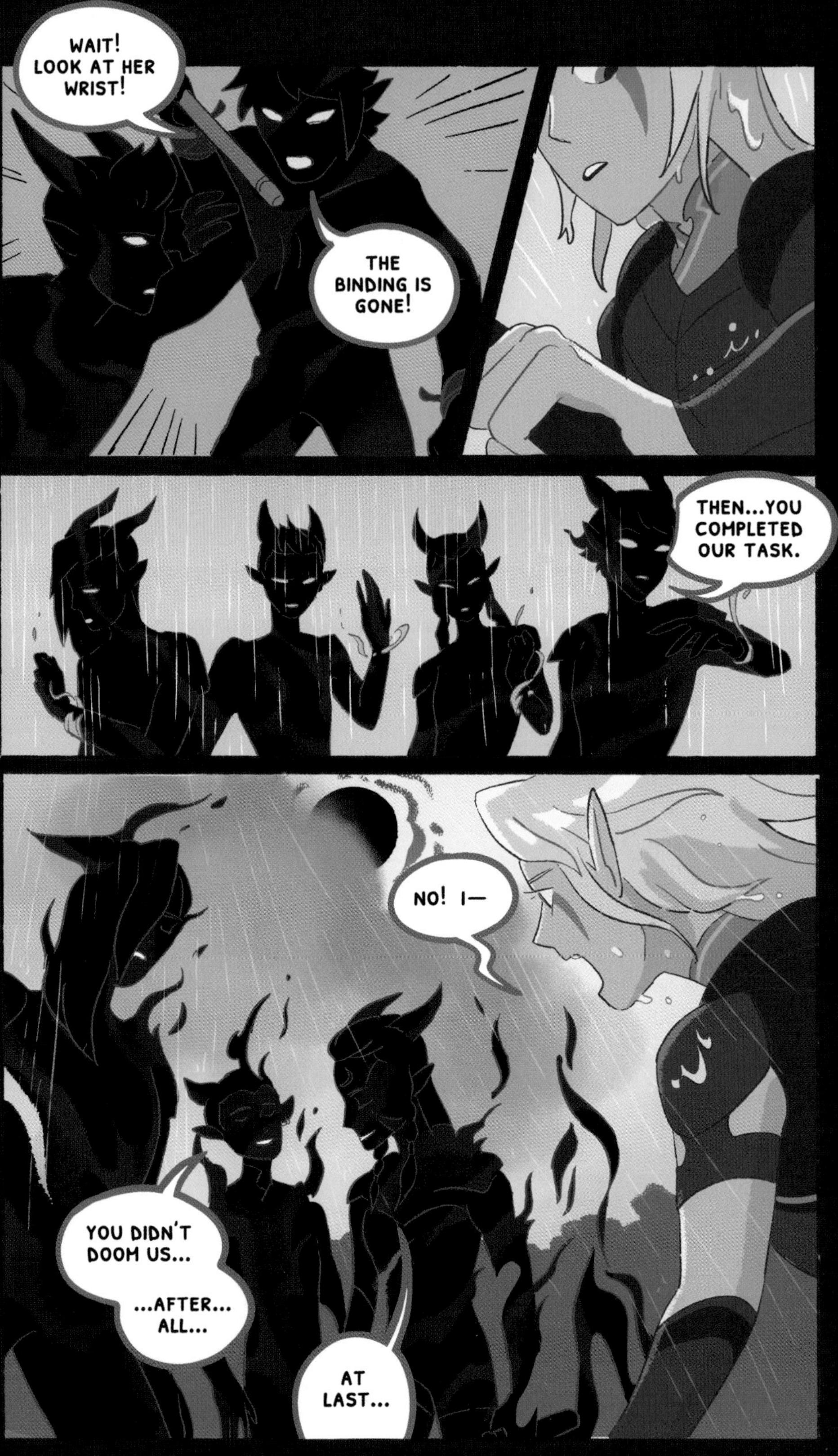
WAIT! LOOK AT HER WRIST!
THE BINDING IS GONE!
THEN...YOU COMPLETED OUR TASK.
NO! I—
YOU DIDN'T DOOM US...
...AFTER... ALL...
AT LAST...

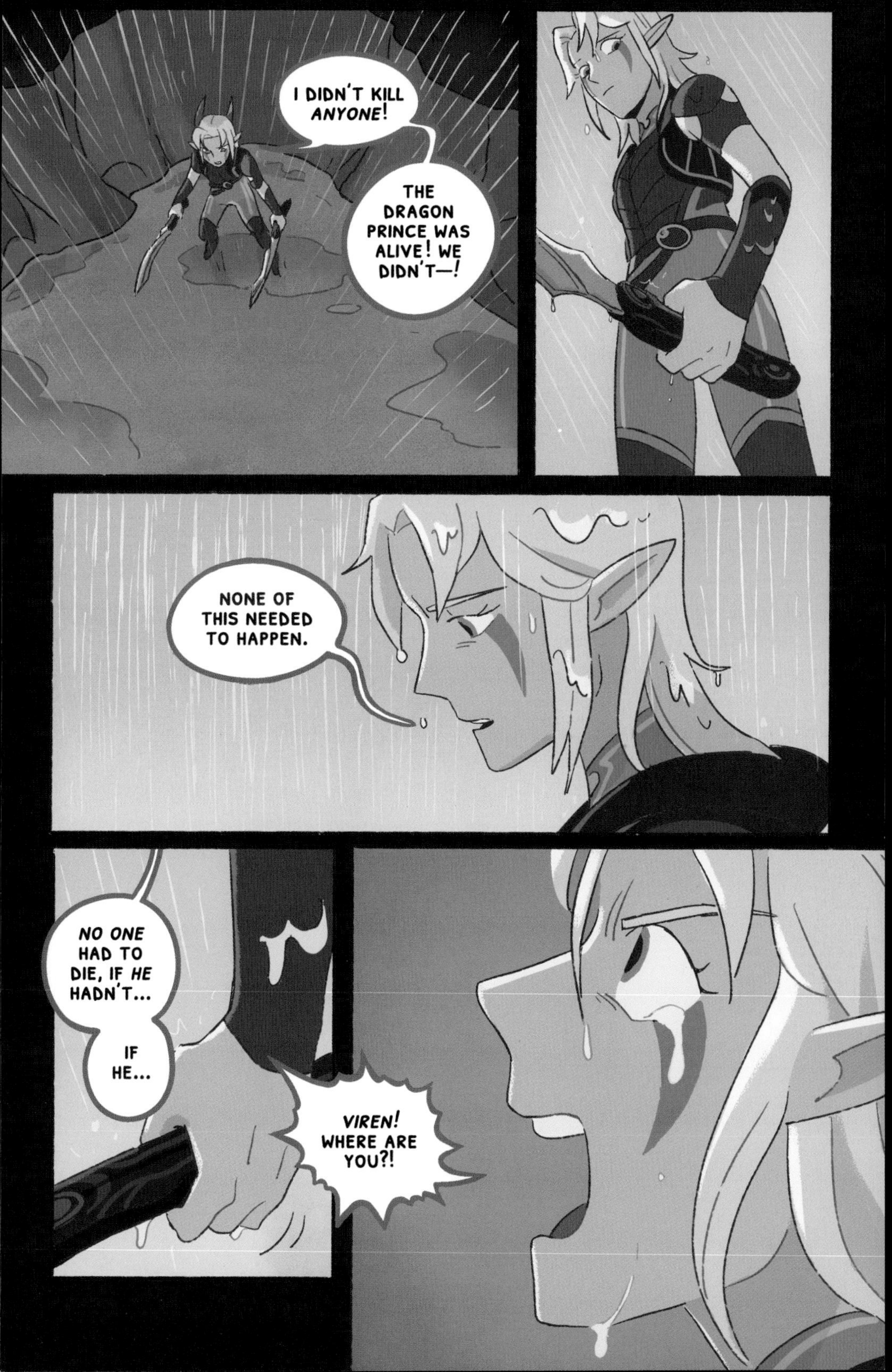
I DIDN'T KILL *ANYONE*!
THE DRAGON PRINCE WAS ALIVE! WE DIDN'T—!
NONE OF THIS NEEDED TO HAPPEN.
NO ONE HAD TO DIE, IF *HE* HADN'T...
IF HE...
VIREN! WHERE ARE YOU?!

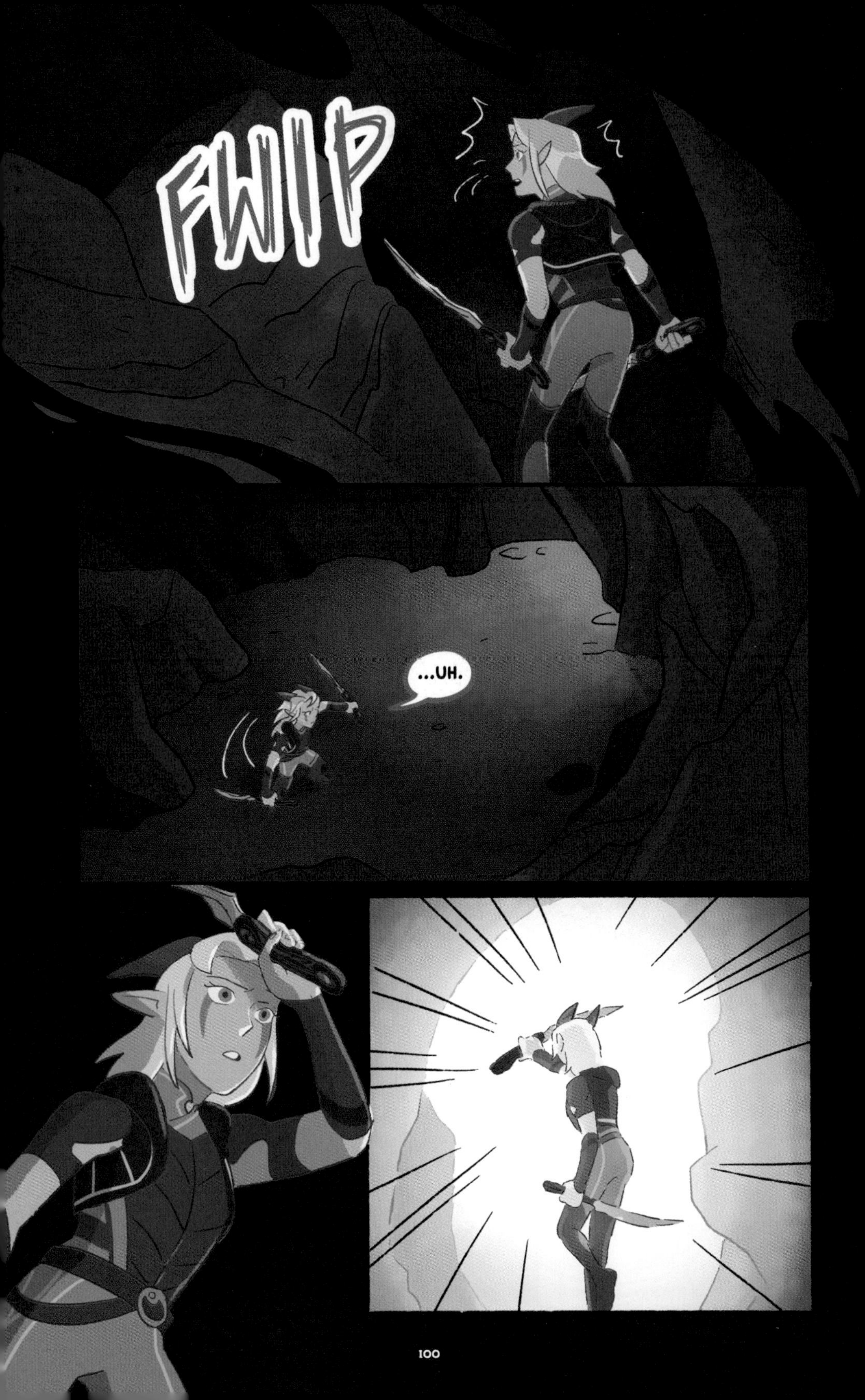
FWIP
...UH.

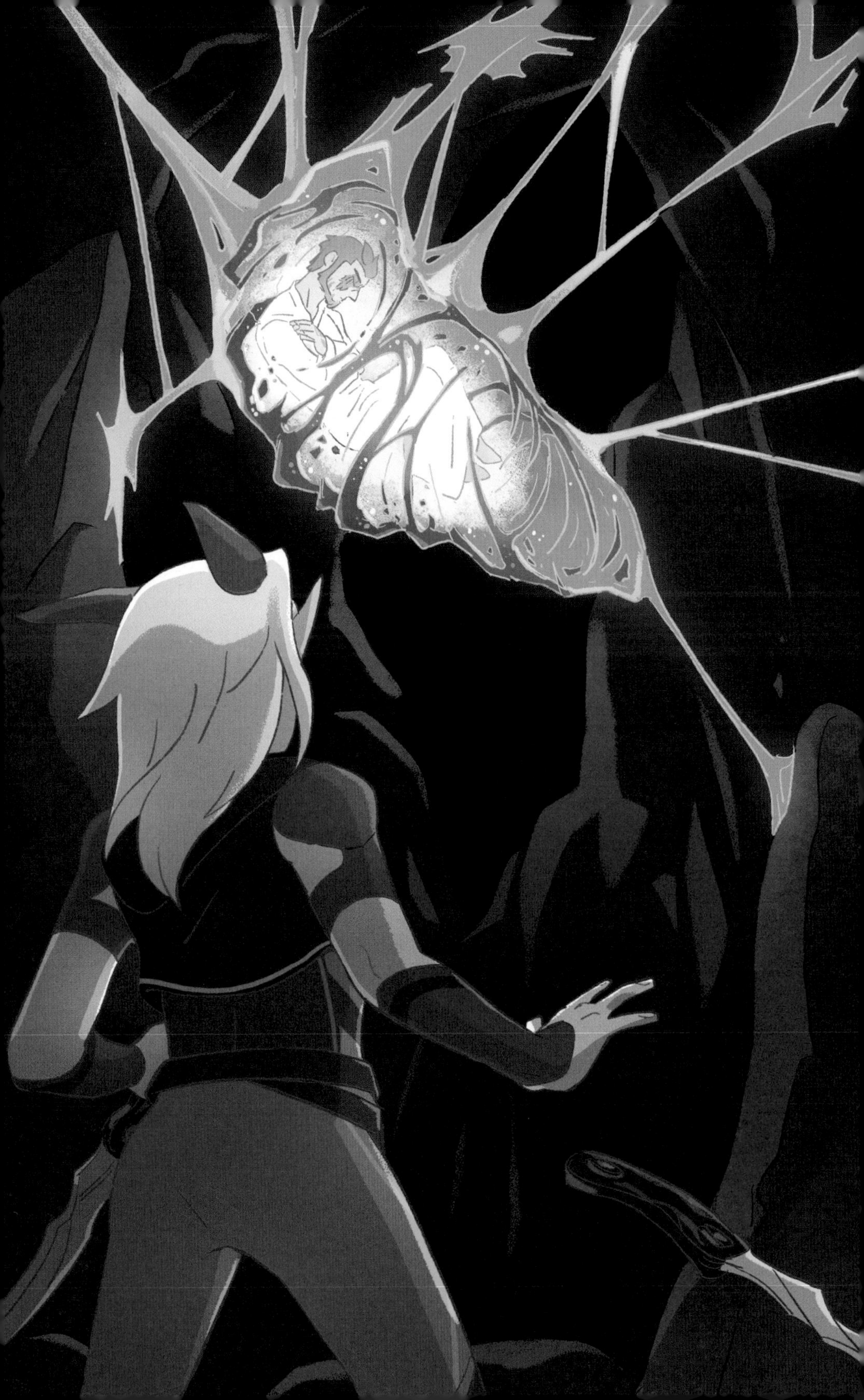

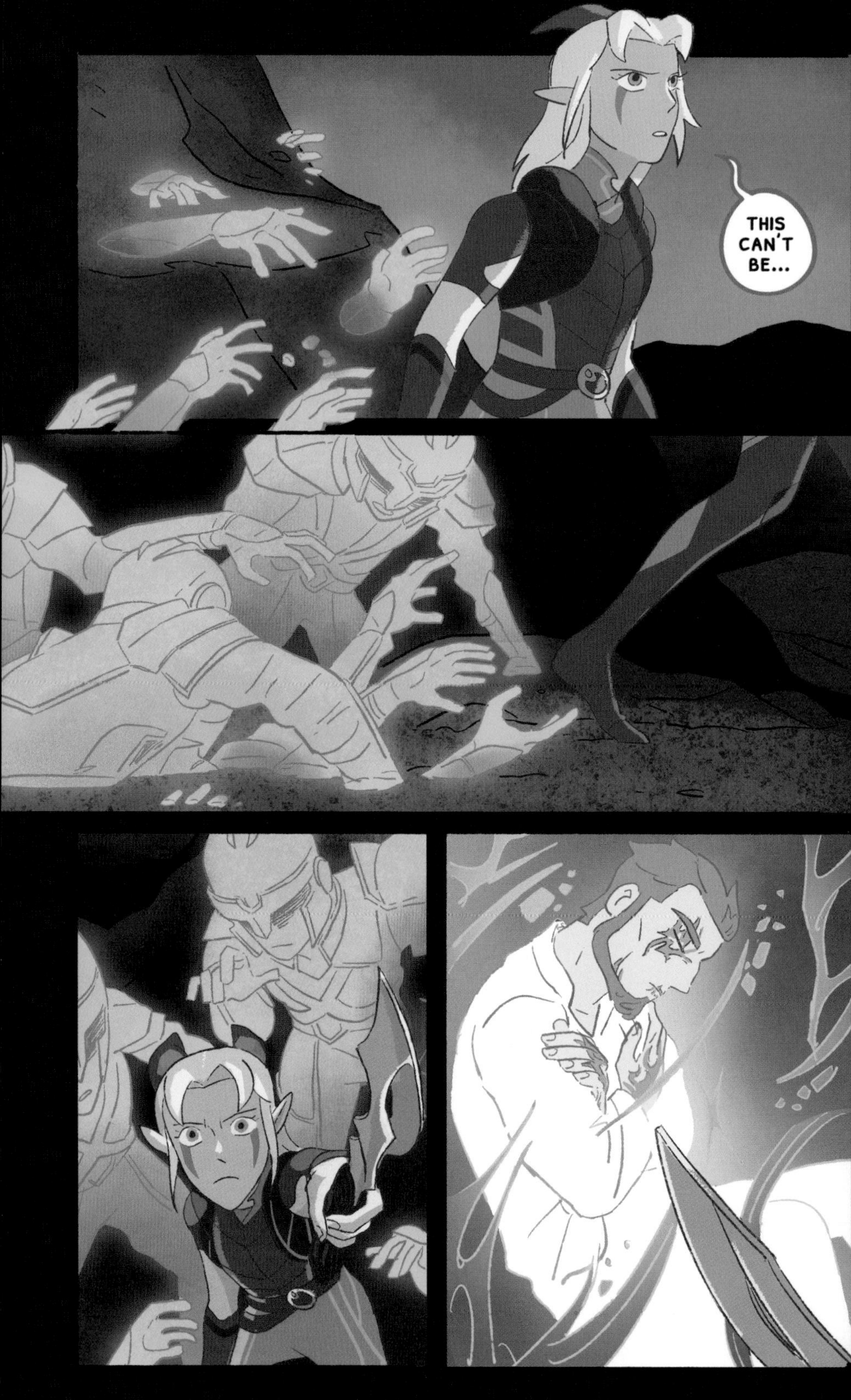
THIS CAN'T BE...

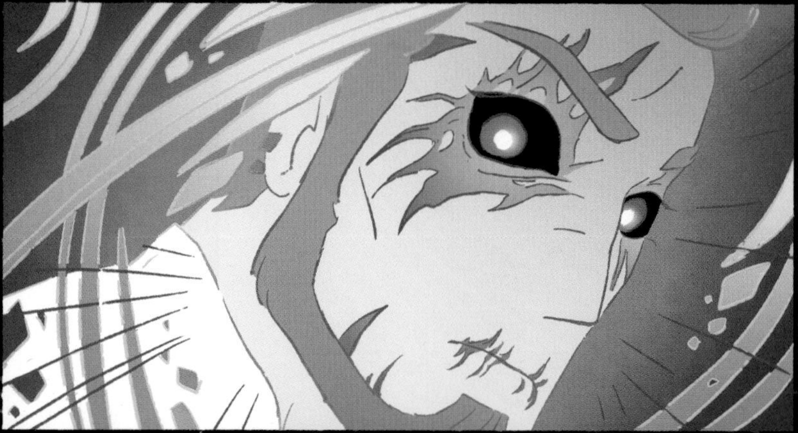

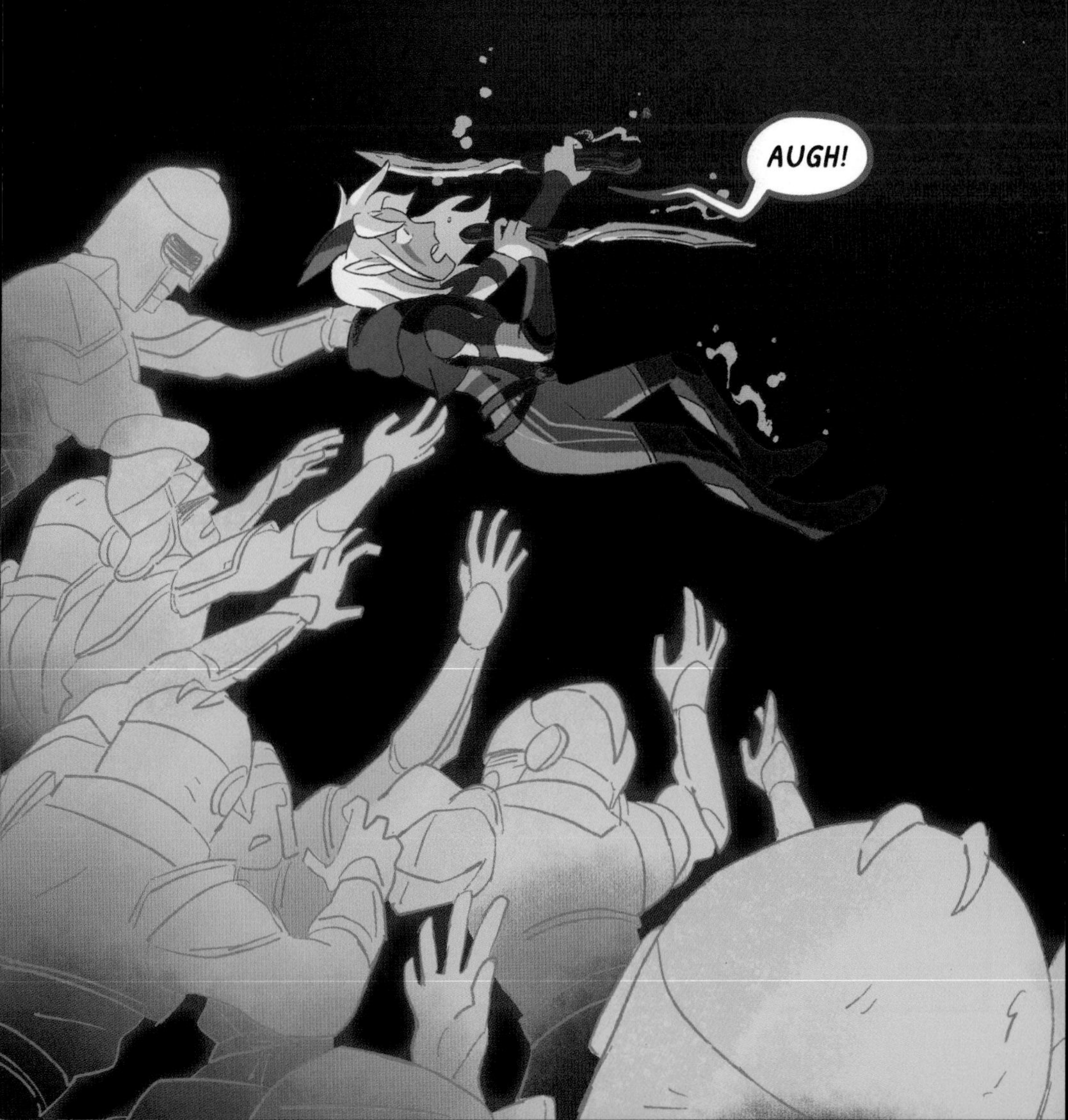
AUGH!

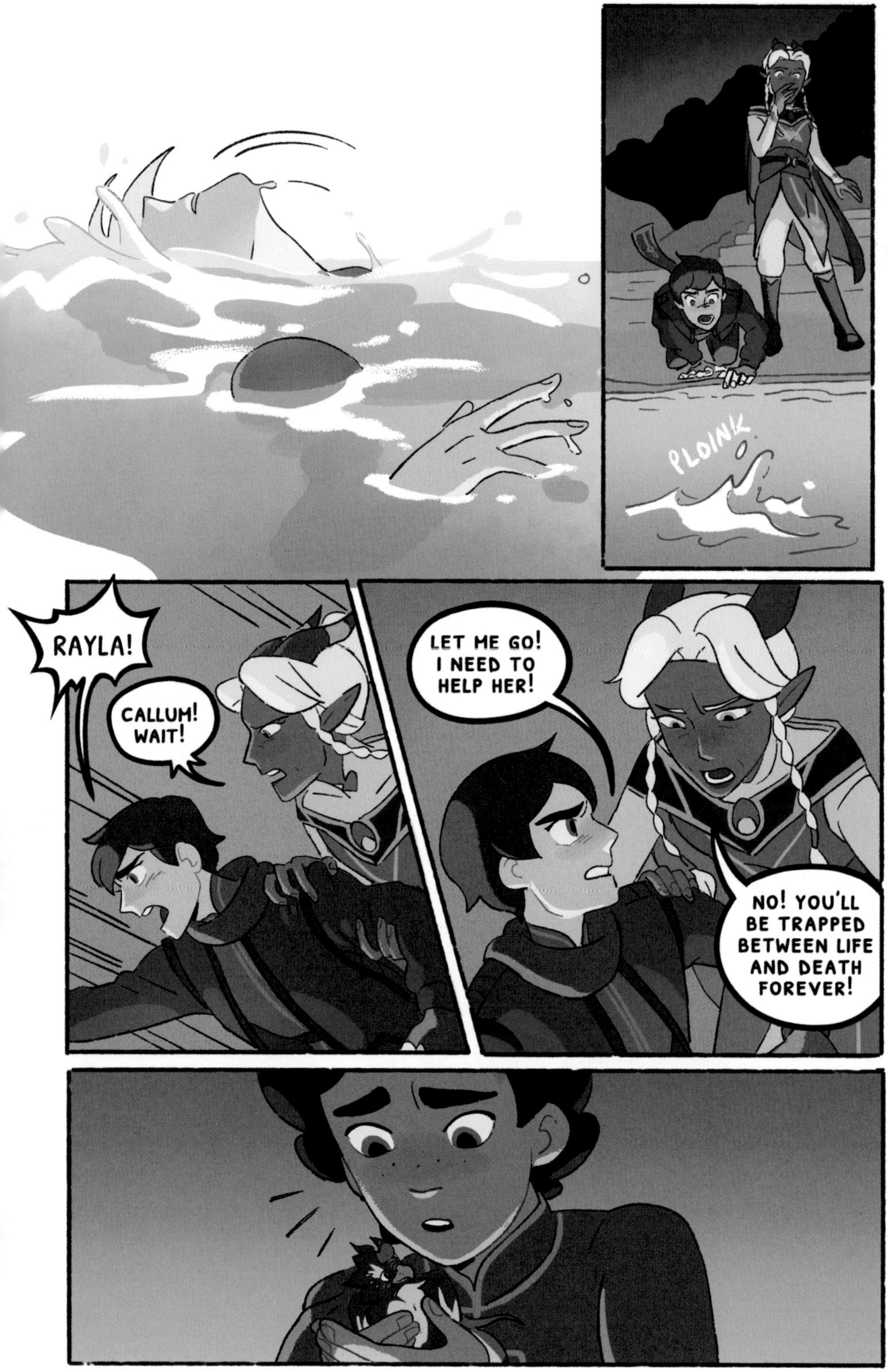
PLOINK
RAYLA!
CALLUM! WAIT!
LET ME GO! I NEED TO HELP HER!
NO! YOU'LL BE TRAPPED BETWEEN LIFE AND DEATH FOREVER!

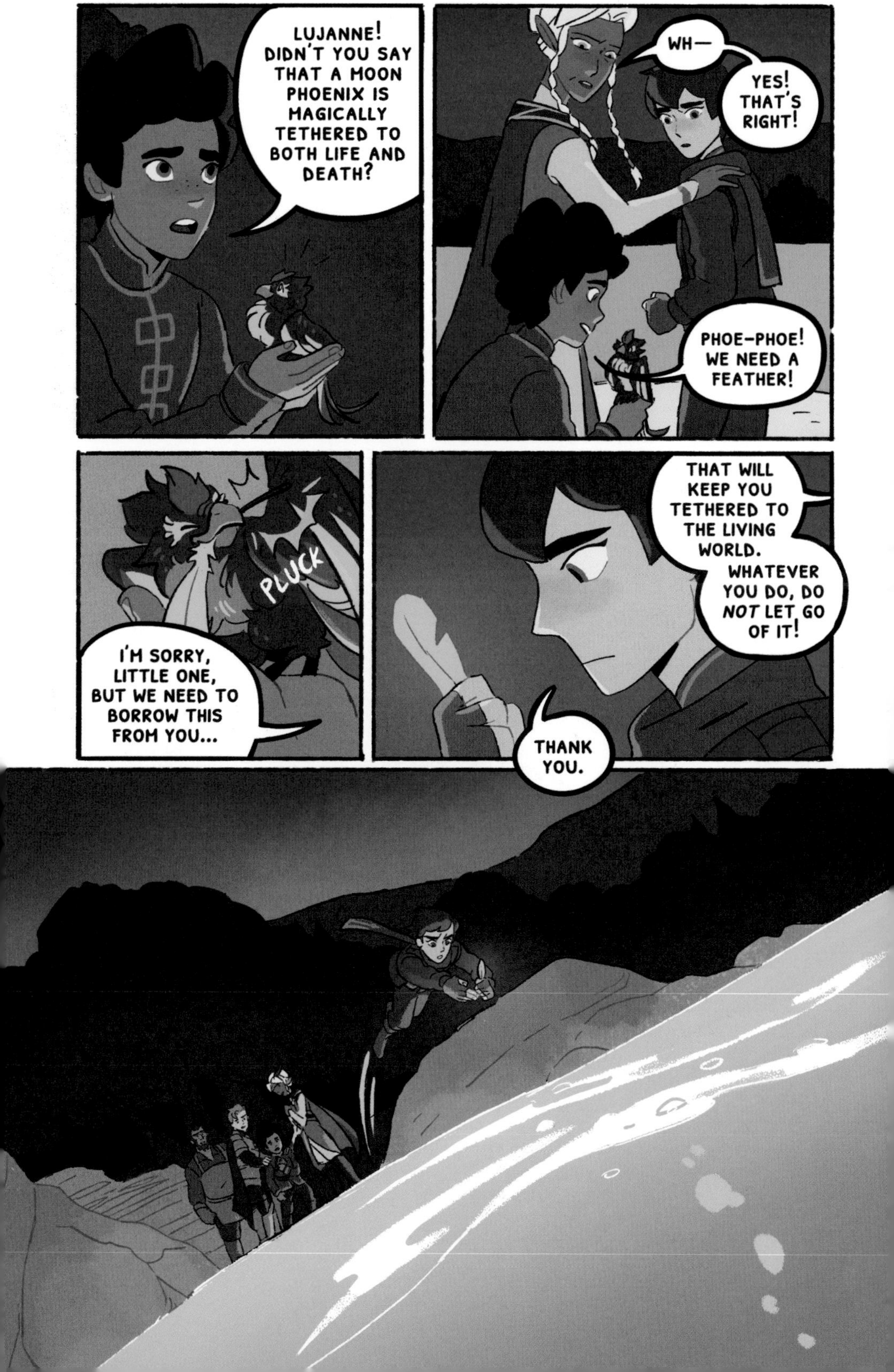
LUJANNE! DIDN'T YOU SAY THAT A MOON PHOENIX IS MAGICALLY TETHERED TO BOTH LIFE AND DEATH?
WH—
YES! THAT'S RIGHT!
PHOE-PHOE! WE NEED A FEATHER!
PLUCK
I'M SORRY, LITTLE ONE, BUT WE NEED TO BORROW THIS FROM YOU...
THAT WILL KEEP YOU TETHERED TO THE LIVING WORLD.
WHATEVER YOU DO, DO *NOT* LET GO OF IT!
THANK YOU.

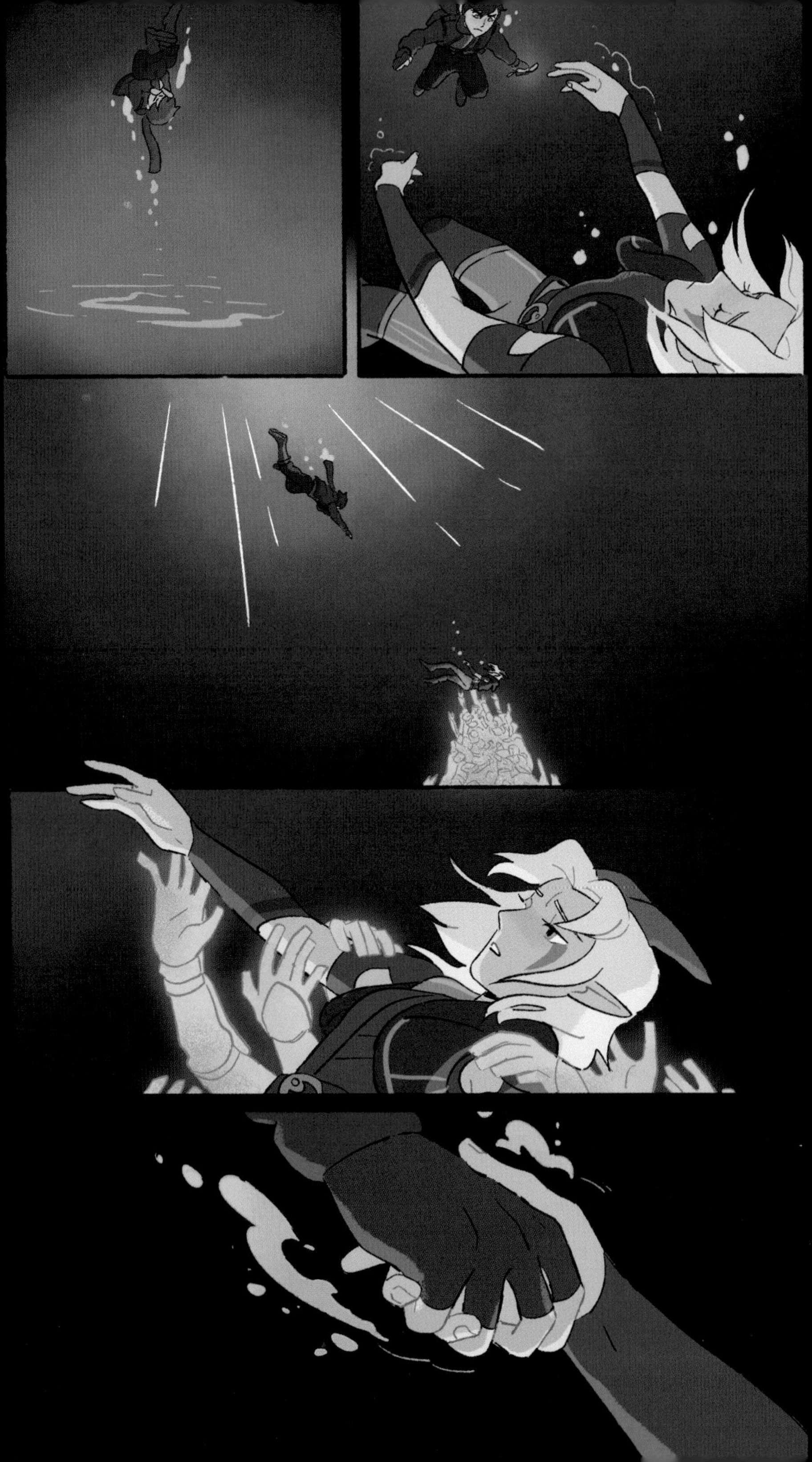

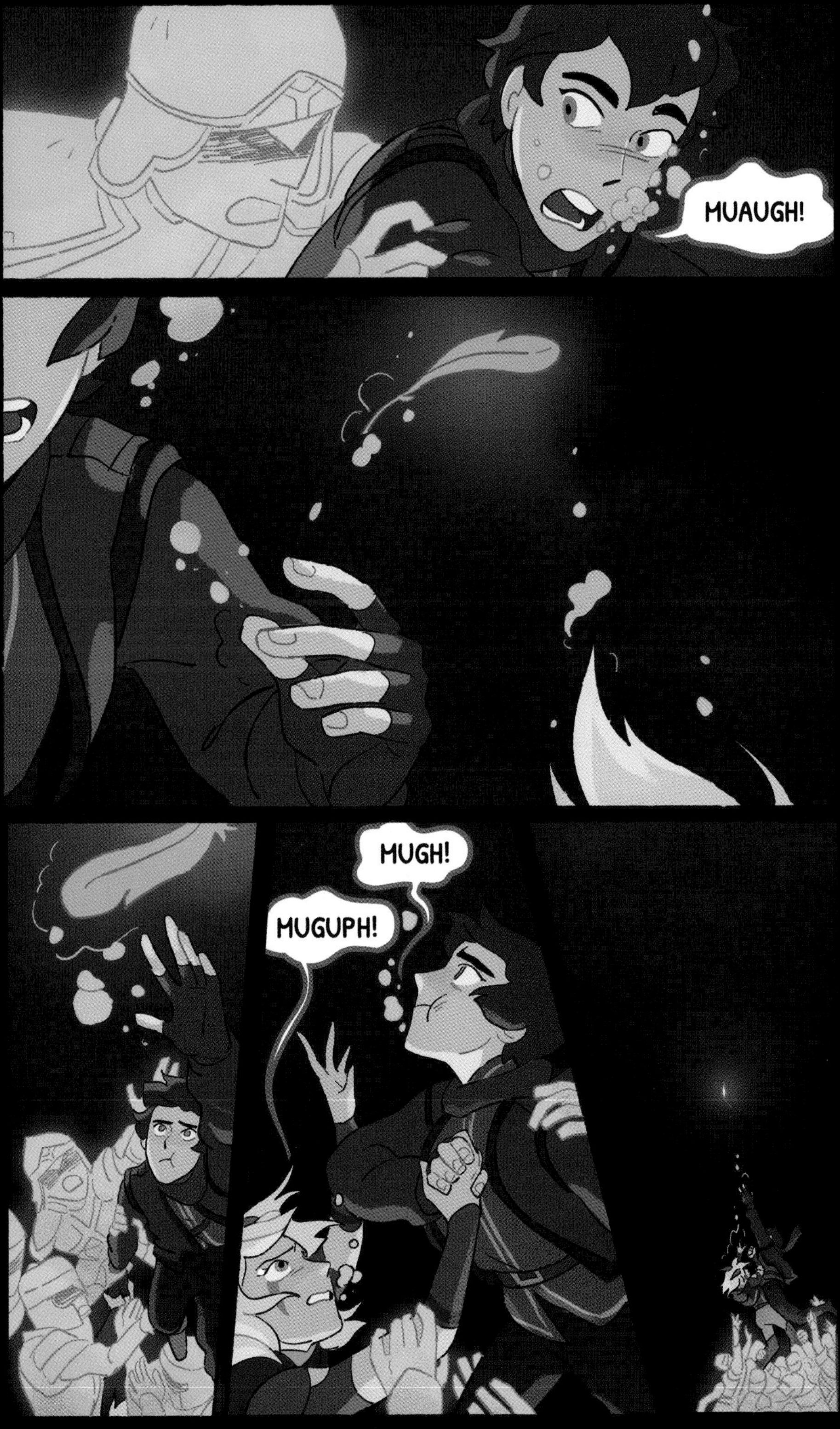
MUAUGH!
MUGH!
MUGUPH!

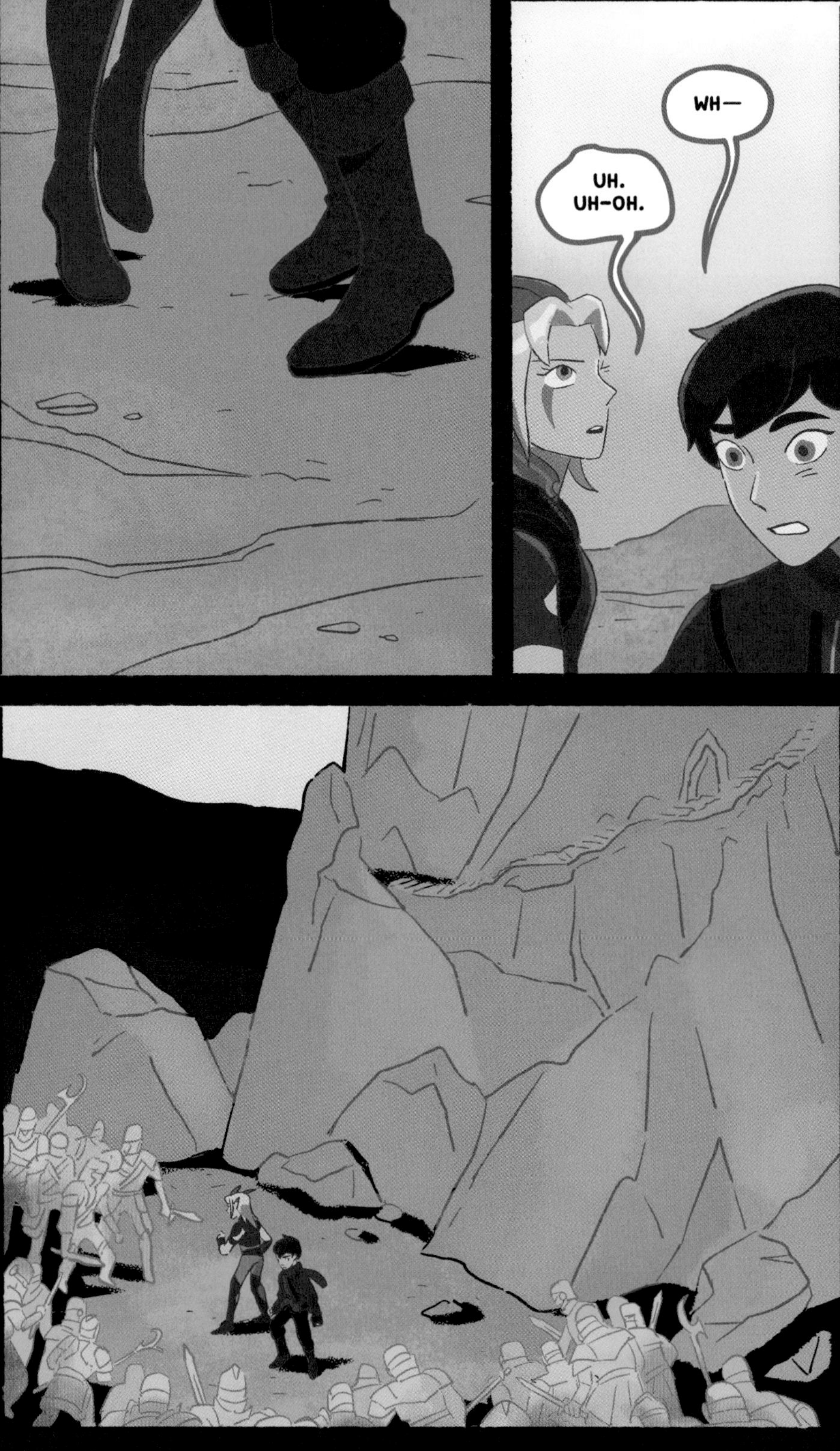
WH—
UH.
UH-OH.

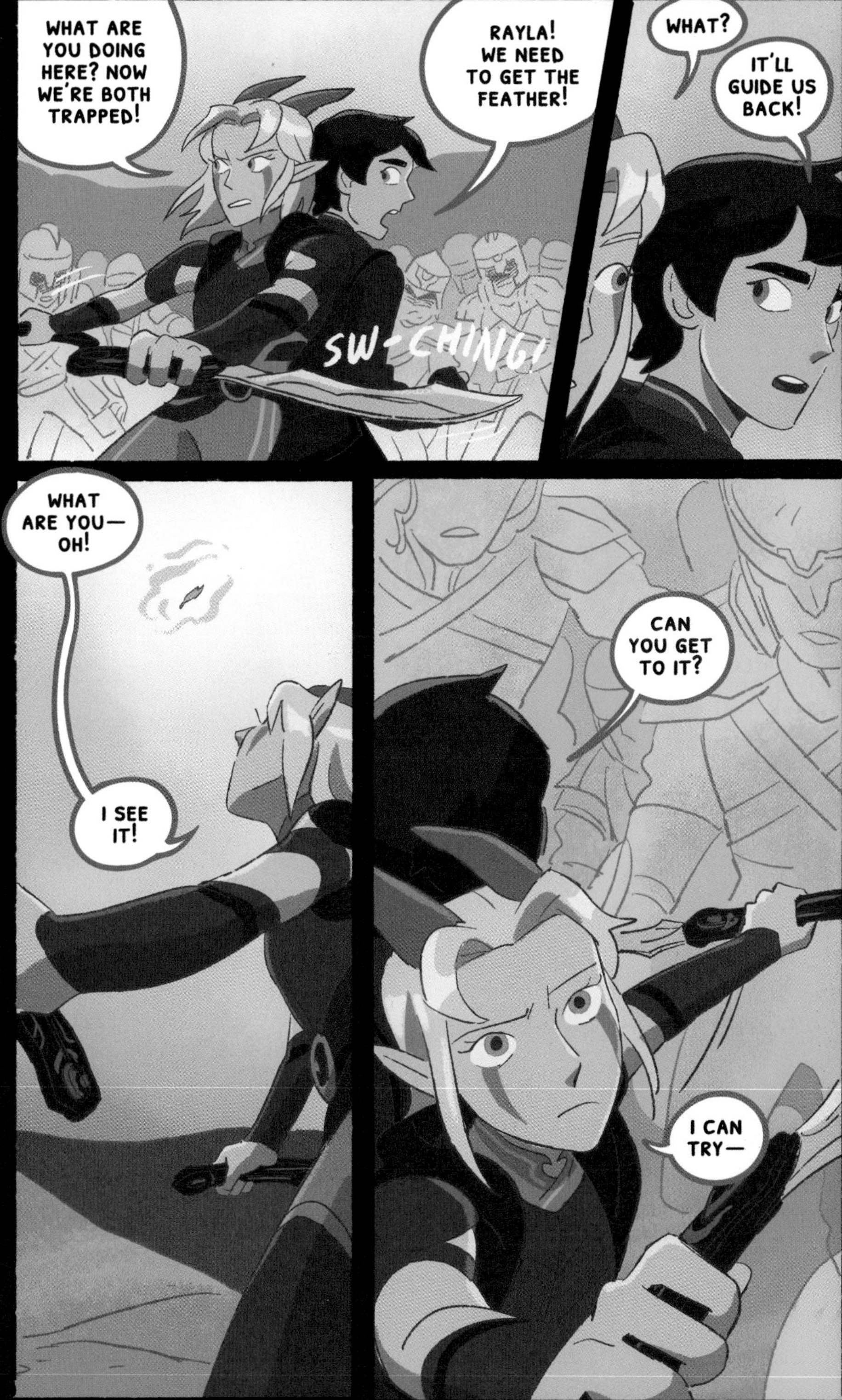

WHAT ARE YOU DOING HERE? NOW WE'RE BOTH TRAPPED!
RAYLA! WE NEED TO GET THE FEATHER!
SW-CHING!
WHAT?
IT'LL GUIDE US BACK!
WHAT ARE YOU— OH!
I SEE IT!
CAN YOU GET TO IT?
I CAN TRY—

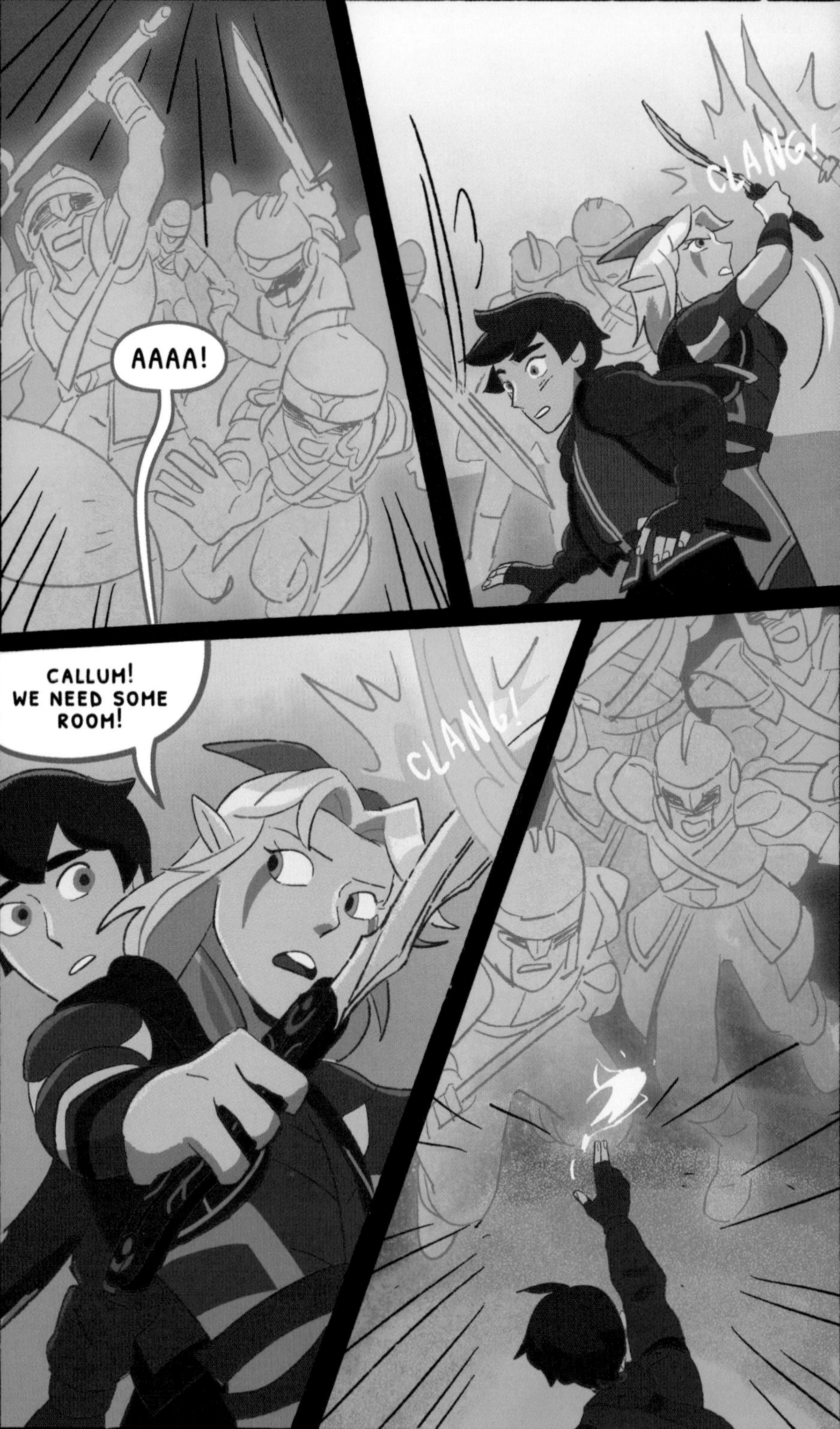
AAAA!
CLANG!
CALLUM!
WE NEED SOME
ROOM!
CLANG!

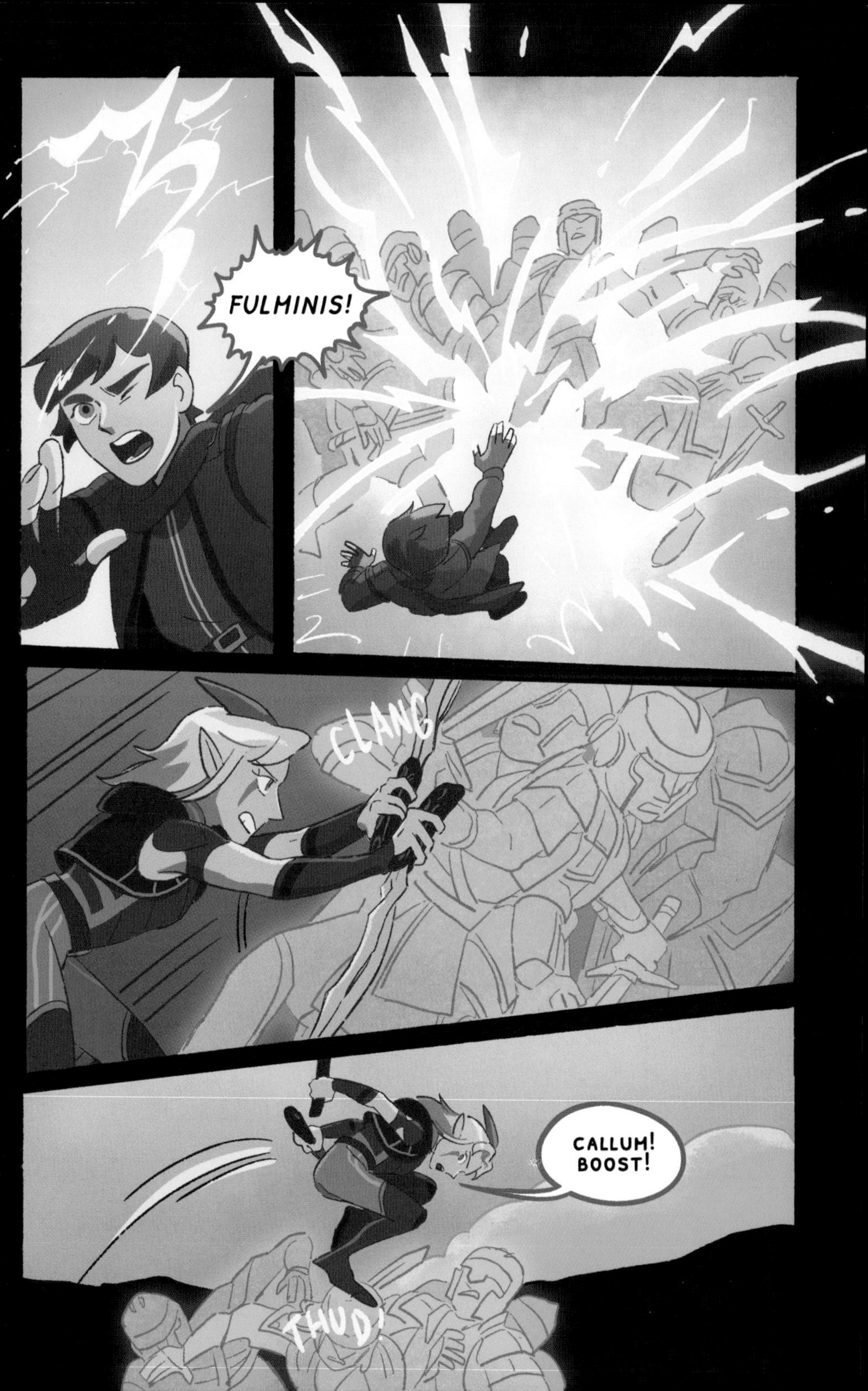
FULMINIS!
CLANG
CALLUM! BOOST!
THUD!

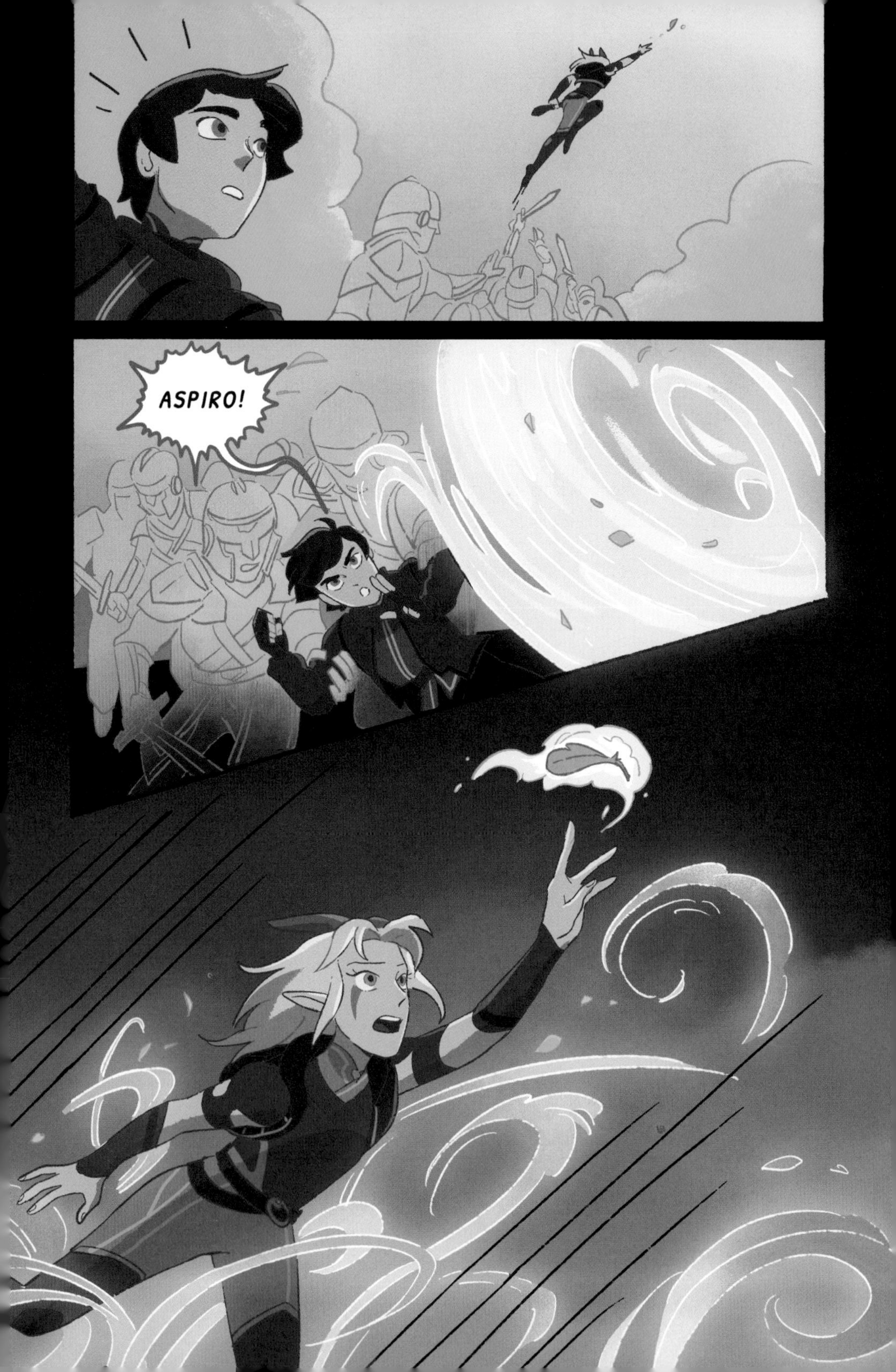
ASPIRO!

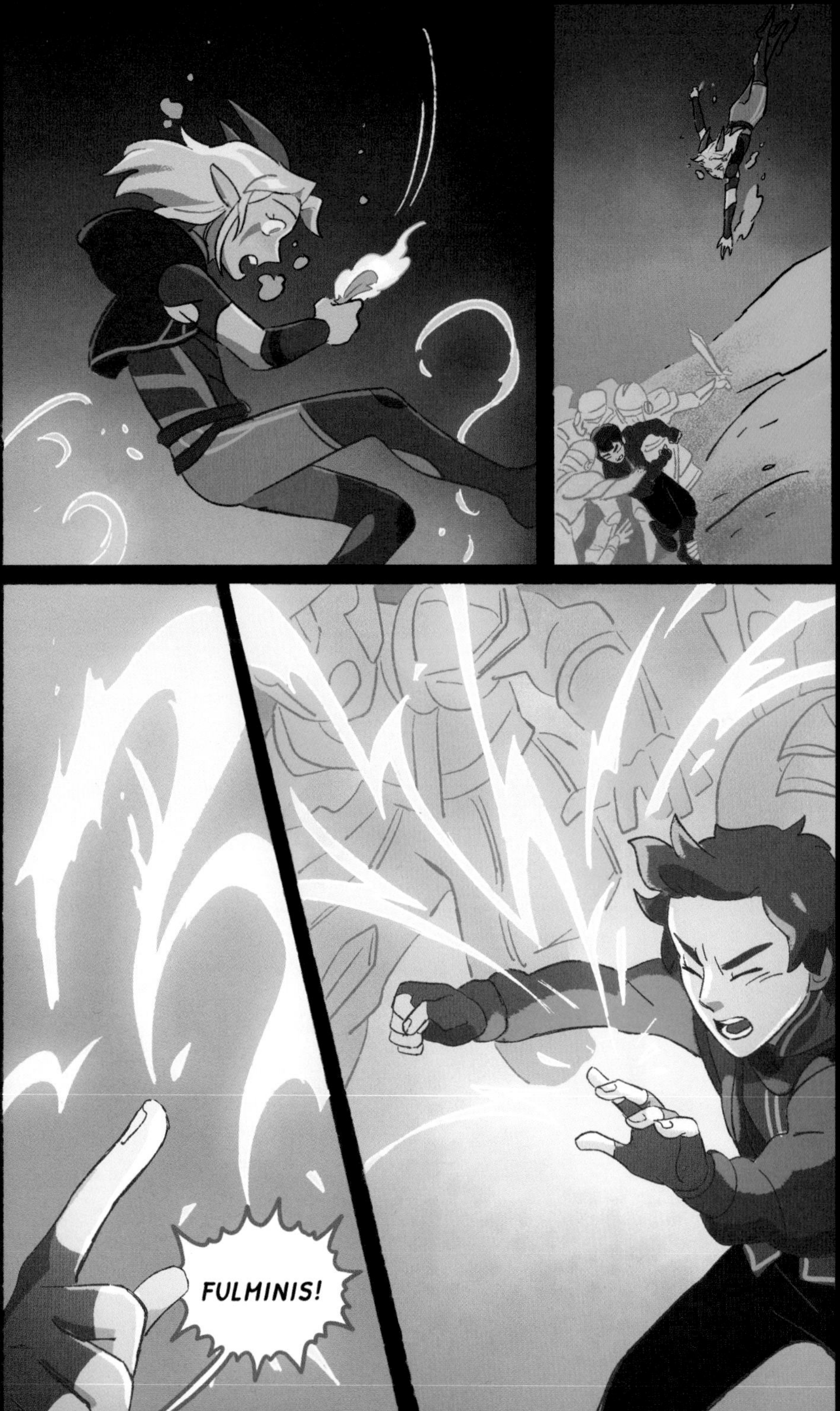
FULMINIS!

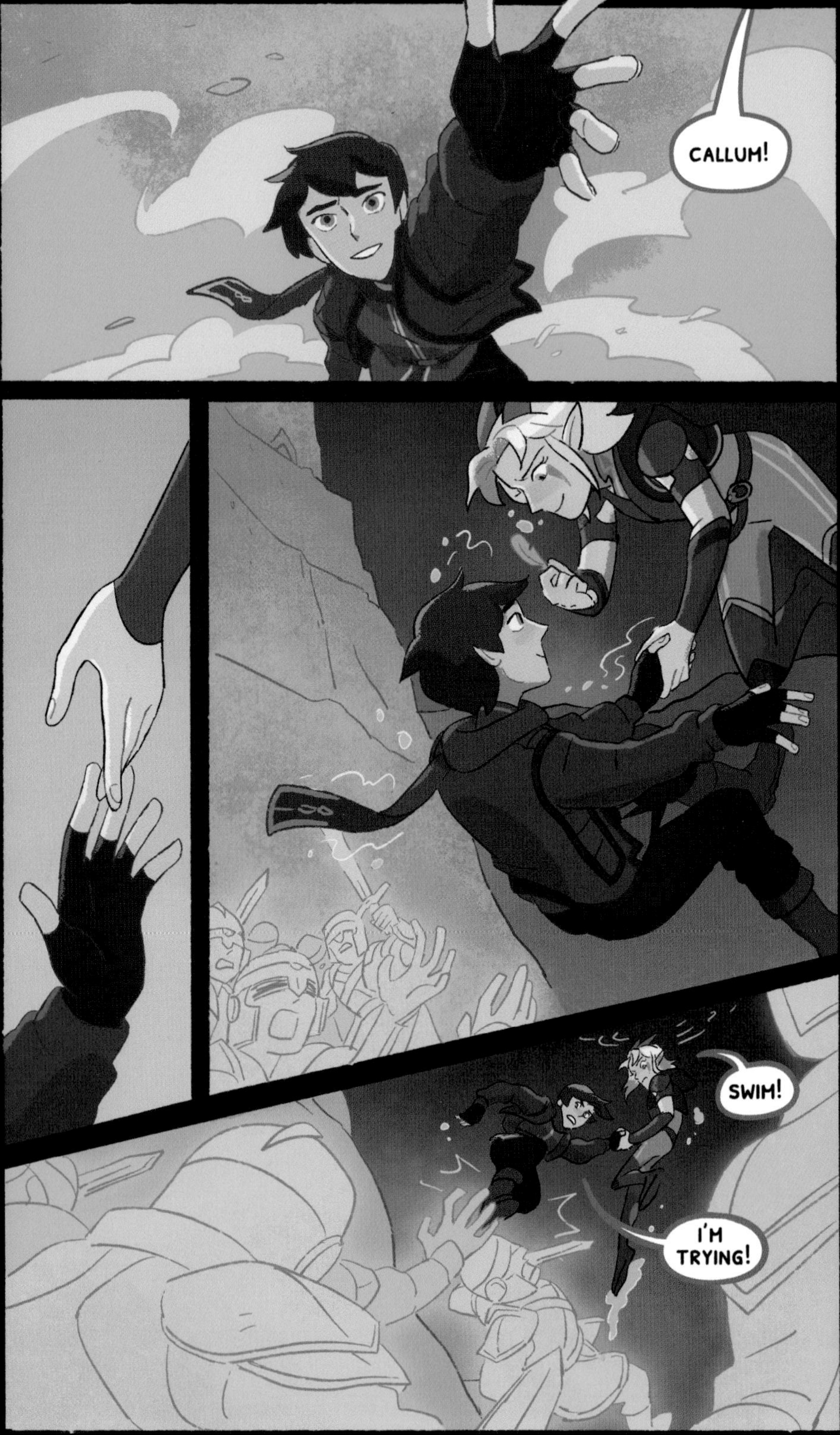
CALLUM!
SWIM!
I'M TRYING!

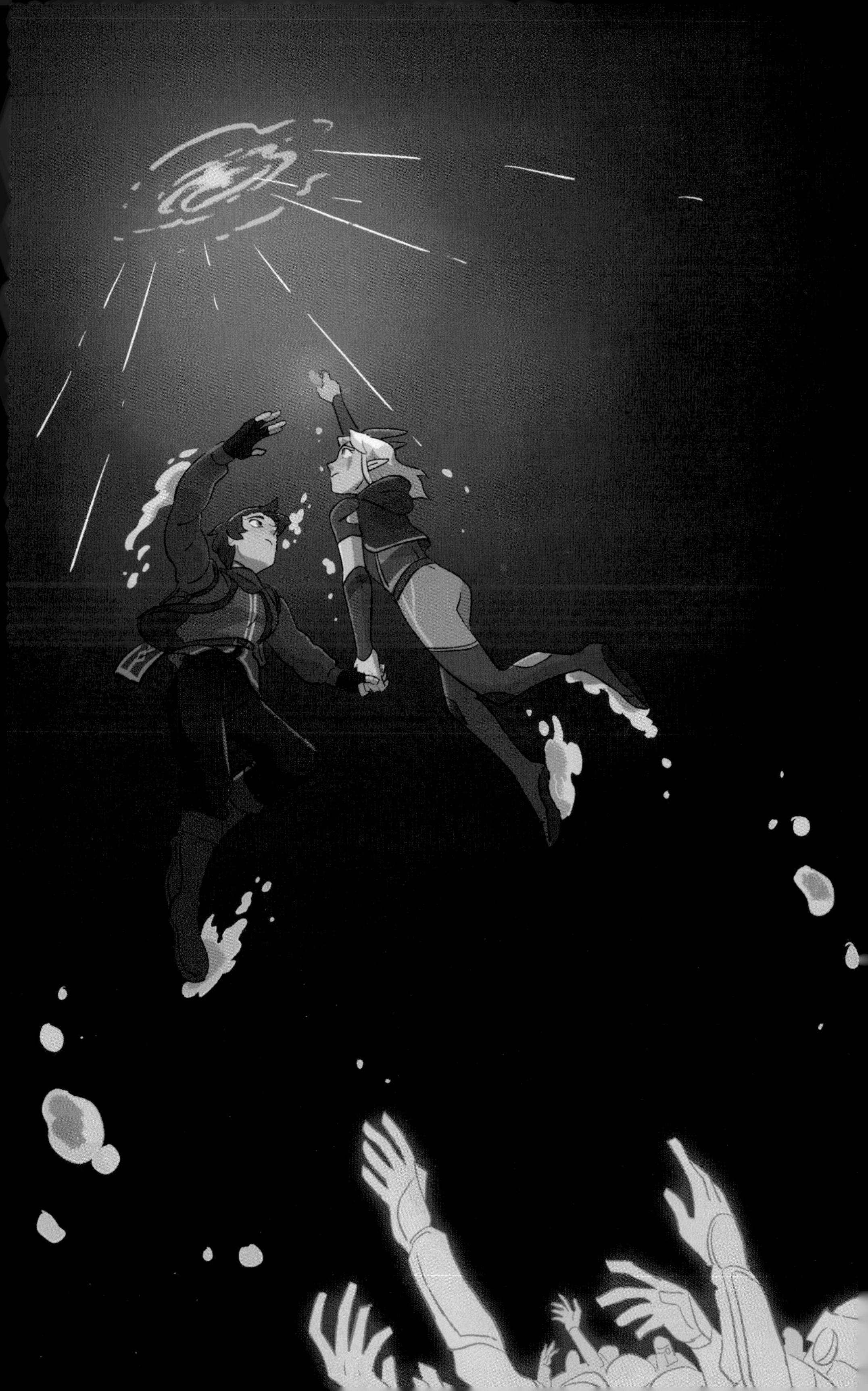

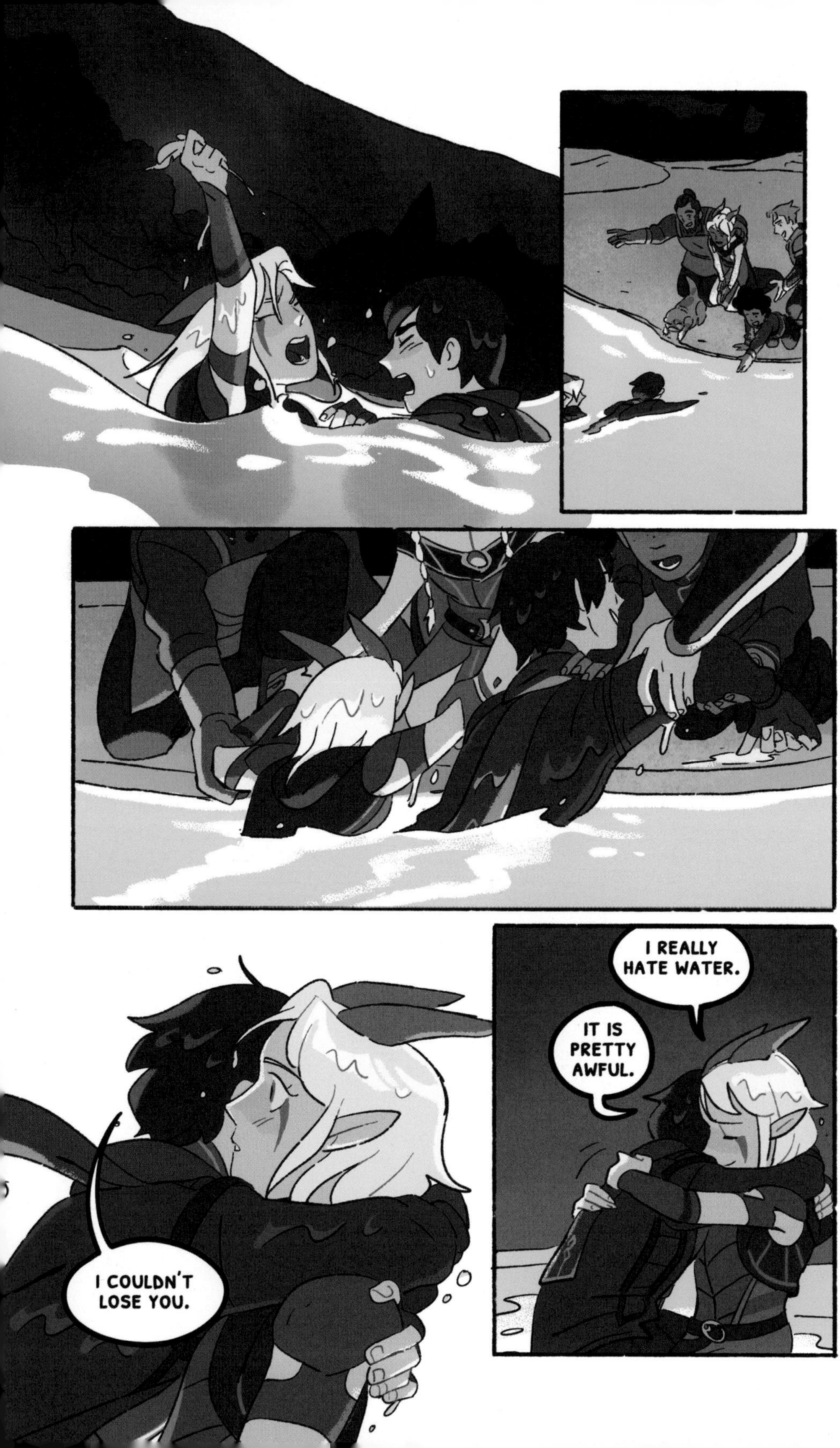
I COULDN'T LOSE YOU.
I REALLY HATE WATER.
IT IS PRETTY AWFUL.

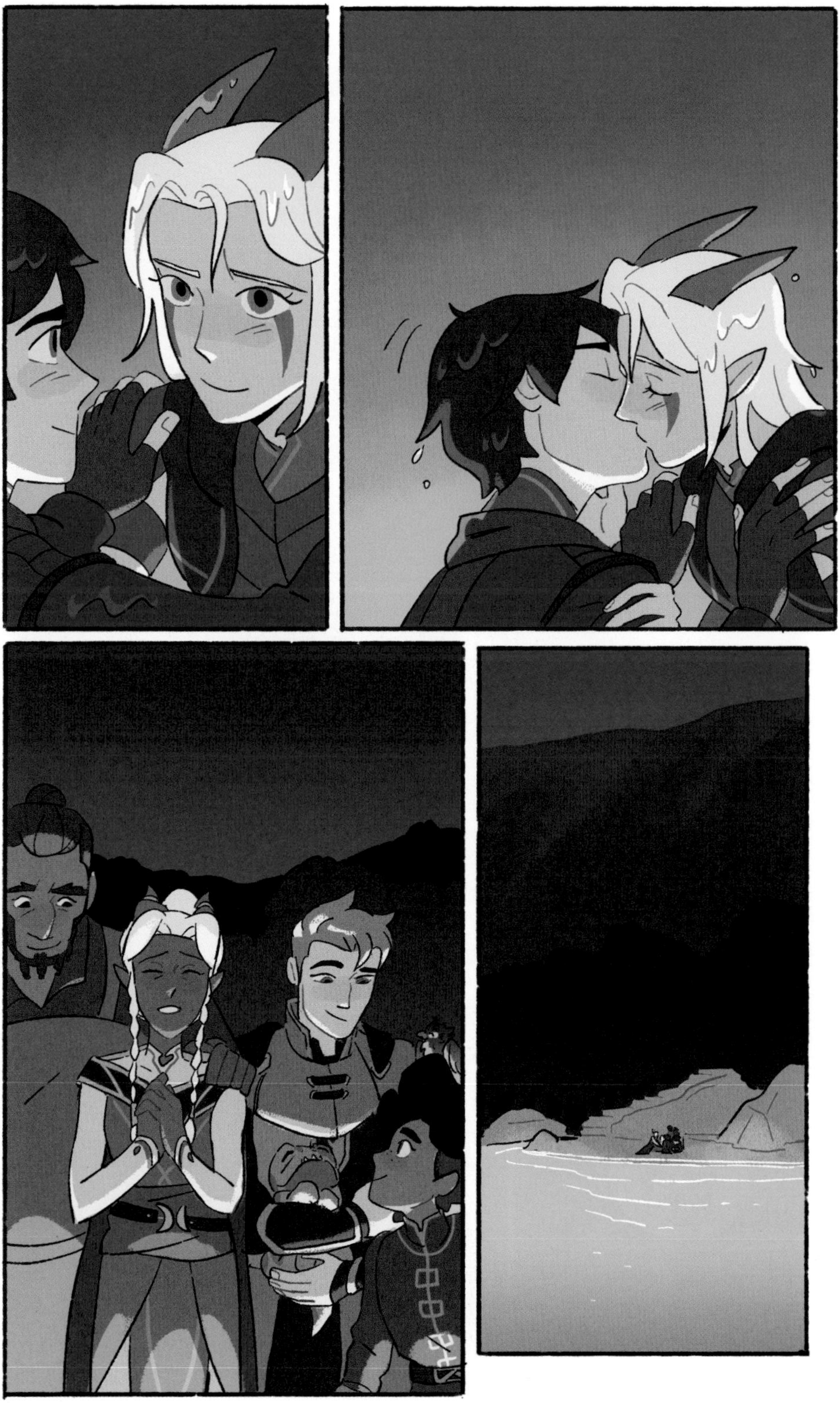

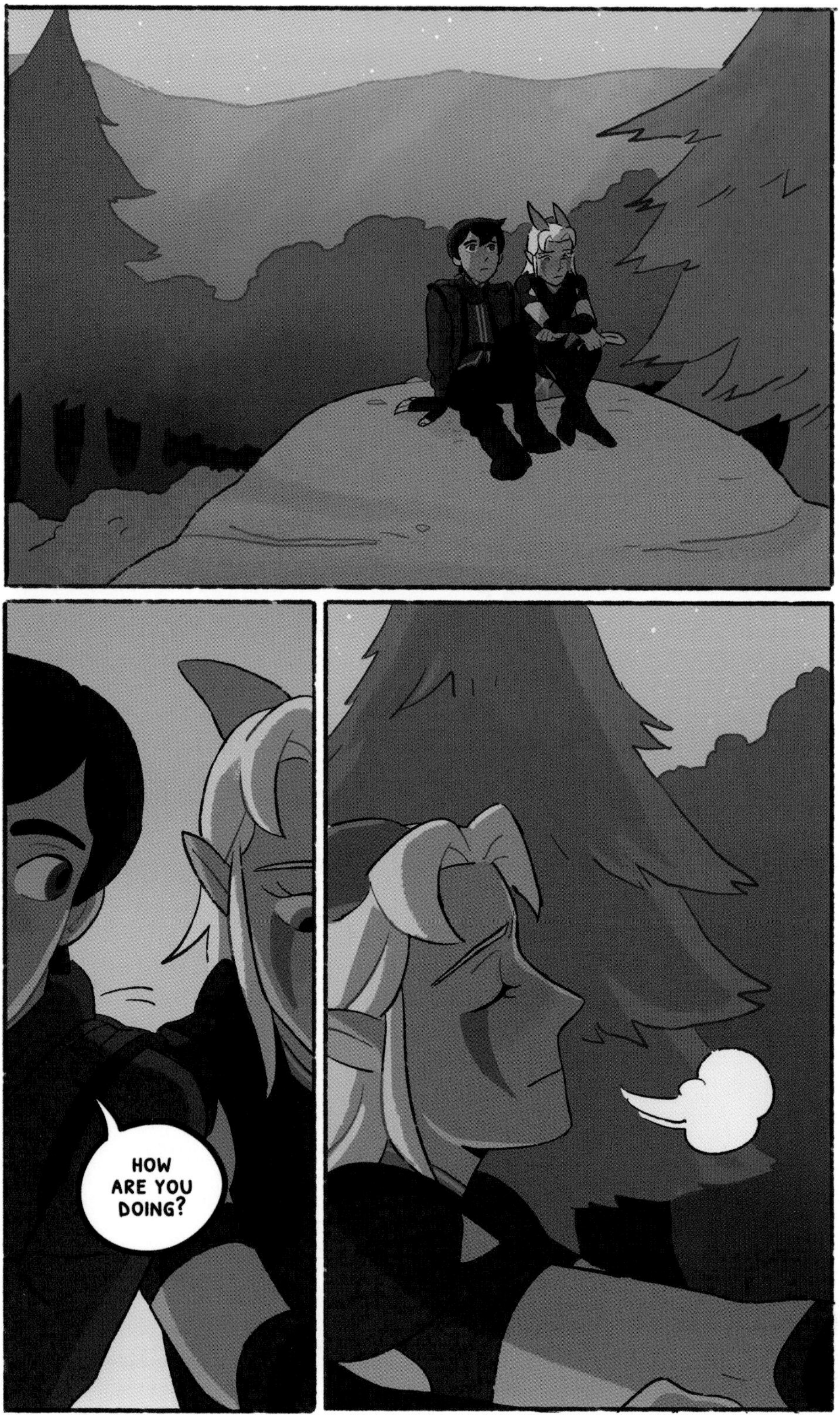
HOW ARE YOU DOING?

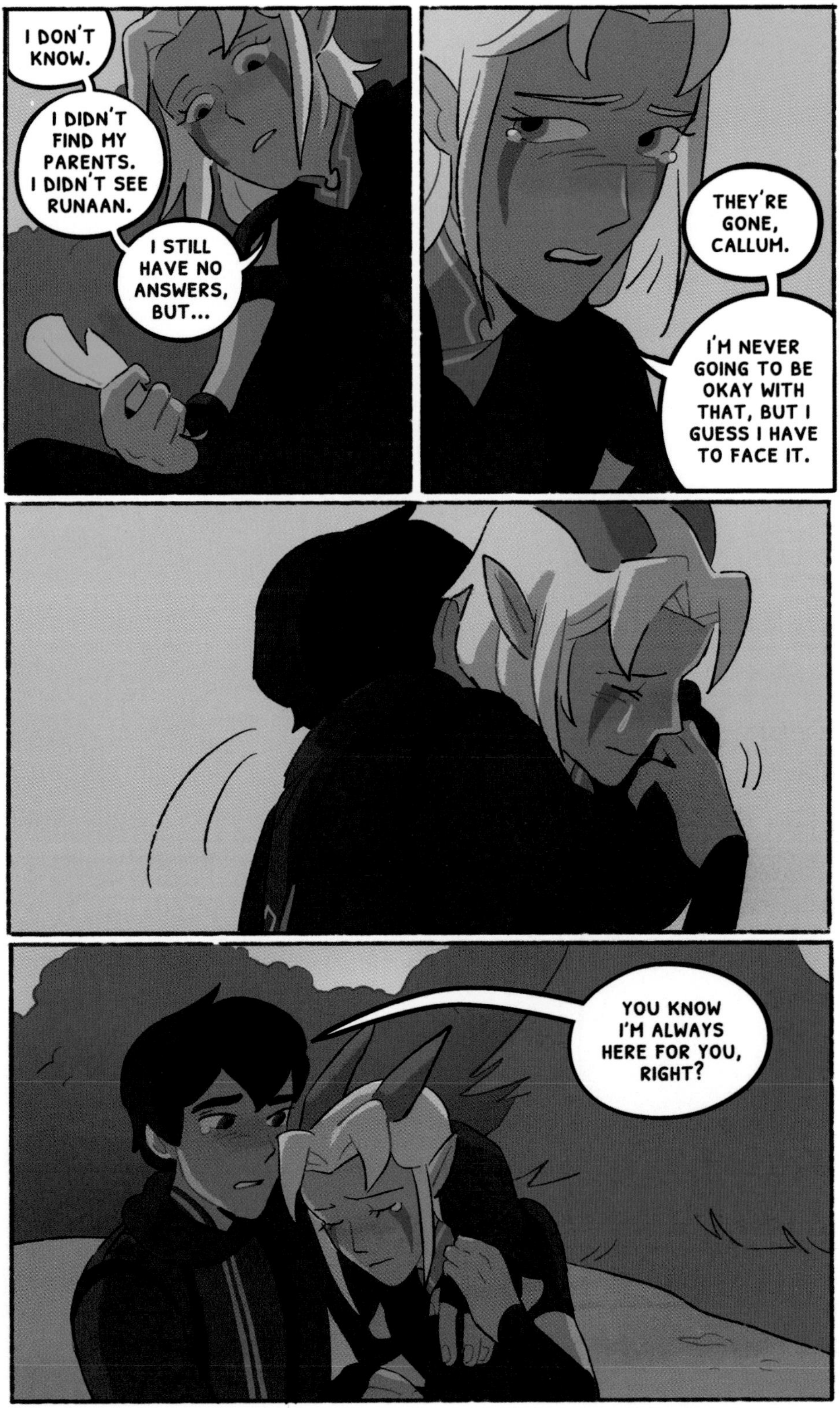
I DON'T KNOW.
I DIDN'T FIND MY PARENTS. I DIDN'T SEE RUNAAN.
I STILL HAVE NO ANSWERS, BUT...
THEY'RE GONE, CALLUM.
I'M NEVER GOING TO BE OKAY WITH THAT, BUT I GUESS I HAVE TO FACE IT.
YOU KNOW I'M ALWAYS HERE FOR YOU, RIGHT?

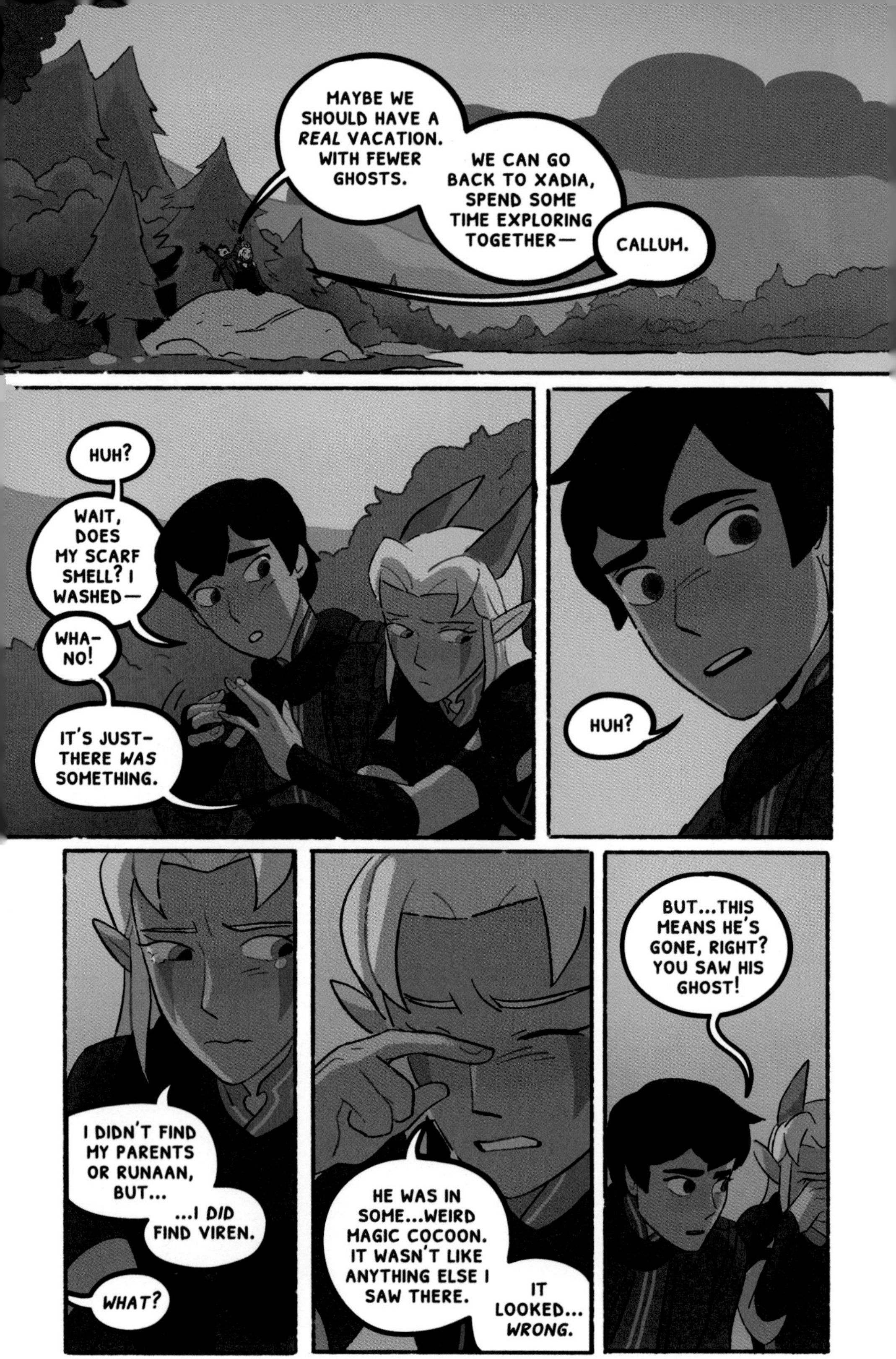

MAYBE WE SHOULD HAVE A *REAL* VACATION. WITH FEWER GHOSTS.
WE CAN GO BACK TO XADIA, SPEND SOME TIME EXPLORING TOGETHER—
CALLUM.
HUH?
WAIT, DOES MY SCARF SMELL? I WASHED—
WHA— NO!
IT'S JUST— THERE *WAS* SOMETHING.
HUH?
I DIDN'T FIND MY PARENTS OR RUNAAN, BUT...
...I *DID* FIND VIREN.
WHAT?
HE WAS IN SOME...WEIRD MAGIC COCOON. IT WASN'T LIKE ANYTHING ELSE I SAW THERE.
IT LOOKED... *WRONG.*
BUT...THIS MEANS HE'S GONE, RIGHT? YOU SAW HIS GHOST!

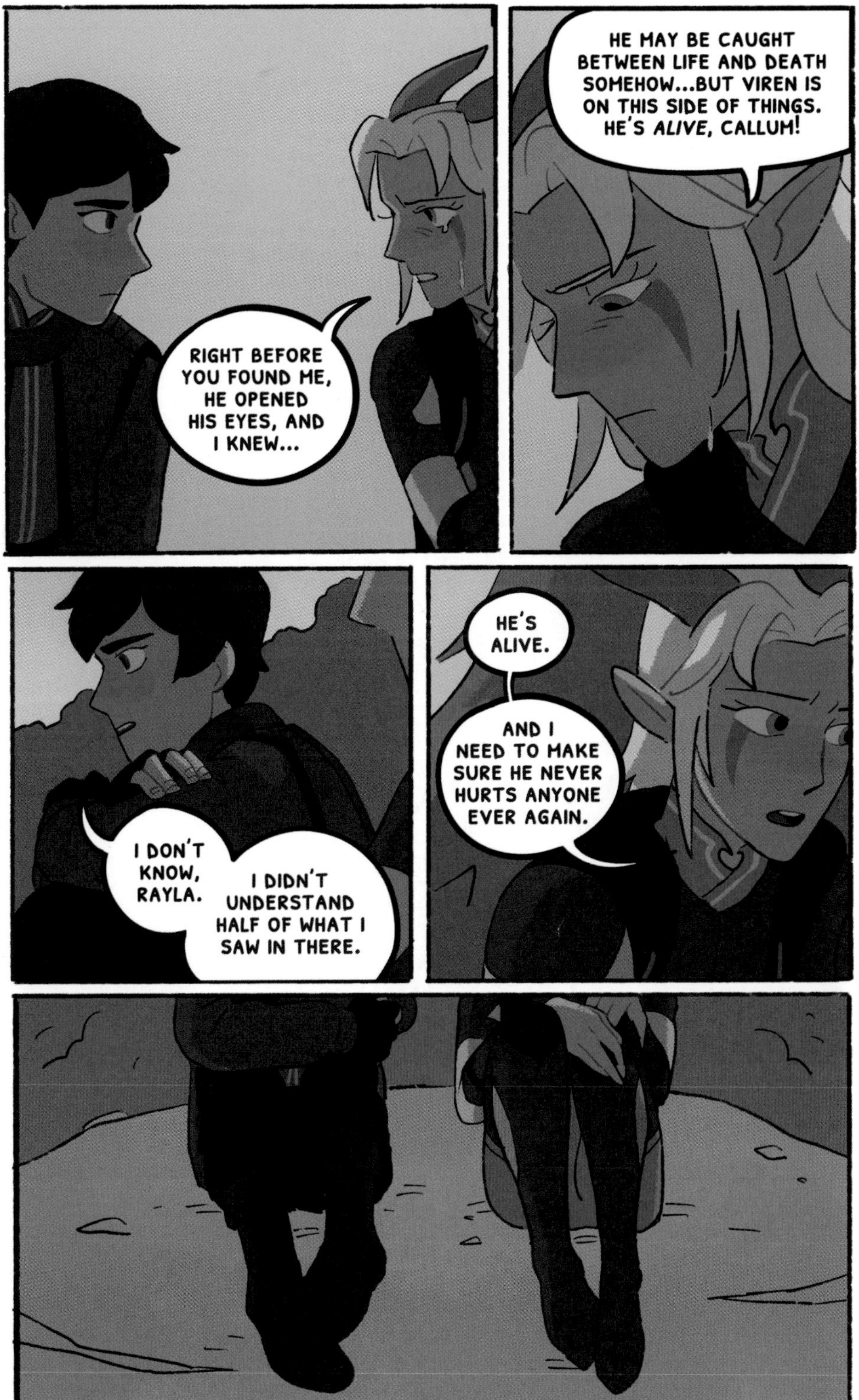

RIGHT BEFORE YOU FOUND ME, HE OPENED HIS EYES, AND I KNEW...
HE MAY BE CAUGHT BETWEEN LIFE AND DEATH SOMEHOW...BUT VIREN IS ON THIS SIDE OF THINGS. HE'S *ALIVE*, CALLUM!
I DON'T KNOW, RAYLA.
I DIDN'T UNDERSTAND HALF OF WHAT I SAW IN THERE.
HE'S ALIVE.
AND I NEED TO MAKE SURE HE NEVER HURTS ANYONE EVER AGAIN.

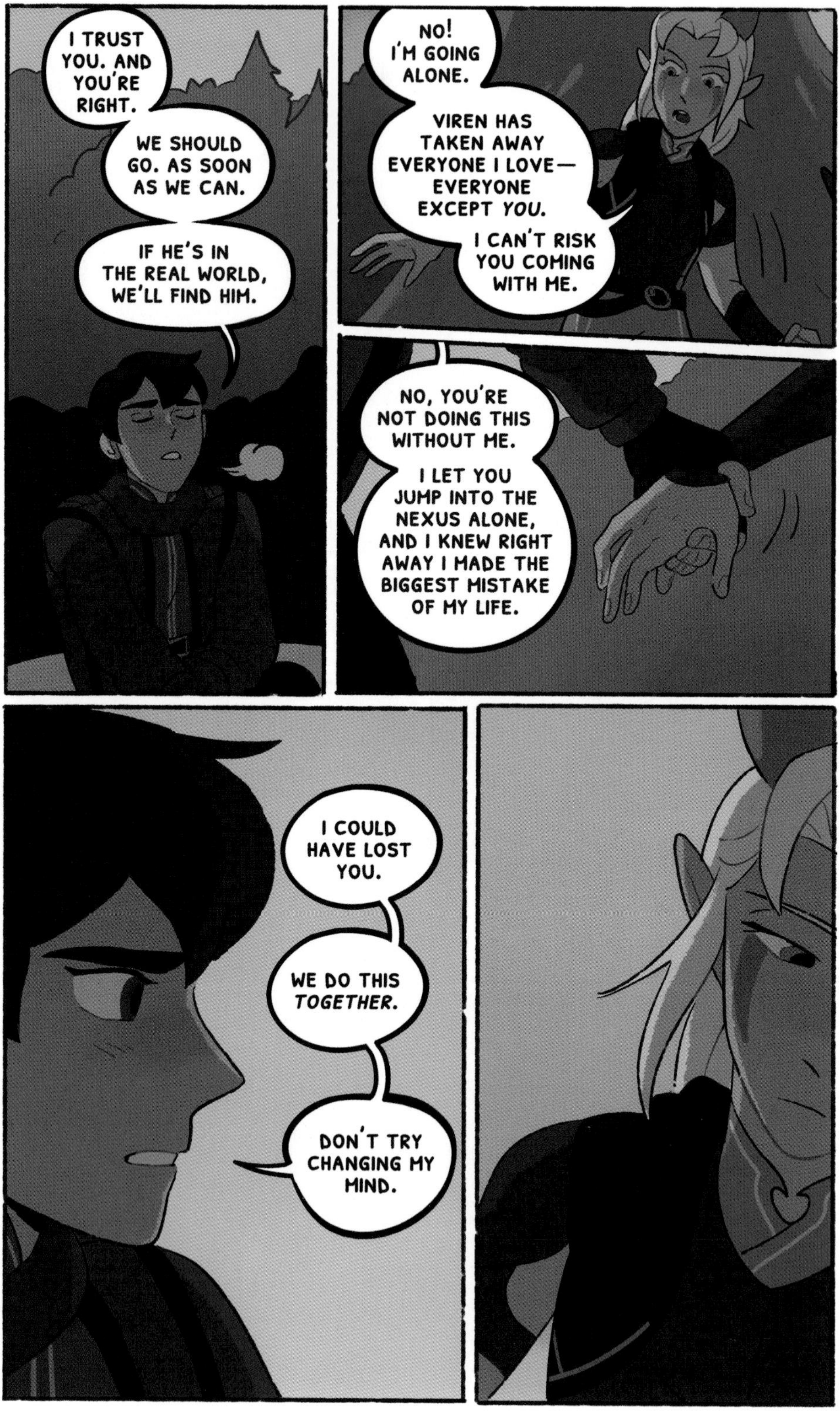
I TRUST YOU. AND YOU'RE RIGHT.
WE SHOULD GO. AS SOON AS WE CAN.
IF HE'S IN THE REAL WORLD, WE'LL FIND HIM.
NO! I'M GOING ALONE.
VIREN HAS TAKEN AWAY EVERYONE I LOVE— EVERYONE EXCEPT *YOU*.
I CAN'T RISK YOU COMING WITH ME.
NO, YOU'RE NOT DOING THIS WITHOUT ME.
I LET YOU JUMP INTO THE NEXUS ALONE, AND I KNEW RIGHT AWAY I MADE THE BIGGEST MISTAKE OF MY LIFE.
I COULD HAVE LOST YOU.
WE DO THIS *TOGETHER*.
DON'T TRY CHANGING MY MIND.

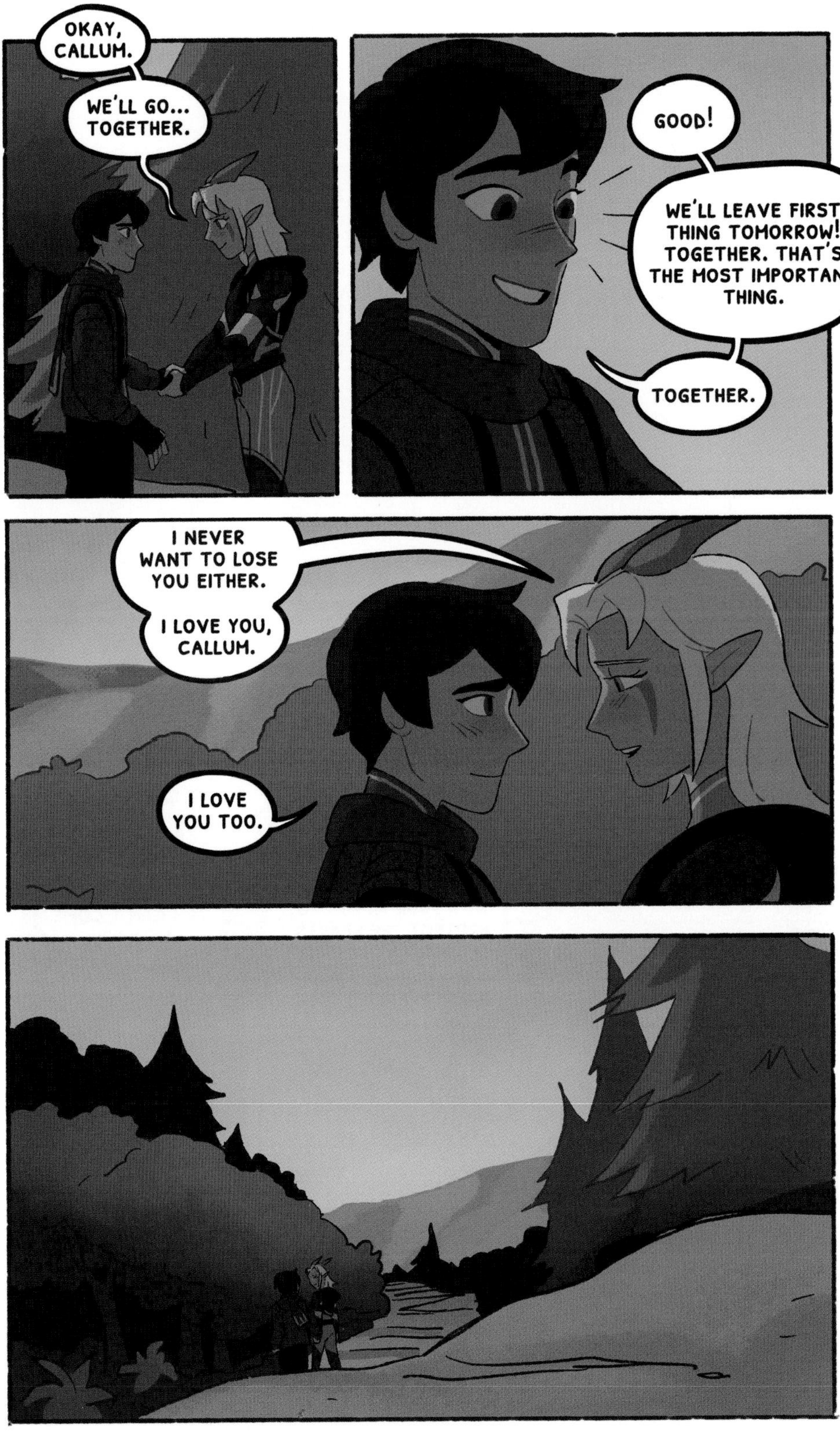
OKAY, CALLUM.
WE'LL GO... TOGETHER.
GOOD!
WE'LL LEAVE FIRST THING TOMORROW! TOGETHER. THAT'S THE MOST IMPORTANT THING.
TOGETHER.
I NEVER WANT TO LOSE YOU EITHER.
I LOVE YOU, CALLUM.
I LOVE YOU TOO.

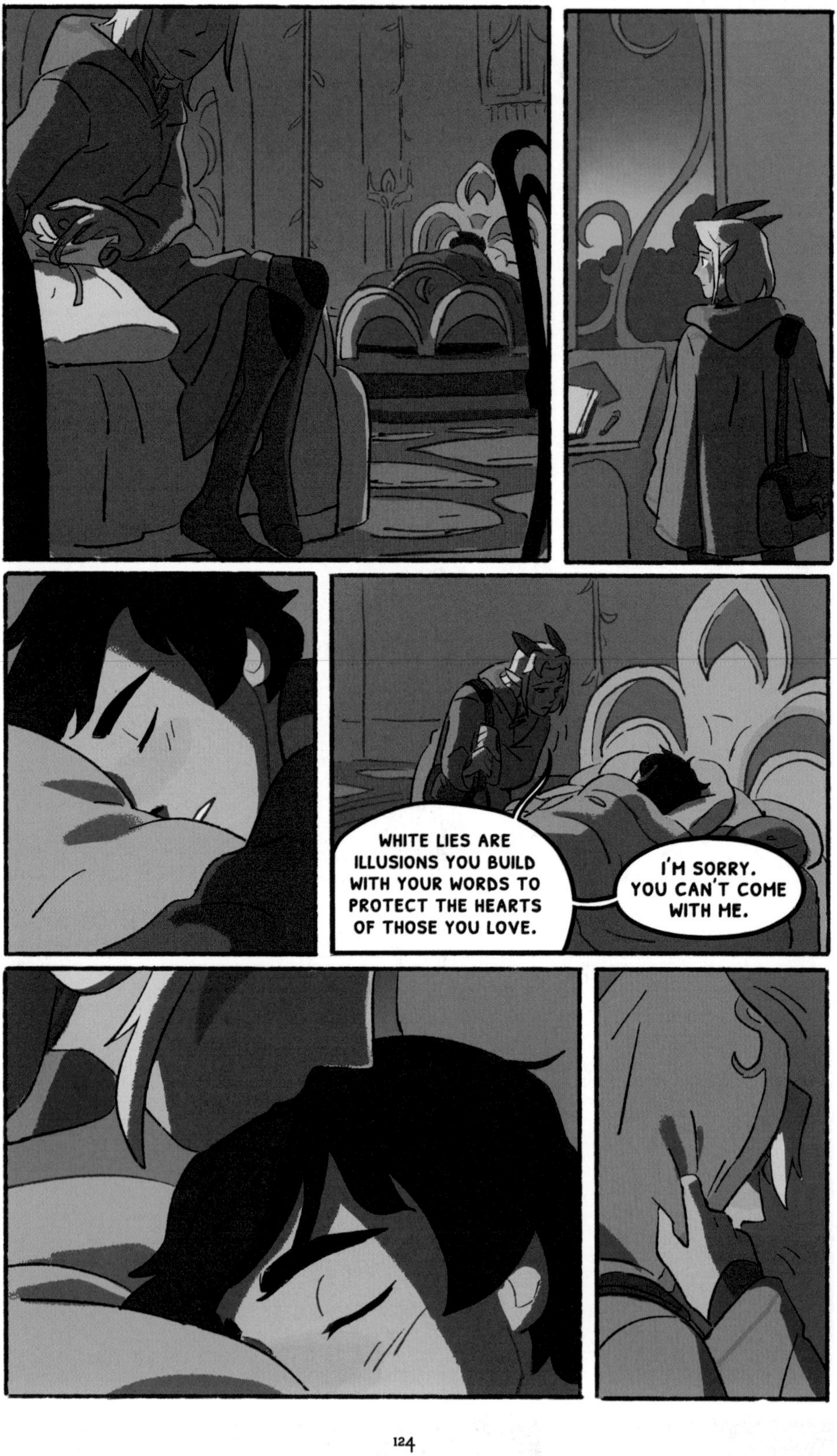
WHITE LIES ARE ILLUSIONS YOU BUILD WITH YOUR WORDS TO PROTECT THE HEARTS OF THOSE YOU LOVE.
I'M SORRY. YOU CAN'T COME WITH ME.

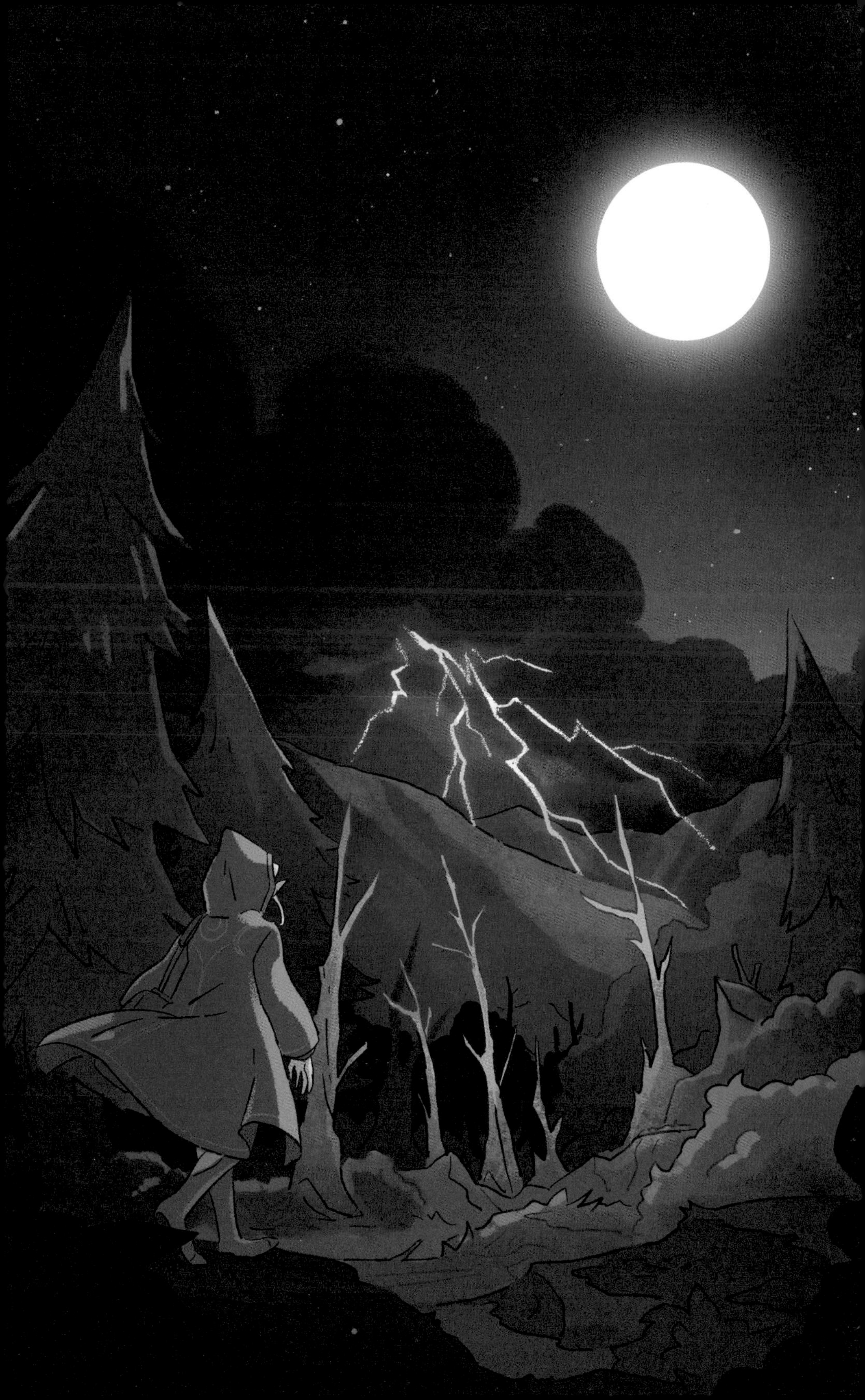

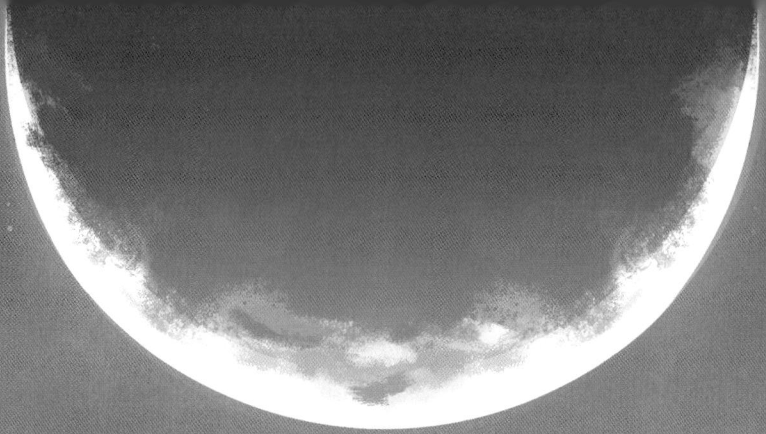

AARON EHASZ and **JUSTIN RICHMOND** are the creators of *The Dragon Prince* and co-founders of Wonderstorm, a media startup in Los Angeles, California. *The Dragon Prince* began as an original animated series on Netflix, and is now being developed into a world-class video game by the same creative team.

Previously, Aaron was the head writer of *Avatar: The Last Airbender*, and Justin was game director on the *Uncharted* franchise.

PETER WARTMAN has been creating stories about monsters, robots, and spaceships since he could hold a pencil. He lives in Minneapolis, Minnesota, where he draws and writes comics pretty much all of the time.

XANTHE BOUMA is an illustrator, colorist, and comic artist for animation and books like the 5 Worlds graphic novel series. Based in Southern California, Xanthe draws inspiration from napping in the beachside sun.

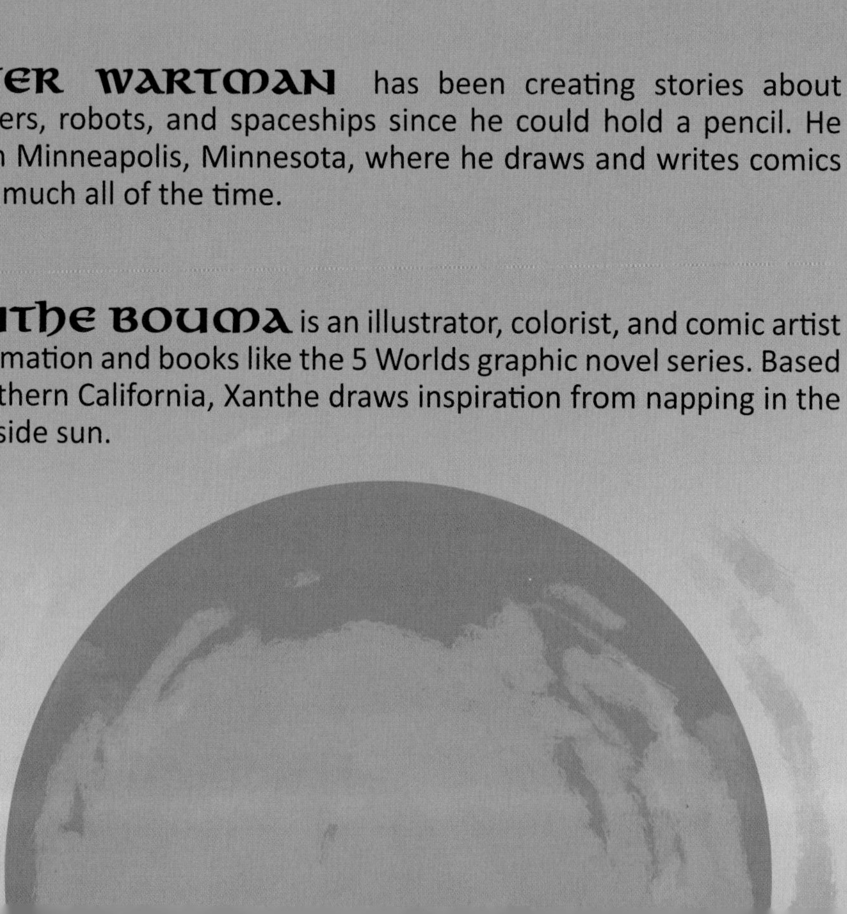